THE
SHAKESPEARE
MURDERS

THE
SHAKESPEARE
MURDERS

SHARON GUPTA

tara
India Research Press

tara

India Research Press

Flat. 6, Khan Market, New Delhi - 110003
Ph: 24694610; Fax: 24618637
www.indiaresearchpress.com
contact@indiaresearchpress.com

2017

THE SHAKESPEARE MURDERS
Sharon Gupta

ISBN 13 : 978-81-8386-141-0

Printed for Tara-India Research Press at *Manipal Technologies Limited.*

*To Papaji, my father-in-law, the late
Dr. Madan Mohan Prasad.*

ACT ONE
ONE

———

Southwark after dark. The kind of place where decent folk feared to tread. A borough, on the southern fringe of River Thames, beginning with a narrow strip of land called the Bankside where arenas for bull and bear-baiting, jostled for space with brothels and playhouses. It was in the early hours of the morning in August Sixteen Hundred and Two that the sounds of horse-drawn carriages rattled through Southwark's main road-High Street- towards London Bridge, the only span across the river. Residents stirred in their beds, some peered out of the windows of their shabby tenements to catch a glimpse of the kind of men who would dare venture in those parts at such a godforsaken hour.

The occupants of the two carriages were well-acquainted with the borough's notoriety and they kept their swords at the ready, prepared for trouble. The first coach carried three men, two in humble attire and one, a gentleman in fine clothes, who appeared to be asleep. The two men kept their eyes peeled against glass windows on either side and talked in low-tones.

"Look sharp now, Tod," the bigger one said to his companion. "'Tis the worst area. These parts supply inmates by the hundreds to Queen's prison and Marshalsea. The streets are filled with cut-purses and coney-catchers and witches."

The other man gave him a dubious look. "Witches, Rod? `Ave you ever seen one? I haven't. Witches! I know they exist but aren't they in caves and heaths?  Ever seen `em on city streets?"

"Aye, I've seen `em, Tod, believe you me. They're fearsome creatures, right devils. One look and they can suck out your soul! Don't be fooled by the quiet streets; the Borough's filled with `em."

"In truth? Everything looks quiet to me."

"That's because it's nearly dawn. They must return to the netherworld at the break of day..."

"What? But I thought it was ghosts that must return..."

"Shh, take care now, you don't want `em hearing you, do you? Look carefully; you might yet catch a glimpse of one as it hides in the shadows."

After another few moments of staring out of the windows and finding no signs of the diabolical creatures, Tod said, "What do they look like, real witches?"

"Ooh, they're ugly, very ugly. You don't want to meet one. Toady eyes, long hooked noses, bad teeth, little horns concealed under pointy caps. Fearsome creatures."

"What about their broomsticks?" the young gentleman said with a chuckle.

Rod and Tod started.

"Sir Geoffrey, you're awake?" Rod exclaimed. "We thought you was in the Land of Never Never. You must be right exhausted, sir, after the voyage from France."

"Of course not; that was hardly an odyssey. The Channel passage wasn't bad but this journey from Dover..." The young man yawned and stretched his long legs. Unlike most men of the day, he was clean-shaven and his sharp features stood out in an open, honest face. "`Don't know when we'll have proper roads in our land. The Romans built great roads centuries ago but we... How much longer to the Bridge?"

Rod peered out of the window. "Almost there, sir. `Just hope we're not too early. Curfew hour isn't over and the Bridge Masters might make us wait."

All gates leading into the city of London were closed from nine p.m. to five a.m. This included two gates on either sides of London Bridge, which was guarded by Bridge Masters. Until the early fourteenth century, Southwark was lawless territory, the abode of robbers and highwaymen and all sorts of nasty characters. Marauding bands of thieves would routinely cross the river in boats at night to rob and pillage the city of London compelling the Mayor and his troops to patrol the north bank of the Thames after dark and keep watch over London Bridge. The situation became intolerable since Southwark's High Street, which travelled from London Bridge through the length of the Borough, was the capital city's only passageway to Dover and the south. Foreign emissaries, tourists and all visitors to London from this direction had to pass through the Borough. Naturally this was detrimental to the aforementioned travellers' safety and to London's fair name. Finally the magistrates of London applied to the King- Edward the Third- for a grant of Southwark and the Borough was reined in.

Although by no means the anarchic place it was before, Southwark still retained much of its rough character at the dawn of the Seventeenth century.

"Come now, Rod, surely you don't think they'll prevent this rig from entering the city," Tod said, "Not when Sir Geoffrey's in it. Our papers are in order. I'm more concerned about the criminals enroute to the Bridge."

The young man made a face. "Stop worrying. You two sound like a pair of old crones."

His gaze travelled through the glass to the deserted borough streets passing by. After the nine o'clock curfew bell sounded the hour of compline, inns and taverns were closed to the public and all traffic disappeared. During this time Southwark seemed like a flat, unremarkable place. Across the river the city of London loomed with high buildings, church spires, Whitehall palace, the formidable Tower and other grand edifices. Southwark made a stark contrast with its low- lying, swampy landscape and cheap dwellings which contained a populace dominated by the poor and the destitute. Only two buildings stood out in the skyline: the Church of St. Saviour's just west of London Bridge adjacent to the Bishop of Winchester's house, and the playhouse called the Globe.

The Globe's unique octagonal circular structure with three tiers and sloping thatched roof huts on top made it tower over neighbouring buildings. Now, as its silhouette came into view, Sir Geoffrey, craned his neck to gaze upon it and then asked his two attendants if either of them had ever been inside.

"I have, once, sir," Rod replied but Tod shook his head. Rod continued, happy with the attention: "It was a few years back. I watched a show called...er...can't remember the name but it was one of William Shakespeare's plays, a comedy about two sets o' twins. Most agreeable, sir."

"You've never visited a playhouse, have you, sir?" Tod asked.

"No," said the young man. "I watched a play once, though, at Court. `A special command performance by the Lord Admiral's Men. It was interesting."

"The Admiral's Men are fierce rivals to Shakespeare's company, the Chamberlain's Men," Rod said. "The players know one another well and some o` them `ave performed together but now they're bitterly opposed. Word is Shakespeare's leading the race right now."

The young man smiled. "It's a different world out there, isn't it? Of plays and stage rivalries. `Surprising that people actually give a fig for such things. I've visited the bull and bear-baiting arenas; those, I can understand. The action there can stir up a man's passions. It's real, it's visceral. But play-acting? How can people flock to playhouses when they know the action is only make-believe?"

"Aye, sir, but the people love it. You should see the crowds outside the playhouses," said Rod. "Correction: outside the playhouse, The Globe. There used to be another two famous theatres, the Rose and the Swan. But the Globe's success forced them to close down, more or less."

"In truth? One playhouse sent them all packing?"

"Aye, sir. Not one playhouse, actually, one man-Shakespeare."

The young man raised his brow. He had heard of Shakespeare, of course, but he wasn't aware of the Bard's impact on the London stage. Shakespeare was a talented chap, he thought, or just plain lucky. There's a problem with good luck, though: it tends to run out...

The rig came to an abrupt halt, sending Rod and Tod nearly flying into their master's lap, and the driver dismounted with an apology from his perch in front. They'd reached London Bridge. Rod and Tod got off with as much dignity as they could, glared at the driver for the awkward stoppage, and then ordered two swordsmen from the carriage behind to guard Sir Geoffrey's coach.

They were at Bridge Foot, the Southwark end of London Bridge. The huge gate leading to the Bridge was shut and four dopey-eyed Bridge Masters lounged about with long swords at their sides. Above the gate the heads of criminals and traitors impaled on poles, served as grisly warnings to anyone harbouring a desire to challenge the queen's authority.

"Ah, there's your great uncle Freddie," Rod teased Tod. "Lookin' good today. The family resemblance is startling."

Tod made a face and tried to come up with a clever rejoinder but one of the Bridge Masters approached them with suspicious eyes and said:

"Ere, what do we 'ave 'ere, goodmen?"

"That we are men is without a doubt," Rod said, "An' that we are good is with report."

Tod pursed his lips in grudging admiration but the guard was unimpressed.

"'Just being polite," he said. "Don't you know curfew's still in force. Bridge-opening time isn't for another half hour."

"Aye, but there's a knight of renown in the carriage over there," Rod replied. "Sir Geoffrey Drake, nephew of the valiant late Sir Francis Drake, on his way back from France."

"Sir Geoffrey?" the Bridge Master's eyes widened and he stood up straight.

"Aye," said Rod. "And I have the honour of being his squire Rodney Peele. This is his squire Tod Makepeace. We request permission to enter the city. You'll find our papers in order."

"Is it really he- Sir Geoffrey himself?" the guard asked, staring open-mouthed at Drake's carriage.

"It was when we checked last about two minutes ago," Tod said.

The Bridge Master grinned, turned around and went off to confer with his colleagues. They exchanged animated words and then all four rushed towards Drake's gleaming black carriage.

Drake's swordsmen moved quickly to block the way.

"No, no, we mean no harm," the senior most Bridge Master said, smiling. "We just want to shake his hand. 'Watched him joust at the tourney on Coronation Day, we did. January this year."

Drake's surly swordsmen eyed them with distrust and didn't seem keen to oblige them but Drake, having overheard the conversation, appeared at the carriage door a moment later and dismounted.

"Ah, my goodmen. What can I do for you?" he inquired.

"Sir Geoffrey! I...we're honoured to meet you," the senior Bridge Master exclaimed. "May I shake your hand?"

"By all means."

Drake shook hands with each of the four men.

"I served with your uncle on board the Golden Hind," another BM said. He was a toothless chap with an ancient-of-days demeanour but his eyes held a proud sparkle. "We fought the Spanish and blew their Armada to smithereens! I still recall the thrill of it all."

Drake's face broke into a smile. "Why, then I'm the one that's honoured to have met you. My dear chaps, I would love to stay and chat, but it's been a long journey." Drake's cheerful smile concealed his exhaustion well. "Will you let me pass? My residence is just across the Bridge at Dowgate. I have the required papers..."

"No, no, sir. Far be it from us to demand papers from you! `Tis not yet the hour of bridge-opening but we can make an exception for you, sir."

Drake thanked him and climbed back into his carriage.

"Godspeed, sir, all the best," said the Bridge Master, "A great honour to meet you."

"Oh, but the honour's mine, as surely as my name is Drake. Many thanks, dear friends. Look sharp now."

"Aye, sir. God save the Queen!"

***

Two

—

A few hours later when the morning's sun rays picked up the first signs of life in the Thames, a group of young boys ran around the city sticking handbills on walls and taverns and pulling down the older ones. On Friday morning these posters had advertised 'Mr. Shakespeare's most excellent comedie *The Merchant of Venice* performed at the Globe in Southwark by the Lord Chamberlain's Servants'. Today the transcript bore the following legend:

'Come and see the right excellent tragedie of *Romeo & Juliet* by Mr. W. Shakespeare at two of the clock at the Globe playhouse in Southwark. Acted by the Right Honourable Lord Chamberlain's Servants.'

As the city stirred and people went about their businesses, some of them making plans to travel across the river and watch the play, professional criers roamed the streets beating drums and singing about the doomed lovers. By ten a.m. they returned to Southwark, from where they'd departed, still singing about the afternoon show.

'Come one, come all,

To the Globe playhall.

For love n' longing this afternoon

Come see young Romeo meet his doom.

If Juliet cannot his fair love be,

He will surely lose his sanity,

His life, his all.

Come one, come all...'

The Globe was situated close to the river in a busy street in Clink liberty called Maid Lane. Anyone passing the playhouse that Monday morning would know, by a mere glimpse of the black flag on its mast, that a tragedy would be performed in the afternoon. The thumb rule was white flag for comedy, red for history, and black for tragedy. But what most people could not have known was that the black flag fluttered in the breeze with dual significance that day: besides indicating the fictional tragedy of Romeo and Juliet, it also served as a sign of mourning, of respect for a recently departed soul. Jeremy Smith, a seventeen-year-old apprentice player who'd been found dead outside the Globe's tall white walls three days ago.

Within the same octagonal walls actors, musicians, prompters and stagehands were hard at work preparing for the afternoon's show. John Heminges, the oldest member of the Company, had taken charge of the rehearsal. He was assisted by Robert Armin, their chief comedian, who also happened to be a Master of Fencing and, hence, usually doubled up as stunt director. Armin was taking their new Romeo through his fencing steps. Heminges' attention was divided. He was watching the stagehands as they rushed about cleaning the amphitheatre and clearing rubbish left over from Friday afternoon's show. Eight of them would assume duties as gatherers at the gate to collect the one penny entry fee. Spectators would pay an additional penny at the bottom of the stairs leading to the galleries on either sides of the stage if they wished to sit on wooden benches. VIP box rooms were also available on the first-floor for a charge of three pence. Once the show commenced and the coin-collection boxes were filled, they would be deposited in the box office, a room behind the stage, which would then be locked by John Heminges, who was also the Company's treasurer-cum-accountant.

Heminges kept an eye on the stagehands but it was Shakespeare that occupied his thoughts. The Bard was a stickler for rehearsals, the main director of each show, but today he was nowhere to be seen. It made Heminges uneasy. Jeremy Smith's death had shocked them all but they were professional players and they couldn't afford to suspend performances over an incident like that. Shakespeare had been so calm on Friday, almost in a daze, and Heminges knew that the full impact of the boy's death would hit him later.

But it's still not right, Heminges thought, we're all grieving for the boy; if we can go on with the show, so should he.

Players usually used long wooden sticks to practise fencing; Robert Armin had, however, permitted the use of the blunt sword that the boy who was to play Romeo would be using since the boy, a twenty -year -old called Thomas Gray, was due to take the stage in a few hours' time.

"Tommy, Tommy, calm yourself," Armin exclaimed as Gray pranced around the wooden stage with the sword in hand. "That's not a plaything. No point thrashing the air in so wild a fashion. Remember what I told you? Fencing is an art, a skill, it doesn't require brutish strength."

Gray grinned sheepishly. "Yes, sir, Mr. Armin. I'll keep that in mind."

"Good." Armin glanced in the direction of the main entrance and added: "And it's a good thing Master Shakespeare isn't here yet; he would've had a fit if he caught you sawing the air like that! Now, let's go over it again. Count the paces in your head like I told you. The stage is forty-three feet across so you'll have plenty of space but Nick will need some room to manoeuvre as well. And he won't give up without a fight."

Armin's reference was to another young actor Nicholas Tooley, who was to reprise the role of Tybalt, Juliet's cousin. Romeo kills Tybalt in a duel in the middle of the play. It was a small part and Tooley had it down pat so he'd been despatched to the city a short while ago on an errand with another player, a senior actor called Richard Cowley. They were to fetch some fliers from the printer for the next day's show of *Troilus and Cressida* and were expected back by noon.

Thomas Gray was a quick learner. He followed Armin's instructions to the 'T' and, after a couple of more sequences, Armin was satisfied. He added as a parting shot:

"Just remember to hit Nick at the correct spot, here." Armin jabbed his thumb between his ribs. "That's where the 'blood' will be. And take care not to strike too hard."

"Yes, Mr. Armin, I'll remember that," Gray said as he strolled off the stage.

To create an impression of blood and gore, the players strapped bladders filled with sheep's blood to their chests or any body part that required to be injured during the show. These were punctured at the opportune moment. The Company also possessed props like fake limbs to be strewn across the stage during battle scenes.

After Gray left, Armin sat down on a bench at the corner of the stage to catch a moment's rest before calling other players for more fencing scenes. His gaze travelled to the balcony on the first floor where the heavy-set figure of Richard Burbage leaned over the railing, watching the proceedings below. Burbage was the Company's lead actor, the original Romeo. At thirty-six, he felt that that was one role he ought not to be doing any longer. This, plus the fact that he was recovering from a bout of flu, was what had propelled young Gray into the leading man's role.

Burbage and his older brother Cuthbert were also co-owners of the Globe and the main stakeholders in the Chamberlain's Men with twenty-five percent shares each. The remaining fifty percent was divided equally amongst four senior players: William Shakespeare (their in-house playwright or 'playmaker', as dramatists were popularly called), John Heminges, Thomas Pope, and Pope's brother-in-law Augustine Phillips (their Company Manager). The rest of the players were hired actors and apprentices.

"It's going well, Robin," Burbage called out. "You will yet make swordsmen of these farming boys."

Armin chuckled. He appreciated what Burbage was doing, trying to lift their spirits since Smith's death had left them all feeling low.

Armin mouthed the words: 'Where's Will?'

Burbage shook his head. No idea.

John Heminges moved into the tiring room directly behind the stage with the boy who was playing Juliet. Women were not permitted to perform on the Elizabethan stage so young male actors played all the female parts. Juliet, that day, was a light-eyed eighteen-year-old boy with a slender figure called Alexander Cooke, whom everyone called 'Saunders'. He was apprenticed to John Heminges. Cooke had played this part before and he was well-prepared so Heminges was merely running through his lines before the show.

Cooke required hardly any prompting. Heminges had the foul papers in hand: rough sheets containing a player's 'side' or part, and he followed Juliet's lines closely but it was hard to concentrate because the playhouse was so noisy. Armin was fencing with William Sly now, Juliet's suitor Paris in the play. Sly was a hefty chap with a pug nose, nothing like his namesake of Iliad fame but he moved with the grace of a dancer. Above them on the second level, musicians were practising in the huts on the roof. Stagehands still rushed about cleaning the playhouse. All in all, there was an awful din.

In the level directly above the stage, where Burbage was standing, steps led to the property room where the Company's props and costumes were stored. This level also contained the gentlemen's boxes, rooms that were privy to all kinds of spicy goings-on since their occupants were invariably the genteel kind that preferred to watch shows discreetly, oftentimes with ladies who were not joined to them in holy matrimony.

"Mr. Heminges, I think I'm through here," Alexander Cooke said, tapping Heminges's shoulder. "Can I go now?"

Heminges started. He'd been so distracted that after the first couple of minutes, he'd barely noticed the boy's rehearsal.

"You've practised your lines? Feeling confident, lad?" Heminges asked. He had a slight stutter that became pronounced when he was under stress.

Cooke nodded. "Can I go? I promised to help Ollie decorate the balcony."

"Ah, Juliet's t- t- terrace, eh? Go on, son."

Cooke left the tiring room and climbed to the next floor from the staircase behind the stage. He found Henry Condell in the property room engrossed in his work. Condell, another senior player, was the Wardrobe Manager. He was sorting out costumes from the wardrobe boxes. The approach to the balcony was through this room.

As Cooke walked away, Heminges noticed the slouch of his shoulders and his dolorous demeanour and his heart went out to the boy. Jeremy Smith's death seemed to have hit him the hardest. They'd been close friends, Smith, Cooke and another young apprentice Oliver Downtown. They lived close to one another in Hill's Rents, one of the cheaper parts of Southwark.

It was not just Smith's death but also the manner in which his body had been found that was so distressing. Face down in the slush outside the Globe's walls just two hours before show time.

The old flower seller's wail still seemed to reverberate through the theatre.

"A dead boy, a dead boy! Anon to the walls. He's one o' yours! A dead boy, I say, a dead boy!"

She'd been the first witness, the one who'd discovered the boy and raised the hue-an-cry as required by law. But then she had vanished. The local constable and some of the players searched for her but she'd seemed to have gone underground.

"This is Southwark, what do you expect?" Heminges said on Sunday night when Thomas Pope had come round visiting. "You'll never find anyone that doesn't want to be found."

"Aye, but why doesn't she want to be found?" Pope wondered. Grief had etched deep lines in his chubby face. Smith had been apprenticed to him. An orphan with no family of his own, Smith had endeared himself to Pope and the others in the Company with his affable nature and cherry disposition. The unmarried and childless Pope had come to look upon the boy as a son.

That Sunday night, as he discussed Smith's death with Heminges, he railed against the flower seller. "What if she knows something, John? What if she saw something? Isn't it her duty to report it? Suppose she killed him? Don't you think her disappearance is suspicious?"

"Come now, Tom, be reasonable. Maybe she doesn't want to get involved. She's an old woman; you know that the constable and the Justice of the Peace would've harassed her just because she was the first witness. Why, in the absence of other suspects, they might have arrested her. How can you expect...?"

"But she must've seen something. Or she's guilty. Jeremy didn't just drop dead; he was killed, murdered! I'm sure of it."

"We can't know that for sure. You saw his body; there were no marks, no signs of injury."

"No apparent injury marks. We're not doctors, John. If only someone had inspected the body properly. Damnation! And the Coroner won't even conduct an inquest!"

"He's far too busy, Tom. From his point of view, young Jeremy might've had a seizure or gone into cardiac arrest.

There were no witnesses, no suspicious circumstances..."

"No suspicious circumstances?" Pope's eyes bulged in his rotund face. "A seventeen-year-old lad suddenly drops dead and the person that discovers his body disappears. Isn't that suspicious enough for you? How can you play the devil's advocate? The boy was seventeen! His eyes had barely opened to the world."

They lapsed into an uncomfortable silence, each communing with his thoughts.

"And I can't get over what a cold-hearted bastard Will is," Pope spoke up again. "He actually said 'The show must go on.' How could he say that? How could we go ahead and perform when Jeremy's body hadn't even gone cold?"

Heminges rolled his eyes with no small measure of exasperation. They'd gone over this before.

"You're being unjust, T- T-Tom. The crowds were straining against the gates; people had come from afar to see the show. They'd bunked work. How could we turn them away? Did you really expect Will to cancel the show?" He added with a raised forefinger as Pope was about to protest: "And to what end, Tom? Jeremy was da-da-dead. Constable Sprat had arrived on the scene. There was nothing else for anyone to do. You'd decided to remain with the body..."

"I couldn't have left him," Pope said in a choked voice.

"Yes, I know. But, tell me, what would we have achieved by not performing *The Merchant of Venice*?"

"What would we have…? We would have shown the dead boy proper respect, that's what. Might I remind you, he was one of us?"

"Of course he was and we will always remember him. But you ca-can't blame Will for continuing with the show. He ca-cares, you know he does. But he's committed to the audience, too. Mind you, in case you've forgotten, Dick Burbage was keen on doing the show, as well."

"Naturally he was; he's the boss. How else does he keep filling the Company's coffers?"

"Not j-just the Company's, yours, too, Tom." Heminges' tone had been irenic thus far. He'd always played the role of peacemaker during disputes amongst players, his senescence attributing some degree of authority to his position. But his patience ran out with Thomas Pope that night. He thought the portly player was being selfish in ascribing dubious motives to Will Shakespeare, who possessed an open and honest character, at least in his dealings with the players. Nothing was done in hugger-mugger or secrecy in this Company. So Tom Pope's reasoning was flawed.

Heminges' sharp tone took Pope by surprise.

"You're a sharer, too," Heminges continued. "Just like I am. So let's not accuse Will and Dick of caring about finances. Look, I know you loved the boy…"

"I did. And he loved us. He had no one else," Pope said in a small voice.

"I know. He had us. He won't go unremembered, I promise you. We're burying him on Tuesday morn in a true Christian service. Need I say more?"

As they concluded the conversation, Shakespeare's elegiac line about Juliet's death sprang into Heminges' mind: Death lies on her, like an untimely frost upon the sweetest flower of all the field.

And Heminges had to swallow hard to make the lump in his throat go away.

The same line popped up during the rehearsal on Monday morning and Heminges found it oddly disconcerting.

It was eleven o' clock and Shakespeare still hadn't shown. Half-an-hour back he had sent a stagehand round to Shakespeare's flat, a small tenement in a lane close to St. Saviour's Church. It was a mere seven minutes' walk from the Globe. The boy had returned within a quarter of an hour saying that the flat was locked and that the landlady Mrs. Humphreys who lived on the ground floor, said that she'd seen him leave home about an hour ago.

So where was he?

***

THREE

———

The stage trembled. Four men shouted and rushed at one another with outstretched swords. Montague versus Capulet men in a street brawl. Abraham and Balthazar on the Montague side were played by James Sands, apprentice to Augustine Phillips, and John Sinklo, a senior player famous for his lean physique akin to Stanley Laurel of modern times. Their opponents were actors Charles Heminges, John Heminges' younger brother, and Christopher Beeston, former apprentice to Augustine Phillips and now a hired player. They were reprising the roles of 'Sampson' and 'Gregory', Capulet men.

It was almost noon.

Still no news of Shakespeare.

Until a few years back, the Elizabethan stage was nothing more than a stark, bare platform bereft of props and backdrops except black cloths hung for tragedies and coloured ones for comedies. Audiences were expected to suspend disbelief altogether. But lately, sweeping changes had been introduced. Props were getting sophisticated; special effects like strong winds were simulated by blowing dead leaves across the stage; trap doors in the wooden floor were used to make players appear or disappear suddenly. Stage Managers were becoming increasingly inventive in their use of backdrops. That day the Chamberlain's Men were using three different backdrops for replicating Italian scenes. The first one was the public place in Verona; the second, interiors of the Montague household; and a third was hung behind the balcony above to provide the background for Juliet's terrace.

The players were fencing when a familiar figure strode onto the stage, threw his hands up, and exclaimed:

"Why are you sleepwalking today? Where's the passion in your words? You're moving around as if in a dream and you're squeaking the lines, not speaking them."

"Will!" Armin exclaimed. "There you are, at last. What kept you? We were beginning to worry..."

William Shakespeare nodded distractedly at him and continued addressing the players.

"Don't go hysterical. Don't overdo it but the scene won't work if you don't show some passion. You're sworn enemies, remember? Charlie, you're Sampson, a petty, choleric chap, quick to take offence. I want to hear the growl in your voice when you say: Draw, if you be men!"

"Fine, Will, I'll be happy to growl for you," Charlie said lightly.

"Don't growl for me," Shakespeare said, "For the play, Charlie, for the play."

"But it's your play."

"So long as I'm writing it, yes. But once it's out there it's yours, the Company's, the spectators'. My job is done." He turned to Armin and added: "Their fencing skills have improved greatly. Good work, Robin."

"Many thanks, Will. What kept you this morning? We were wondering..."

Shakespeare brushed the query aside. "Tell you by and by. Now, men, are you ready to have another go at Scene One?"

The players nodded and took their positions again.

Shakespeare, instead of waiting there to watch them on stage, went into the tiring-room, greeted John Heminges, and then climbed up the stairs to reach the balcony. The tiring-room took its name from the backstage area covered by a curtain where players changed their 'attire'. They would return to the stage either the same way or from two arras or side doors at stage level. The tiring-room plus the property room on the first-floor and the balcony about twenty feet above stage level together constituted the tiring-house.

Henry Condell and Oliver Downtown were updating the Company's wardrobe inventory. Robin Hood's green suit needed mending; two Roman togas were torn at the hem; Ophelia's gown was missing a few buttons... Condell rifled through these, examining the extent of damage and wondered if he should send them across to the seamstress Mrs. Dogoody, who lived in Hill's Rents and was, in fact, the dead boy Jeremy Smith's landlady. Oliver Downtown was entrusted with the task of delivering such garments to her and then fetching them once they were set right.

"Will, good to see you," Condell said as Shakespeare strolled through.

Shakespeare nodded at him and at young Downtown, who was given to standing to attention whenever the Bard came near.

The balcony was adorned with flowers and pretty ribbons. Shakespeare complimented Alexander Cooke, who was applying the finishing touches, as Burbage looked on.

Cooke flushed with pride. "Thank you, sir, but Ollie did most of the hard work. I was busy preparing for Juliet's part."

Shakespeare glanced in Downtown's direction and smiled.

Oliver Downtown was a curly-haired, dark-eyed boy who had joined the Company only a fortnight back and had quickly made himself indispensable. He wasn't much of an actor but he was a useful odd-jobs man. The only thing Shakespeare found strange was that he didn't smile much.

"Wonderful aroma," Richard Burbage remarked as Shakespeare turned to him.

The profusion of roses, lilies, marigolds and other sweet-smelling plants wafted around the stage and swirled through the galleries in a most agreeable manner.

"So you've got your sense of smell back, then?" Shakespeare said in reference to Burbage's lingering cold. "Feeling better today?"

Burbage shrugged. "I've been worse. So, what's your excuse? Where've you been? We were worried. John even sent a stagehand- Peter, I think- to your flat but you weren't there."

"What did he do that for? Why would you all worry about me?" Shakespeare sounded annoyed. "Let's not lose our heads over this, Dick. I was..."

He paused as the rehearsal concluded on the stage below and the four players glanced up for his approval.

"Excellent," Shakespeare said and they all smiled. "Who's next?"

"I think we're ready, Will," Heminges said, emerging onto the stage from the tiring-room. "We've done this play so many times that most of us know it by r-r-rote. We're ready for the show."

"What about Tommy? It's his first time as Romeo."

Thomas Gray waved from a seat in the eastern gallery, where he was relaxing. "I'm ready, sir."

Shakespeare smiled and turned his attention to Burbage again.

"You were about to tell me what you were doing this morning," Burbage said.

"I was, wasn't I?" Shakespeare said and his dark brown eyes brooded over. "I retraced his steps, Jeremy's. Hill's Rents to our playhouse. I took three different routes, went via High Street and the Clink; then the direct way from Hill's Rents past the Rose; and finally I walked all the way from Hill's Rents via Paris Garden. On no occasion did it take me more than half-an-hour. So Jeremy could not have come directly from his digs in Hill's Rents to us on Friday morning, not if he left earlier than usual as his landlady testified. He must've taken a detour. But, why? To meet someone? His killer, perhaps?"

"His killer?" Burbage repeated sharply. "We don't know that he was killed, Will. You know we can't be sure of it. He might've died of natural causes..."

"Come now, Dick. You don't really believe that."

As he said this, Shakespeare shot quick glances at Cooke and Downtown. They'd both ceased work and stood staring at him with desolate looks on their faces. Henry Condell also paused his inventory work and waited for Downtown to put a magician's costume into a box.

"My fault," Cooke said in a strained voice. "If I hadn't fallen ill..."

Since they were close friends and practically neighbours

Smith, Cooke and Downtown walked from their tenements to the Globe together every morning. But on Friday their routine had broken. The three of them had been out drinking at St. George's tavern near Hill's Rents the previous night, after which Cooke suddenly took ill. He began to be sick on the way back home and complained of a severe stomach ache. He thought he'd get over it by the morning but when Downtown had come calling at nine the next morning, Cooke said he was still reeling from the effects of his stomach infection- food poisoning or ale-sickness, whatever it was. He asked Downtown to make his excuses to Burbage. Fortunately Cooke was not playing a major part in that day's show, *The Merchant of Venice*. Christopher Beeston, who had just completed his training under Augustine Phillips, was reprising the role of the heroine Portia. Jeremy Smith was supposed to play the part of Nerissa, Portia's nurse. It was his most significant part thus far and he was nearly levitating with joy. He had promised to reach the Globe by nine-thirty sharp so that he could rehearse his lines on stage over and over again before the others arrived.

"I reached his place at a quarter past nine and found that Jeremy had left already," Downtown had said on Friday when Smith's body was discovered. "I asked Mrs. Dogoody about him and she said Jeremy had left earlier than usual. I assumed, naturally, that he'd come straight here, to the Globe like he said he would."

"But he couldn't have," Shakespeare said now as he, Burbage, Cooke and Downtown stood on the balcony. "If he had, he would've reached well before you, Ollie. I was here by nine-thirty that day; you came in soon after. But Jeremy... something must've detained him somewhere."

"Someone, you mean," Burbage said. "And you think that that person followed him or accompanied him here and then killed him?"

Shakespeare pursed his lips. "Isn't that probable?"

"But why here? Why kill him right outside our playhouse?"

"So that we'd find him. If Jeremy was killed someplace else, we might not have found his body for days. It's clear that the killer wanted him found."

"But, why?"

Shakespeare shrugged. "If only we knew...To think he was lying there in the dirt until the flower seller raised the hue-and-cry...How come no one noticed him before...? O, what unfeeling curs we are, walking past a dead boy and assuming he was a drunk or a tramp? Dear Lord, when did the iron enter our souls?"

He paused and the turmoil was only too evident in his face. At the age of thirty-eight Shakespeare was balding prematurely and this caused him no end of grief but it did nothing to diminish the attractiveness of his fine brow, his aquiline nose, and neat beard. His was the kind of face that stood out in a crowd. His demeanour most of the time was kind and compassionate, a commendable fact considering his fame and wealth. He had chosen modest dwellings in Southwark, a two-room flat on the first-floor in a row of houses in a quiet lane between St. Saviour's Church and Winchester House. His main holdings were in his hometown Stratford-upon-Avon, about eighty-five kilometres north of London, where his wife Anne lived with their two young daughters Suzanne and Judith. Their mansion was luxurious, the second biggest house in town, and Shakespeare was thinking of buying a farm, too, on the outskirts of the town.

"Come now, Will, I think it's unjust to consider this incident as a reflection of a character flaw of the entire human race," Burbage said. "The old woman did, after all, alert us to Jeremy's body. She did a brave thing."

Shakespeare made no reply but the old woman's persistent knocking on the Globe's gates and her banshee-like wail still rang in his ears.

'A dead boy! A dead boy! Anon, anon, to the gates, I say...'

Then, suddenly, the gates rattled.

Nobody moved.

A loud, knocking sound.

The players remained frozen as if in a weird re-enactment of the burning of Sodom and Gomorrah, all of them about to be dissolved into pillars of salt.

The knocking continued but- mercifully- it was unaccompanied by crying and wailing.

Shakespeare swept his gaze over the players to make sure they were all accounted for. Armin and the fencing four were walking off the stage; John Heminges was back in the tiring-room; Thomas Gray and another actor called Duncan Sole were amusing themselves with a game of marbles in the western gallery. Sounds of music and chatter from the huts above testified that Thomas Pope and Augustine Phillips were still there, rehearsing the bawdy jig they would perform after the play. Henry Condell was in the Property Room. Burbage, Cooke and Downtown were on the balcony...Suddenly something slithered in the pit of Shakespeare's guts. Richard Cowley and Nicholas Tooley weren't back from the printers' yet; could the knocking be because one of them...

"Davey," Burbage called out to one of the gatherers at the entrance. "Get the gates, will you?"

***

FOUR

Phillip Henslowe was the go-to man in times of trouble. Theatre impresario, owner of two playhouses, producer of plays, financier and money lender- Henslowe thrived on the adversity (and stupidity) of others. He had the enviable knack of bailing people out of trouble and ensuring they remained in his debt for a long, long time. It was a heady feeling, having power over lesser mortals and he ought to have been a contented man, secure in the knowledge that as producer of plays for the Admiral's Men and financier of a new company the Worcester's Men, there was none to rival his power on the London stage. Yet when he stood at the Globe's gates that Monday afternoon, it was a feeling of incompetence that overwhelmed him. This was where his Spanish Armada had been sunk by the prodigious talent of one Englishman. William Shakespeare.

Henslowe gazed at the Globe's logo proudly displayed on the arch above the main entrance: Hercules holding up the globe (as a temporary replacement for Atlas, who'd gone off to pick the golden apples of Hesperides). A legend in Latin ran across its crest: *Totus Mundus Agit Histrionem*. Or, in plain English, 'The Whole World is a Playhouse'.

Yes, Henslowe thought grimly, Shakespeare's playhouse.

He glanced at his son-in-law Edward Alleyn, who stood beside him, and his dark mood intensified. The tall and broad-shouldered Alleyn, popularly called Ned, was one of the most famous actors of the day. He dwarfed the crowds outside the gates. One p.m. and spectators were milling outside the Globe in the hope of getting the best standing space in the pit in front of the stage. Alleyn's rendition of parts like Tamburlaine and the Jew of Malta, both eponymous plays by the late Christopher Marlowe, had won him many admirers. Several spectators recognized him outside the Globe, and excited cries of 'Ned!' 'Greetings, Ned' 'Welcome back, Ned Alleyn!' filled the air. Alleyn basked in the attention and shook hands all round, conveniently neglecting to mention that he was not there to perform on stage in the Bankside but only to accompany Henslowe, who had business with Richard Burbage.

How can he be so cheerful? Henslowe wondered. Doesn't he know that fame is as fleeting as the summer breeze and that it depends on the quality of plays performed, not on individual actors?

Henslowe had no dearth of actors; it was his repertory

of good plays that was getting depleted at an alarming rate. His chief playmaker Benjamin Jonson was a talented, learned chap but he wasn't in Shakespeare's league. His two most popular plays *Everyman in His Humour and Everyman Out of His Humour* were no match for Shakespeare's *As You Like It or A Midsummer's Night Dream* or *A Comedy of Errors...*or any Shakespearean comedy, for that matter.

The Globe's gates opened after an interminable wait and Henslowe entered with Alleyn at his side. The Chamberlain's Men were present in full force. The stage was set with a backdrop describing a public square, and players were moving about purposefully in their costumes. Clearly, a performance was about to begin. Shakespeare and Burbage were looking down from the balcony above the tiring-room. Juliet's terrace, no doubt. It was adorned with beautiful, multi-coloured flowers and the air was redolent with their pleasing fragrances.

Alleyn took out a penny from his pocket and asked with a crooked smile: "How much for a seat in the gallery, good sirs?"

"No charge for you," Burbage called back in reply. "Come in, come in, both of you."

There was only the slightest trace of annoyance in his tone.

Fancy having the Admiral's Men turn up just before a show. `Can't be a good omen. Would the queen, for instance, relish having Philip the Second of Spain casting his evil eye over her Coronation Day celebrations? When your bitter rival is around, you may safely assume that misfortune is hovering about as well. Burbage knew in his heart that something would go wrong that day. He and Shakespeare turned away from the balcony and made for the stairs so that they could greet the newcomers but Henslowe raised his hand and said:

"Don't bother coming down. We'll join you."

A hush fell over the playhouse. All eyes focussed on the slim, fifty-two-year old Henslowe and his tall, grinning son-in-law as they walked towards the rear lip of the stage and then up the wooden steps.

"Congratulations," Henslowe said, panting a little once he reached the first-floor, where Shakespeare was standing to receive him. "The crowds outside: wonderful. The kind I was accustomed to when the Rose was at her peak."

Shakespeare smiled, shook his hand warmly, and said: "I remember. Those were good times, Mr. Henslowe, and not so long ago. Hello. How nice to see you. Hello, Ned. Welcome."

Alleyn shook hands, too.

"Three years, isn't it, since you put this place together?" Henslowe said. "Beam-by-beam. A truly Herculean effort; it's good you've put him on the gate. I watched the Globe rise like the Phoenix from this muddy plot of land. I knew then..."

Henslowe paused and deleted the rest of his intended sentence:...that the Globe would be a roaring success and that my days in Southwark were numbered. He swallowed hard. The memory of the building of the Globe always evoked mixed feelings in him. There was admiration, of course, for who would've thought such a thing was possible? In Fifteen Ninety-Seven it seemed that the Chamberlain's Men would be forced to disband. Cuthbert and Richard Burbage's father James Burbage had built one of the first playhouses in London, the Theatre in Shoreditch. The brothers inherited it after his death and performed there as the Chamberlain's Men from Fifteen Ninety-Four onwards. Three years later, the lease on the land ran out and the landlord, an unsmiling Puritan (is there any other kind?) called Giles Allen, refused to renew the contract. It was a major blow for the Company. Lesser men might've given in, either closing down the Company, or returning to the old touring ways when players travelled around the countryside performing in inn yards and noblemen's houses. But the Burbage brothers and Shakespeare didn't lose heart.

Cuthbert Burbage reasoned that although the lease on the land had expired, the theatre building was still theirs. It had been erected by their father not Giles Allen. So he suggested they use the building's material to put up a new playhouse. They chose Clink liberty on the Bankside since it was outside London city's Puritanical authorities. The project took a while to fructify and complete secrecy had to be maintained since Giles Allen would've been none too pleased if he'd got wind of their plan. Miraculously, it all worked out.

While Giles was away celebrating Christmas in his country house, the Chamberlain's Men and a dozen labourers or so began, on a cold December night in Fifteen Ninety-Eight, to dismantle the Theatre and carry it across the Thames, which happened to be frozen that year. The men carried twelve-inch beams that were later used to form the Globe's main frame. The material that could not be transported across the river was stored in the carpenter Peter Street's warehouse in Bridewell. Street and his team worked a steady pace and erected the Globe within six months. Henslowe still recalled that day in Fifteen Ninety-Nine when the new playhouse opened with a booming trumpet call, heralding the performance of William Shakespeare's new Roman saga, *Julius Caesar*. And he knew his days in the Bankside were numbered.

Two years later when he and Alleyn stood before Burbage and Shakespeare on the Globe's balcony, there was a lot of excess baggage amongst them.

"Heard about your dead player," Henslowe said directly. "My condolences. Who was he?"

"A young boy, apprenticed to Tom Pope," Burbage said. "Jeremy Smith. Just seventeen."

Henslowe shook his head regretfully. "Too bad. What happened? I heard that his body was found outside just before the show. How did he die?"

"We don't know; that's what's so distressing. He seems to have just dropped dead..."

"It was foul play," Shakespeare interjected. "I'm sure of it. But since there were no injury marks, no blood, we've no idea what happened. Misfortune can be met with stoicism if the cause is known. This kind of uncertainty is very hard to deal with."

"But surely the coroner must have some suggestions about the cause of death," Alleyn said.

Shakespeare grimaced. "Natural causes, he said. No other explanation. He couldn't be bothered with a proper inquiry. The boy was an orphan; we were his family but without a real next of kin, Her Majesty's Coroner is hardly bothered..."

"Dear me. I'm very sorry to hear all this," Henslowe said. "Let's hope you have no more bad luck." Then he glanced around and said: "So it's *Romeo & Juliet*, eh? Great play but one of your best lines is from *A Midsummer's Night Dream*. Never did the course of true love run smooth. One of your best lines, if I may say, Will, because of the truth in it. I suppose one can say the same of true friendship, what?"

Shakespeare smiled. Henslowe was in quite a mood today. Not surprising. He was getting on, after all. But the spark in his eye had not diminished, the burning ambition to over-reach himself, to claim the Golden Fleece, to rule the London stage... Their last meeting had been acrimonious with Burbage accusing Phillip Henslowe of plagiarism. For when the Globe's success caused a decline in the fortunes of the other two Bankside playhouses- the Rose and the Swan (owned by one Francis Langley)- Henslowe decided to cut his losses and move in the opposite direction, to Shoreditch outside the city limits. There he built the Fortune. Much to the Chamberlain's Men's consternation, the new playhouse was architecturally identical to the Globe. Henslowe had even employed the same carpenter, Peter Street.

Alleyn ran his fingers along the balcony's railing and said:

"Lovely. Every inch is covered. Who is Romeo today?"

"A new boy, Thomas Gray," said Burbage. "We're trying him out..."

"Ah, let's hope it's not too trying for the audience!"

Alleyn chuckled at his own joke and Burbage's face darkened. Henslowe put a restraining hand on his son-in-law's shoulder.

Alleyn and Burbage were natural enemies. Alleyn was famous mainly for Tamburlaine and the Jew of Malta; Burbage was hailed for his masterful turn as Richard the Third, Brutus, Romeo, *Hamlet*...the list went on and on, commensurate with nearly each of Shakespeare's awesome lead characters. Over a decade ago the two actors had performed together at the Theatre in a play called *Dead Man's Fortune*. They'd gotten along quite well even though it was evident to everyone that they were competitors. But the bonhomie didn't last long. They got entangled in a petty dispute over wages and Alleyn left in a huff, accusing the Burbage brothers of withholding a week's earnings due to him. And Richard Burbage heaved a sigh of relief; at he had the stage to himself...at least at his own theatre.

Now, as Alleyn towered over him on the balcony, Burbage snapped: "It's nearly opening time. Have you come to see the play or is there some other purpose behind your visit?"

"There is a purpose," Henslowe said. "Sorry, I know we should've come straight to the point. I can see you are occupied. It's just that...well...we're closing the Fortune for a while..."

"What? Already?" Burbage said with ill-concealed delight. "Is business so bad in Shoreditch now?"

Shakespeare gave him a sharp look and a silent rebuke. Henslowe ignored the bad feeling and said:

"It will only be for a week or so. Our playhouse requires some minor renovations. Street and his team are standing by but first I thought I'd talk to you."

He paused.

Shakespeare and Burbage waited expectantly.

"We were wondering about performing here in the Bankside again," Henslowe continued. "The Rose is still functional. I let it out three days a week to the Worcester's Men. Talentless upstarts, they are, aren't they? The Earl of Worcester thinks he can ride on our success, ours, the Admiral's and the Chamberlain's Men. He doesn't realize that one must first have a solid foundation. That is solid works, plays, upon which to build a company. They have only a few minor works and Thomas Dekker. Who's he? A mere pamphleteer who doesn't know the first thing about real drama. Can't even spell 'Aristotle', I'm sure, much less understand the Theory of Drama. He hangs about Ben all day thinking he can imbibe some of Ben's talent. Pooh, pooh, that's what I say. Anyhow, I let out the Rose to them and wish `em luck. They prefer using the Boar's Head Inn courtyard most evenings, anyway. `No competition from you all in the Bankside, see?"

"The Boar's Head Inn in the city? How did Garrard permit that?" Burbage said, referring to the Lord Mayor of London.

A Puritan sympathiser, Garrard hated players with the kind of passion Nero once displayed towards the Christians. Like the erstwhile Fiddler of Rome, Garrard would, if he could, joyously serve up actors and playwrights as fodder for lions. But since this presented certain technical constraints, he lost no opportunity in closing down playhouses at the slightest provocation and in arresting stage actors on charges of vagrancy. Naturally, he was not buddy-buddy with the Lord Chamberlain or with the Lord High Admiral.

"The Worcester's Men are too insignificant to warrant Garrard's attention," Henslowe said with a dismissive wave of his hand. "Now, I was wondering if we might come to some arrangement?"

"We?" Burbage said in surprise. "What do you mean, sir?" Then it dawned on him. "You want to perform here? At the Globe?"

Henslowe nodded.

Burbage looked like he'd had the wind taken out of him. He stared at Henslowe and Alleyn and then at Shakespeare. It wasn't unusual for other companies to use the Globe on rare occasions. They could hire it for a day or for an evening but the Admiral's Men...?

"But...what about the Rose?" he stuttered. "You...you've let it out but it's still yours, isn't it?"

"The Rose is not what it used to be," Henslowe said with a sigh. "It's hardly been maintained since we moved two years back. Besides, I've already committed it to the Worcester's

Men thrice a week for the next two weeks. Somerset, the earl of Worcester, is a prickly chap. I don't relish being the cause of friction between him and our Lord Admiral. And I hardly need to sing paeans to the Globe's reputation; you have a devoted audience. Ned and I have a better chance of drawing them in here than at the Rose."

"But what kind of arrangement...? Surely you don't expect us to vacate our playhouse for you?"

"Certainly not, Dick. You know me better than that. Give us the mornings; we'll perform at nine o'clock. You can have the theatre back by one, after noon. There'll be enough time for you to prepare the stage for your two o'clock show."

"What about wardrobe? Props? We don't share..."

"We'll bring our own, of course. Both sides will need to accommodate one another, Dick. This request is not without precedent. You performed at the Rose a number of times before the Globe sprang up. This is a business proposition. I'm giving you the chance to enhance your Company's profits for a week; we'll pay your hiring fee, of course."

Burbage hesitated, scratched his brown beard, and then said: "All right, twenty-five percent."

"Twenty-five?" Alleyn exclaimed. "Have you taken leave of your senses?"

Henslowe clenched his teeth and muttered: "Ten percent. That's normal. That's fair and you know it."

"Twenty-five," Burbage insisted.

"Why?" cried Alleyn. "You charge others ten percent of their earnings; I know that. So why are you discriminating against us? Afraid we'll steal your audience, Dick? Hasn't Pa just explained that it's a temporary arrangement? One week, that's all. Will...?"

Alleyn looked askance at Shakespeare, beseeching him to take a stand. He was a senior stakeholder, 'the' Bard, and Dick Burbage's closest friend. His word carried weight.

Shakespeare's face clouded and he glanced at Burbage in silence. But he chose not to interfere.

"Twenty per cent," Burbage said. "That's my final offer."

Henslowe shook his head.

"You're envious, that's what," Alleyn said. "You can't bear to see anyone else's success. You all destroyed the Rose, the Swan- everything on the Bankside! Francis Langley died of a broken heart because of you."

"Langley?" Burbage repeated incredulously. "You can't blame us for his downfall. He was the most self-destructive man in the world, his own worst enemy."

Francis Langley had led an adventurous life and he was frequently in trouble with the law and with the Revels Office, the royal department under the Master of the Revels that issued licenses to playhouses and monitored all public performances. He died in January that year. Like the Rose,

Langley's playhouse the Swan also suffered on account of the Globe's success and it fell into disuse a few years back.

"Oh, you all will never admit your complicity in anything," Alleyn said. "You've always been jealous of me, too. Why don't we step outside and settle this like men, eh?"

Alleyn advanced menacingly at Burbage. He appeared even taller and bigger than he was and it couldn't have been much fun for Burbage to discover that his nose was level with Ned Alleyn's chest. But Burbage stood his ground and didn't even flinch.

Shakespeare made a move to restrain Alleyn. The image of Alleyn giving Burbage a leg over the balcony suddenly flashed across his mind and it wasn't a pleasant sight.

"Ned, let it go," he said.

"Why? You all know I'm right," Alleyn continued. "Dick can't deal with the truth- that the Queen prefers me to him. Everybody knows I came out of retirement only because she asked me to."

True, true.

Ned Alleyn had abruptly exited the stage five years back. He and Henslowe had already bought an interest in the bear-baiting business in Bear Gardens on the Bankside and Alleyn decided to concentrate on it. The next year, 'Ninety-Eight, he and Henslowe tried to get appointed to the office of Master of the Royal Game of Bulls and Bears after the death of the incumbent Ralph Bowes. But another enterprising chap John

Dorrington beat them to it and the duo had to be content with a deputyship under Dorrington. It was still enough to keep Alleyn occupied. He also bought some land in St. Leonard's parish, Shoreditch, and leased out tenements in an area called Alleyn's Rents. One of the Chamberlain's Men- Richard Cowley- was his tenant.

Alleyn's departure left Richard Burbage as the sole superstar on the London stage, a situation most agreeable to him but his delight was short-lived. Queen Elizabeth began to miss her favourite actor and she instructed the Master of the Revels Edward Tilney to coax him to return.

"I want my Tamburlaine back," she said in open court.

Who could refuse summons like that? So Edward Alleyn returned to the stage in Sixteen Hundred and performed at the new Fortune playhouse.

"Destroyers, that's what you are," Alleyn railed and shook off Shakespeare's hand. "May God forgive you, for I won't."

"We didn't destroy or steal anything," Burbage retorted. "People simply chose the better Company."

"Look sharp, Dick, I get the whiff of pride," Henslowe said, tapping his nose. "It's a nasty odour indeed. Remember what the wisest king said: Pride goeth before destruction and a haughty spirit before a fall. Proverbs, Sixteen, in case you want to look it up. We came to you with a business proposition but if you're not interested, that's all right."

The gates rattled just then. Quarter-to-two. Time to admit

the crowds. The gatherers at the gates glanced up at Burbage and Shakespeare. Burbage signalled to them to wait.

"We'll be on our way anon," Henslowe said. "The Admiral's Men have weathered many a storm; this is no more than an intrusive breeze. It will blow over. We won't be ruined if we don't earn for a week or so."

"That's right, Pa," said Alleyn. "Besides, our fee for the command performance at Court ought to tide things over for a while."

Having said this he paused, and got the reaction he'd hoped for: flashes of surprise in Shakespeare's and Burbage's eyes.

"What? Haven't you heard?" Alleyn said gleefully. "We're performing in Court the day after tomorrow. Her Majesty is hosting a banquet in honour of King Christian of Denmark, who's just arrived in London. We've been invited to perform- what else?- *Tamburlaine*. Yours truly will, of course, reprise his most famous role. Will you be there, watching from the sidelines?"

Burbage pursed his lips and exchanged a look with Shakespeare that said it all: How could this happen? The Lord Chamberlain managed the royal household; they were the Chamberlain's Men. How could he permit another company to perform before the queen and a royal guest? Why, the Chamberlain's Men hadn't even received an invite to the banquet.

"Marry, you didn't know?" Alleyn rubbed it in. "No

invitation, either? Tut-tut. I suppose we won't be seeing you then."

"Ned." Henslowe's tone was mildly reproachful. "Our business is concluded here. We'd best leave now. Good day, Will, Dick. All the best for the show."

He turned to leave.

"Fifteen percent," said Burbage.

Henslowe paused at the head of the stairs, cocked his head to one side, and said:

"Nah, Dick. I'm afraid the Globe's too small for both our companies. Farewell."

He left.

Alleyn gave Burbage and Shakespeare wry smiles and followed his father-in-law down the steps.

As the gates opened to let them through, spectators began to stream inside in a disorderly queue. The gatherers quickly got into position with their coin-collection boxes.

"Tom! The trumpet," Burbage called out to Pope, who was still in the hut above with Augustine Phillips and other musicians.

"I hear you," Pope responded and promptly sounded the trumpet.

There'd be three calls about two minutes apart.

Burbage tried to avoid Shakespeare's eye and turned away from the balcony.

"Come on, Will, let us repair to the tiring-room. We can watch from there."

"You could have just said 'no'," Shakespeare said. "There was no need to treat them like that, especially Henslowe."

"Marry, Will, don't go all sentimental on me. Of course I have deep regard for Phil Henslowe but Alleyn is a conceited bastard. He's getting worse all the time. Saw the way he was gloating? Damn, why didn't the great Lord Carey do something about it? What kind of Lord Chamberlain is he? Alack, to think they'll be performing before the King of Denmark!"

"Ned is the Queen's favourite," Henry Condell said from the Property Room. "No getting away from that."

"Thanks, Harry, that makes me feel so much better," Burbage shot back. "What were the names of Job's comforters? Wasn't one of them called 'Henry Eliphaz Condell'?"

The Wardrobe Manager shrugged. "I'm just saying...And *Tamburlaine* is a wonderful work, poor Kit's best. He must be turning with joy in his grave."

Christopher 'Kit' Marlowe had died in a tavern brawl nine years back.

"But aren't we famous for *Hamlet*, the Prince of Denmark?" Oliver Downtown said in a soft voice. He and Alexander Cooke had stood by and watched the balcony from the Property Room when Henslowe and Alleyn were visiting. "If the Danish King is visiting, shouldn't we...?"

"*Hamlet* is a tragedy and it doesn't portray the Danish court in a favourable light," Condell said. "You've been with us for two weeks; haven't we performed *Hamlet* while you were here?"

"I...er...don't know," Downtown said with a nervous glance at Shakespeare.

"We have," said Shakespeare.

"We did it ten days ago," Alexander Cooke said. "You had just joined."

"That's why you don't recall the line 'Something's rotten in the state of Denmark'!" Condell said with a chuckle. "I don't think that would fill the Danish king's heart with joy, would it?"

"I...suppose not, Mr. Condell."

"We needn't have done *Hamlet*; we could have performed any other play," Burbage said, still sulky. "But I suppose it's quite certain we won't get the chance..."

"Have patience, Dick," Shakespeare said. "It's not like we've never performed in Court. Opportunity will surely knock our way again soon. As of now, let's concentrate on today's show. See, the Globe is full; people are waiting. I do believe we are about to be transported to the city of Verona!"

***

FIVE

The floor of the pit in front of the stage was lined with straw. About a thousand spectators were packed into the area. Double that number thronged the galleries where they'd paid two pennies to sit on wooden benches. In the balconies on either sides of the stage, the three penny customers sat on cushioned seats. Will Sly stumbled once and there was a heart-stopping moment all round since he nearly fell onto the pointy end of Beeston's sword. But Beeston pulled the blade away just in time and so the tension dissipated.

The play was so popular that many people in the audience knew it by rote. Shakespeare was amused to see a couple of women in the pit mouthing Romeo's lines along with Thomas Gray.

Love is a smoke raised with the fume of sighs;

Being purged, a fire sparkling in lover's eyes...

His landlady, a roly-poly widow called Mrs. Humphreys, was an ardent admirer and a repository of helpful advice and street smart wisdom.

"Why don't you go home more often, sir?" she had asked him once and he had stiffened. "It's been four months since you visited Stratford last, hasn't it?"

He averted his eyes from her bulging gaze. "I don't know; I haven't been counting the days."

"Well, I have, if you don't mind me sayin' so. A man needs to be with his family. Otherwise there's no point in life. My poor Johnny couldn't bear to be away from me for more than a few days, he couldn't. We was happy. But you spend months and months..."

"It's because of my work here, Mrs. Humphreys. You know there's so much pressure for new plays. The audience is very demanding nowadays. We have to give them new things all the time."

"Aye, but four months?"

She had hit a nerve and he had half a mind to tell her to go stuff herself. But he'd held his peace and just clammed up instead.

Stratford was his home and he knew he would live there after he retired. But there were no real ties to bind him there anymore; his wife and he were together for their daughters' sakes only. He took his responsibilities seriously but his heart was not there anymore.

She —his true love-was here; his heart was here. It was all he lived for.

Duty weighs you down but love carries you up like a buoy in water...

***

He had decided that everyone would remember him as the best Romeo ever. Thomas Gray put his heart and soul into every gesture, every line that he spoke. Most of the spectators had watched the play before and they were riveted, waiting for their favourite scenes. Gray was unaware of them; he was sensitive only to the presence of his fellow actors in different scenes. Every nerve in his body felt raw and so alive! He had rehearsed his part well and dearly hoped Shakespeare would be satisfied. If so, there might be more lead roles for him. Maybe he would become a regular replacement for Richard Burbage, whenever the great actor needed a break. Gray possessed a ruddy and eager disposition. His gestures had just the right amount of restraint. He knew how Shakespeare hated the players overdoing anything. He slipped up a few times with his lines but the prompter John Heminges was right there, whispering the words he needed, and the show went off smoothly- Until the balcony scene in the middle of the play-

***

"A bottle of Ale, sir? Ha' penny packet of nuts?"

The smiling vendor stood before Shakespeare in the western gallery, where the Bard was sitting with Henry Condell and watching the show. Shakespeare nodded absent-mindedly, though he really meant 'no, thank you.'

"Cakes, then, sir?" the vendor persisted and tried to hand Shakespeare something.

"Uh, no, nothing," Shakespeare brushed him aside and gazed over his shoulder. The balcony scene was about to commence and the audience was in a tizzy with anticipation. It was a fun sequence in which Romeo meets Juliet in her chamber and then flees by climbing down the bier when her mother Lady Capulet arrives. The crowds loved it and cheered each time Romeo made good his escape.

"Sir." The vendor dropped his tone and said: "A lady in Box Three gave me this for you."

He pressed a small piece of paper into Shakespeare's hand.

Shakespeare's heart leapt. Even without opening the note, he knew it was from her. She was here! He smiled at the vendor and rewarded him with a penny. The fellow winked and walked away.

Shakespeare stole a glance at Condell; fortunately, his friend had been too engrossed in the on-stage action to notice the exchange with the vendor.

"I'll be back anon," Shakespeare said to Condell, and

hurried towards the steps leading to the balcony where the boxes were located. He opened the note and grinned. Yes, it was their secret sign: the sketch of a heart with an arrow piercing it. Beneath was the number 3. Just in case the vendor forgot to mention the box number.

She is a pearl, whose price hath launched a thousand ships- that's how he'd described Helen of Troy. But it was not the legendary queen of Sparta who'd inspired him while he was working on *Troilus & Cressida*; it was the woman waiting for him in Box Three. His heart soared and he felt like he was levitating as he rushed towards the small room. The merest glimpse of those grey-green eyes or of the lovely dark hair that cascaded down her slender shoulders or even of her wrists (a la Nausica of the slim ankles in The Odyssey) could make his legs all gooey and his heart ram against his ribs, as if seeking a means of escape.

Moments later he'd entered the box and there she was.

"My darling!"

His appearance brought a big grin to her face and she leapt into his arms. Her maid smiled and withdrew to wait in the corridor outside.

"How are you, my love?" she murmured with quivering lips and he kissed her hard and with great emotion.

"I am in heaven, now that you're here," he said after drawing away. He clasped her hands to his chest. "When did you come?"

"It's been about five minutes. I can't stay long, William."

"Oh? You won't stay for the show?"

"Would love to but I can't. We're in London for the day. I managed to get away by telling him that I needed to visit the shops, the drapers on Lombard Street. He let me go with Louise. But I must hurry back. William, I had to come to warn you. I think he knows..."

Her voice trailed off and Shakespeare put his hands to her lips. Lovely lips, full and red and swollen with the taste of strawberries. He kissed her again.

"William, you're not listening! I fear you are in danger."

He smiled. "Say that again."

He loved her accent, the way she said 'Weeliam' and 'danjeur'. He wondered why the French ever tried to speak correct English.

"Oh, you're impossible. Why don't you listen?" Her eyes were troubled, greener and deeper than usual.

"My darling Marie, I don't care about my safety; it's you I'm concerned about."

"Please, William, promise me you will be careful. I can't stand the thought of losing you. This is not one of your plays; it's real life."

"All right, I'll be careful." He gazed into her eyes again. They were the colour of the sea on a warm summer's day when the sun beats down in a cloudless sky and the water takes it in, sending back gorgeous hues of emerald and muted silver...

"I have to go. He will begin to miss me..."

"Are you sure no one followed you here?"

Marie rolled her eyes. "*Enfin*! So you have been listening to me. No, I was not followed. Louise is very careful."

"How can you be sure he knows?"

Marie hesitated. "It...it's silly...I'll tell you later. I just know. Promise me you will take this seriously, Mon Cher..."

"I promise."

"Farewell, farewell! One kiss, and I'll descend," Romeo declared, ready to climb down the chord offered by Juliet's nurse, played by Nick Tooley.

Gray's and Beeston's lips met briefly and awkwardly. Then Gray got one leg over the railing and began to descend.

Shakespeare and Marie watched from the VIP box.

Sepulchral silence filled the amphitheatre. Then a cracking sound cut through the air. The players paused, confused. The crowd murmured. The sound became louder, the balcony's railing came apart, and three thousand spectators watched in horror as Thomas Gray went hurtling down head first onto the wooden stage below-

***

Four days later.

Whitehall Palace.

Enter the Lord Chamberlain George Carey the second Baron Hunsdon with his usual retinue of four men in attendance, all walking briskly along the dank corridors towards his office chamber. Their faces were taut and tense. Occasionally one of them glanced out of the large windows on either side and sighed at the miserable wet weather. As if the Lord Chamberlain's troubles weren't enough, the rain gods had decided to pour buckets that Thursday morning. The sky was grey and gloomy like an enormous maelstrom shrouding the city.

"Have they arrived? Where are they?" Carey demanded of his secretary, a dour-faced chap called Bleach, who reminded one of a victim in a Dracula tale. Even his lips were bloodless.

"Yes, sir. They're waiting in Your Lordship's office," Bleach replied in a whinny voice.

"Good. Have they said anything yet?"

"Yes, sir. They asked: 'When will His Lordship arrive?'"

Carey scowled. "No, you fool, I meant, did they say anything about the last incident?"

"Er...no, sir. They wait upon Your Lordship's leave."

Carey harrumphed. "They'd better have some answers for me. I can't let this go on."

"No, My Lord."

His attendants rushed ahead to throw open the heavy office doors and Carey strode into his official chamber with a flourish, his red velvet cape swinging behind him, his black shoes gleaming with spit and polish.

To the left of the room, a wooden desk was piled high with state papers, ink pot and quills. Carey went and stood behind it while Bleach began to sift through papers and files. Hanging on a wall across the room was a large and colourful map of England, the first accurate representation of the rivers and towns in the country. It was the work of a man called Christopher Saxton, whose painstaking research had yielded thirty-four maps, county by county. Each county was printed in a different colour and when stuck together, they formed a picture of the whole country.

Two men were standing in front of this map. They bowed gently and greeted Carey.

"My Lord."

The Lord Chamberlain gave them hard looks and didn't acknowledge the greeting. Instead, he took off his black gloves, sat heavily on a wooden straight-back chair behind the big desk, and then launched into a tirade.

"Master Shakespeare, Mister Burbage, can either of you enlighten me? Can you tell me who, or what, has brought this evil upon us? Three incidents in a week! Two players dead; one, worse than dead. This has become a tragedy, a Grecian tragedy, not one of yours, William. Now tell me, what do you propose to do?"

Silence.

A rhetorical question, surely. They were still struggling to come to terms with the previous night's incident.

"No plans? Are you just going to stand by and let that son of a whore John Garrard walk all over me? This is exactly the kind of opportunity the fat sod's been waiting for! Trouble in the Chamberlain's Men. Shut down the Globe. That's his aim, mind you. But, no. No, sir, I will not give him the satisfaction. That dog!"

Silence again.

But Shakespeare and Burbage nodded in agreement with Carey's vitriol. They shared his sentiments regarding the Lord

Mayor of London and frequently expressed these in much ruder terms.

"I don't need to tell you how this makes me look," Carey said, and proceeded to do exactly that. "Stupid. Helpless. Impotent! Garrard must be laughing behind my back. I can almost hear him hacking...How come no one's dying in the Lord Admiral's Company? Or in Pembroke's Men? Or in that upstart Lord Worcester Somerset's Company? What's it called?"

"The Worcester's Men," Shakespeare, Burbage and Bleach said in unison and then started in surprise.

"Yes, yes. Worcester's. He's a fool, you know, thinks he can leapfrog over us. Don't you have any ideas at all? What shall we do to stop this murderer?"

"Er..." said Burbage.

Shakespeare stroked his beard and said, "Umm..." as if in deep thought.

Carey narrowed his eyes. "Suppose it's not me they're after? What if it's one of you? William, could it be a rival? A jealous playmaker?"

"Perhaps, my Lord."

"But, who? All playmakers must be envious of your success. Does one of them hate you enough to target your players?"

"Maybe, my Lord, I'm not sure."

"And feelings are so unreliable, as Your Lordship knows surely," Burbage interjected quickly with a restraining hand on Shakespeare's arm. 'We don't know anything. We have no proof of anybody's involvement in these terrible, terrible incidents. My Lord, if we knew anything..."

"What about creditors?" Carey demanded. "Are you concealing some facts from me? Is the Company in financial trouble? Do you owe anybody money?"

Burbage shook his head.

"Someone might be extracting his money's worth in blood," Carey said, screwing up his nose with distaste. "Like that fellow in your play, William, The Merchant of Venice. He wanted his pound of flesh, didn't he? What about that litigious fellow, Francis Something?"

"Francis Langley, my Lord," Burbage said. "He died earlier this year. My Lord, I assure you that the Company is flourishing. You have nothing to be concerned about on that account. We've run everybody else out of business in Southwark."

"Then what is it? Who could be behind all this?" Carey demanded, thumping his desk hard and startling Bleach, who was still rummaging through official papers.

Carey had a square face with thick eyebrows and an ample brown beard. His eyes, quick and impatient, reflected his personality. A man adept at multitasking, always on his toes. Understandable, given his position as Manager of the Queen's household.

"Who is trying to harm us like this?" he railed. "A jealous husband? William, I've heard rumours about you and a certain dark lady...?"

Shakespeare stiffened.

"Seems that you poured out verse after verse in her praise when you dedicated those poems to Southampton. Who is she? Perhaps it's her husband...?"

Shakespeare said nothing and Burbage quickly made light of the whole thing by chuckling and saying:

"Husbands, my Lord; surely Your Lordship means husbands, plural! They're so many. But I hardly think they would kill our players."

"Bah, you two are useless," Carey exclaimed. "I can't let this continue. You had a narrow escape last year; now this? Southampton! Good Lord, William, didn't you dedicate your long poem to Wriothesley, as well?"

Shakespeare nodded grimly. "Yes, my Lord, The Rape of Lucrece and Venus and Adonis. The Earl was my patron at the time."

"Ah, so he was, wasn't he? You certainly know how to pick them, your patrons, I mean."

Carey laughed and failed to see that the sarcasm was misdirected since he was Shakespeare's patron now.

"My Lord, I couldn't have known."

Shakespeare's protest was as sullen as he could afford, and Carey quickly sobered up.

"I know, I know. None of us could've foreseen it. That's why you all were spared. That, and your friend Augustine Phillips's spirited defence. He proved to be a remarkable orator."

Orator, my foot, thought Shakespeare. Phillips's defence had consisted mostly of tearful assertions of the players' loyalty to the Queen and of emotional protestations of innocence. The charges: collaboration with the Earl of Essex Robert Devereux and his friends, who had rebelled against the Queen in February Sixteen Hundred and One. The eighth of February, to be exact. A few days before, Essex's close friend Sir Gelly Meyrick approached the Chamberlain's Men and asked them to perform Richard the Second on the seventh of February. Prima facie it seemed like an innocuous request. The players were accustomed to having noblemen come to them with requests for command performances. Naturally they obliged whenever possible. This time they'd dithered because Richard the Second was an old play and no longer high on the audience's popularity list. They feared the Company would suffer a loss for performing it. Not to worry, said Meyrick, they would be compensated handsomely. He paid them the generous sum of 2p40s, an extraordinary amount, and the play was performed at the Globe in public.

Richard the Second was always controversial because of its elaborate deposition scene: King Richard giving away his throne and sceptre to the pretender Bolingbroke, who became Henry the Fourth. It struck at the very heart of the 'Divine Right' theory of kingship. Shakespeare did, of course, portray Richard as a weak and ineffectual king, nothing like the current monarch. But, with Queen Elizabeth in her late sixties, unmarried and childless, the issue of succession was an important political concern. John Hayward, who'd written a history of Henry the Fourth, was imprisoned for his portrayal of a perceived analogy between QEI and Richard II. To compound his troubles, he had dedicated his work to none other than Robert Devereux.

Oblivious to its sinister implications, the Chamberlain's Men performed Richard the Second that afternoon in February 1601. Twelve of Essex's supporters watched it. Henry Wriothesley, the Earl of Southampton and Shakespeare's erstwhile patron, was one of them. The performance was intended as a deliberately incendiary act. Essex and his misguided band raised their rebellious flag the next morning by marching through the city streets and hoping that the populace would rise up with them. Their stated objective was not to depose the Queen but to make her see reason, to expose her close confidants Robert Cecil and his father the Lord Burghley, who was heading the Privy Council.

It was a disastrous rebellion, hardly worth its name. Essex and his cronies were swiftly overpowered and arrested. The public did not support them. The Queen set up an inquiry committee and, in the days to come, the Chamberlain's Men's role was questioned. Shakespeare wasn't singled out because Richard the Second was an old play and everyone was aware of the deposition scene, which had previously been edited by the Master of the Revels. It was the timing of its performance that was suspect. The Company was asked to prepare its defence and appear before the Committee of Inquiry. Any senior player could represent the Chamberlain's Men.

The dice fell on Augustine Phillips.

Slim, athletic, a witty speaker and one who had ample experience in the business, Phillips proved equal to the task.

The Chamberlain's Men were absolved of all charges and they were even invited to perform before the Queen on the day she signed Devereux's death warrant. Devereux, Meyrick, and five others were beheaded. Henry Wriothesely's neck was spared on account of his mother's influential appeal; he was imprisoned in the Tower for two years.

That was the end of the sorry affair and Shakespeare's close brush with political conspiracies.

"I'm calling in assistance from outside," Carey said, pacing the floor of his office. "Someone with no connection to plays and playhouses. A young man with a sharp, analytical mind. A knight of renown." Carey rubbed his hands together and went on: "I've got it all worked out. He will be my agent in the Company. He'll join you as an apprentice, get to know everybody, and solve this damned case. We must stop the killer before he finishes off all my players. Bleach, will you stop rummaging in those papers? You remind me of a rat sometimes. What's so important anyway?"

He turned to confer with Bleach and left Shakespeare and Burbage open-mouthed and staring at each other in dismay.

An outsider?

A spy in their midst?

Carey's agent?!

Bad idea! They certainly didn't relish the thought of having Carey's appointee poking his nose into their affairs. The company at the Globe was a cohesive unit. They had their share of internal squabbles but whenever a stranger appeared on the scene the players closed ranks in a manner reminiscent (or so they liked to think) of a Spartan phalanx. It would be hard to accept a new player and make him privy to Company secrets.

Carey grunted, put his quill to paper, handed the paper to Bleach, and then turned to the other two again.

"So, as you see, the problem should be sorted out soon. The young man I've chosen is brilliant, take my word for it. He's a real problem-solver."

"May we know his identity, My Lord?" Burbage asked in a neutral tone.

"Oh, haven't I mentioned his name? The two of you are the only ones that will know. You've heard of Francis Drake..."

"Sir Francis? My Lord, but he is..."

"Long dead, six feet under. Yes, I am aware of that, Richard. Don't pre-empt me. Didn't I say this gentleman was young? It's Drake's nephew Geoffrey, his brother's son. Francis Drake died childless so his coat-of-arms, property and everything went to his younger brother John. Geoffrey is John's younger son. A fine Knight Bachelor. Have you heard of him?"

"Of course, My Lord," Burbage and Shakespeare said together. Who hadn't heard of the gentleman?

A celebrated knight.

Twenty-four-years old.

A dashing chap, whose lance and sword had won him top honours at the tournament held on Coronation Day three years in a row. He was one of the Queen's favourites and was expected to be invested as a Knight of the Garter sometime soon. It was the highest honour accorded to a knight. All very well, but how would any of these attributes make Sir Geoffrey a successful spy? If anything, his flamboyance and high profile should preclude him from dissembling. But who could make the Lord Chamberlain see reason?

Burbage mustered up his courage and said, "With respect, Your Lordship, I have a concern."

"Yes?"

"Well, er...we know of Sir Geoffrey but would a knight of his stature fit in with us- Your Lordship's lowly servants- at the Globe?"

"He'll have to, won't he? He will have to go down to your level for the plan to succeed. It's all I can think of at the moment. I simply cannot sit back and do nothing. Drake's the best man for the job. Have either of you met him before?"

They shook their heads.

"You shall, soon enough. Both of you will prevail upon him to accept this assignment. Prepare for a journey. We leave tomorrow morning."

"Leave, My Lord?" Shakespeare said in surprise.

"Yes, for Suffolk. We'll find young Drake there. Haven't you heard? There's going to be a big celebration. The Queen and King Christian are going there. Christian the Fourth of Denmark. You do know he's visiting, don't you? By the way Howard's Men- rather, the Admiral's Men as they call themselves now- put on a brilliant show the other night. Marlowe's Tamburlaine. They performed at the Queen's banquet. Alleyn is a brilliant actor, isn't he? Any chance of his defecting to our side?"

Shakespeare stifled a grin but colour rushed to Burbage's cheek and he replied stiffly:

"No, My Lord;most certainly not."

"Pity. Anyhow, Her Majesty and our royal visitor are bound for Suffolk at the earl's invitation. They left this morning." Carey added with a wry smile: "Thomas Howard is one of the few earls left with unblemished records. The Queen was exceedingly glad, a tad relieved even, to receive his invitation. He's hosting a tourney and, of course, Drake's taking part. So we'll have to catch him there. `Can't afford to waste any more time waiting for his return to London. Suffolk is a two days' journey. We ought to make it by nightfall the day after if we leave early tomorrow. `Won't be a smooth ride in this damned weather but it can't be helped. You both will travel with me in my carriage."

"Oh, Your Lordship is too kind," Burbage exclaimed. "But..."

"Yes?" Carey snapped.

"Er...if I may be so bold, My Lord, Charlie's barely cold. We were hoping to attend his funeral."

"When are you burying him?"

"We don't know, yet, My Lord. The Coroner will conduct an inquiry first..."

"I know that, Richard. I was the one that insisted on an inquest. But you can't just sit around doing nothing until then. The inquest might take a few days, maybe even a week. No, you two must accompany me to Suffolk. The others can take care of Heminges's funeral."

Burbage said nothing.

Shakespeare said nothing.

Both of them loathed leaving the rest of the players at a time like this. Charlie's death had shaken them all; John Heminges was heartbroken and the others were in mourning, too. Chin -Chin -Charlie had been a popular chap and he was about to get married. That's what the previous night's party was about: celebrating the end of Charles Heminges' bachelorhood. How ironical that it should end with his death. As in the case of Jeremy Smith, there were no apparent injury marks on the body. He, too, was found lying face down in the dirt outside the Mermaid's Tavern.

"So it's all settled then," Carey said. "Today's Friday. We should reach Ipswich, the Suffolk capital by Sunday night. Good timing, since the tournament will probably commence on Monday. You both are likely to be away for a week or so, once we take the journey time into account. Go on and make some arrangements for the playhouse. It's not yet noon; you have the whole day ahead of you. Surely you can interest some company in hiring the Globe for a week?"

Shakespeare smiled quietly. Burbage swallowed hard.

Henslowe. `God, Burbage would have to eat a humble pie and approach the Admiral's Men! Now Henslowe and Alleyn could rub his nose in the dirt.

"We'll do our best, My Lord," Burbage said weakly.

***

SEVEN

———

The rain had let up by the time Shakespeare and Burbage departed from Whitehall but the streets were masses of slush and puddles. Shakespeare walked briskly towards the riverfront, his thoughts knocking about in his head and matching his stride.

His leaving London at this time was the worst thing for the Company. After Charlie Heminges' death the previous night, a terrible fear had gripped the players: fear of a curse, a hex upon the group; the kind of irrational anxiety that lodges itself in the brain like a worm and doesn't give up until the entire being is consumed. Personally he didn't subscribe to such wild imaginings but he knew how potent their effects could be. He felt the need to remain close to the players and to keep performing on stage. That was the only antidote to these venomous misgivings.

It was hard to remain rational, though, in the face of such horror.

Smith. Gray. Charles Heminges.

Who was next?

His own lines from *Hamlet* returned to haunt him.

When sorrows come, they come not single spies/ but in battalions.

What had seemed so appropriate for the Danish tragedy was becoming frighteningly real to him.

Thomas Gray had survived the fall but only just. His collarbone was broken, his spinal cord snapped, and the physician said he would never walk again.

"Would that I'd broken my neck and died, instead of this!" Gray had screamed and there was not a dry eye in the parish infirmary.

"It doesn't make sense," Robert Armin said. "How could the balcony's railing just break off like that?"

"It was an accident," John Heminges said. His was the voice of reason until then. "These things happen in playhouses, Robin. How often do we check our props?"

"But Will, Dick, you were on the balcony a short while before the show commenced. You two leaned on the balcony, didn't you?" Armin asked. "Did the railing feel loose to you?"

Shakespeare shook his head.

"No, but I didn't really pay attention," Burbage said. "Perhaps it was getting loose at the time and we didn't notice."

That was three days back when the four of them were standing outside the hospital early evening waiting for the doctor's prognosis on Thomas Gray. The show had been abandoned after Gray's fall. In the ensuing melee, Shakespeare hadn't got the chance to say goodbye properly to Marie. She'd. made a quick exit with her waiting woman. The image of her slim retreating figure was burned on his brain.

The litheness of a gazelle.

The poise of a princess.

The body of a very sensual woman...

"Saunders and Ollie Downtown were in charge of the props today," Armin said slowly. "I think we should have a chat with them."

Heminges raised a bushy brow. "What are you suggesting? Surely you don't think one of them loosened the railing!"

"Well, someone did."

"Robin, it was an accident. How can you think otherwise? Saunders and Downtown are wee boys; don't go chasing after ghosts, for Heaven's Sake."

"I'm not, John, I'm not. But don't you think we should consider the fact that they were somehow linked to Jeremy's death, too?"

"What? How so?"

"What d'you mean by 'how so'? Weren't they the ones that were supposed to walk with him to the Globe every morning? Suddenly Saunders takes ill on the very day of Jeremy's death. We have only his word for it."

"And Downtown's," Heminges pointed out.

"Precisely. And Downtown's. In both incidents it's Alexander Cooke and Oliver Downtown. Who introduced Downtown to our Company?"

Heminges fell silent.

"Cooke, wasn't it? Or 'Saunders', as we call him?" Armin said and the other three nodded.

"This is mere conjecture," Heminges said, still unconvinced. "I can't see them as a murdering duo; they're good lads, Robin. And why, O why, would they commit such violent crimes? These boys have a stake in the Company's future. They're not sharers, but they might be someday. So why would either of them...? Will? Dick? What do you think?"

"I think we should consider Ned Alleyn as a suspect, too," Shakespeare said and three pairs of eyes stared at him.

"You can't be serious," Heminges said.

"Why not? He was up there on the balcony with us just before the show. As I recall, he paid special attention to the railing and the flower arrangements on it. Who has a greater motive to see our downfall?"

"Will, that's ridiculous," Burbage said. "I hate Ned's guts; in fact, I'm not too keen on his little toe, either! But Ned Alleyn is not a murderer, no way."

"He would love to see us fall from grace," Shakespeare insisted.

"Yes, but so would Ben Jonson and Thomas Dekker and the Earl of Worcester and the late Langley's relatives and the Lord Mayor of London! The list of our ill-wishers would stretch from here to France. But surely all of them can't be plotting to top our players! Besides, Henslowe was on the balcony, too. Are you suggesting he's involved? No, Will, Robin, today's incident was a freak accident, like John says. Let's accept it as such."

Burbage caught up with Shakespeare when he'd almost reached the riverbank.

"Will, Will, slow down," he called out, panting. "I'm not as fit as I used to be. We're both getting on, you know."

Shakespeare made a face. "Thanks, but I could do without such a reminder. You need to stop feeding your face. Remember, I had to make *Hamlet* fat and scant of breath because I knew you'd be struggling in the fight scene!"

Burbage chuckled good-humouredly. "Too much of the good life, eh? Actually, it's my wife's cooking."

"Lucky man."

"Yes, I am." Burbage wanted to make a quip about

Shakespeare's wife's cooking but he held his peace since he knew his friend didn't take kindly to any references to his family. Instead, he said: "I know you're troubled. We all are. And now we'll have to miss Charlie's funeral but...have patience and endure."

A quote from one of Shakespeare's recent comedies, *Much Ado About Nothing*.

Shakespeare rolled his eyes and responded with a line from the same play: "There was never yet philosopher that could endure the toothache patiently. Please, Dick, don't quote my words back to me. It's very annoying."

Burbage laughed.

"What are you so cheerful about?" Shakespeare demanded. "Are you relishing the idea of going to Henslowe with a begging bowl?"

Burbage was unfazed. "Water off a duck's back, Will. I'm a practical man. I've a business to run. So I'll visit Mr. Henslowe with nary a care in the world. He knows how things work. I'm sure he'll agree to hire the Globe at the usual rate of ten percent per day."

"Ah, so now it's ten percent?"

"Yes, now it is. Can you fault me for trying to drive a hard bargain? I thought they were desperate."

"Phil Henslowe is never desperate. He owns more players, playbooks and playhouses than the rest of us put together."

"True, but he doesn't have one thing: you. He can never hope to draw in the kind of crowd that you do." Then Burbage paused, looked askance at the Bard of Avon and said: "What were you thinking, back there in Carey's office? Were you about to give them a name? Would you have really accused Ben Jonson of murder?"

"I might've suggested his name as a suspect. He's killed before and he's no stranger to the nick. I can't help feeling he was somehow involved in Charlie's death last night."

Burbage pursed his lips. "A few days ago you were suggesting Ned Alleyn was a killer."

"Well, they're both with the Admiral's Men. You were there last night; you saw what happened."

"Yes, I was and I tell you, you're out of your mind! Ben could not have killed Charlie. Seriously, Will, you can't go around accusing people like that. You know what Carey will do. His reputation as torturer is only a couple of notches lower than Topcliffe's."

"So? Maybe Ben Jonson deserves to have his limbs torn apart."

"No, he doesn't and you know it. Deep down, you two are very fond of each other."

"We are not. That is to say, I am not favourably disposed towards him and I feel the sentiment is mutual."

They'd reached the river and they jostled for space in

the unruly queue that waited for the next ferry. The air was redolent with the odour of eel and herring and other Thames fish; these combined with the usual cacophony of riverside London, boatmen cursing, swearing and shouting 'Eastward Ho!' and 'Westward Ho!'

The two men suspended their conversation as they climbed into a boat, paid the sixpence fare each, and rode across the river. Previously, whenever he neared the Globe and saw its sparkling, steep white wall and proud flags, Shakespeare experienced a rush of adrenalin. This was his place, the seat of his craft. He'd written his recent plays with the Globe's stage in mind. The masque scene in *Much Ado...*; the senate in *Julius Caesar*; Arden forest of *The Twelfth Night*; the battle scenes in *Troilus and Cressida-* all these were conceived with the Globe's platform in his mind's eye. He knew every spot, every corner of the stage, the location of the trapdoors. He'd calculated the precise number of steps it would take an actor to walk from the edge of the stage to its centre and vice versa. The balcony was useful as ramparts of a castle or as an upper storey. This theatre had become part of his consciousness and he always looked forward to entering its gates. But that day, for the first time, an overpowering sense of dread came over him. His chest constricted as if with heartburn, he started to perspire, and he wondered if he was having a heart attack. Slowly and painfully, the sensation passed. He found himself clutching the ferry's railings and nearly throwing up over the side.

Presently the boat docked at the Southwark bank and passengers filed out noisily, the boatman egging them on so he could start his return journey. Shakespeare went along with the flow, barely aware of his surroundings. His legs felt leaden and his stride increasingly heavy as he walked towards the playhouse with Burbage.

What evil was in store for him today?

***

EIGHT

——

Charles Heminges had stared at his image in the mirror (for the last time, unknownst to him) and critically examined his physical appearance. He didn't look thirty-five, no; his face was much more youthful than his older brother's. John Heminges didn't wear his years well; Charles did. Maybe there was something about bachelorhood. What a contrast the two made. John, with his brood of seven and counting; Charles, yet to become a father. He didn't really regret having been single for so long. He'd had his fair share of women. But then he'd met Esther Castleton and everything changed. She was virtuous, wide-eyed and buxom and the mere thought of her turned him on.

It's my good time, By George, it is.

Tomorrow I will be *Hamlet*!

He wasn't sure what excited him more: the chance to play *Hamlet*, or his impending marriage. All these months of being Dick Burbage's understudy had paid off. Burbage, not yet fully recovered from the flu, said he wanted a few more days off so it fell upon Charles Heminges to reprise the very popular role of the Prince of Denmark. Charles was so excited; he'd spent every waking moment rehearsing his lines. Practically levitating with joy, he decided to treat his colleagues at the Mermaid's Tavern. Drinks and supper on him. It was an extravagance since the inn in Cheapside just east of St. Paul's Cathedral, was quite sophisticated as compared with their usual Southwark watering holes, the Bear's Inn and the George.

Everyone hadn't come. Richard Cowley and Augustine Phillips went home to their families. Thomas Pope, Nick Tooley, Duncan Sole and John Sinklo went bear-baiting instead. So the Chamberlain's Men numbered ten that night: Shakespeare, Dick Burbage, John and Charles Heminges, Robert Armin, Henry Condell, James Sands, Alex Cooke, Chris Beeston and Oliver Downtown.

An even number, that's good, thought Charlie.

When they walked into the tavern, the first person they laid their eyes on was Ben Jonson. Dressed immaculately as usual, the Admiral's Men's chief playmaker was sitting at a table-for-two directly in line with the main door with a pint of ale before him. Tall and powerfully built with a dark beard and beady black eyes, Jonson had an arresting physical presence. He smiled when he saw Shakespeare & Co. Beside him was Thomas Dekker, pamphleteer and playmaker for the Worcester's Men.

"Marry, this is a surprise," Jonson said. "The Chamberlain's Men in full force...well, almost. What brings you all to this neck o' the woods?"

"Hello, Ben," Shakespeare said. "Tom, good to see you."

John Heminges and James Sands greeted Jonson warmly and pulled up a couple of chairs to join him and Dekker at their table. Shakespeare, Burbage, Armin and Condell took the next table. The youngsters- Beeston, Cooke and Downtown occupied a table in a corner. Charlie joined them.

"What's the occasion?" Jonson asked again. "One doesn't usually see you chaps outside Southwark."

"Charlie's getting hitched," Heminges said and added sotto voce: "Finally."

"You don't say? Really? How nice." Jonson raised his mug and congratulated Charles Heminges.

Dekker added his felicitations.

Charles grinned and waved back.

"The drinks are on him," Heminges said. "Feel free to order what you like, Ben. You too, Tom."

"Thank you, that's very generous," Jonson said.

Heminges laughed. "I'm not paying."

"Who's the lucky lass?" Jonson asked.

"An Esther Castleton. Ever heard of her?"

"Er...no, I don't believe so."

Dekker said wickedly: "It's a good thing if Ben hasn't heard of a woman!"

Heminges and Sands laughed.

"Come now, Tom, what do you take me for?" Jonson said with mock-seriousness. "I'm a loyal husband. Mind you, I would cherish my freedom were it given back someday. I keep telling the missus, let me go, let me go. But she's dug her claws in."

"Claws, Ben?" James Sands echoed. "Are you suggesting your woman is a shrew?"

"Aye, and one that cannot be tamed!"

They all laughed again.

A waiter arrived and took their orders. Tankards of ale, roast beef, and mashed potatoes.

The small talk continued for a while. Then they began to discuss business at the Fortune.

Jonson said that the audience was different in North London, more genteel and harder to please. He said he missed the energy of Southwark. Then he turned to Shakespeare and Burbage at the next table and said:

"Sorry to hear about your recent troubles. A boy named Smith? And then another boy falling from the balcony? Must've come as a big jolt to you all. How is he- Thomas Gray?"

"In bad shape," Burbage said. "The physician says he's lucky to be alive. Lucky? He doesn't see it that way."

"What will become of him?" Dekker asked.

"He was injured during the course of a performance; the Company will take care of him. It's in the contract. Any injury sustained during a performance or a rehearsal...practically covers twenty-four hours. We'll look after him."

"What about the boy Smith's death?" Jonson asked. "I heard that you all suspect murder?"

"Oh, we can't be sure of anything at this stage," Burbage said with a weary shake of his head. "There were no marks on his body to suggest the cause of death but it's hard to believe that he just dropped dead because of some quirk of fate. The woman who raised the hue-an-cry vanished. So it's going to remain a mystery for now."

"How did you hear about our woes?" Shakespeare asked.

"Bad news has swift feet," Jonson replied.

"In truth? You're still interested in what goes on in our Company?"

"Of course I am. Why wouldn't I be? We all go back a long way, Will."

Their orders arrived and the conversation was interrupted. There was only the glug-glug sounds of ale being poured into mugs and the clanking of knives and forks. The men began to dig into their meal. Jonson glanced at Shakespeare and seemed to want to say something but Shakespeare, although aware of the eyes on his back, refused to acknowledge the gaze.

"You didn't mean that, did you, Ben?" Heminges asked.

"I did. Why wouldn't I? I am interested in you…"

"No, I meant earlier, when you said you'd be happier as an unmarried man."

Jonson chuckled. "It was meant in jest but, come to think of it, the life of a single man is more interesting. Wouldn't you agree? No encumbrances, the freedom to do as you please…"

Jonson was married to a woman called Ann Lewis and they had a young son Benjamin Jr.

"There are some of us, however, that do our will regardless of our marital status," Jonson added pointedly. "We continue with old flames and ignore our legally wedded wives."

The others stiffened. Was this directed at Shakespeare? They all knew he had a mistress but her identity was a secret; Shakespeare had been extremely discreet.

Shakespeare heard the remark but he refused to take umbrage and continued with his drink and meal as if oblivious to the others.

"That's all right, I suppose," Jonson continued, "If all the parties involved are reconciled to the situation, why should anybody else interfere?"

"Socrates knew all about love", Jonson said, happy to put his knowledge on display. "Yes, but that's the only knowledge that Socrates claimed; of love," Shakespeare interjected unexpectedly from the next table. "His most famous line is: I know that I know nothing, but love. He linked it with a love of wisdom."

"What? Love makes us wise?" Armin exclaimed.

"Well, according to Socrates!"

"Marry, I thought it made me lose me marbles!"

Everyone laughed.

"It drives me insane," Armin continued in the same vein. "Certainly doesn't make me clever. What did you call it, Will? A madness most discreet, a choking gall, and a preserving sweet?"

Shakespeare smiled. "I didn't; Romeo did."

"Romeo? Aye, perhaps I can play Romeo next time, eh?"

"Of course, and we'll have the audience rolling in the pit with laughter," Heminges cried. "The fool playing Romeo? Nay, nay, Robin dear, you can play the fool, that's all."

Armin lashed out at him in mock-seriousness and the others laughed heartily. Heminges avoided the blow, knocked his ale mug over by mistake, and the room erupted with more laughter. Everyone was tipsy by now and enjoying themselves thoroughly.

"Getting back to the Greeks," Jonson said in a sonorous tone, and all eyes turned to him again. "Long passages of the Symposium are devoted to praising Eros, the god of love. Plato talks of Eros accomplishing two things: leading men towards eide or the transcendent world, and pouring heavenly streams from Zeus into the souls of the lover and the beloved. This leads to greater knowledge and, hence, love is connected with wisdom."

Jonson paused and a momentary hush fell over the two tables. Then Armin, Burbage, Sands and Heminges dissolved into laughter once more.

"Streams from Zeus?" Burbage exclaimed, thumping the table and sending his drink slushing around. "That...that's hilarious, Ben!"

Shakespeare chuckled but held back his laughter. He saw Jonson's face darkening, his brow getting colder and heavier, and his knuckles whitening around the mug's handle. The heat from Jonson's rising temper was making the room stuffy. Clearly, the Admiral's Men's playmaker did not relish being laughed at even if it was all in good humour.

To compound matters, Robert Armin gazed into his mug and exclaimed, "I'll be damned if I don't find wisdom in my ale. Tommy, James, Dick, take a look; see any Zeus droppings in it?"

Burbage and James Sands laughed out loud but Thomas Dekker, out of loyalty to Jonson, stifled a smile and ended up looking constipated. Jonson sat there bristling like a pot of boiling soup.

Presently, Armin sobered up and turned to Jonson. "That's hogwash, Ben," he said in a surprisingly coherent tone. "Love, if there's such a thing, stems from and is sustained by this, and this alone." He made a crude gesture towards his crotch. "That's all there is to it. Once a lassie loses her charms, her man won't give a fig for her. To hell with wisdom and 'ee-day', or whatever the Greeks called it. And, tell me, if the Greeks spent all day sitting and talking philosophy, how did they earn an honest living? Did they go about begging for alms or send their wives a-whoring?"

"Ah, now that's a point," Burbage agreed, and thumped his friend on the back.

"You're talking like an ignorant, ill-bred cur," Jonson snapped at Armin. "But that's no surprise, for it is, indeed, what you are! A fool upon a fool!"

Jonson's phrase was a reference to a pamphlet called *Foole upon Foole*, written by Armin, in which he'd discussed the art of comedy.

Armin made no retort but Burbage sprang to his defence.

"Aw, Ben, that was uncalled for."

"His remarks were uncalled for," Jonson shot back.

"Why are you getting all hot and bothered? We're all just having fun; no harm meant."

"Fun?" said Jonson. "Why do you denigrate what you don't understand? Why get into arguments you have so little knowledge of? Little learning is a dangerous thing, Robin."

"I have learned more than I need," Armin said. "I'm no gentleman, Ben, and I don't hang about university wits all day long. I'm the son of a tailor and I know that fancy clothes don't make a fine man."

Jonson pursed his lips. "The kind of love you referred to is base, common love. It doesn't last because the object of that love doesn't last, either. The Eros that's praiseworthy is the one that encourages us to love in the right way. It's the creative force in man that..."

"Love is not love, which alters when it alteration finds," Shakespeare cut in with a line from his own sonnet (CXVI). "Love's not Time's fool...and love bears it out even to the edge of doom!"

Everyone, except Jonson and Dekker burst into spontaneous applause.

"Wonderful!" Charles Heminges called out from his corner table. "Must remember to use those lines in my wedding service."

Shakespeare grinned and raised his mug to all.

"That, dear Ben, is true love," he continued. "The adjective 'common' is incongruous, like yoking together a tailor and a philosopher. Who is of more use to me? I'll take the tailor any day; I have more need of good clothes than of fancy ideas."

"Hear! Hear!" Burbage cried.

Armin and Sands thumped their table, while Heminges let out a happy whistle.

"That's because you're already swollen with ideas," Jonson retorted.

He took a shilling from his pocket to pay for his drinks and nodded at Dekker.

"I'll be on my way. You coming?"

Before Dekker could reply, Shakespeare railed at Jonson: "I'm swollen with ideas? And you're swollen with what? Pedantic wit?"

Burbage patted his arm. "Let it go, Will; he's retreating from the battlefield."

Jonson rose, glared at them both, but said nothing.

"There'll be many more opportunities," he murmured. "Even though our objectives are different, our paths will cross every now and again."

"Different? How so?"

Jonson hesitated a moment and then said:

"Neque me ut miretur turba, laboro;

Contentus paucis lectoribus."

The tavern fell silent. No one seemed to have a clue about what he'd said.

Shakespeare smiled and translated from the Latin:

"I don't work to be gaped at by the mob, but am happy with a few readers. Horace, if I'm not mistaken?"

The others stared in surprise. Jonson looked like he'd had the wind taken out of him.

"And you think I want art!" Shakespeare exclaimed with obvious triumph. "I don't have to depend on borrowed words and ancient ideas to puff myself up, Ben. And whatever I might lack by way of learning, nature has compensated. Be on your way now. We have no use for your badge of learning."

"Will, please..." Burbage restrained him anxiously. He didn't like the look of contempt on Jonson's face and glanced at Armin and Heminges for support.

Jonson gritted his teeth and glared at Shakespeare, little coals of fire shooting from his eyes. Shakespeare stretched his legs in a languorous way that was most annoying. For a moment it seemed as if the big chap was going to strike him.

The other players tensed.

Shakespeare wore a cool façade but the muscles in his neck were taut and under the table, his hands gripped the edges to control his temper.

Violence was simmering just under the surface.

Then Jonson shrugged, dropped the coins on the table with a loud clang, and made his exit with much ceremony. John Heminges wanted to remind him that the drinks were on his brother but, under the circumstances, he considered silence a better option.

Dekker was half-way out of his chair, unsure of whether to follow Jonson or to remain with Shakespeare & Co.

"Stay a while," Heminges said. "You're an observer of London life; you'll find much of it here in the tavern. Remain here and you might get some fodder for your pamphlets."

Dekker nodded and sat down again, relieved to have been invited to stay.

"Round One to the Bard of Avon!" Heminges exclaimed and signalled to a serving boy. "Top us up, will you?"

He turned to address his brother at the corner table. "Charlie, `hope you're loaded tonight..."

Charles Heminges wasn't there.

"Where's he gotten to?" Heminges asked Alexander Cooke, who was sitting there alone.

Cooke put up his little finger. `Gone out to pee.

"Didn't Ben look mad angry tonight?" James Sands said. "I thought he was about to hit you, Will."

"Would've come as no surprise. He's no stranger to violence, is he?" Shakespeare said. "But I was ready for him tonight."

"I'm glad there were no fisticuffs," Burbage said. "This is a happy occasion; Charlie is getting married."

He glanced in the direction of Charlie's table. Downtown and Beeston had rejoined Cooke but there was still no Charlie.

"Maybe one of us should go and have a look," Cooke said. "He's been a while."

"What? Won't you let my brother take a leak in peace?" Heminges said. "He'll be a cuckold soon, unable to take a breath without permission from the missus! Let him be."

"Speaking from experience, John?" Burbage teased.

Heminges made a face and rolled his eyes dramatically.

The heavy mood had lifted now like mist clearing up under the mid-day sun. Shakespeare, Burbage and Heminges struck up a conversation with Thomas Dekker about the latest action in the bear rings. Bull and bear-baiters were natural allies with theatre actors since they had common enemies: Puritans and the Lord Mayor's office. Despite strong opposition, bull and bear-baiting remained a popular sport. The Queen also visited the bear rings occasionally. It was the only business that hadn't been affected by the Globe's success even though the Bear Garden was adjacent to the Globe.

Thomas Dekker echoed a popular sentiment when he said that Puritans opposed bull and bear-baiting not because they cared about the beasts but because it gave the spectators pleasure. So intent were they on being judgmental and miserable, they couldn't tolerate one happy face.

"True, true," Heminges agreed. "Will, you should put them in one of your comedies. They won't laugh at anything but that doesn't stop us from laughing at them."

Shakespeare smiled. "That's an idea."

Heminges glanced across at the corner table again.

Beeston, Cooke and Downtown were there chatting away nineteen to the dozen but Charlie still hadn't returned.

Where had he gotten to?

Heminges rose and pushed his chair aside. A vague sense of unease came over him.

***

NINE

———

Love and hate are two sides of the same coin. Extreme emotions that drive you insane with passion. Consider King Saul and David. How the king loved him and hated him, too. These were the thoughts playing around in Charles Heminges' mind when he stepped out of the Mermaid's tavern twenty minutes ago. Will and Ben were still bickering inside. It's only when you care about someone that you admit these two demons- Love and Hate- into your life; otherwise there's just indifference. He knew all about indifference. Until now he'd never felt strongly about a woman. But Esther had changed all that.

Will and Ben were intensely fond of each other; that's why they were always at loggerheads. When Jonson remarked casually to one of his university wits that Shakespeare 'wanted art', it truly rankled the Bard. Everyone knew he'd felt hurt.

Now why would he care if he didn't secretly admire Benjamin Jonson? Shakespeare had acted in Jonson's famous play *Everyman in His Humour* a number of times. He seemed to enjoy it thoroughly. No pressure from the public, no expectations; it enabled him to unleash the actor within. They had so much in common, Jonson and Shakespeare. Even their wives shared the same first name- Ann/ Anne.

Men like them led charmed lives. Great success; great rivalries.

He- Charlie- was just a player, an ordinary man that wanted to make most of the fortuitous opportunity life had thrown his way. Playing *Hamlet*! All these months of practise and he'd never really expected to get this chance. Not *Hamlet*. Richard Burbage was *Hamlet*. But...what a stroke of luck, Dick still not keen on doing a major part. Charles was determined to excel himself, to surpass everybody's expectations. He only hoped he'd remember the lines. Will's soliloquies could go on and on. Quite a nightmare for the bravest of players. But he had put his heart and soul into the rehearsals and he felt ready to take the stage tomorrow.

He recalled Shakespeare's instructions to think about the character all the time.

"Consider, for instance, *Hamlet*'s anguish when he cries: O! What a rogue and peasant slave am I! To what is he enslaved? To his sorrow? To his position as prince? To his love for his mother? Or merely to his own indecisive nature? All of these must flash upon your mind when you breathe the lines. But, for heaven's sake, don't overdo it. Too often a player mistakes vehemence for passion. We're holding up a mirror to nature, remember?"

The tavern's door swung open and a familiar face peered out.

"Here I am," Charles Heminges said, stepping out of the shadows. "Looking for me? It's a bright night. The moon has risen in its full orb, see? So, has the battleinside ended?"

"Yes."

"Good. I'll be there in a moment. The tavern's a little stuffy and tonight's a lovely night to be outdoors. How I wish..."

He never did get to articulate his last wish. Charles Heminges' words died in his throat. He felt a shooting pain in the side of his neck and his eyes bulged as he slumped to the ground. A terrible choking blocked his throat and the narrow passages of his windpipe. He couldn't breathe. He lay writhing on the ground for a few moments, panic and hysteria overtaking his mind.

'This can't be happening! What's wrong with me? I can't breathe! Oh God, I can't...'

His legs went numb, the pain abated and ascending muscular paralysis cut off the oxygen supply to his heart.

Fifteen minutes later John Heminges found him lying face down in the muddy ground.

Exit Charles Heminges.

***

ACT TWO
ONE
———

The Lord Chamberlain's carriage travelled at a canter through deep green woods with a posse of four horsemen accompanying it. Another carriage followed closely behind it with the secretary Bleach, the Lord Chamberlain's manservant-in-waiting, and his personal tailor in it. George Carey was a fashionable man. He was going to a party where the Queen and a foreign monarch would be present; God forbid he should make a faux-pas in his choice of vestment or suddenly find himself in need of a new cape. His tailor Abe Swift would be at hand to combine cloth and thread to ensure that his lord would not be found wanting in the couture department.

Carey had nodded off soon after the journey began and his two companions, Shakespeare and Burbage, also fell asleep after trying to chat sotto voce. The route was bumpy and the carriage seats hard but the two players were overcome with slumber. Perhaps it was because of the rhythmic beat of the equestrian hoofs. When they awoke about an hour later, they saw verdant wet woods rushing by as the carriages passed through Middlesex County. On the seat opposite Carey was chomping on an apple and enjoying the view from his own glass window. Shakespeare straightened up, mumbled an apology, and nudged Burbage in the ribs. Burbage awoke with a start and sat erect when he realized where he was. Carey gave them an indulgent smile and offered them apples from a basket beside him, which they accepted, and then he remarked on the beautiful countryside.

"Wonderful, isn't it? We don't realize what we miss when we're in London. I'm half expecting Robin Hood and his merry band to pop out from behind the trees!"

"Robin Hood stole from the rich and gave to the poor," Shakespeare said with a wry smile. "I fear he would not be favourably disposed towards Your Lordship."

Carey chuckled. "You're right; I'd forgotten that. It's a good thing we have horsemen to protect us." Then he suddenly changed the subject and said: "Have you any idea how one ripens an apple out of season?"

"An apple, My Lord?"

"Apples, yes."

Shakespeare exchanged a perplexed look with Burbage.

"I'm wondering if Howard will do a Carew for Her Majesty," Carey said.

"A Carew?"

"You have no idea what I'm talking about, do you? You weren't there. Fifteen Ninety-Nine, during Her Majesty's progress in Bedington. Francis Carew, the earl, delayed the ripening of cherry trees in the county to coincide with the Queen's arrival. It signified that her presence brought spring out of season. Magnificent effect." Carey shook his head and chuckled to himself. "These provincial leaders will go to any lengths to impress our Sovereign, never mind the costs. So, I was wondering what Howard has arranged in Suffolk. `Ever visited a county estate during the Queen's progress?"

The two men shook their heads.

"Ah, then you're in for a treat, particularly because you are accompanying me. You'll be accorded the same courtesy that's shown me."

***

TWO

County roads were nothing more than dirt tracks and the Lord Chamberlain's cavalcade made slower progress than they'd expected through the muddy paths. They had started out at a good pace but the intermittent rain left a slushy, slippery wake and the entourage had to halt frequently to rest the horses, refresh the travellers, and wash the coaches' wheels. They camped at inns in Essex both nights- Friday and Saturday- with boarding and lodging facilities arranged by the Justice of the Peace. After Robert Devereux's rebellion and subsequent execution Essex lost its earl and the Queen baulked at the prospect of another Earl of Essex. So the Justice of the Peace Theodore Cowdrey, an elderly gnome-like gentleman who seemed to be blind as a bat, as the senior most official of the county, was the Lord Chamberlain's host.

Shakespeare gave Cowdrey a sympathetic look as he

hovered about the VIPs at supper on Saturday night but Carey winked at the playmaker and quipped:

"Don't feel sorry for the old crone. He must be a rather effective justice; isn't justice supposed to be blind?"

Carey laughed aloud at his own joke, sending spittle of wine into the air between them, and it was all Shakespeare could do to refrain from making a retort. He conjured up an image in his mind of Carey being drowned in a barrel of ale, coughing and gasping for breath, and it made him feel better. He even managed to give Carey a broad, fake smile.

They reached the main Suffolk town Ipswich on the third day after their departure from London. Monday, mid-morning, bang in the middle of the festivities. One of Carey's mud-spattered horsemen rode on ahead to inform the local officials of the Lord Chamberlain's arrival. The rest of the group waited at the town's entrance. Everyone got out of the carriages to stretch their legs and admire the decorations. Every tree in the vicinity was covered in colourful ribbons and streamers. Cloth banners hung on posts every five hundred yards or so with signs like 'Long Live the Queen', 'God Save the Queen', and 'Hail, Beloved Queen' painted on them. The road leading from the city entrance to the Earl's castle was strewn with colourful flowers, the aroma of which filled the air.

Shakespeare inhaled a lungful of sweet air and smiled. Now this was something he'd never experienced before, Nature joining in the royal celebrations. The Tudor rose was all-pervasive, staring at them from every banner and signpost. Soon after, the reception-committee arrived: Carey's outrider and four horsemen led by the earl's Steward of the Household, a fair-haired thickset man of about forty called Peter Lennox. He greeted Carey with due courtesy and conveyed the earl's apologies for not being there to receive Carey in person. Apparently the earl Lord Howard was attending upon the Queen and King Christian at a mid-day banquet on the castle lawns.

"The Earl requests Your Lordship to join the banquet at the earliest," Lennox said. "Along with Your Lordship's esteemed companions." The chap tilted his head towards Shakespeare and Burbage. "That is, of course, after My Lord has refreshed himself at the castle."

"Thank you, my good man," Carey said. "Please inform the Earl that we'd be honoured to join the banquet shortly. Lead on to the castle."

As he and his entourage began to climb back into the carriages for the short ride to the castle, Carey added to Lennox:

"My compliments on the decorations. The city looks beautiful. Have the revels begun?"

"They have, My Lord. They began yesterday. We had archery contests, tightrope walkers, fire-eaters and things like that. Now a dance is in progress, the Pavane. Then musicians will perform. Finally, at one o'clock, the jousting will commence."

"Ah, that is what I'm looking forward to," Carey exclaimed. "Is the splendid young Drake taking part?"

"Yes, My Lord. Sir Geoffrey's one of the jousters. He's the favourite to win the tourney."

"Excellent. We, too, are rooting for him. Let's make haste to the castle and, thence, to the banquet. Lead on, lead on."

***

Queen Elizabeth, pragmatic to the core, knew better than to permit her provincial nobles to become power-centres in their own right. Bitter experience had shown her the dangers of encouraging her earls and barons beyond a certain limit. As a consequence she made sure that non-royal castles were not strongholds but luxurious palaces instead. This went down well with the aristocrats, who were only too happy to indulge in enhancing their material comforts. Had they lived a few centuries later, many of them would've snapped up Marie Antoinette's offer of cakes instead of bread! With the increasing use of gunpowder and cannons, the old Norman castles lost much of their impregnability anyway. Crenulations on top of castle towers and walls were not permitted any longer. These ramparts contained solid portions (aka 'merlons') and crenels (or gaps) two to three feet long in between for firing arrows. Moats were filled up or provided with many drawbridges. The Earl of Suffolk's castle was, however, and exception.

Situated on the estuary of the River Orwell, Ipswich was close to the coast and the nearby town of Woodbridge was an important ship-building site. The area had been hit hard during the Danish invasions of the late tenth century.

The Viking monarch Sweyn Forkbeard took King Ethelred the Second by surprise, leading to the latter's unflattering moniker 'Ethel the Unready'. But the Danes didn't rule for long. Forkbeard died within twelve months and Ethelred, who'd taken refuge in Normandy, romped back home (And, presumably, took greater precautions and kept himself battle-ready since the Danes didn't succeed in invading England again). Emotional scars of the invasion remained. They were prominent enough to cause Queen Elizabeth to permit the fortifying of Lord Howard's castle. Hence his was a strong stone structure with battlements and a moat- the works- but the interiors were luxurious rather than Spartan.

The Lord Chamberlain and his guests were led across lavish carpets that crept over a large staircase to the West Wing of the first-floor. The Queen, King Christian and their entourages were lodged in the opposite wing on the same floor. The interiors were brightly lit with large torches on the walls at regular intervals, swathing the place with amber lighting. But the castle didn't smell good. The rooms were small, damp and unpleasant, their stone walls moist to the touch. Even Howard with all his wealth could not beat the English weather.

Carey withdrew into his special guest chamber with his manservant and asked Bleach, Shakespeare, Burbage and Abe Swift to be quick about freshening up. They were already behind schedule; no point missing the banquet altogether. He dismissed the rest of his party, saying they were free to relax for the remainder of the day. Lennox's assistants led them away to the staff quarters below.

Lennox escorted Shakespeare and Burbage to a chamber just down the hall, which was smaller than the Lord Chamberlain's but not wanting in luxury. The furnishings and fixtures were all gold and velvet and colourful. Two big four-poster beds stood at either ends of the room, each with ornate bedposts and red canopies from which gold-coloured tassels hung all around the edges. A small meal was spread out on a table at the centre of the room: wine, bread, cheese and an array of fruits. The two men dug into the food. They'd snacked all through the journey but the sight of so much grub refuelled their appetites.

"Let's not overdo it," Shakespeare warned. "We're going to a banquet, remember? We can't be too long."

"I know, I know, but this cheese....umm," Burbage said with his mouth full. "By George, isn't this castle magnificent? And these arrangements...How much do you think it must've cost Lord Howard?"

Shakespeare shrugged. "Must be five hundred pounds at least. It's a good investment for him. He's highly favoured with the Queen at present; 'reaped much benefit from Essex's rebellion. Remember, he was made Constable of the Tower of London in addition to Earl of Suffolk. But he must be well aware of how quickly one's fortunes can change."

"Yes, like Devereux's. He was a charming fellow, actually."

"In truth? Well, the devil acquires a pleasing shape, too."

Burbage winced, realizing he'd brought up a sensitive subject. Shakespeare still chafed at the memory; to be used thus for inciting a revolt against the Queen! It was one of the worst things he could've ever imagined.

"Marry, let bygones be bygones, what?" Burbage said and went across to the sole window in the chamber. It was nothing more than a square shaped hole in the wall, covered by a thick curtain to keep out icy winds. "Look at that!" he exclaimed. "What a spectacle! Come quick, Will. We can see the banqueting table from here. The castle lawns are directly beneath. Look, look."

Shakespeare joined him at the window and they took in the panoramic view of the carnival-like scene below. Bright banners, flowers, and canopies adorned trees, hedgerows and banquet tables. Elizabeth was depicted in tapestries as a fairy queen, a rural goddess, and as the usual 'Gloriana', blessed sovereign with a divine right to rule.

Half-an-hour later Shakespeare and Burbage were gawking with delight as they joined the Lord Chamberlain's train and made their way towards the banquet table, which consisted of a series of wooden tables with brightly coloured cloths spread over them, stretching seamlessly for nearly a quarter of a mile.

Jostling crowds thronged the outer ring where the Earl's guards on foot and on horseback formed a cordon to protect the royal guests. The Queen's personal guards, armed with swords and muskets, stood on watch around the banquet table.

Queen Elizabeth was sitting in the centre nearly swamped with the multitude of fruits, meats, wines and desserts laid out before her. The Secretary of State Robert Cecil was seated to her immediate left, followed by Thomas Howard, the Earl of Suffolk. King Christian sat at her right hand. Then came his translator Hans, his Secretary of State Ericksson, and a few more Danish officials. Christian was a pleasant-faced chap with narrow eyes and a golden beard. He looked older than his thirty-three years and made a fitting companion to the Queen, who was pushing seventy. She wore her usual tiara and neck frills. Shakespeare thought she looked a little tired amidst all this excitement. Her expression was mostly inscrutable thanks to layers of make-up that filled in every wrinkle and blemish; but her eyes said it all.

Howard rose when he saw Carey and his small group approaching. He greeted them with warm handshakes, welcomed them to Suffolk, and asked if they'd been properly attended to by his staff. Carey assured him that his hospitality was not lacking in anything.

"Very decent of you to say so, George," Howard said with a hand on the Lord Chamberlain's shoulder. "But I feel terrible that the Lord Chamberlain was received in my county by my servants instead of me! It couldn't be helped. My sincerest apologies. I'm sure you understand; I couldn't get away. Her Majesty has been inquiring after you. This way, please."

He led them to the banquet table.

"Ah, George." Queen Elizabeth smiled when Carey bowed before her. "You've arrived at last. About time, too; what kept you?"

"The passage from London is rough and uneven, Madam. In this weather..."

"Don't complain about the weather. This is England; what else do you expect?"

"Yes, Madam. I only meant the route..."

"I know, George, I took the same route two days ago. Don't complain about the roads, either. You're the Lord Chamberlain. Why don't you get on the case? Chew up Bob's ears till he does something about it."

She looked askance at Robert Cecil and he froze, fearing she might launch into one of her famous tirades. But she turned to Carey again and glanced over his shoulder.

"Master Shakespeare. Mister Burbage. How nice to see you. Are you performing here today?"

"No, Your Majesty," they chimed.

"We came to see you," Shakespeare added.

Eyebrows went up at his forwardness but the Queen looked pleased; she was all for mild flirtation.

"Well, you're welcome," she said. "Come, take your seats. Oh, first you must meet King Christian. George, won't you do the introductions? They are your players."

"Of course, Your Majesty."

Carey cleared his throat and addressed the Danish King.

"Your Majesty, may I present Master William Shakespeare, gentleman playmaker of my acting Company, the Chamberlain's Men. And this is Richard Burbage, lead actor of the same."

Both men bowed before the King.

At the mention of Shakespeare's name, the King stiffened and launched into a pow-wow in his native tongue with his translator. Hans was a chubby, fleshy fellow, who looked like he'd never learnt to smile. Now he bobbed his head several times and then turned to Shakespeare with a gaze filled with derision.

"His Majesty wishes to confirm," he said in a sonorous, affected tone. "Are you not the one that wrote a play about our country called *Hamlet*?"

Shakespeare's eyes widened in surprise and he floundered for an adequate response.

"Ham...let? Yes, in actual fact, there are many versions of this play. I...er...drew upon a number of sources but, yes..." It had to be admitted. "I believe mine is the most recent."

Hans translated rapidly and then the Danish monarch said:

"*Glad for at gøre dit bekendtskab.*"

"Pleased to make your acquaintance," Hans elucidated with all the warmth of a frosty night.

"*Deres Majestæt, jeg er beæret,*" Shakespeare replied, much to everyone's astonishment.

"What's that?" Queen Elizabeth demanded.

"He says he is honoured," Hans spat out.

"Good Heavens, William!" Queen Elizabeth exclaimed. "Since when did you start speaking Danish?"

Shakespeare smiled mysteriously.

It was a little known fact that Thomas Pope had once been part of a group of instrumentalists in the entourage of the Danish ambassador to England Henrik Ramel. It was way back in `Fifteen Eighty-Six before the Chamberlain's Men were formed. He also accompanied Ramel when the ambassador went home to Elsinore, and worked as an entertainer at the Danish court for nearly a year. Pope had provided Shakespeare with valuable background information and local colouring for *Hamlet* as well as a smattering of the language.

King Christian was not amused. His eyes turned into thin slits as he added in a tone laden with sarcasm:

"Der er noget råddent i staten Danmark, eh?"

"Something's rotten in the state of Denmark?" Hans translated with an expression that revealed how rotten he thought Shakespeare was.

The Bard did not reply.

"Go on, give it back to them," the Queen egged him on.

But Shakespeare shook his head.

"My apologies, Madam, I'm afraid that's the extent of my

Danish. I only know a few words and phrases."

"Oh. How disappointing. I thought we could show you off."

"I'm sorry, Your Majesty." Then he turned to the King and said: "I must beg Your Majesty's forgiveness if my play gave offence; it's just...a play. It's not real."

The King glared back for a moment and then responded with: "*Din Hamlet er en tåbe, hej?*"

This meant, according to Hans the Hun: "Your *Hamlet* is an imbecile, yes?"

Shakespeare responded with a disarming smile. "Your Majesty, I couldn't agree more!"

That seemed to pacify the hoary monarch and he sat back in his chair with a smug expression on his face.

Queen Elizabeth chuckled. "Well, well, Master Shakespeare, trust you to arrive and liven up the proceedings! What a morning. Howard here has been most generous in his entertainments. This time round I was welcomed into town by my mirror image, a fairy queen. Spenser's tradition. I have been received in the past by the Lady of the Lake, by Roman deities, and by all sorts of interesting creatures; most amusing, all of them. But the highlight of today's festivities is the tournament, isn't it?" She threw Howard an inquiring look. "When will it begin?"

"Shortly, Madam, in a couple of hours."

"A couple of hours?"

"Yes, at one o'clock."

"But, why? It's only eleven now."

"Well...I...we assumed you might like to rest awhile..."

"Rest? Why should I rest in the middle of the day? Are you suggesting I have one foot in the grave?"

"Oh, no, Your Majesty!" The Earl flushed with embarrassment. "Far from it. That...that thought is farthest from my mind..."

Queen Elizabeth raised her hand to cut him short. Then she leaned over and murmured to King Christian:

"Beware. A few years down the line, and they'll be writing your obituary, too."

Hans translated and Christian looked perplexed.

"Well? What's next then?" She demanded of Howard. "If we're compelled to wait for the tourney, what is on offer now?"

"Music, Your Majesty."

"Music? All right."

She craned her neck to glance at Shakespeare, who was seated at the far end of the table to her left.

"William, what was that wonderful line about music in one of your plays?"

Shakespeare beamed with delight. What an honour to be

acknowledged in public like this!

"Your Majesty, it's 'If music be the food of love...'"

"...Play on," she exclaimed. "Yes, that's the one. I'll say it in French for the benefit of our royal guest. Do you know he speaks every language under the sun except ours?" She glanced at Christian and said:

"Si la musique est la nourriture de l'amour, jouer sur. Isn't that lovely?"

King Christian replied with a flirtatious line in the same language:

"Pas aussi belle que la reine Elizabeth."

"Not as lovely as the Queen Elizabeth," Hans translated red-faced and quite unnecessarily since everybody at the table understood French and they were all smiling and applauding.

The Queen chortled girlishly and said with a hand at her heart: "Oh, I'm flattered; you're quite a one, sir!"

When things had quietened down, she tilted her head at the Earl of Suffolk and said in her characteristic brusque manner:

"What are we waiting for, Howard? Let the musicians begin. Get on with it. We have a long afternoon ahead."

***

THREE

"Charlie Heminges is a very lucky man; I envy him. Would that I could trade places with him! Mr. Condell sir, Mr. Armin sir, please help me. Put me out of my misery."

Thomas Gray's impassioned plea brought tears to the two senior players' eyes. Gray's mother, with tears streaming down her own face, shushed him.

"Ye must not say such things, Tommy, please. `Tis a sin, lad, a terrible sin."

"But it's the truth, Mother. Day and night I lie here longing for death. How I wish someone would supply me with a cup of poison or pour some extract of ebony in my ear like they did for poor *Hamlet*'s father...anything to spare me from this life."

"Nay, Tommy, nay. Ye cannot say... cannot think such things. Have ye no fear of God? Ye'll be sent to hell, son, no more of such talk."

"Sent to hell? I'm there already, Ma!"

Armin and Condell looked at each other helplessly. What can one say to a boy whose life is reduced to an existence without movement, without promise and with no hope of recovery? Gray was painfully aware of the fact that he'd be a burden on his family for the rest of his days.

When Condell and Armin came calling on Sunday evening and informed him about Charlie Heminges' death, a terrifying suspicion started dwelling in his mind. It hissed and hissed at him like an ugly snake all through the meeting until he could bear it no longer.

Condell had just managed to find some words of comfort ('Have courage, Tommy', 'Miracles do happen,' 'You're young, don't lose hope' and so on) when Gray burst out:

"You'll hate me for it but I think I know who killed Charlie and...nearly killed me!"

"What?" The other two looked stunned.

Condell was bemused. "But you weren't even there, lad, when Charlie died. How could you...?"

"I'm right, I tell you; I know who it is."

"What on earth are you saying?" Condell cried. "Who do you suspect?"

Thomas Gray's lips pursed into a bitter line. "You might think I'm a nutter, that I'm imagining things because of my state, but I heard them talking..."

"Who?" cried Condell and Armin.

When Condell and Armin left Gray's place in Southwark half-an-hour later, their expressions were stiff and their faces lined with the burden of what they'd just heard. Neither of them spoke for a while as they walked towards the riverfront to take a ferry across the Thames to go home. Then Condell said:

"The lad is loony, that's all there is to it. `No wonder, too."

"He sounded quite convinced," Armin said hesitatingly.

"Convinced, my foot. He's had a horrible accident, Robin, gone potty in the head. To even think such things..."

"I suppose you're right."

"Suppose?"

"All right, you are right."

"His allegations are nothing more than the murmurings of a very sick boy. Can you blame him?"

"No, I can't, not really. But, Harry, what if...?"

"There's no 'if'! We never heard this, do you understand? Tommy Gray never said a word to us. Get that, Robin?"

"Ye..es, I suppose." Armin stretched his answer too long.

"We didn't hear a thing," Condell repeated.

Armin said nothing.

"Thank Heaven he isn't fit to depose in the inquest tomorrow."

"Yes, thank heaven," Robert Armin agreed.

***

The Coroner William Danby was an elderly gentleman, who seemed to be born for this profession. The sparse white hair on his head, his wizened face, and failing eyesight spoke of a man that was accustomed to dealing with death on a daily basis. His manner was severe and he had the capacity to stare down witnesses until they wilted and told him exactly what he wanted to hear. Half-truths evaporated like water from seaside salt, leaving behind the truth all hard and crystallized, perfect for use in his legal cuisine.

On Monday morning around the time that Shakespeare and the Lord Chamberlain's entourage were cantering into Ipswich, Danby and his assistants were preparing to enter the dank chamber where Charles Heminges' mortal remains were interred and witnesses had gathered for the deposition.

Danby's scribe, a short young chap called Little Dan, began with a roll call, acknowledging those present: John Heminges, older brother of the deceased, Robert Armin, Henry Condell, James Sands, Christopher Beeston, Alexander Cooke and Oliver

Downtown, all of whom were at the Mermaid's Tavern on the night of Charles Heminges' death. In addition, Thomas Pope and Augustine Phillips were attending at their own request.

"Further, the following persons summoned have made themselves available for deposing before the inquest today: Master Benjamin Jonson, playmaker of the Lord Admiral's Men; Mr. Thomas Dekker, pamphleteer; Mr. William Johnson, landlord of the Mermaid's Tavern and Mr. Joshua Harvey, waiting man of the same tavern. Lastly, we have Constable James Sprat."

The scribe proceeded to swear-in everybody and then the inquest began.

Charles Heminges' body was laid out on a table naked except for a loin cloth. John Heminges was asked to make a formal identification before the rest of the witnesses, or rather 'jurors', as they'd now become according to the prevailing law. Heminges did so and quickly stepped back beside Condell, who placed a comforting hand on his shoulder.

Little Dan read out a brief summary of the facts of the case. Then the scribe paused to catch his breath, glanced around him, and dropped the bombshell:

"Upon close examination of the body, the Coroner has discovered a small puncture mark on the left side of the neck. The wound is thought to have been caused by a small needle or some such sharp instrument."

"A puncture mark?" John Heminges exclaimed. "What? Where? We...we didn't know, didn't notice anything."

Danby nodded. "It's easily missed. Come and see, Mr. Heminges. A tiny hole at the side of his neck.

Everyone crowded around the corpse. Charles Heminges' mortal remains were not a pretty sight. It was the fourth day after his death and decomposition was setting in fast. The Coroner's assistants had applied some kind of fluid to slow down the decay process and they'd filled the room with incense sticks that, mercifully, muted the stench. Without this, none of them would've been able to linger near the deceased as they did now.

The hole in his neck was barely visible; it was a tiny incision about three inches beneath his left ear.

"The killer must have come up from behind and speared him with a tiny dart or needle," Danby said.

"So it was murder!" Armin exclaimed.

"It appears to be," Danby replied. "Obviously, one cannot be absolutely sure but that is my conclusion. As you can see, there are no other revealing injuries on his body. However, look at the lips. Can you see what I see?"

All eyes duly focussed on the dead man's lips.

"His lips are blackened," Ben Jonson said.

"Precisely; that's it," Danby sounded elated. "The poor chap was poisoned, no doubt by a needle or dart. Clever bastard, the murderer, I mean. `Such an easy way to kill."

"Dear God in heaven," Heminges murmured. His eyes

were dilated with a glazed look of horror. "Who would do such a thing? Why?"

"Good questions, both of them," Danby said. "I have no answer, of course. One would require an intimate knowledge of poisons to carry out such an act; the exact dosage is important. Nowadays wood-based poisons are quite popular but Hemlock has been a favourite of poisoners for ages. Remember Socrates? And there's Belladonna, too, one of the easiest to procure. It's a pretty plant called the Deadly Nightshade. One can grow it in one's garden and then, with a rudimentary knowledge, extract the poison from its leaves or roots or berries. The whole damned plant is toxic. Child's play, actually." Danby paused and added to himself: "What an awful thought. Anyhow, let's get on. You may all step back. Let me have the details now. I will begin by asking some questions and then Little Dan here will record your statements. Master Jonson."

Ben Jonson started at being singled out like that.

"You left the tavern just before the deceased's body was discovered. He was found a little to the left of the main door; did you not see him, dead or alive, when you made your exit?"

"Did I...? No, I did not, sir."

Jonson's sense of alarm was justified. He had suffered run-ins with the Law before and was therefore anxious to have his name cleared at the earliest.

The room fell silent and the Coroner regarded him with a sombre expression.

"That is a little strange, Master Jonson," Danby said. "If the deceased had been alive when you left, he would have been standing quite close to the entrance since that's where his body was found. You could not have missed him. And if he were dead by then, surely you would have noticed...?"

"I didn't see anything," Jonson said hotly. "I...er...left in somewhat of a state. Shakespeare and I had been arguing and I was annoyed with him. I left the tavern preoccupied with other thoughts. I'm afraid I didn't notice anything out of the ordinary."

The Coroner shrugged and turned away from Jonson "Who else left the Mermaid's after the deceased went out?" Danby asked. "I have two names: Oliver Downtown and Christopher Beeston. Step forward, both of you."

They complied.

"Did you leave together?"

"No, sir," they chorused.

"Who went out first?"

"I did, I suppose, sir," said Downtown, all alert and eager-eyed.

"He did," Beeston agreed.

"Why did you go out?" Danby asked.

"For a bit o' fresh air, sir," Downtown said. "The tavern was gettin' heated, like, with the arguments n' all. I thought I might clear me head."

"And did you see the deceased outside, dead or alive?"

"No, sir. I went in the opposite direction. I saw no one until Mr. Beeston here came out."

"Is that what happened, Mr. Beeston? Anything you'd like to add?"

"No, sir. Oliver is correct. It happened like he said."

"Did you, either of you, see anybody else outside?" Danby asked. "The killer, perhaps?"

"No, sir."

"All right, you are excused for now. You may step back. Mr. Johnson..." Ben Jonson started again. "No, not you," Danby said, much to his relief. "I meant Mr. William Johnson, of the Mermaid's. What can you tell us? Anything you can add to these good men's testimonies?"

"No, Sir, nothing."

"So you saw nothing unusual?" Danby continued after a brief pause. "Mr. Johnson, nothing to denote the players' dislike of the deceased?"

"Dislike?" William Johnson's eyes widened in surprise. "By George, no, sir. Charlie was the most popular man in the tavern that night, he was; the drinks were on him, sir."

"Aye, true, true," came the chorus from the others.

The Coroner nodded, signalling the end of this particular line of questioning.

"Just one thing, I must mention," William Johnson said unexpectedly. "I was going to let it pass but, seeing that we are all gathered here- all honest men under oath- I must say this. You, sir, you were missing from your table, too." His finger pointed at Alexander Cooke. "You went out before Charlie Heminges' body was discovered, didn't you?"

"Me?" Cooke sounded incredulous. "No, sir, I did not. That's not true."

"Ah, but you was missing from your table, lad. I was keepin' an eye on that table since Charlie Heminges was paying. You were gone, too, for a short time."

All eyes turned on Cooke, hostile and inquiring. The sudden shift in mood was palpable "It's not true, I tell you; I never left the tavern." Cooke's voice was tremulous. "I...I only got up to see where the others had gotten to. They'd all gone. Charlie, Chris Beeston, Ollie. So I got up, opened the door, and looked out. But I didn't see anything or anyone, I swear it. I sat down again and waited for them to return. I must've left my table for thirty seconds, no more. But I never went out, I didn't."

Nobody spoke for a few moments.

The Coroner regarded Cooke with a cold, hard eye. "Why didn't you come forward and say this earlier, Mr. Cooke?"

"I...I didn't think it mattered. You asked if anyone had left the tavern; I hadn't. I swear I didn't step out of the Mermaid's. I only went out when the others did, after Mr. Heminges rushed in shouting that his brother was dead."

"All right, you're excused for now," Danby said. "Mr. Sprat, your turn next. Please tell us, in your own words, what you saw when you arrived at the scene that night."

***

FOUR

———

Jousting was once a legal way to settle disputes even to the point of death. Knights and noblemen, a breed known to be irascible and easily offended, would take up arms at the slightest provocation and challenge an opponent to a duel. Bloodshed on this account became so common and so outrageous that Queen Elizabeth intervened and outlawed this ancient tradition. Duelling became illegal except in tournaments and it was strictly regulated by the Office of the Heralds, which was entrusted with the task of running and scoring the event. Knights and noblemen qualified to bear arms could take part in the lists with their shields and surcoats bearing their emblems. These coats-of-arms (or simply 'arms') were unique to each knight and his family.

In counties like Suffolk starved of theatres and other 'city' forms of entertainment, a tournament was an eagerly awaited event. The venue for today's tourney was a large ground adjacent to the Earl's castle at the edge of a sylvan wood. People had begun gathering there from the previous day. They'd come from the farthest end of Suffolk and its neighbouring counties.

Shakespeare and Burbage reached the ground half-an-hour before time along with Carey and the other dignitaries. The buzz in the air was infectious and it put them all in a good mood. Festivities had begun early that day with archery contests, performing bears and various circus acts to keep the milling crowds entertained. Similar events had taken place the previous day as well. By now the spectators were all wound up, tipsy with gallons of ale in them, and restless for the jousting to begin.

"By my troth, I never knew there were so many people in all of England," Burbage exclaimed.

The galleries were brimming over with spectators. Young people hung like ripened fruit from every tree in the vicinity. The seating arrangements in the galleries were rather basic: coarse carpets on the floor and rows of wooden benches set upon them. But colourful tapestries and fluttering ribbons hanging from canopies in the galleries made up for the simple seating.

The royal gallery in which Shakespeare and his companions took their places was the grandest of them all. It had cushioned chairs for all and two throne-like arm-chairs on a dais for the Queen and King Christian. Squires, pages, and pretty young maidens dressed in brightly coloured liveries waited in the enclosure for the VIP guests. It was a sunny day and the colours on the ground sparkled, sending brilliant shafts of light all across the arena.

"Hope the weather holds up," Carey said. "As things are, the damned rain has left the ground rather soggy; our valiant knights are going to struggle a bit, slipping and sliding all over. Can't be helped, I suppose. At last we'll be seeing young Drake in action. Not real action, though. Jousters can't kill one another these days. `Pity. It used to be wonderful and manly, all that blood and gore, ah!"

Carey was nearly salivating at the recollection and Burbage managed a weak smile. Shakespeare grimaced and considered the Lord Chamberlain's remarks quite inappropriate in view of their reason for being there. Deaths in the Company. Not blood and gore, but no less horrifying. The Coroner's inquest would be underway now; he wondered about the outcome. Would ol' Danby discover anything new? What would his findings be?

Murder, no doubt.

His mind reeled at the thought of a murderer in their midst.

And how were they getting along with the Admiral's Men? It was an odd feeling to have 'surrendered' the Globe to Henslowe and party for a week. An inexplicable sense of loss. His stomach churned at the thought of Alleyn, Ben Jonson and the others stomping around his stage and enacting their plays, not his.

"There he is," Carey exclaimed, cutting off Shakespeare's train of thought. "Geoffrey Drake!"

He pointed towards the southernmost end of the field where the jousters' tents were pitched: six colourful pavilions with different coats-of-arms emblazoned on shields, flag posts, and canopies. The tents' cords were of the same colour as the knights' uniforms. Geoffrey Drake was dressed in black and silver. He'd inherited his arms from his late uncle Francis Drake, who was knighted many moons ago in Fifteen-Eighty-One. Francis Drake returned from his maritime expeditions after defeating the Spanish Armada and brought booty of gold, silver and other treasures for the Queen. She was delighted and promptly knighted him on board his ship The Golden Hind. Sir Francis died heirless in `Ninety-Six and his arms passed on to his younger brother John, and John's sons. Geoffrey was the younger son. The arms were attractive, a wavy horizontal fess (band) between two stars argent against a sable backdrop. The silver of the stars reflected flashes of sunlight while Drake and his team prepared for the challenge ahead.

Geoffrey Drake was in full armour: black breeches and breastplate with streaks of silver in them; a sword at one side, and a dagger at the other. One of his squires carried his lance, another his shield and helmet. A third squire and Drake himself were inspecting the horse, a strong, black steed.

"I see there are six contenders today. Will they all face off?" Carey inquired of the squires standing by.

"Yes, My Lord," the squire said, pleased at the privilege of explaining things to the Lord Chamberlain. "They'll begin with general combat, three knights on either side. Then it shall come down to two."

"This is it? The tourney ends today?"

"Aye, My Lord; His Majesty departs for his native land tomorrow morn."

"And then everyone can heave sighs of relief," Carey muttered under his breath.

Pleasant as King Christian's visit must've been, Carey knew that his hosts would be glad to see the back of him. He was an important ally- a Protestant monarch- keen on maintaining good relations with England. He was the Scottish king's brother-in-law, too. But who could forget that the Danes had once invaded and briefly occupied parts of England? Even though it had been six centuries back, a strange unease lurked beneath the surface when King Christian and his entourage were around. Two Viking ships were docked at the Suffolk port waiting to carry their monarch safely back home. A posse of the Earl's men kept constant vigil on them.

"The odds are on young Drake, I suspect?" Carey said to the squire.

"Indeed, My Lord. Everyone's hoping it will come down to Sir Geoffrey versus Sir John, like it was on Coronation Day this year."

Carey chuckled. "A great joust, wasn't it? Geoffrey made short work of John, didn't he? John's no pushover, though, and he must be thirsting to avenge his defeat. I wager they'll be at outrance today."

Being at outrance signified the use of sharp weapons. In tournaments like this one, arms of courtesy were usually used, these being the reverse ends of lances with flat boards fixed upon them; no danger of serious injury save from a fall from the horse or a violent blow to a vulnerable body part. But sometimes jousters chose to fight with sharp weapons.

"One question, Squire, if I may," Burbage said.

The squire glanced at him inquiringly.

"Isn't it customary to appoint a Queen of Love and Beauty for the duration of a tournament?"

"Er...yes, it is but..." The squire shifted uncomfortably from one foot to another.

"Yes?" Carey prodded him.

"My Lord, it was felt that such a...a...thing might not be in order. I mean, why would we need a fake queen when Her Royal Highness is here?"

"Oh! Of course. You're right, you're right," Carey laughed. "'Hadn't thought of that. We already have a Queen of Love and Beauty, don't we? There's your answer, Richard."

Burbage reddened and mumbled: "Yes, yes, My Lord. Thank you."

Shakespeare grinned at him and whispered: "No prizes for that one."

Still smiling, Carey thanked the squire and dismissed him.

Burbage, smarting from his faux-pas, whispered back to Shakespeare: "Dear God, I really put my foot in it; the squire must think me an imbecile."

"Indeed, for he seems to be a discerning young man," Shakespeare quipped.

Burbage glowered at him. "Very funny. Wait till you make a mistake like that. You know what I've been thinking? All this pomp and ceremony's reminding me of your histories, especially *Richard the Second*. Why don't you do another one with a full jousting scene, not an aborted one?"

"It is a thought," Shakespeare conceded but he didn't sound enthusiastic. "I don't know if I'll write another history but I do have an idea floating around in my head, a Scottish theme with lots of blood and action; a murderous couple, husband and wife, how about that?"

"Husband and wife?"

Shakespeare nodded.

"Why, I like it already! But I thought you were working on that Moor from Venice?"

"Othello." Shakespeare grimaced. "The Moor of Venice; still grappling with him. He's not an easy one."

"Won't be pleasant to perform, either. I'll need lots of grease paint. You said he strangles his wife?"

"Maybe. I'm not sure. I think he'll smother her instead, with a pillow."

Burbage raised a brow in mock-horror. "You're in a merry mood, aren't you?"

They were still chatting away about Shakespeare's future projects when a young boy came running towards the royal gallery. He was a common lad of about eight or nine, dressed in a tattered brown tunic. One of the squires barred his way but the boy outmanoeuvred him and, to Shakespeare's astonishment, ran directly to him. Grabbing the edge of Shakespeare's sleeve, he cried:

"A penny, sir, won't you spare a vail for a poor boy?"

Shakespeare froze.

"Sir? Sir?"

The boy stood there with an outstretched palm.

Shakespeare stared at the folded piece of paper the boy had just thrust into his hand.

"A vail, sir?"

A squire grabbed him by the collar and told him to clear off. "Now don't be pesterin' good gentlemen. Be off, lad, be on your way."

Shakespeare gaped at the boy. The term he'd used- vail- signified a tip for an errand, monetary reward for services rendered.

Who would risk sending him a secret message in such a public place?

Only one person he knew.

"Wait," he said to the squire. "Let him go; he's just a boy."

"Marry, sir, you don't want to go round encouraging them beggars."

"At ease, Squire, he's a child. Here, boy."

Shakespeare gave him a penny.

"Thank you, sir, thank you. God bless you, sir." The boy grinned and then scampered off after sticking his tongue out at the squire.

"Why did he pick on you?" Burbage asked Shakespeare. "Wonder what he really wanted."

Shakespeare was nonplussed; Burbage's remark indicated that he'd not seen the note. He quickly closed his fist and shrugged.

"No idea."

Burbage grunted and took no further notice.

Shakespeare's pulse raced like a galloping horse. Who could it be, the sender of the note? Marie, it had to be her. But how could she reach him here?

He stepped back, away from the group in the most innocuous manner possible, and quickly fumbled to open the note.

There it was, the drawing of the heart with an arrow through it. Their code.

Above it were three words in French.

Attention! Il sait.

Beware! He knows.

Shakespeare's heart lurched. So she was here, at this very tournament with her husband!

Wonder-full.

Just when he thought things couldn't get any crappier, here comes the whole heap of shit.

His eyes darted all over; where was she?

Of all the towns, of all the counties in England, she has to descend upon Suffolk when he was there!

Suddenly the trumpets sounded, thunderous applause shook the galleries, and spectators began to wave and shout praises of their sovereign.

Queen Elizabeth had arrived at the ground with her retinue.

Shakespeare stared in dismay as he saw that the royal party included, besides the King of Denmark, Robert Cecil, Earl Howard and their assistants, the Viscount Lord Henry Blackburn and his wife, the beautiful Countess Marie.

The other afternoon at the Globe their meeting had been hurried and then abruptly cut short when Thomas Gray fell from the balcony. After Marie was gone, Shakespeare had felt he'd hardly seen her. They hadn't had the time to do anything.

Now here she was gliding along in the Queen's entourage looking every bit the noblewoman she was.

As for her face, it beggared all description.

It was a line he'd thought up for a tragedy he was contemplating about Cleopatra and Mark Antony. But Cleo had been ugly with a hooked nose and bad skin; Marie was pink and perfect. Her long dark hair served to highlight the milky white perfection of her skin. Her eyes, dark and lively, swept through the crowd.

Shakespeare withdrew into the background to avoid making eye contact with the viscount. The urgency in Marie's note was disturbing. She'd been quite certain that her husband knew about their affair and she'd said so at the Globe that day. So why was the note necessary now? Something must've happened since then. Something had troubled her enough to send him the warning. He'd better keep a low-profile now. He could not risk a public meeting with her.

He knew all about love, what a terrible master it is. That busy Archer had struck and left a wound so deep that nothing could ever fill it. He was condemned to endure the knowledge that the woman he loved was possessed by another man more powerful than he. Those lovely arms, smooth thighs, proud breasts- they would suffer another's caresses night after night, and he was powerless to stop it. Sometimes, when his despair became too great, he would consider ending it all. He lived in the sporting district; no dearth of women there. He would go to the harlots and satisfy himself. When spent, he would lie in the dark thinking: This is how it must be for her. A meaningless conjoining of bodies; no emotion, no feeling. He imagined that Blackburn was a ravishing beast and she, a hapless Leda. She was forced into submission; she would never submit willingly... Were they in another time he would rescue her from this earthly hell, he would.

Today, as he shrank away from the royal party, he was seized by another, more disturbing thought: what if- when he saw her with her husband- she did not look distressed? What if she actually looked happy?

No, no, please, no. That would be too hard to bear. What suffering lover wants to see his beloved in a joyous state? No, she must be as miserable as he.

What if Juliet rose at the end of the play and said with a short laugh: 'Dear Romeo, dead and gone? Ah, free of that whinny wimp at last. Romeo, O, Romeo, wherefore art thou Romeo? Up in heaven, I pray. God bless your soul. Leave this earth to us mortals to laugh and dance and play!'

Trumpets sounded again and a hush fell over the lists. Queen Elizabeth and the King of Denmark took their seats and then, according to practice, the Queen gave the herald the signal to proclaim the laws of the tournament. Two marshals on horseback would enforce these laws during combat. This being a general tournament, the Knights challengers would face each other in two groups of three men each. The last two knights left in combat would be judged winner and runner-up.

"Now, at Her Majesty's signal, let the tournament begin," the herald cried, "Glory to the brave!"

"Glory to the brave!" the spectators shouted.

At either ends of the ground the Knights challengers waited on horseback to enter the field. The crowd cheered them by name and Geoffrey Drake certainly got the loudest cheers when he entered the field.

Shakespeare noted that even at a distance, amidst so many brave peers, Drake stood out. He sat erect on his black horse, a slim and dignified figure. His horse was disciplined, too, standing quietly whereas the other beasts had begun neighing and stomping about in all the excitement. Like the rest of the crowd Shakespeare, too, was caught up in the spectacle and momentarily forgot his own turmoil. Countess Marie had taken her seat directly behind the Queen. She didn't glance back and Shakespeare saw that Blackburn had her hand in a vice-like grip.

Soon after, the trumpets blew for the third time and Shakespeare's attention was diverted.

The six jousters entered the ground on foot with their horses marching gently along to present themselves before the Queen and the crowd. As each one passed the dais, the herald announced his name, and the crowd cheered lustily. From the northern end of the lists came three men: John Huntington (the one who'd lost to Drake on two previous occasions), Phillip Taylor and Samuel Francis. Opposite them were Geoffrey Drake, Frederick de la Mer and John Rothsfeld. A loud cheer went up from the crowd when Drake's name was called. Shakespeare and Burbage got their first view of him.

A very young and very handsome face with short blond hair.

He looked more Nordic than English. He exuded confidence and there was a trace of pride in the way his mouth curled into a half-smile. As he passed by saluting the royal gallery, Carey leaned back and whispered to Shakespeare and Burbage:

"A fine specimen of manhood, isn't he? We'll go to his pavilion after the joust. You haven't forgotten the purpose behind our visit, I hope?"

"Very nearly, My Lord," Shakespeare said cheekily.

Carey narrowed his eyes. "Well, refresh your memory, then. We aren't here for the party, William. Don't let all this pomp and ceremony sway you."

"No, My Lord."

"And don't forget that somebody is murdering players in my Company."

"I won't, My Lord."

Carey gave him a nod and then sat forward again.

The knights did a round of the lists to acknowledge the crowd's support and then returned to either ends of the ground for combat.

"For England! For Her Majesty the Queen!" the herald exulted. "Glory to the brave!"

His last few words were drowned in the clamour of trumpets and then the knights rushed at each other.

***

He looked more Nordic than English. He exuded confidence and there was a trace of pride in the way his mouth curled into a half-smile. As he passed by saluting the royal gallery, Carey leaned back and whispered to Shakespeare and Burbage.

FIVE

Miserly sods. They earn hundreds of pounds but they're too mean to pay a poor ironsmith. They perform *The Merchant of Venice* and make a villain of Shylock; why, they're all Shylocks, every one o' them. Okay, so the boy is dead but that's not my problem, is it? I still need my dues. I have hungry mouths to feed, don't I? Blah, blah, blah...

Benjamin Finch's thoughts became darker and angrier as he entered Maid Lane and saw the steep white walls of the Globe. He'd passed the Rose along the way and cursed loudly. Greedy bastards, the lot; he was glad to see the grand old theatre in near-disuse. He knew that further west in Paris Gardens the Swan had died, too. Good, good, good.

He wasn't a Puritan and didn't have a grudge against players per se; it was their mendacity that got his goat. They lured people into playhouses, performed fantastical dramas, earned pots of money and yet reneged on their dues. How could they live with themselves?

Today was the day, he'd decided. He would knock on the gates and demand payment. A shilling, not an impossible amount but not insignificant, either. Twenty-five curtain rings; four padlocks with duplicate keys; and two bolts- he'd written down the order, thank goodness. He still couldn't get over the fact that no one had come forward to pay him. They boy had assured him that the money would be sent by the evening.

His fault for letting them have the stuff on credit.

He paused at the gates, swallowed hard to steady his nerves, and then knocked on the gates.

A young boy answered.

"Benjamin Finch," he said in a sonorous tone. "Ironsmith from Kent Street market."

"Aye? What do you want?"

"I want to speak to the owner of this playhouse, that's what. You men owe me money. It's been over a week and no one showed up at my shop. I will take my payment today, thank you."

"We owe you money? For what?"

"For what?" Finch held up a grubby piece of paper. "For this; can you read?"

The boy averted his eyes. Evidently, the question stung. He was a mere usher, not an apprentice. No, he couldn't read.

Finch smirked. "Get me someone who's in charge and be quick about it. I have a business to run, you know."

The boy hesitated. "They...the Chamberlain's Men, most of them are still at the Coroner's inquest. There's only the Admiral's Men here. Wait, let me see if anyone...Wait here."

Finch grunted.

It took about five minutes. Finch grunted some more, shuffled his feet, and dusted his doublet. Moment by moment, his annoyance mounted. Finally a portly chap of average height emerged from the gates and said:

"I'm William Sly, player with the Chamberlain's Men. What do you want?"

"My dues, that's what."

He stuck the paper in Sly's face.

Sly read it, his brow creased in concentration, and then he said: "What's this?"

Finch let out an exasperated sigh. "What's this? What does it look like, Mr. Sly? By George, you all are...It's a list of items your boy took from my shop, isn't it? I let him have it in good faith and he promised to pay..."

"What items? Which boy?"

"The boy, that one that died- Jeremy Smith. He took them

from me on the morning of his death, didn't he?"

Sly was gobsmacked. "I'm sorry, Mr. Finch, I don't know what you're talking about. Jeremy took these items from you? Twenty-five curtain rings? That...that's very strange. I'm quite certain his pockets were empty when we found his body. I'll have to check with Mr. Heminges; perhaps you've got the day wrong. It couldn't have been on the day he died. You say we haven't paid you?"

"Of course you haven't. Would I leave my shop and walk all the way here if you had paid me? And, no, I have not got the day wrong. It was on the day he died. He showed up at my shop early morning and said he'd received a note instructing him to fetch these items positively before going to the Globe. Twenty-five curtain rings; four padlocks; bolts... He was in a bit of a state, I can tell you. `All keyed up about some big role."

William Sly felt the hairs stand at the back of his neck.

"Jeremy came to you the day he died? You're sure of it? This is very strange. Are you sure he said he had been instructed to fetch these items?"

"Am I sure? Bloody right I'm sure. He showed me the note, too. I can read, can't I?"

"Yes, yes, of course you can. What did the note say?"

"Just what I told you: that Jeremy was to procure these items before going to the Globe that morning. It was signed, too."

Sly stiffened and his voice dropped to a whisper. "Do you remember whose signature it was?"

"I remember that well. `Saw it with my own two eyes. It was signed by Richard Burbage. That was the name. Richard Burbage. Now, am I or am I not going to get paid today?"

***

The six knights clashed in the middle of the field in a cloud of dust and, at first, all that was visible was a blur of horses accompanied by loud shouts and the sound of clanging metal. Lance met shield and in a few moments the first rush was over. The spectators strained their eyes to see who'd been felled and who'd emerged unscathed. Much to everyone's delight, Drake and Huntington were still astride, apparently none the worse for the first round. Two knights were unhorsed; one of them- John Rothsfeld- received a debilitating blow to his right arm and was forced to leave the field. His squires assisted him but his lance and shield were picked up by the pursuivants (the herald's assistants). The other knight, Phillip Taylor, rose shakily and dusted himself and walked away slowly with his weapons intact.

Two knights down, the herald announced, four more to participate in round two.

The jousters returned to their ends of the ground. Frederick de la Mer noticed that his shield had cracked so his squires hurried onto the field with a replacement.

After a brief interlude, the second round began.

The four knights rushed at one another and as they clashed in the centre, Drake's lance crashed into Huntington's shield and broke it in two. Such was the fury of the blow that Huntington lost his grip on his lance and it fell to the ground with a thud.

"Shame! Shame!" the crowd chanted.

Huntington steered his brown horse aside and waited for his squires to bring him a new lance and shield. In the meantime, the other two knights turned on Drake as if to avenge Huntington. They thrust their lances at him. Drake proved equal to the challenge. In a display of excellent horsemanship, he dodged one lancer at the last moment, brought his steed up on its hind legs and caused his opponent to flail wildly and lose his balance. The man crashed down onto the muddy field, taking his horse with him. Then Drake blocked the second lancer's blow with his own lance and followed up with a swift counterattack: a sharp blow to the middle of the lance, breaking it apart. The crowd cheered wildly as both Drake's antagonists withdrew to the trumpet's call and duly accepted defeat.

Round three.

As predicted, only Drake and Huntington remained in the contest. Excited chatter passed through the galleries. Everybody anticipated a good fight. The two challengers retreated to the opposite ends of the ground for a short break. They drank some water and their squires inspected their lances and shields for damage.

"He's going to do it again; By George, Drake's going to win," Carey exulted. "It'll be four times in a row. `Amazing, just amazing."

The Queen smiled, looking pleased, but refrained from making any comment.

King Christian said something and Hans translated:

"His Majesty wishes to know how the Lord Chamberlain is so certain of Sir Geoffrey's victory. The other knight is bigger and older so he must've seen more combat than the young man."

"True, true," said Carey, "But Drake's a natural, just wait and see."

The herald was about to call the third round when one of Huntington's squires ran up to him and said something. The herald looked surprised. Then he nodded at the squire and approached the Queen.

"Your Majesty, it appears that Sir John wishes to exercise his right to outrance."

"Outrance?" Queen Elizabeth exclaimed. "Good Lord, he's in a choleric mood today, isn't he?"

She turned to Robert Cecil for advice. He shrugged and said: "You may stop the combat any time you wish, Madam."

"And so I shall," she said. "I won't have knights killing each other over a mere trophy. Oh well, all right. Herald, we permit Huntington to challenge Drake but we won't let it get out of hand."

"Very good, Your Majesty."

The herald bowed and returned to his position from where he declared, much to the crowd's delight, that the next round would be fought with sharp weapons.

Lusty cheers went up from the galleries. But first Huntington would have to complete the formality of challenging Drake. So he rode across the field to Drake's side and touched Drake's shield with the sharp end of his lance.

"I accept, sir," Drake said.

Huntington acknowledged this with a nod and then returned to his end.

An expectant silence descended upon the galleries. The mood suddenly turned sombre as the spectators realized that the knights might receive grievous injuries during this round of combat.

Shakespeare glanced around him and saw that as usual women appeared in great numbers at this event. Their expressions were taut and excited, every bit as eager as the men. Blood and violence didn't seem to affect them. The proportion of women to men at public hangings, bull and bear baiting, and other such events had always taken him by surprise. It was nearly fifty-fifty. Women had a stomach for this sort of thing. They might scream out in horror; occasionally one of them might swoon. But by and large, ladies were avid spectators on occasions generally considered as contrary to their natures.

This time when the trumpets sounded the air was so thick with excitement that Shakespeare found it hard to breathe. The two knights set spurs to their horses and charged down the ground from opposite directions. Huntington used his brute force to thrust hard at Drake, hitting his breastplate and nearly unhorsing him. It was the first shock young Drake had received in the tourney and exclamations went up from the crowd. Some women shouted:

"Beware, Drake, Beware!"

The young knight was shaken. He'd managed to avoid the ignominy of being thrown from his horse only because of his equestrian skills but he would have to look sharp now. He recovered his balance. Clasping his shield close to his left side, he turned his horse towards Huntington and waited for him to charge. He maintained a safe distance of about four feet from Huntington, thereby reducing the latter's advantage of physical strength, and dexterously blocked Huntington's lance with his own. Huntington pulled back and thrust at the younger man again. Drake presented his shield in defence and then, with astonishing swiftness, reversed his lance and used the blunt end to deliver a strong blow that threw his opponent off balance. Huntington went crashing down with a loud cry.

The galleries erupted with joy. Spectators chanted Drake's name. Shakespeare and Burbage cheered loudly. The Queen looked pleased but remained decorously silent. King Christian looked like he was enjoying himself and kept making rapid exchanges in Danish with his aides.

Once a knight was unhorsed, his antagonist was not permitted to continue the duel on horseback. So Drake dismounted, threw his lance down, and drew his sword, waiting for Huntington to rise. Huntington got to his feet slowly and unsteadily and tried to gather his wits about him. His helmet had fallen off to reveal an angry square face with bushy eyebrows and a thick beard. He looked nearly fifteen years Drake's senior though he was just seven years older. His was the kind of visage that age withers quickly. The two men were of nearly the same height but Huntington was more powerfully built and looked capable of demolishing the lighter, younger man. But strength alone has rarely favoured infantry combatants; it's of little use unless accompanied with skill and agility. Huntington picked up his shield, unsheathed his long sword and rushed at Drake, sawing the air wildly and altogether missing his target. Swords clanked noisily, the blades gleaming in the sunlight, as the two knights fenced with all their might like in a real fight to the death. As Huntington came at him, Drake used the senior knight's bodyweight against him, stepping aside and thrusting upwards between Huntington's waist and breastplate. It was a vicious slash and Huntington cried out as blood gushed from his right side.

His scream mingled with shouts from the spectators.

Queen Elizabeth raised the baton and lowered it, exclaiming: "Halt! Stop the combat!"

Immediately, the Marshalls galloped onto the field and shouted for the knights to cease combat.

Both knights obeyed.

Drake sheathed his sword and raised his hands to acknowledge the cheers all round. Chants of 'Brave Knight!' and 'Geoffrey Drake! Geoffrey Drake!' filled the air.

Huntington collapsed, holding his side and his squires were quick to the rescue. A physician was waiting in his pavilion.

Drake approached the royal gallery on foot flanked by two Marshalls.

"Your Majesty, today's victor!" one of the Marshalls said. "Geoffrey Drake!"

The young knight knelt before the Queen to the sound of deafening applause and cheers.

Queen Elizabeth smiled broadly. "Congratulations, Sir Geoffrey, on a well-deserved victory. You and your sword brought alive the legends of King Arthur and Excalibur; of Ilium's Prince Hector and his sword Durendal. I dare say you met with a better fate, though. Does your sword have a name?"

"It does, Your Majesty," Drake said, grinning. "I call it Verbera."

"Verbera?" the Queen chuckled. "Latin for 'Scourge', isn't it?"

"Yes, Madam. You are right, as always. And I remain your ever-loyal servant."

Elizabeth nodded. "Now, your reward. Pray rise, Sir Geoffrey."

Drake got to his feet.

A page boy brought a trophy on a gleaming silver tray. It was a gold-plated figurine of a knight on horseback with the globe at his feet.

"For everlasting glory," she said. "May your fame spread throughout the world."

Drake accepted it with a deep bow and everyone could see how thrilled he was. His face beamed with joy. Then one of the pursuivants arrived at the gallery with the reins of an exquisite white horse in hand. The Champion's prize.

"That's yours, Geoffrey," the Queen said affectionately. The way she was beaming, it was obvious that she was very fond of the young man.

Drake's eyes sparkled. The steed was a beauty and he was the envy of every nobleman in the arena. He took the reins from the pursuivants and stroked the horse's neck. Then, in a display of his dexterity, he mounted the animal in one swift move without saddle or stirrup. The horse neighed in surprise and stomped about for a few moments but it soon fell prey to the young man's charms. Calming down, it strutted around with Drake comfortably astride. Both knight and horse received thunderous applause as they did a victory lap around the field.

The Queen and King Christian waited until Drake completed the round and then they left the ground with their retinues. Carey signalled to Shakespeare and Burbage to remain behind. Once the others had left and only a handful of squires lingered in the pavilion to look after Carey and his group, Carey whispered to his players:

"We'll give Drake fifteen minutes to refresh himself and then we'll meet him in his pavilion. I trust you've sharpened your powers of persuasion?"

"Persuasion? Hardly, My Lord," Shakespeare said with a touch of irony in his tone. "Who can refuse the Lord Chamberlain?"

Carey rolled his eyes. "Come now, William, do you really think I'd coerce Drake into a project like this? Of course not. He won't succeed in catching the killer unless he participates in this willingly. Understand?"

Shakespeare nodded.

"My Lord, if I may...?" Burbage said.

"Yes?"

"My Lord, at the risk of sounding impertinent, I may say that...well, we've witnessed Sir Geoffrey's prowess with the lance and sword but he won't need those to track down whoever's responsible for the murders in our Company. Not unless it comes down to hand-to-hand combat. So I'm wondering...?"

"Why I've chosen him?"

"Yes, My Lord. I don't mean to be so bold but..."

"That's all right. Curiosity is a good thing, Richard. I

know I'm under no compulsion to explain myself to you but I don't mind enlightening you."

"Thank you, My Lord. You're most kind."

"I know, I know. First, however, I must say your assertion is wrong. Do you think that Drake's skill with lance and sword is divorced from his personality? Why did he win today? Because of a sharp mind, and courage in combat. Both these qualities are invaluable to a person who's trying to track down a killer. But, yes, there is another reason, too, and I think I've mentioned it before."

He paused and the other two gazed at him in rapt attention. Carey smiled, enjoying himself.

"It's a little known fact that Geoffrey Drake is a mystery-solver. Despite his young age, he's been invited into select circles in the past to solve problems; the kind of problems that require the strictest confidentiality. You'll be surprised at the strange goings-on in the lives of noblemen! I was a witness in one such case and Drake left an indelible impression on my mind. But that's a story that bears telling at leisure. Maybe I'll narrate it during our journey back to London. As of now, I think it's time we met the young champion, eh? Come on; let us now be up and doing and all that."

***

Six

————

Geoffrey Drake's pavilion was a loud, raucous place where his squires and attendants were drinking, dancing and celebrating his victory. Twenty-odd men were packed into the tent. Some of them were sitting on a carpet; others were hanging about a long wooden table where all sorts of delectable refreshments were laid out. Wine flowed freely in silver goblets. It was evident that Drake had anticipated his victory and prepared for it.

The man of the moment was sitting on a chair surrounded by his friends as a tipsy musician played a lyre nearby.

Presently Drake's squire Rodney Peele, who'd been standing at the entrance, announced that the Lord Chamberlain was there and that he wished to meet Sir Geoffrey.

Drake sprang to his feet. "The Lord Chamberlain? Lord Carey? Escort him in, Rod; you can't keep him waiting, for God's sake!"

Rod nodded and disappeared for a moment, returning with Carey and two men.

"My Lord!" Drake exclaimed with a big grin. "How kind of you to grace my tent with your presence. You do me an honour, sir."

Carey smiled back, shook Drake's hand and also thumped him on the back. "The honour's all mine," he said. "Heartiest congratulations on an excellent victory."

"Hear! Hear!" Drake's men cried applauding, and the victorious knight gave them all a gentle bow.

Carey gestured towards his companions.

"Geoffrey, I'd like you to meet the most talented men in all of England. From my players' Company, William Shakespeare..."

"Master Shakespeare?" Drake's eyes widened with delight. "My word, I am honoured today, doubly honoured. I've heard so much about you."

Shakespeare beamed as Drake shook his hand warmly. A small sigh of relief escaped Carey's lips; thank goodness Drake was familiar with the London stage. He'd had his doubts.

"Have you ever visited the Globe?" Carey asked him.

"No, My Lord, but I've passed by several times. I must confess I'm not an avid playgoer but I did see a show at Court one day. I...er...don't recall the name of the play but it was immensely enjoyable."

"In truth? Let's hope it was one of ours. Geoffrey, here is one of the most famous actors in our land..." Carey began, by way of introducing Burbage.

"Delighted," Drake said, extending his hand to Burbage. "You must be the one and only Edward Alleyn! Everybody talks about you. I saw your play. *Tamburlaine*, ah, that's what it was called. Wonderful, quite wonderful, sir."

Carey sputtered, Shakespeare stifled a guffaw, and Burbage's jaw dropped in dismay.

Drake saw their expressions and realized something was amiss. Burbage looked as squashed as a wet cabbage leaf.

"Oh, oh, have I got it wrong?" Drake inquired. "I thought...well, you did look thinner and taller at the time. Oh, you're not Edward Alleyn, are you?"

Burbage shook his head.

"This is Richard Burbage," Carey said heavily. "Ned Alleyn works with the Admiral's Men."

"By Jove, I am sorry! I beg your pardon, Mr. Burbage." Drake reddened and smiled sheepishly. "I really put my foot in it this time. Mr. Burbage, welcome to my pavilion. This way please, sirs, My Lord. Please share a drink with me."

He led the way to a set of chairs and signalled to his servants for food and wine. Carey, Shakespeare and Burbage sat down, Burbage looking sullen and the other two, amused. Drake apologized again and explained that he wasn't much of a playhouse person. Carey said that was evident.

Drake's attendants hung around while the guests were served wine, bread and fruit.

"I hear you've just got back from France," Carey said to him. "Was your visit fruitful?"

Drake grimaced. "In a sense, yes, My Lord. I suppose I should say it was fruitful because it made me decide what I do not want!"

Carey raised his brow. "Indeed? So there'll be no wedding bells for the Drake family and the Pompadours?"

"Not as far as I'm concerned."

"But why? The young lady was not to your liking?"

"No, My Lord, she was not."

"That is unfortunate. Your mother must be very disappointed."

"She is, since they're her distant relatives. But, My Lord..." Drake lowered his voice and leaned toward Carey. "...can you imagine marrying a woman who was called 'Mademoiselle de la Pompadour'? The name's enough to put you off! And she was as pompous as her name. So I made a hasty exit; Mother's still there trying to smooth the ruffled feathers."

Carey chuckled. Then he said he would like a word in private; could Drake ask his men to clear the tent?

Drake was surprised. He clapped his hands, calling everyone to attention, and said: "Please excuse us, all of you. The Lord Chamberlain and I have some business to discuss. Leave us for now."

His men scrambled up, murmuring amongst themselves, and filed out of the tent. One squire remained behind, Drake's bodyguard Rod Peele. But the knight rolled his eyes to indicate that he should leave as well. The Lord Chamberlain was hardly likely to assassinate him in his own pavilion! Rod complied and Drake knew he'd be right outside the tent's flap, straining his ears for every word. Loyal chap; worth his considerable weight in gold.

Drake turned inquiringly to Carey. "My Lord, how can I be of service?"

"Do you spend much time in London?" Carey asked.

"I? Why, yes, My Lord. Our ancestral home is in Devon but we have an establishment in Dowgate, near London Bridge. It belonged to my late uncle, Francis."

Carey nodded. "I know. Tell me, how well acquainted are you with the theatre? I know you don't watch plays but are you aware of the Laws of the Companies and things like that?"

"Er...no, My Lord, I can't say I am. I do have a general idea...I mean, everybody knows the Globe, where your men perform. And I know of the Admiral's Men. I've also heard of the other playhouses, the Swan and the Rose. But that's about it."

Carey pursed his lips and adjusted his lace collar. "I suppose this is good in a way. For if you haven't been frequenting playhouses, the usual playgoers won't recognize you. The downside is, of course, that you'll have to start from scratch and learn everything about playhouses."

"May I ask why, My Lord?"

"Yes. We're in trouble, Geoffrey. Somebody is trying to ruin me, or at least, my Company."

Drake's blue eyes widened. "Ruin you, My Lord? In what way?"

"By murdering my players."

"Murder? You don't say!"

Carey nodded grimly. Drake stared at Shakespeare and then Burbage with incredulity written all over his face. They bobbed their heads, too.

"Two actors have been killed so far and a third is disabled for life," Carey continued. "We're quite sure there'll be more deaths unless the murderer is caught."

"Good Lord! How long has this been going on?"

"About ten days."

"That sounds rather desperate, a matter of concern, yes. Three incidents in such a short span of time. How did the two men die?"

Carey turned to Shakespeare. "You're the wordsmith; go on, tell him."

Shakespeare cleared his throat and then explained about Jeremy Smith, Thomas Gray and Charles Heminges.

Drake listened intently and then asked about the Coroner's inquest.

"There was no proper inquiry into the first two incidents," Shakespeare said. "But now, thanks to the Lord Chamberlain's insistence, the Coroner is conducting an inquest into Charlie Heminges' death. It was scheduled for this morning; we'll learn about his findings when we return to London."

"In the first instance, the death of Jeremy Smith, you say an old flower seller was the first to discover the body. Wasn't she questioned?"

"No. She disappeared after raising the hue-and-cry. No one's seen her since."

Drake pursed his lips. "That's not good. She can provide you with vital clues. No one found her? Not even the Constable?"

"The Constable's an ass," Carey said. "He's lucky if he can find himself! He's a newbie called Sprat and I'm told he's quite out of his depths in Southwark."

"The recent death of Charles Heminges, who discovered his body?"

"His brother, John Heminges," Shakespeare and Burbage chorused.

"I see. And this John Heminges; is he a player, too?"

"Yes, the senior most member of the Company," Shakespeare said. "He's our treasurer, too."

"So, obviously no one's questioned him?"

"Question John?" Shakespeare started.

"That's out of the question," Burbage exclaimed. Then he remembered himself and apologized.

Drake smiled. "No need to be sorry; I understand how you feel but the obvious conclusion, with the information you've given me so far, is that the murderer is a player or a worker in your Company. No one else would be privy to intimate details about your movements on a daily basis. So it's important to keep everybody under suspicion. Master Shakespeare, were they- the three victims- supposed to play important roles in your plays just before they died? Or, in Thomas Gray's case, before he fell from the balcony?"

"Not the first boy Jeremy. He was playing Nerissa, a minor character in *The Merchant of Venice*."

"So his death did not disrupt that day's show?"

"No, sir."

"And the other two?"

"They were doing lead parts. Tommy Gray was playing Romeo, while Charlie was going to be *Hamlet*. Richard usually does *Hamlet* but he wasn't keeping well."

"And Charlie had been my understudy for a while,"

Burbage added. "He was so keen..."

Drake lapsed into a long and thoughtful silence. His brow furrowed and Shakespeare couldn't help observing what a good-looking chap he was. His youth shone through in a face that was clearly noble. Women must swarm all over him.

"Mr. Burbage," Drake said abruptly. "I hope you are keeping your guard up?"

"I, sir?"

"Yes. It puzzles me; why hasn't the killer tried to eliminate you by now? What's he waiting for? You are the lead actor; your death would surely cripple the Company for some time. It would be a terrible blow. So unless you are the murderer, you're probably the next target!"

"Well, I..." Burbage sputtered, unsure of whether to be worried or offended. "Of course I'm not a murderer, sir, and I have no intention of dying, either!"

"Good. I'm sure all of us are in agreement with that!"

"But how can I be on guard, sir? Against what? Whom?"

Drake shrugged. "We don't know yet, do we? Just stay close to those you trust."

"That would be every player in the Company!"

Burbage's exasperation was well-received. The other three exchanged troubled looks.

"Geoffrey, I need you to get to the bottom of this," Carey

said. "I want you to join the Company as a player and find out who the killer is. Richard and his brother own majority of the shares and they're the ones that hire players so..."

"A player, My Lord? Me?" Drake shook his head. "Surely you jest, My Lord! I cannot act; I...I'll be found out in an instant. I'm useless with words and poetry, things like that." He pointed at his scabbard hanging from a nail on a wooden post in the tent. "That's all I'm good with."

"But how else will you get inside, become one of them?" Carey asked.

Drake turned to Burbage. "What kind of apprentices do you have?"

"None like you, sir, they're all common, very common."

"There you are," Drake said to Carey. "My speech will give me away; I can't disguise that. Even if I were to do some small, preferably dumb parts, the other players will become suspicious. But...I do have an idea."

The other three looked at him expectantly.

"Master Shakespeare," he said. "You're a gentleman; what if I arrived at the Globe pretending to be your long lost cousin? Wouldn't that work? I could call myself Geoffrey Something or the other from....let's say, France?"

Shakespeare smiled. Brilliant idea; why not?

"That sounds fine, sir, it could work," he said.

Drake grinned at Carey. "It will work, My Lord, as surely as my name's Drake. If I'm Master Shakespeare's cousin who's just visiting London for a while, I'll have an excuse to hang around the playhouse and become pally with the rest of the players. They won't perceive me as a threat or as a competitor. I really think it's a plan that can succeed."

Burbage nodded. "I agree, sir."

"Excellent," said Carey. "I knew you'd find a way, Geoffrey. William, Richard, didn't I tell you he was smart?"

All four men were grinning now, their minds churning with details of the charade. Suddenly it seemed doable. They'd have to think it through and ensure there were no loopholes in Drake's fake back history. None of the others- not even Cuthbert- were to be told about this plan. The success of the operation depended upon the strength of Drake's cover.

"I'm fluent in French and I really have spent many years in France," Drake said, pacing the floor with nervous excitement. "Master Shakespeare, I'll be your aunt's son, Geoffrey Dupont, newly arrived from France. Perhaps I'll pretend to be seeking some kind of appointment in Court. Let's keep it vague. I'll reveal a superficial interest in the theatre, too, as if I'm testing the waters. It'll give me the chance to hang around aimlessly for a week or so at the least. As for the rest, I'll improvise as I go along. We'll work out more details, of course. Which aunt? My father's occupation, and so on. How does it sound so far?"

"Very good, sir," Shakespeare and Burbage chorused with big grins on their faces.

Drake raised his finger. "First thing: you'll have to drop the 'sir' bit; you must call me 'Geoffrey', that's all."

"Well, sir...that'll take some getting used to," Shakespeare said with an awkward smile.

"Trifles," said Carey. "You will get used to it. Geoffrey, I want you to know I'm grateful to you for accepting this assignment. If you succeed in catching the killer and saving my Company, I will ensure that you're rewarded richly."

"My Lord, surely not," Drake exclaimed. "No reward can be greater than the honour of being of service to you."

"Good of you to say so, but I know how to show my gratitude, young man. For starters, I'll make sure that your investiture as a Knight of the Garter takes place soon. And then..." "My Lord, please. I am not doing this for any kind of personal gain; I've accepted mostly for the fun of it. I enjoy puzzles. This one seems to be the most challenging one I've encountered thus far since I've never dealt with murder before. But I'm looking forward to solving it."

Carey smiled and rose to his feet. The others followed suit.

"When will you begin?" he asked Drake.

"Directly, My Lord. I shall leave for London first thing tomorrow morning. I would've left now but for the Earl's banquet tonight."

"Ah, yes, the banquet. It'll surely be a grand feast. The Queen and King Christian as honoured guests! Howard must be as proud as a...as a...beaver."

"Peacock," Shakespeare said.

"That, too. Alack, you can't leave too early in the morning, either, Geoffrey; everyone must wait until the royals leave. The Danes will depart first. Their ships are docked nearby; then Her Majesty will leave, around eight o'clock. That's the plan as of now. We'll be free to travel after that."

"Very good, My Lord, I shall plan accordingly. Master Shakespeare, a word with you after the banquet? With you and Mr. Burbage, of course. I need to know everything about the Company and the playhouse before I present myself at the Globe."

"Marry, sir, we'll be honoured," Shakespeare said.

"Excellent," Carey remarked as he prepared to leave. "It all sounds good. Let's hope this tragedy has a happy ending! `Till supper then, Geoffrey?"

"Yes, My Lord."

Shakespeare and Burbage were silent and preoccupied with their thoughts during the short walk from the tournament grounds to the Earl's castle but Carey rambled on. He was in a state of feverish excitement over, what he perceived to be, the success of the first part of the plan. Drake was on board; what a relief. He reposed unshakeable faith in the young man. If anybody could solve this mystery, it would be the illustrious knight bachelor.

"Wait till I tell you two about the matter of Countess Blackburn's will," he said. "Drake was marvellous about it. He really saved the day."

"Blackburn? The Countess Blackburn?" Shakespeare exclaimed in spite of himself.

What was this, all of a sudden?

"Yes, Viscount Blackburn's mother. She had a large fortune and left it all to Henry, her only son, whom we met at the tourney today. Were you introduced? He's a fine chap, Blackburn. But that wife of his..."

Shakespeare's heart sank and he stared at the Lord Chamberlain with an expression of dread.

They were nearly at the castle's door so Carey dropped his voice and continued: "I'll tell you the full story later; suffice it to say that Blackburn owes his inheritance to Drake's skills of detection. Would you believe it, his wife and her lover tried to do him out of his inheritance?"

Shakespeare blanched.

Burbage gasped but for a different reason; he was delighted at this bit of gossip regarding a nobleman's family.

For Shakespeare, the words 'Blackburn's wife and her lover' stung his ears with a pain of a thousand beestings.

"She...has a lover?" he croaked, trying his best to maintain a façade of nonchalance.

"The Lady Marie?" Carey rolled his eyes meaningfully. "A number of them, my dear William. Why do you look so surprised? Do you think noblewomen are virtuous? Marie Blackburn is infamous, busier than a Winchester goose at times." He added with a self-deprecating cough: "I shouldn't be telling you this but considering that you are my men, I can confess that I, too, have...you know...with her!"

Carey winked.

Shakespeare felt his heart freeze under his ribcage. Thump. Stop. A heavy, unmoving stone. He thought he's pass out if the Lord Chamberlain said another word. But Burbage, blissfully unaware of his friend's torment, pressed on excitedly:

"In truth, My Lord? Surely you jest?"

Carey laughed, his brown whiskers twitching as he said: "No, no, I assure you it's the truth. She is an exquisite creature, dear Richard. She has the softest, most voluptuous derriere! But..." He punched Burbage playfully. "You evil chap, getting me to reveal intimate details about a lady! Get thee from me!"

Both men laughed out loud.

They entered the castle. The Earl's men were at hand to receive them and escort them to their chambers.

Carey dropped his voice again and whispered to Burbage as they walked up the huge staircase: "Tonight she'll warm Howard's bed. Would that I could exchange places with him! The lucky sod."

"Tonight, My Lord?" Burbage said gleefully. "But her husband's here."

"Oh, he's a cuckold, `can't control her at all. In any case, he'll be similarly distracted. The Earl will supply him with a couple of beauties and he'll be in another world."

"Incredible. I would never have guessed," Burbage said. "She looks so...so..."

"Innocent? I know. Well, you know how it is. William, what was that line about unfaithful women in *Hamlet*?"

"Frailty, thy name is woman," Shakespeare muttered in a low, guttural voice. "Never was there a truer line."

"Indeed. You really are full of wisdom, William, and you seem to know all about human nature, don't you?"

"Not so, My Lord, you give me far too much credit." Shakespeare's face was drained of all colour, and he thought he'd never make it to his chamber. He felt sick at heart. "I know nothing, My Lord."

Carey frowned and threw him a sideward glance. What was up with him? The playmaker looked like he'd swallowed a horse. Such a melancholic comment.

Burbage stared into Shakespeare's face and was stunned at what he saw there.

And then it struck him: the conversation; the references to Marie Blackburn's sex life (odd that there'd been no reaction from Shakespeare, not a snigger, nor the smallest chuckle);

Carey's revelations about having had her; and Shakespeare's anguish.

And it all came together.

And then he knew...

***

"That's the most ridiculous thing I've ever heard," John Heminges burst out. "Dick sending Jeremy a note asking for hardware? An urgent requirement? Impossible. I'm in charge of stores and purchases and I know we've placed no such order recently. Twenty-five curtain rings? What on earth would we do with 'em? No, it can't be true. This Finn...Finch, whatever his name is, is delusional or a sodding liar."

"He sounds quite convincing," William Sly said, chewing his nails with a perplexed look on his face.

He, Heminges, Armin, Condell and Pope were huddled together in the eastern gallery while Alleyn & co. were enacting *Dr. Faustus* on the Globe's stage.

"Or, rather, he was convinced about what he saw," Sly continued. "The note from Dick, that is."

"There was no note from Dick Burbage," Heminges insisted.

"Okay, let's assume it was a forgery," Henry Condell spoke up. The practical one, the voice of reason. "Why would someone send Jeremy a note like that? What would it achieve?"

The men glanced at one another.

"It would delay his arrival here," Robert Armin said. "The ironsmith probably opens shop around nine o'clock, so Jeremy would've had to wait for him. But surely he would've told someone- his pals, Saunders and Oliver, at the least. They all lived close by. But he didn't tell them."

"How do you know that?" Condell said.

"Alex Cooke was sick, remember? Food poisoning. And Ollie said he went to Jeremy's place, found the room locked, so he asked the landlady about him," Armin said, carefully recalling the sequence of events as he knew them. "He said she mentioned that Jeremy had gone out early, she didn't know where. So, Oliver took off for the Globe alone."

"That's what Oliver Downtown says," Condell pointed out.

Armin shrugged. "Why would he lie?"

Condell shrugged, too. "I don't know why. I'm not saying he lied. Perhaps he forgot; that's all. Jeremy's death must've been hard on him. He's just a boy, after all. Let's ask him..."

"But what could've happened to the curtain rings,

padlocks and all that Finch says he gave Jeremy?" Armin wondered aloud. "We found nothing on him."

"I can't understand what anyone can hope to achieve by playing a prank like that," Sly said. "How did the person get the note across to Jeremy anyway? I don't recall any of our ushers being despatched on an errand like that to Margaret's Hill."

"Of course they weren't because Dick didn't send a note like that," Heminges exclaimed with exasperation. "He wouldn't, I tell you. If he thought we needed some extra locks or rings or what-have-you, he'd ask me to arrange for them."

William Sly said: "We have to ask Dick about it when he returns. For now, let's keep this to ourselves. It's a funny business. I can't figure it out."

"Very funny business," Heminges said with heavy sarcasm. "Perhaps the killer is a comedian."

"Thanks," Armin said drily. "That makes me feel so much better."

***

The guest chamber was warm and brightly lit. Three candelabras bathed the room with amber lights, one on the table and one each on either sides of the room near each bed. It was windy up there and the breeze kept flapping at the drapes of the window, trying to invade the room. Shakespeare could've sworn that the cold draught that hit him as he entered the room had come from the window but Burbage didn't seem affected by it. He sailed into Shakespeare the moment he shut the door.

"You could've told me, you know; you could've trusted me. I thought I was your closest friend, Will."

"What are you talking about?"

Shakespeare moved towards the bed and refused to meet his friend's eye.

"You know what."

"No, I don't."

"That Countess Marie is the one."

Shakespeare said nothing.

"Come now, Will, talk to me, please! I know you're hurting. Why won't you talk to me?"

Shakespeare moved to the window, pushed the thick velvet curtain aside, and gazed out. The tournament grounds were visible beyond the castle's lawns. Things were winding down now. Labourers were pulling down the pavilions and clearing the ground of fences, pennons and other paraphernalia. The earl's men supervised them. Excitement over. The guests would leave in the morning and the county town would return to its humdrum existence. Like the day after Christmas. Everybody living and loving, hating and betraying...

"Will?"

Burbage's rotund face stared into Shakespeare's, his eyes wide with concern, his brow knitted tightly.

"Isn't Marie Blackburn the woman you love?"

Shakespeare exhaled deeply and then nodded.

"Good Lord, I'm so sorry. I had no idea…Carey's remarks must've hurt like hell. Ignore him, Will; you know how he likes to boast…"

Shakespeare pursed his lips. "I don't think he was lying."

"Yes, but you don't know for sure…What a mess. By Jove, you must feel like Paris would have if he discovered that Helen was shagging Hector, Achilles and the whole Trojan army!"

"Hector and Achilles?" Shakespeare gave his friend an affectionate smile. "Nice try, Dick, but they weren't on the same side, you know. Must you resort to such ancient analogies?"

"No, but I thought it rather appropriate since you seemed to have worshipped her."

"Did I? I thought people thought I referred to her as the Dark Lady. I don't recall being particularly rapturous of that person." He shut his eyes and quoted from a sonnet: "In nothing art thou black save in thy deeds/ And thence this slander as I think proceeds. Rather appropriate now, isn't it? When my love swears that she is made of truth/ I do believe her though I know she lies. Marry, if I'd only known…"

"If only? The lines in your sonnets, they're filled with sounds of betrayal and heartache. We all thought you were describing a woman that's constantly tormenting you."

Shakespeare's lips pursed into a wry smile. "Earlier, the only source of my torment was the knowledge of her husband's existence. It chafed my heart to think of her in his arms every night; how was I to know she was bedding the whole of England, too?"

They lapsed into silence for a while. Burbage was at a loss for words. He kept sighing and pacing the floor like a caged animal. Then he said with due hesitation:

"Maybe it's for the best, you finding out like this. You do have a family, Will. Why don't you bring them over?"

"What? To Southwark? You're not serious. Southwark's no place for well-bred young women. And I can't afford a big enough house in the city. No, Stratford's good for them; the air is clean."

"And what about your wife?"

"She's fine." The Bard's tone was brusque. "She's a rich woman with a big house, servants, beautiful daughters..."

"And an absentee husband?"

Shakespeare shrugged. "Yes, well, one can't have everything in life."

The coldness in his tone indicated to Burbage that the conversation was over. If Burbage pushed any more,

Shakespeare was likely to retreat into his shell and the lead actor could hammer away till the end of time but the carapace would not crack. Not until Shakespeare decided to emerge from it of his own accord.

Burbage knew that Shakespeare's romance with his wife had ended years back; now they remained in a state of matrimony for the sake of appearances only. But he also knew that his friend nursed a strong sense of duty towards his daughters, nineteen-year-old Susanna and Judith, who was two years younger. Judith's twin Hamnet had died six years ago at the age of eleven. That had been the breaking point for Shakespeare's emotional attachment to his family. He hadn't been around much when the children were young since he'd been recruited by an acting troupe- Leicester's Men- in Fifteen Eighty-Five, the year of the twins' birth. In those days players travelled through the countryside performing in inn yards, so Shakespeare was constantly on the move. Once the acting troupes became better organized, formed companies and started performing at fixed venues like the Theatre and the Rose, Shakespeare's visits to Stratford became fewer and farther between. He missed his children, especially Hamnet and Burbage recalled the glow in his eyes when he'd boasted of his son's intelligence.

"You should hear him read, Dick, he's just a wee boy but his Latin is fluent; better than mine ever was! He reads quickly and clearly. I dare say he'll devour Homer and Horace before his twelfth birthday."

Sadly, that day never came.

When theatres were shut down for two years (Ninety-two to Ninety-Three) because of the plague, Shakespeare spent nearly the entire time at home. He enjoyed the hiatus, wrote the two famous long poems and his sonnets and spent many happy hours with his children. His affair with Marie had just begun and he was ecstatic. Strangely enough, he got along well with his wife, too. The plague ended in 'Ninety-Four and Shakespeare rushed back to London to start earning again. It was but natural that all players and playmakers worked overtime to recover lost ground. As a result, Shakespeare didn't see much of his children for a while.

Then, in August 'Ninety-Six came the crushing news: that Hamnet was gravely ill. His body was racked with fever and he wasn't responding to any treatment. Shakespeare was basking in the success of *The Taming of the Shrew*, a new play at the time, when he received the letter from Anne. He immediately hired two horses and rushed home with Henry Condell accompanying him. They reached a day late. Anne had hung on for his arrival, keeping their son's body so that Shakespeare could say goodbye one last time...

When Shakespeare held his son's cold, limp hand, he felt that something inside him had died. No matter what he did henceforth, whatever praise and riches may come, they would be meaningless. The best part of him was gone. Now his work would be just that- work, labour, meaningless toil to sustain him and provide for the boy's mother and sisters. That's what they would always be to him: Hamnet's mother; Hamnet's sisters.

'Grief fills the room up of my absent child," he wrote in *King John* soon after. 'Lies in his bed, walks up and down with me/ Puts on his pretty looks, repeats his words...Then I have reason to be fond of grief.'

Nothing was more painful than the loss of his son. Tonight as he brooded over the revelation of Marie's true nature the pain, although it seared through his heart, was no worse than a dull toothache. He felt more angry than jealous.

Ten years! They'd been lovers for a decade and all the while she'd been carrying on with other men?

"Will, it's supper-time," Burbage shook him gently. "We ought to be going down; `won't do to arrive after the queen."

"I can't attend the banquet tonight. Please make some excuse; tell the Earl I'm ill or something."

"Will, you can't avoid this. You're the Queen's favourite playmaker; your absence will be missed."

"No, I won't be missed. They're so many important people here tonight. Please, Dick, make my apologies. I can't face her...I don't want to see her tonight. And her husband will be there, as well. I'm just not up to it."

"But what about supper?"

"Oh, there's plenty to eat here. See, that table is full. I'll help myself to something. You go on ahead without me."

Burbage made a face. "I don't feel like attending the feast without you but Carey will have a fit if we both skip it."

"You must go. I will be grateful for some time on my own."

"If that's what you really wish. I suppose I'd better be getting on with dressing for the banquet. I brought a new doublet that was gifted to me by my mother-in-law. She's a talented seamstress, you know. 'Wish my Winifred had inherited some of those skills..."

And so Burbage prattled on.

Shakespeare nodded absently but he'd shut him out. He wished Burbage would leave quickly; he longed for solitude. He needed to sort out his thoughts. 'The oaths of a woman I inscribe on water,' Sophocles said. So true. If only he'd done that instead of branding her vows on the walls of his heart. Memories came flooding back to him of happy hours they'd spent by River Avon hidden from the world on 'their' bank. It was a secluded spot nestled in a grove of elms near the river's edge. When they made love he felt that their hearts were tied together with strings of gold that no one could tear asunder. He remembered clearly the feel of her breasts against his chest.

Burbage left.

Shakespeare reclined in bed with his shoes on and contemplated his next move. Should he go and confront Marie? But he had no idea where her chamber was. There might be a guard posted in front; how would he get past?

The chamber's door opened and a stocky young maid entered with a jug in hand.

"Sir," she exclaimed, as if startled to see him there. She obviously expected him to be at the banquet like everybody else.

He glanced at her inquiringly.

"Fresh ale for the night," she announced.

He gestured towards the table.

The woman curtsied and went across to the table. Shakespeare watched her in an absentminded way. She rearranged plates and bowls, checked the fruit, checked each candle to ensure it would last through the night, and then fiddled with the drapes at the window. Then she disappeared into the adjoining bathroom. He could hear her clanging about.

Nothing unusual. Her actions were like those of any chambermaid except...were those breeches he'd noticed under her skirt?

Shakespeare sat up with a start. He knew enough about men dressing as women to tell one from the other. No matter how skilled an artist was, to the discerning eye a man was always a man. Shakespeare could always tell. And this 'chambermaid' hadn't even done a good job of disguising himself; the breeches revealed he'd been in a hurry when he donned the maid's clothes. He hadn't had the time to shave his legs.

But, why?

Why would a man pretend to be a chambermaid?

The 'maid' emerged from the bathroom presently and gasped in surprise to find Shakespeare sitting there upright and alert.

"Sir." Another curtsey, most unnecessary.

There. Shakespeare saw the breeches again. Now he was sure.

The 'maid' started for the door.

"Wait," Shakespeare called out.

The maid paused with his/ her back to him.

"What's your name?"

"Kate, sir."

Shakespeare sat very still. No more falsetto- the voice was male now.

"What did you want? Why did you come to this chamber when you're not really a maid?"

It was a question he would wish he had never asked.

***

TWO

"By my troth, Master Shakespeare, you do have a way of attracting trouble," Geoffrey Drake exclaimed. "You say this woman...man tried to murder you?"

"Yes, sir, he did. I...I can hardly believe it, either. The dagger...I saw it just in time!" Shakespeare was still panting from the encounter. "He lashed out at me without the slightest provocation! Not the slightest...I can hardly believe it."

"Disbelief weighs heavily in my mind, too," Drake said, watching Shakespeare intently. "Why would a chambermaid, or somebody disguised as a chambermaid, try and kill you?"

"I don't know, sir. I swear it, he just attacked me..."

"Was he trying to steal something?"

"I don't believe so, sir. He was about to leave the room. I noticed his breeches and asked him...perhaps he intended to rob us but couldn't because I was in the room. He did look startled to see me when he first entered the room."

Drake nodded. "He must've expected you to be at the banquet like everybody else."

They were standing in the centre of Shakespeare's chamber, staring down at the would-be-killer's immobile body. A deep red blot was spreading across the chap's chest like spilt wine on a table cloth.

"Why didn't you attend the banquet?" Drake asked. "I overheard the Lord Chamberlain asking Burbage about you; he sounded displeased."

"I wasn't feeling well, sir."

Drake narrowed his eyes and said in an icy tone: "Don't talk like a lily-livered lass. What d'you mean you weren't feeling well? You're the Earl's guest, the Lord Chamberlain's playmaker; your presence is expected at a banquet where the Queen is a guest of honour. You'll have to come up with a better excuse, Shakespeare."

"But that is the truth, sir. Perhaps it was something I ate earlier." Shakespeare rubbed his stomach to drive home the point. "I am indisposed."

Shakespeare knew it was a weak excuse but it was the best he could do under the circumstances. He couldn't let on about Marie, after all.

Drake gave him a shrewd look. "That's better. Now tell me again, slowly, what happened?"

Shakespeare took a moment to gather his wits about him. He gulped down a mug of ale and it made him feel better. He stared at his hands; they were stained with the dead man's blood.

He narrated the sequence of events succinctly to Drake.

He'd been lying in bed when the door opened and the chambermaid entered-'She' seemed surprised to see him-She had a jug in hand and said it was fresh ale- she pottered about for a bit and then turned to leave- he asked the maid what 'she' had come for- the fake maid suddenly lunged at him with a dagger in hand.

Shakespeare paused as Drake knelt down and retrieved the dagger. It was a nasty little pointed knife easily concealed in a person's clothes, not the longer double-edged basilard used in real fights; nevertheless, it could cause grievous injury as it evidently had, in this case.

"Go on," he said.

"Well, I was stunned, sir, but I managed to grab his hand and twist the knife into his chest. Unfortunately it went in too deep."

"Unfortunately? Would you rather it was you lying dead right now?"

"N...no, sir, but I've never killed a man before."

"It's not easy the first time," Drake agreed.

He had a calm and introspective look on his face. He'd left the party as soon as the royal guests retired for the night, and decided to look in on Shakespeare since the Bard hadn't shown up for the feast. He wanted to gather details about the Company and the playhouse before showing up at the Globe. He and Shakespeare would also need to work out a solid back history since they were supposed to be cousins.

But when Drake entered the chamber, he saw Shakespeare standing over a limp body with blood on his hands.

"He attacked me! He tried to kill me!" Shakespeare had cried.

"He?" Drake repeated in surprise for the body was clothed in a woman's attire. Then he'd looked closely and seen that it was, indeed, a man.

"Death didn't come easily," Shakespeare continued, trembling and wild-eyed. "He was gasping for breath. It was horrible. I kept asking him who he really was and why he wanted to kill me but he said nothing. He was just gasping and choking...no words..."

Shakespeare's voice trailed off. Drake continued to watch him intently. He seemed badly shaken up.

They stood there in undecided silence for a few moments.

Then the door was flung open and Burbage entered in high spirits.

"Will, you missed a great feast!" he slurred and then stopped dead in his tracks.

"Sir Geoffrey? Will! Good Lord, who's that? What happened? Is he...is that a 'he'?"

The sight of the recently departed had a sobering effect on the portly actor.

"Marry, Will, is this man dead? What happened?"

Shakespeare told him.

Burbage's hand flew to his mouth. "Dear God in heaven! Are you sure you're all right, Will?"

He wrapped his friend in a tight embrace. "Are you hurt?"

"I'm fine, I'm fine. I just wish I hadn't killed the chap. Now we'll never know why he attacked me."

"But we do know why: somebody is trying to ruin the Company. Sir Geoffrey, this is exactly what the Lord Chamberlain was talking about this afternoon. First Jeremy Smith, then Gray, then Charlie, and now Will! It's the same pattern."

"I'm not so sure about that," Drake said with a pensive look on his face. "This wasn't an attack on your Company; it was an attack on one man."

"But this man is the life and soul of the Company, sir."

"Dick..." Shakespeare interjected.

Burbage brushed him aside. "This is no time for modesty. Sir Geoffrey, William is the reason we've driven out all competition from Southwark; if he were to die today, the Chamberlain's Men would collapse. Boom! Kaput! Finis! It's the truth, sir, no exaggeration."

"I don't doubt a word you've said," Drake returned. "But there's a problem with that theory. If we assume that the same person or persons responsible for the previous attacks on players in your Company were behind tonight's killer 'chambermaid', tell me, how did they know you two would be arriving in Suffolk today? Didn't Lord Carey decide on the spur of the moment that you'd be accompanying him here? So if it's the same killer, he would've had to have been in- what? the Lord Chamberlain's retinue?"

"In our group?" Burbage was incredulous. "But that's impossible, sir. Our entourage comprised only of Lord Carey's personal attendants; I'm sure their loyalty is beyond reproach."

"Then what are the alternatives, if we're to assume that the killer tracked you here from London?" Drake said. "Was he part of Robert Cecil's retinue, or Lord Blackburn's?"

As he said this, Shakespeare and Burbage exchanged a quick look. Drake went on apparently obliviously; if he'd noted the communication, he gave no indication of it.

"That's unlikely, too, since the Blackburns arrived before you did; ditto Sir Robert. He travelled with the Queen. No one could've known that you, Shakespeare, would be coming here. It isn't customary for the Lord Chamberlain to travel with his players, is it?"

Shakespeare shook his head.

"I thought as much. No, I think this attack was unpremeditated, as surely as my name's Drake. No matter; we'll get to the bottom of this. But first we must inform Lord Carey about this attack and the poor devil's death. The Earl, too, must be informed since this is his castle. Burbage, would you go and fetch them? Get hold of the nearest guard. He'll take you to them. Hurry now. The night is growing old and the body is going cold. Have a cup of wine, Master Shakespeare, to gain some Dutch courage. You'll have some explaining to do."

***

"Cherie, tu es la femme la plus belle du monde," Thomas Howard, the Earl of Suffolk, gushed at the naked woman in his bed.

She giggled, leaned against his large velvet pillows and playfully clasped the sheet around her waist. He'd just told her that she was the most beautiful woman in the world and she liked hearing it.

"You're not so bad yourself," she cooed.

Howard was in the process of getting undressed. His cape and boots were off but he was still in his doublet and breeches.

With his gaze fixed on her smooth, slim neck and the swell of her breasts below, he put his hands into his shirt pocket and fished out a heavy gold necklace with a huge emerald pendant dangling at the end. He slid this over her neck, smoothed his hands over her breasts, and said:

"Now you are perfect."

Marie Blackburn traced her fingers over the jewel and her eyes sparkled. It was the biggest stone she'd ever seen.

"Mon choux, where did you get this from?" she asked, "It's beautiful; it's too much."

Howard gave her a leery grin. "Don't worry, my dear, you're going to earn it."

She batted her lashes at him. "I 'ave no idea what you mean."

"I'll show you!"

They were in the middle of round two when a discreet knock interrupted them. It was followed by a self-deprecating cough from the Steward of the Household.

"Lennox?" Howard called out sharply. "What in the devil...?"

"Deepest apologies, My Lord, but it is an urgent matter."

"Damn!"

Howard cursed some more and rolled off Marie. She quickly pulled the sheet up to her neck.

Howard slipped into a dressing gown mumbling to himself, and jerked open the door of his chamber.

"This had better be bloody good."

Lennox was standing in the antechamber with a peculiar, stressed look on his face. The veins of his thick neck were sticking out.

"I am so sorry for disturbing Your Lordship..."

"What is it?"

"My Lord, there's been an incident. A death, My Lord. Murder, it appears, in one of the guest's chambers."

"Murder?"

"I'm afraid so."

"Good Lord! In whose chamber?"

"A member of the Lord Chamberlain's entourage, a player called William Shakespeare's..."

"What? Shakespeare's been done in? In my castle?"

"My Lord, it's not...He's not..."

"There's a killer on the loose? Have you alerted the Queen's bodyguards?"

"My Lord, the death was in..."

"Answer me, damn it! Have you alerted...? Oh God, King Christian's here, too. You must tell the royal guards to look sharp."

"I've done that already, My Lord."

"You have? Excellent, good man. What about Carey? Tell him, too. I'll inform Cecil. `God, Carey will be awfully sorry. Shakespeare was a brilliant playmaker. By George, a murder in my castle? It's like one of poor Shakespeare's plays: the Tragedy in the Castle."

"But, My Lord, Shakespeare is not..."

"Was, Peter, was. Past tense. Give me five minutes. I'll get dressed and we'll go to the chamber. Marry, it's incredible. Why would somebody kill a playmaker?"

"Er...we don't know, My Lord."

"Yes, yes. Wait here."

The Earl was in such a state of agitation that he hadn't listened properly. He rushed back into his chamber where Marie was sitting propped up against pillows with the bed sheet barely covering her modesty. She glanced at him inquiringly.

"My dear, I'm afraid I have to go to one of our guests' chambers. There's been a murder," he said and spoke a volley while putting his clothes back on. "Would you believe it, a murder in my castle? It seems that a player had been topped. You must've met him today. William Shakespeare. He's a playmaker, actually with Carey's Company. He's just been killed; can you believe it? I must go to his chamber at once." Howard paused, noticing the way the colour drained from Marie's face. "What's the matter, Cherie? You've suddenly turned pale. `Must be all this talk of murder and death. Forgive me; how insensitive of me to lay it on you. Wait here; I'll be back soon."

His lips met hers briefly. "Be patient. I know just the thing to make you feel better..."

When Howard stormed into the guest chamber, he was surprised to find a large crowd there. Carey was in the centre of the room. Robert Cecil was there, too, along with Carey's Secretary Bleech, Hans the interpreter, Geoffrey Drake, a cook, Richard Burbage and...William Shakespeare in the flesh, very much alive albeit ashen-faced and wobbly on his feet.

Howard glared at Lennox. "Shakespeare's alive; why did you tell me he'd been murdered?"

"With respect, My Lord, I tried to explain but Your Lordship misunderstood."

"Who's that?" Howard pointed at the corpse on the carpet.

"The killer, My Lord," said Lennox.

"But he's dead."

"Yes, My Lord. Master Shakespeare says this fellow tried to kill him and that he acted in self-defence..."

"Who is he? And why is he dressed like a woman?"

"He's Gregory, the pot-boy. I suspected it was he so I summoned the cook to identify the body."

"Good thinking," said Howard. "But do all our pot-boys like to wear women's clothing?"

"No, My Lord. This fellow must've done it to disguise himself."

"But, why? What did he want?"

"Perhaps he entered this chamber with the intention of theft," Drake spoke up. "The banquet was on and he must've assumed that everyone would be in the dining hall. 'A golden opportunity for thieves, My Lord. Dressed as a chambermaid, he would have had a good excuse to enter the guests' chambers."

"That's a possibility, Geoffrey," Carey said, "But isn't it also possible that he wasn't acting alone? That he was sent by someone to kill Shakespeare? I told you about our Company's troubles; was this attack on Shakespeare linked to the conspiracy to ruin my Company? Did someone hire this fellow to murder Shakespeare?"

"But why would anyone want to murder your playmaker?" Earl Howard wondered aloud. He didn't know details about the incidents in the Chamberlain's Men. "I'm sure that none of our staff has travelled to London recently, let alone watched one of his plays."

Howard's remark raised a few chuckles from the others.

"That's a rather extreme thought," Robert Cecil said lightly. "I hardly think Master Shakespeare's plays make people want to murder him! The odd person may dislike his work but they're hardly likely to try and kill him for it!"

Everybody guffawed again and Howard reddened.

"I didn't mean..."

Carey waved him away. "Never mind, Tom. Just concentrate on finding the man responsible for this, will you? I'm sure the pot-boy did not act alone. He must've been coerced or lured into trying to commit murder. Remember, whoever has done this, has attacked me. Shakespeare and Burbage are my players."

The others nodded gravely.

Howard gave an assurance that the conspirator would be hounded even if he had to shake the gates of hell to find him.

Robert Cecil said that that was all very well but he would have to inform the Queen about this. He was loathe to intrude upon her at this hour since she'd had a long day (and she wasn't getting any younger- was his unsaid addendum) but he would brief her in the morning.

Hans the interpreter expressed similar views about his monarch. Christian had retired for the night and certainly could not be disturbed so he would be told in the morning as well.

"Kaerlighed til penge er roden til alt ondt," Hans murmured.

"What's that?" Howard asked, "`Sounds Greek to me."

"My native tongue," Hans replied hoitily, "Danish for

'The love of money is the root of all evil'. `From the Book of Proverbs in the Bibel."

"Ah, yes, the love of money," said Howard, "Also, love."

"Love?" Hans echoed, his brows shooting up. "Are you saying that love is the root of all evil?"

"Well, not all evil but you'll be surprised at how love spurs a fellow towards murder every now and again."

"Truly, sir?" Hans said with a dubious look.

The others didn't seem to bother with Howard's remark but Shakespeare's heart was pounding.

Marie had warned him!

Was she right, then? Was her husband behind this attempt on his life?

Howard ordered his steward to remove the body. Lennox and the cook did so. Then Howard addressed the gathering.

"As your host I offer my apologies for tonight's incident. Master Shakespeare, I am relieved to see you are alive and I wish you live a long and happy life. I shall deploy two guards outside your chamber tonight, so rest easy now. We've all had a busy day and we'll be off to an early start tomorrow. So I suggest we all retire now. As I've said, there'll be a thorough investigation and we will find the conspirator behind this attack. Good night now. Let us hope tomorrow is a happy day!"

***

THREE

———

The Earl's guests left in quick succession the following morning. The weather was holding up nice and sunny and everyone wanted to take advantage of it. King Christian was the first to depart. Two large, impressive long ships would sail him home through the North Sea to the town of Ribe on the south-west coast of Denmark. Queen Elizabeth bade him goodbye in her chamber and gave him a trunk full of gifts. Then Earl Howard, Carey and Robert Cecil escorted him and his retinue to the outskirts of town in a cavalcade of twelve carriages and two posses of four horsemen each. There, the Danish carriages peeled away with two Suffolk coaches accompanying them. The Justice of the Peace was given the charge of seeing the Danes off right up to the seaside. He would remain there until the foreign guests were safely (and surely) on their way.

"Master Shakespeare."

Queen Elizabeth beckoned to him with her forefinger. She was about to climb into her shiny black carriage with Robert Cecil and her lady-in-waiting when she'd spotted Shakespeare standing in line with the rest of the farewell committee.

Shakespeare started in surprise and hurried forward.

He bowed low. "Madam."

"You look well this morning," she said. "None the worse for the wear, I see. We were told you had a rough night."

"Yes, Your Majesty."

"But you are in good health this morning?"

"Yes, thank you, by Your Majesty's grace."

"Good. I hope my grace is sufficient for thee."

It was an irreverent remark, a reference from the New Testament. The old queen seemed to be in top form that morning.

"It is, Your Majesty," Shakespeare replied.

"All right, carry on."

Shakespeare bowed again and returned to his place in line, quietly falling back behind Carey, Bleach and the others. The next retinue to leave would be the Viscount Blackburn's and he couldn't bear the sight of Marie and her husband. His would-have-been killer? He'd already had his share of histrionics a short while ago when he'd walked out of the castle and found Marie standing there, waiting to join the farewell line-up...

The Queen's procession moved slowly through the streets of Ipswich to enable the maximum number of people to see her and greet her. She waved gaily from her glass windows.

Blackburn waited for Howard to return after taking her leave at the town-limits. Then he and Marie left in a smaller cavalcade of four carriages. Next was the Lord Chamberlain's turn. Shakespeare dithered. He was desperate to avoid Carey's coach today; he just wasn't in the mood for randy talk about Marie. He knew that Carey would get started on his tale about Geoffrey Drake's detective skills at the earliest opportunity. That would include his account of Marie's deception, too. He didn't want to know about it. There were two more coaches in the cavalcade; he could find a seat in either of them. But how would he extricate himself from Carey?

He couldn't think of a way.

Before he knew it, the door of the coach swung open and he and Burbage were ushered in. Carey followed directly behind. He hung out of the window for a while, waving goodbye to Howard and the local officials. Then, as his coach picked up speed, he settled down, stretched his legs, and said:

"Excellent visit, wasn't it?"

His companions stared back. Surely he was joking.

"Oh, last night's incident?" he said, waving dismissively as if referring to a broken button or a torn stocking. "Think nothing of it. You're alive, William, that's all that counts. The killer is dead; we're going home."

Neither Shakespeare nor Burbage said a word. They didn't know whether Carey was being factitious or just plain insensitive. Last night he was the one touting conspiracy theories; so why was he being so dismissive this morning? Wasn't the real killer- the man behind the attack- still out there? Perhaps he was stealing away in Blackburn's entourage at that very moment! The words in Marie's warning note flashed into Shakespeare's mind's eye.

Attention! Il sait.

Who was the 'he'? It had to be Henry Blackburn, who else?

But what could he do about it?

Shakespeare's chest tightened as he recalled the look on Marie's face when they met outside the castle an hour ago.

"Oh, William, I am so glad you're all right," she gushed. "I was so afraid. He...they told me you had been killed..."

"I'm fine, thank you," he returned curtly. "Don't concern yourself about me."

"Oh, but please be careful. I told you, he knows. You see, the portrait of you, the small one I `ave, is missing. I think he's taken it to give to a contract killer or someone like that. I'm so afraid..."

"Don't concern yourself about me, Marie. I'm sure you have other men to worry about."

The knowledge of her betrayal seared through his brain like a hot iron. Was it true that she'd slept with half the men in England? The Lord Chamberlain, too? And what about Earl Howard? Had she shared his bed the previous night?

As they stared at each other, Marie's hand went to a gold chain that adorned her slim, white neck. An enormous emerald pendant hung from it. Looked new. A gift from the Earl? Shakespeare wondered. From what he knew, her husband was too tight-fisted to splurge on her. So the necklace must've come from a very rich man.

A silly little ditty sprang to his mind.

'Lord Howard the Earl

Bought a bright pearl

Round and nice and of great price.

Not his to possess

Everyone's to caress

And then she'll be gone in a thrice.'

How could she do this? She was no better than a whore! The very thought of her with the Earl made him sick in the guts and Shakespeare had quickly turned away. The farewell committee was forming nearby.

He started to walk towards it.

"William..."

Her voice carried in the wind.

He paused without looking back.

"Please do not condemn me. Remember, *je n'ai pas le choix.*"

Bollocks, he mused. Everybody has a choice. It wasn't like these men were raping her.

When he reached the line of noblemen, knights and sundry local officials waiting to greet the Queen as she left, Burbage was there in conversation with Geoffrey Drake. They were talking in low tones, their heads tilted towards one another, and Shakespeare knew they'd be going over details of the plan again. It had been decided that Drake would show up at the Globe three days later, i.e. Monday, and pretend to be Shakespeare's long lost cousin. Drake seemed to be engrossed with Burbage but Shakespeare had seen him watching as he'd walked away from Marie; had the shrewd young knight noticed the intimacy between them?

"Is Drake ready to pose as your cousin? Does he know enough about your family history, William, to fool your friends?"

Shakespeare said nothing so Burbage replied. "Yes, Sir Geoffrey seems to be well-prepared."

"I hope so for some of the older players might think it odd that William has never mentioned this cousin before," Carey said.

"Yes, My Lord. I suppose we'll just have to be very convincing."

"William," Carey said sharply. "Why aren't you replying? Drake's posing as your cousin, after all, not Richard's. Are you with us? You seem to be in another world."

Shakespeare flushed with embarrassment. "Forgive me, My Lord."

"All right. Now, the pair of you must be waiting eagerly to hear about Drake and the Blackburn will. Shall I tell you the story?"

"Yes, My Lord, we can hardly wait," Burbage said with all the enthusiasm he could muster.

Shakespeare managed a weak smile.

He had no choice; he would have to bear it. Perhaps he could tune out the Lord Chamberlain.

Carey sat back with a satisfied expression, opened his snuff box, took a few quick sniffs and began the story.

***

"It was about six months back. I was informed on a cold winter's night in February, the twenty-first I think, that the Countess Clarence Blackburn had died. The Blackburns' county estate lies in Hertford. Since it's just north of London, several of us nobles turned up for the funeral. Blackburn is a viscount, after all. The Queen chose me to represent the Crown and personally picked out a sombre wreath for the coffin.

When I arrived at the Blackburn estate, I found a large crowd there. The Earls of Sussex, Kent and Suffolk- our recent host Lord Howard- were present, among others. So was young Drake. The coffin was placed in the centre of the drawing room and everyone had gathered there to pay their respects. Blackburn's father had passed away several years ago and Clarence had been quite the matriarch. She was the one that owned much of the estate. It was also common knowledge that she and her daughter-in-law couldn't see eye to eye. They say that while Henry Blackburn was blind to Marie's philandering, the old lady had known exactly what was going on. Just before Clarence's death, when she was confined to bed with illness, a young fellow called Gerard Guilbert arrived from France. Marie claimed he was her cousin." Carey chuckled. "Much the same way Drake's going to pretend to be your cousin, William."

Shakespeare gave him a polite smile. He dreaded the rest to come and wished he could do the disappearing act like magicians did. If only they were on stage at the Globe, he could've escaped through a trapdoor.

"Whether Guilbert was her cousin or not, Marie did seem excessively fond of him," Carey continued with a gleam in his eye. "There was the servants' gossip, too, of suspicious goings-on in the dead of the night."

"Now here's where the story gets really interesting. Pay

attention, both of you," Carey said. "The Blackburns have an old solicitor, a Mr. Tripplethorn. He had custody of Clarence's last will and testament, one that she'd drawn up the day before her death. There was an earlier will, too, of which both Henry and Marie had copies. I learnt later that the older one had been drawn up many years before, when Marie had first come into the family. Clarence had left her a considerable fortune in that. Oh, I forgot to mention that Drake had arrived at Hertford the previous night and stayed over at the Blackburns' estate."

The Blackburn manor was large and luxurious. The drawing room extended across an area large enough to accommodate two centre-courts at Wimbledon. Heavy velvet drapes concealed two glass windows and a door that led into Blackburn's private garden. Besides those, the only other door was a heavy mahogany portal that admitted people through the hallway in the front of the house. It was through this door that everyone passed on the day of the funeral. A cold wind blowing across the estate ensured that all other doors and windows were tightly shut.

After the guests paid their respects to the dearly departed, the solicitor Tripplethorn rose, cleared his throat and announced that he would begin reading the last will and testament of Countess Clarence Blackburn. He fished out some papers from a bag and stood behind a small square wooden table that was placed beside the coffin.

"This is the last will and testament of the Countess Clarence Blackburn, sadly departed yesterday," he began. "It was drawn up in my presence on the Nineteenth of

February Sixteen Hundred and Two, that is, two days ago. I am its executor and the Countess' Personal Secretary Mr. T. Bolsworth was witness to the signing of the will."

All eyes turned to Bolsworth, a fellow of considerable bulk with hairy ears and a tunic bursting at the seams. He was seated a few chairs away to the left of the coffin with an expression suitably funereal, and he rose a few inches from his chair to acknowledge the august company.

As soon as Tripplethorn mentioned the will's date, Marie's hand had flown to her mouth in an expression of alarm. She had a copy of the earlier will rolled up like a scroll in her hand. She glanced at this and bit her lower lip. Guilbert hastened to her side and they had a quick exchange in low-tones.

Then Tripplethorn informed the gathering in a sonorous tone that the countess had left her entire estate and all her personal fortune to her only son, the Viscount Henry Blackburn. She also made several small bequests but nothing, not one penny, to her daughter-in-law Marie.

The colour drained from Marie's face when she realized what had happened. She had been cut-off; she would be completely dependent on her husband from now onwards. Guilbert looked agitated, too. Blackburn went to her side, clasped her hand and told her not to worry; he would take care of her like he'd always done. Guilbert left the room. Servants re-entered with another round of refreshments. About five minutes later, Guilbert returned. Presently a manservant came in and said something to Marie. She nodded and excused herself.

Suddenly a shrill cry pierced the air.

"Mon Dieu! Mon Dieu! Non, Mama!"

French. Marie, unmistakably. Henry Blackburn sprang to his feet. The guests followed him. So did Guilbert. They found Marie in a swoon in the hall assisted by her maid Louise.

Blackburn, who was the first to reach her, held out a small piece of paper.

"A letter," he said, "Bad news from France. Her mother..."

It was a brief communication in French saying that the Lady Marie's mother Edith La Croix had passed away the previous week after falling sick with consumption.

The guests pressed around the viscount and Marie and offered their sympathies. The solicitor also emerged from the drawing room.

Marie thanked everybody and begged their leave to retire to her chamber. Blackburn nodded at the maid, who led her away sobbing. The group filed back into the drawing room, talking amongst themselves in low, respectful tones.

Tripplethorn returned to his table. Suddenly he let out an exclamation of surprise and groped around the table and in his leather bag as if searching for something.

"What's the matter?" Blackburn demanded.

"The will! The will! It's gone," Tripplethorn sounded strangled. "It's missing, My Lord. I...I was just reading it but now it's gone."

The room erupted with murmurs of excitement.

"How can a parchment vanish like that?"

"What if the will is not found?"

Amidst the din of voices, Drake asked the pertinent question: "Don't you have copies of the will, Mr. Tripplethorn?"

The old man was ashen-faced. "No, Sir Knight, I'm afraid not! I meant to get it done but the Countess passed away so soon..."

"But what's the problem?" Lord Howard said. "We all know what's in the will; you just read it out. Just transcribe it again."

"That's not possible."

"Why not?"

"Because..." Tripplethorn hesitated.

The room fell silent. The solicitor wiped sweat from his brow. The guests gazed at one another.

"Without an authentic copy, the will won't stand up in court," Tripplethorn said, "You see, none of you saw it; you only heard me reading from it. What if I had made it up? There's no proof, for instance, that the countess made any bequests...My word alone won't be good enough."

"Isn't there another will?" Radcliffe asked.

Tripplethorn exchanged a quick look with Henry Blackburn. "Er...the terms and conditions of the earlier will are different," he said.

"May I see it?" Drake asked boldly.

The old man handed it over. Drake read in silence. Then Carey went through it. It was clear that they'd just witnessed a very clever deception; the letter from France had been a diversion. God alone knew how Marie and Guilbert had succeeded in getting the timing so right. "Sir, we have to do something," Drake whispered to Carey. "We must search the guests - the men - physically."

Carey's brow shot up. "Are you serious?"

"Deadly serious, My Lord. There's a thief among us and we must not let him get away. He's in this room as we speak."

"He must be, but, Geoffrey..."

"Please, My Lord. The viscount deserves better."

Carey rubbed his chin thoughtfully. "What about the ladies?"

"There are nine ladies here and all of them rushed out of the room when we heard Lady Marie's scream. They returned after most of us, men, had come back into this room. So, none of them would've had the opportunity to filch the will."

Carey glanced admiringly at the young man. "Does anything escape you?"

"George, what's going on?" That was from the Earl of Suffolk. Howard approached Drake and Carey and asked them what they were hobnobbing about. Carey conveyed their suspicions.

Howard, who was about as subtle as an elephant in a garden, blurted out: "What? There's a thief in this room?"

"A thief?" the noblemen chorused in horror.

Sharp exclamations erupted from the gathering. The ladies nearly swooned; the gentlemen looked like they were on the verge of collective, spontaneous combustion. To be accused of stealing was almost up there with treason! Murder wasn't as bad; there could be extenuating circumstances, after all. But robbery was downright crude and demeaning, something unbecoming of a genteel society. It was unthinkable that someone in this crowd would steal.

"Have you taken leave of your senses?" Henry Grey, the Earl of Kent, demanded. "These are serious allegations."

"They are, My Lord," Drake answered, "As is the crime." He turned to the solicitor. "Mr. Tripplethorn, you were the last person to leave this drawing room, weren't you?"

"Yes, Sir Knight. I didn't intend to leave the document unattended but then I also felt it would be improper to ignore the Lady Marie, who was obviously in some distress. The gentleman told me she'd fainted."

His gaze travelled to Gerard Guilbert.

"I noticed something," Drake said. "That Tripplethorn was the last to leave this room and all of us, who'd left earlier, have now returned. Except Lady Marie, of course. This means, as I said earlier, that the thief is still in our midst, in this very room..." He added as indignant voices exploded in a cacophony: "...and so is the missing will!"

"Are you certain of this?" Henry Blackburn asked.

He'd been a mute spectator thus far. He looked utterly crushed. Who would relish such a scene in his own home? Especially with so many noblemen present? What ignominy! And what if Geoffrey Drake was wrong? He would be ostracized. But there was something about the young man, the way he held his ground in this esteemed company; he possessed unwavering nerves.

"There is only one way to be sure," Drake said, "We must first eliminate the possibility that someone has hidden the document on his person. Perhaps the Lord Chamberlain, as the senior most nobleman and Her Majesty's representative, would oblige by having us men searched?"

"Strip-searched," Carey added.

Drake nodded.

Shakespeare gave Carey a bemused smile. "So Your Lordship actually stripped about twenty-five noble men?"

Carey chuckled. " I just watched as they disrobed one by one. Drake offered to be the first."

"Quite a surreal experience, it must've been," Burbage said, laughing.

"'Telling me? If only it were the ladies who were stripping," Carey said. "I do know now who amongst my peers have the best physiques. Howard is not bad but the best is Drake's, no prizes for guessing there. The boy is chiselled like a Greek God! Were I a woman, I would've become his mistress in an instant."

"What about Your Lordship?" Burbage asked impertinently. "Did you also...?"

Carey laughed out loud. "I offered to disrobe but no one wanted me to. They all agreed it was unnecessary. As Drake put it, I was among the first to leave the drawing room; I was with Henry and Marie all the time; and I was among the last to return to the drawing room. So I wouldn't have had the opportunity to nick the will."

"What happened next, My Lord?" Burbage asked.

"Well, the document was not found on any of us.

We thought the thief had outwitted us all."

***

FOUR

———

"Now what?" Earl Howard demanded of Drake in a belligerent tone. "The peek show is over and the damned document is still missing. What do you intend to do next? Strip the dead countess's body?"

Drake met the earl's gaze evenly and said, "No, My Lord, for I don't believe the thief had the time to open the coffin, hide the will there, and close it again. He had less than a minute's time, remember?" Drake's eyes travelled around the room again and, suddenly, his expression brightened. He turned to Lord Carey with a look of suppressed excitement. "My Lord, may I be so bold as to request everybody to clear the room this time?"

"What?" Carey was taken aback. "Really, Geoffrey, I think you've tried our collective patience quite enough. Let's accept the fact that the will in question is irretrievably lost..."

"Not at all, My Lord, I know where it is!"

"In truth? You know where it is?"

"Yes, My Lord. But I require about half a minute alone in this room to recover the document. Please bear with me."

A rumble went through the gathering.

Carey looked at Blackburn. The viscount's shoulders drooped and he said to his guests: "Let us take a walk in my garden."

So the noblemen trooped out again, most of them throwing dagger-looks at Drake.

None of Blackburn's guests were in the mood to converse with nature. They were bristling with indignation at the treatment meted out to them. Geoffrey Drake came in for much criticism. Impertinent fellow. What did he think of himself? Were he not Francis Drake's nephew...and the Queen's favourite...Huh. Wait till she hears about his behaviour today. No chance of his making it to the Garter.

Presently, the heavy door leading into the garden opened and Drake stood there with a triumphant smile on his face.

Twenty-six pairs of eyes focussed on him.

"Well?" Carey demanded.

Drake's smile broadened and he spoke a volley: "My Lord, I have one word to say, a quotation from the Greek philosopher

Archimedes, second century B.C, I believe. It's what he said when he discovered that goldsmiths had adulterated the gold in Hiero, King of Syracuse's Crown. The word, I've heard, is eureka!"

He held up a document for them all to see.

"The last will and testament of the dearly departed Countess..."

"You did it, By Jove, you did it!" Carey exclaimed and nearly snatched it from Drake's hand.

Tripplethorn begged for permission to examine it and when Carey gave it to him, the old man clasped the document to his chest as if it were fashioned of pure gold.

"Yes, yes, this is it," he said a moment later.

Everyone marched into the drawing room for the third time that afternoon. There was excited chatter and the obvious question:

How did Drake find it?

The ladies were invited back into the room.

"So where was it, Geoffrey?" Carey asked when they'd all settled down.

"First of all, by your leave, I wish to say something," Drake began. "Since the will has been found, let us agree that there's no thief in this company. Let's just say that someone borrowed it and now it's been returned. The identity of that person shall remain secret; I shall convey my suspicions to our esteemed host and he may take whatever action he deems fit."

Drake paused, and a strange silence descended upon the gathering. The young man's discretion surprised them.

"Now, to answer the question on everybody's mind," Drake went on. "How did I find the will? The reason I requested to be left alone in this room was because I wanted to sit in the very seat that the erstwhile thief sat in before all the commotion and wonder where I would hide a document if I had to keep it out of sight for some time. You must remember, the perpetrator only wanted to hide it until he could return to this room alone and retrieve it after everyone else had left. So, where did he hide it? Any guesses? No? Well, my Lords and Ladies, are you familiar with the phrase 'swept under the carpet'? The thief certainly is!"

***

Three o'clock in the afternoon.

Friday, the day after Shakespeare and Burbage's departure from Suffolk.

Fierce winds blew. The sounds of fishermen's shouts mingled with the noises of a busy marketplace. Figures moved purposefully across the stage against the painted backdrop of a harbour where ships and boats bounced on choppy waters. The audience watched spellbound as the story of The Jew of Malta unfolded before their eager eyes. It had been a while since this play had been performed in Southwark. Alleyn's tall, imposing figure strode across the Globe's platform in a black cape and black hat, reprising the role of Barabas, the Jew of Malta. Barabas was an anti-hero, a rich merchant whose wealth is wrongfully seized by the Christian governor of Malta to appease marauding Turks. This embitters him and he wreaks vengeance upon his enemies. He doesn't even spare his own daughter Abigail when she converts to Christianity, and poisons the nunnery where she has taken refuge. Finally he becomes governor of the city but the Maltese turn against him, kill him, and regain control of their island.

Ned Alleyn revelled in the role of Barabas. His manner was so dark and menacing that he caused many in the audience to gasp and shrink back in fear. Christopher Beeston, Alexander Cook and Oliver Downtown were also part of the audience that had its gaze fixed upon the stage in the gallery to the left of the stage. They had walk-on parts in the play as members of the Maltese public.

"Isn't he brilliant?" Cooke said with a small sigh. "I can never be like that."

"Aye, he's the best," Beeston agreed.

"Not so. Mister Burbage is the best," Downtown said. "He's much more..."

"Burbage?" Beeston echoed, "No need to try n' kiss his arse, Ollie; he isn't around today. Ned is way ahead of him, everybody acknowledges that. Just see how conflicting emotions play upon his face. See how well he brings out the contradictions in Barabas's character?"

"What contradictions? The chap's a villain, that's all," said Downtown.

"No, that's not all. Haven't you been paying attention? Barabas is a victim as much as he's a villain. He's been wronged, remember? How would you feel if you were stripped of everything you own?"

There was nothing understated about this performance. Ned Alleyn's Barabas was utterly compelling and brimming over with hate. One of the hired boys of the Admiral's Men was directly behind the stage with foul papers in hand to provide Alleyn with cues in case he forgot a line. But Alleyn never dropped a line. He'd played his roles so many times that it was second nature to him.

"Don't know how he does it," Beeston gushed. "It seems like he's in a trance, like he actually becomes the character he's playing.".

"Hush, you two, you're missing the action," Alex Cooke hissed. "Watch now; Barabas has just learnt that his daughter has become a Christian. He is about to poison the nunnery."

Beeston and Downtown suspended their argument and turned their attention back to the stage. The mood in the playhouse had darkened suddenly with the audience's foreknowledge of the tragedy to come. The Admiral's Men's stage director had employed a number of special effects to heighten the dramatic tension. He had engaged stagehands to provide the shouts and sounds of a harbour from the sidelines; he also created the effect of strong winds by having dead leaves fanned across the stage with large hand fans from either side. There was no ghost in the story so the trapdoors remained unutilized.

"There is no music to a Christian's knell," Alleyn said in his turn as Barabas and then shut his eyes in a trance-like state. "How sweet the bells ring, now the nuns are dead."

"Lord ha'mercy!" a woman cried out in the pit in front of the stage. Others crossed themselves.

Beeston grinned at Downtown and Cooke. "Didn't I say Ned's marvellous? Isn't this a fitting finale to a great week?"

"A week without incident," Cooke added quietly.

"Yes," Beeston agreed and sobered up as they wondered about the days to come. "Perhaps it's a sign; maybe the killer's blood thirst is satisfied."

He got wry looks in reply.

"Things have been far too dull," Downtown said. "Were I the killer, I'd be itching for another kill."

"Marry, Ollie, you sound frightening," Cooke exclaimed with an amused grin. "I sorely hope you are not the murderer! I wonder who'll be the next victim. Any guesses?"

***

FIVE

Richard Burbage returned from his Suffolk trip Saturday evening to a warm welcome from his wife Winifred and two young children Richard and Julia. Richard Junior was all of two-and-a half and Julia was an infant, just seven months old. Both kids flung themselves into his arms. He hugged them tightly, his heart swelling with affection. What a fortunate man he was, truly blessed.

"Dick, I know you must be tired but I hope you don't mind..." Winifred said with a hesitant smile.

"Yes, Dear?"

"John Heminges and Harry Condell have been around twice looking for you. They said they wanted to speak to you urgently. So I...er...I sent so I sent Martin off to fetch them as soon as I heard you at the gate."

Martin was their servant boy.

Before Burbage could respond, they heard the sound of the gate creaking open.

Winifred wrung her hands. "I'm sorry, dear, I should've warned you." Burbage glowered at his wife and then turned around to greet his friends in the drawing room. The servant Martin smiled at him and then went into the kitchen to assist Mrs. Burbage.

"John, Harry, how are you?"

Heminges and Condell responded warmly and the three men made small talk for a while.

"So, what's the urgency behind this visit?" Burbage asked, finally. "What happened at Charlie's Inquest? Is that what this is about?"

"No, Dick, this has nothing to do with Charlie's death," Heminges replied. His expression was sombre under his bushy brow. "We...we'll tell you a..all ab...about the inquest later..."

"But at least tell me if the Coroner made a ruling on the cause of death," Burbage said.

Heminges nodded. "Charlie was poisoned."

"Poisoned?" Burbage repeated in surprise. "But, how? He was with us all the time. We ate and drank together. How in the world did someone poison him?"

"The Coroner thinks the killer used a poison-tipped

needle," Heminges explained. "He found a small puncture mark at the side of Charlie's neck. Here."

Heminges pointed to his own neck, the left side.

"By Jove, that's incredible." Burbage shook his head in wonder. "A poison-tipped needle? Who would've imagined...? Good Lord, that's what must've happened to Jeremy as well. None of us noticed but there might've been a puncture mark on his neck as well."

"Jeremy Smith," said Condell. "That's what we need to talk to you about."

"Have you ever heard of a man called Benjamin Finch?" Heminges asked.

"Benjamin Finch? No, `can't say I have," Burbage replied, "Who is he? What's he got to do with...?"

"He's an ironsmith in Kent Street market."

Burbage screwed up his nose. "Nasty area."

"Aye, nasty area with nasty people," Heminges agreed. "Finch is one of them. It sounds ridiculous but he says that on the day of Jeremy's death, the boy visited his shop early in the morning and took some hardware on credit, things like curtain rings, padlocks and bolts..."

Heminges paused and Burbage looked astonished.

"Curtain rings? Padlocks? Why? What on earth would he do with them?"

Heminges shrugged and continued: "According to Finch, Jeremy said we had requisitioned these items. Apparently he'd received a note saying he was to procure these things from the market before going to the Globe. Finch says we owe him a shilling."

"A shilling? That's ridiculous. The fellow's lying, of course. None of us would've asked Jeremy for things like that. Finch is lying, that's all there is to it. Ignore the fellow."

An awkward look passed between Heminges and Condell.

"What is it?" Burbage demanded. "What are you keeping from me?"

Condell sighed. "Finch says he saw the note and that it was signed by 'Richard Burbage'."

"Signed by me?"

"That's what he says."

"But...but that's preposterous. It's a lie," cried Burbage. "I never...Dear God, what does this mean?"

They lapsed into silence for a while.

"Perhaps it was a robbery gone wrong," Condell said but the hesitation in his tone revealed that he didn't believe his own theory. "What if someone saw him buying these things, tried to steal them and when Jeremy resisted...But would anybody kill for a shilling's worth of hardware?"

"Yes, people have killed for nothing," Burbage said.

"Perhaps a beggar would've but the said robber would've done him in at Kent's Street, wouldn't he? Why follow him all the way to Maid Lane and kill him outside our playhouse?"

"The flower-seller," Heminges said with a start. "By George, maybe she was the one! Maybe she tried to sell him flowers and when he resisted she stole…Okay, that's ridiculous, too. She's an old bat; Jeremy was a strapping young lad. But there's something about her. Why did she disappear?"

"Never mind all that," said Condell. "What do we do about Finch? He won't keep quiet. I think he's telling the truth; he really did see a note like that…"

"With my name on it," Burbage said, his brow creasing with anxiety. "Perhaps we should just pay Finch and get it over with?"

"Can't do that," Condell objected. "If this ever gets out, it would look bad for you. Yet, if we don't pay up, he's threatening to go to Court."

"Over a shilling?" said Burbage, "As our dear William said in *Julius Caesar*, 'Has reason fled to the beasts'?"

Condell spread his hands helplessly. "Well? What do we do about Benjamin Finch?"

"Stall him," said Burbage.

"Stall him?"

"Yes, Harry. Tell him we're verifying our stocks; give him any excuse. Buy us some time so we can try and figure out what this is all about."

"Aye?" said Heminges said, "And, pray, how do we propose to do that?"

Burbage permitted himself a small smile.

Geoffrey Drake, that's how.

He couldn't tell them, so he gave them a lame excuse: "I'll think of something."

Heminges and Condell looked unconvinced but they didn't argue further.

"Be quick about it," Condell added a parting shot. "Finch won't be put off for long."

***

Six

A quarter past five and the show hadn't begun. There was barely standing room in the inn yard and the spectators were getting restless. Rambunctious shouts and catcalls rose up from them. Thomas Dekker gazed in distress at his actor, who'd passed out on the tiring-room's floor in an inebriated state. This is what happens when you try and convert an inn into a playhouse.

The tavern was just right of the entrance. It seemed like the Boar's Head Inn still couldn't decide if it was an inn first and also a playhouse, or a playhouse where actors and troupes could perform in its half-covered yard, and also a tavern where the public could wet their throats after, before and during show time.

The proprietor Oliver Woodcliffe wanted to cash in on the popularity of the stage so he renovated the Boar's Head Inn in Fifteen Ninety-Five. London city was bereft of playhouses since the regular ones were concentrated in the sporting district. Woodcliffe thought he'd fill the void. He also decided to begin shows later than usual- five o'clock instead of two. That way, regular theatregoers could still ride across the river, watch a show in Southwark and then return to Boar's Head inn for another play. Since the inn was primarily a tavern, crowds were accustomed to staying there late, until curfew hour.

The Worcester's Men had chosen the Boar's Head as their more or less permanent home after obtaining their licence in February that year. Sometimes the inn yard was packed; on other occasions the crowd was sparse. The Worcester's Men were only too aware of the hard work required to draw audiences away from the Globe and the Fortune. Dekker, who was their main playmaker, was not in the same league as Shakespeare or Ben Jonson. He was primarily a pamphleteer and the few plays he'd written had been at best moderately successful. That day, however, the Worcester's Men were hopeful of having a packed house since it wasn't a Dekker play they were performing, but *Hamlet* instead. They claimed, for public consumption, that it wasn't Shakespeare's *Hamlet* but an earlier version that they'd adapted for the stage. No one believed this. Crowds flocked to the inn yard to see the play they knew and loved.

But things hadn't begun well.

Fifteen minutes past opening time and the show hadn't started. The spectators, with strong ale coursing through their veins, seemed like they were about to launch into a full-scale riot any time now.

"Come on, let's `ave it," cried one, "Where's the ghost of `Amlet?"

"Aye, get on with it. We ain't go'all night yer know."

"Tommy Dekker, you tryin' to fool with us?"

Dekker wrung his hands in despair. His Horatio, a player called Eliot, was still out for the count.

"Marry, I'll do the part," Dekker said with a sigh. "I think Eliot's costume will fit. Hopefully Horatio was not known for his fashion sense! Roger, you'll have to prompt me."

Roger Jenkins, a hired player, bobbed his head but held the foul papers with reluctance as if they were aflame.

The Worcester's Men didn't have an authentic copy of Shakespeare's play since playbooks were jealously guarded by each company. They had deputed Jenkins and another youngster Mark to the Globe to copy down the lines on the previous two occasions that *Hamlet* was staged. Jenkins and Mark weren't the brightest of fellows and their notes were dodgy. Dekker hadn't even read them properly but the company had decided to give it a shot anyway.

With Dekker outfitted as a stand-in Horatio, the performance finally got underway at twenty-past five. The first scene went off smoothly: short exchanges between a pair of guards, then between the guards and Horatio. Jenkins and Mark had made some major gaffes in capturing the dialogue but, fortuitously for Dekker and Co. the audience seemed not to notice.

When the guard Bernado spoke the line: 'In the same figure, like the king's head' instead of the original 'In the same figure, like the king that's dead', Dekker cringed but the crowd was quiet.

Dekker sent up a silent prayer of gratitude.

He was taken aback when Jenkins prompted him with the lines:

'What art thou that usurps this time of night,

Together with that worm-like form,

In which the majesty of Denmark is buried...'

Worm-like majesty??

Dekker nearly passed out. He was painfully aware of the confused looks in the audience. Something wasn't quite right; these weren't Shakespeare's lines.

Damn that Jenkins and Mark. Imbeciles with pea-sized brains! Dekker fumed in silence. He must use better scribes next time round.

As soon as the scene was over, Dekker dashed into the tiring-room, picked up the foul papers and began speed-reading, something he should've done much earlier. He held his head in his hands. The papers were disastrous, sheets and sheets of rubbish!

Outside, the player doing Ophelia drew laughs and whistles from the crowd when he said of *Hamlet*:

"He took me by the wrist and went all hard."

Not 'went all hard', Dekker wanted to scream, it's 'held me hard'; he knew that much by rote.

Damn, damn, what a cock-up. He just hoped the crowd was too drunk to notice the drivel being dished out. The cash boxes were jingling nicely; if they could just get through the show without incident...

Then came *Hamlet's* famous soliloquy in the middle of the play, and all hell broke loose.

"To be, or not to be, that is the question," the player Michael Green began with high emotion. And then:

"And a very good question it is.

Whether suffering is noble in the mind or fortune..."

Murmurings in the audience.

"I shall take up arms against the sea and oppose it..."

Sploch. A rotten tomato went sailing through the air and landed at Green's feet.

"Charlatan! Cheat!" someone called out from the crowd.

"That's not Shakespeare," said another.

Green tried to put up a brave front.

"To sleep, or dream..." he continued.

Clump. Thump. Sploch.

Eggs and rotten tomatoes went flying and Green beat a hasty retreat, ducking into the tiring-room for refuge.

"Shame! Shame! Cheats!"

The cacophony from the crowd was deafening.

"Mon-ee back or we'll put you on the rack!"

Woodcliffe and Dekker took the stage to try and placate the crowd. Of course they'd get a refund; if they'd only be so kind as to form an orderly queue...

"Orderly? Do you mean to say we're dis-orderly?" a big fellow demanded, eyes goggling. "You lead us here by deception and then accuse us?"

"Nobody's accusing you of anything, Good Sir," Woodcliffe said. Beads of perspiration gleamed on his forehead. One false step and there'd be a riot. Because of the Puritans' dubbing his inn a den of vice, the Lord Mayor had washed his hands of the Boar's Head. So the authorities were unlikely to come to his rescue if the place was being trashed; more likely they'd join in with the rioters.

Dekker put forth a feeble excuse, that this play was not Shakespeare's *Hamlet* but another version. But his dissembling impressed no one, least of all Woodcliffe, who remonstrated at once.

"Shut your mouth, Tom, for the love of God! D'you want to be lynched by this mob? Tell your accounts manager to bring out the penny boxes and return the entrance fee to these good people."

"Hear! Hear!" the people responded.

"Go on, be quick about it."

For the crowd's benefit Woodcliffe gave Dekker a kick in the butt, and spontaneous applause broke out.

Dekker was red-faced and left with no choice. He went into the tiring-room to confer with his manager.

Geoffrey Drake watched the proceedings from a bench in a corner of the eastern gallery. What a stroke of luck, his being here tonight. He had decided to wait another day before showing up at the Globe. He wanted some insight into the theatre-scene. The Boar's Head Inn hadn't seemed like the right place to begin. It was Whitechapel Road, after all, not Southwark. But when he's stopped by for steak and a goblet of wine earlier- alone, much to the dismay of his squires Rod and Tod- he heard that the Worcester's Men were performing *Hamlet* in the inn yard that day, so he decided to stay on for it. Now, despite the play being cut short, he was pleased that he'd decided to stay. For he'd learnt so much. He'd discovered that all he'd heard about Shakespeare's stature as a playmaker was true. Other companies stole his plays? How's that for flattery? And he was impressed to find that the audience knew Shakespeare's works well enough to spot the fraud.

Once they got their money back, a number of men in the audience headed for the Boar's Head's tavern. Drake followed the crowd and chose a spot at a corner from where he could sweep his gaze across the room. Cheap furniture, dirty tables, grimy floors, noise, noise, noise- not his idea of the ideal watering hole. His men were appalled when he said he'd be dining there. It wasn't pleasant but it gave him an insider's view into the world he must become part of for some time. He saw servings men rushing about and spilling ale all over, even on their customers but no one seemed to mind. The landlord, a fat, sweaty fellow as all landlords tended to be, wore a harassed expression but Drake sensed he must be delighted at the sudden spurt in business.

Drake ordered a goblet of wine and sipped it slowly as he watched the motley bunch eat and drink and make merry.

Presently, Thomas Dekker came through the door with a mousey-looking young fellow in tow. They stood at the entrance, scanning the crowd, and then the young chap's face fell into a scowl.

"That's `em, Mr. Dekker," he exclaimed, pointing at two chaps seated at a table next to Drake's.

"Them?" Dekker set his jaw grimly. "I should've guessed."

"You know them?" the boy asked.

"Aye, I sure do, Jenkins. Come on."

He and the chap called Jenkins strode up to the table in question.

"Well, well, if it isn't the Chamberlain's Men," Dekker said frostily. "Sent here to stir up trouble, lads?"

"Stirrin' up trouble?" said the older of the two, a ruddy-faced boy just over twenty. "All I've ever stirred up is soup, Mr. Dekker, with you in it!"

"Dekker in the soup," said the other boy in the same cheeky vein. He was smaller and younger with curly dark hair and quick eyes. "Is that the name of a new play, then? A comedy from the Worcesters' stable?"

Both boys burst into laughter and Jenkins surged forward as if to strike them. But Dekker placed a restraining hand on his shoulder.

"Easy, Jenkins." Then, to the other two: "The pair of you was at the Mermaid's the other night when Charlie died. But I don't believe we've been properly introduced. You're Christopher Beeston, aren't you?"

The older one.

"Aye, that's the name I was christened with. And this is Oliver Downtown."

The curly-haired chap gave Dekker a haughty look but said nothing.

"Rabble-rousers, both of you," Jenkins snarled. "They were the ones that started it, Mr. Dekker. 'Mon-ee back! Mon-ee back!' That was from them, sir. We ought to teach them a lesson, what?"

"Is he the one you sent to copy down our *Hamlet*?" Beeston said, jerking his thumb towards Jenkins. "I was Ophelia; I'm surprised he recognized me."

"All the chalk in the world can't hide your ugly features," Jenkins sneered.

"That's enough," Dekker cut in. "You run off now, Jenkins. I'll deal with this. Go on."

Jenkins made a face.

"Head off now," Dekker said firmly. "I'll join you anon. Go, go."

So Jenkins glared at Beeston and Downtown and then stalked off.

Dekker pulled up a chair and sat down heavily.

He was a plain-faced man of average height and build but there was a look of cunning in his eyes that could not be ignored.

"What did you come here for?" he asked.

Gone was his bellicose. Beeston and Downtown's insolence seemed to have got the better of him. Now he just looked apprehensive.

"Who sent you?" he inquired. "Shakespeare himself? Burbage? John Heminges? Who?"

Beeston smiled. "We heard rumours about our plays being performed- you know- unauthorized. Mr. Armin also noticed two of your chaps jotting down parts of *Hamlet* the last time we performed it. One of them was Jenkins, wasn't he? Word got round that you were doing our play here today so everyone thought we should verify this."

"In truth? And what are your findings?"

"A poor attempt to copy us. You really need better scribes, Mr. Dekker. Everybody's going to laugh their heads off back at the Globe when they hear about this."

"So you've decided to tell them?"

"Course we will; why won't we?" Downtown said at once.

Beeston nodded. "You've really put your foot in it this time, Mr. D. We'll be off now to inform our friends about this. Master Shakespeare will make a formal complaint to Lord Tilney in the morning."

Dekker flinched at the mention of the Master of the Revels. Oh, how Tilney would enjoy this; he would simply revel in it! A great opportunity to wring the Worcester's Men dry. A ten pounds fine at least, plus humiliation for the Earl, Lord Somerset. No doubt the Chamberlain's Men would produce a host of witnesses to support their allegations.

"I've always been on good terms with Shakespeare and the rest of you thus far," Dekker said, "But, yes, I suppose Shakespeare will report me to Tilney." He paused, leaned back in his chair, and added: "If you tell him, that is."

"Why wouldn't we?" Beeston asked with an innocent expression but there was a sly gleam in his eye.

"Perhaps I can persuade you."

"How's that?"

Dekker's face broke into a smile. His shoulders relaxed and the tension seemed to exhale from him. He sensed that the storm had blown over; these two were just hired players, after all, mere boys.

"I could make it worth your while," he said. "Ten shillings each?"

The boys didn't reply but a quick look passed between them. Ten shillings was bloody good money, more than their week's earnings.

"And an offer of employment," Dekker added.

"Employment?" Downtown screwed up his nose. "Why would we leave the best company and perform with yours?"

"Better terms, better pay."

"Not a chance, Mr. Dekker. Nothing can beat performing with the Chamberlain's Men; you're far behind."

Downtown's refusal was direct but Beeston's silence screamed with meaning. He was a picture of restraint. Dark eyes rolling about in a smooth face, a mind churning and contemplating his options.

"What terms?" he asked finally.

Downtown sat up with a jolt. "Chris! How can you...?"

"Relax, both of you," Dekker intervened to seize the initiative. "There's nothing to worry about. No harm's ever come from listening, has it? You're both fine young lads and talented players. Will you hear me out?"

***

SEVEN

Shakespeare held his breath and tried to stave off the onset of a panic attack. Tuesday morning, and still no signs of Geoffrey Drake. They were rehearsing *A Midsummer Night's Dream*. The players insisted on performing comedies only until the killer was caught, as if humour was their talisman to ward off misfortune. Now that Charlie's death was confirmed as murder, they all knew that a killer was on the loose. Shakespeare had to relent. They were all on tenterhooks now that he and Burbage were back. The past week had gone by without incident, the Admiral's Men enjoying an unexpectedly good run. This confirmed the players' worst suspicions: that the Chamberlain's Men were, indeed, the killer's target. Shakespeare and Burbage specifically?

He wasn't sure how Burbage felt but Shakespeare had begun to empathize with Jonah. He was certain his colleagues would toss him overboard if the need arose.

They performed *As You Like It* on Monday and today it was *Midsummer...* The players were busy with their elaborate costumes and the rehearsal went off well but Shakespeare couldn't shake off the lingering unease in his mind. Like a dull toothache, an ominous warning of worse to come. The previous evening he had despatched Beeston and Downtown to the Boar's Head Inn to verify rumours about the Worcester's Men plagiarizing his work. But they'd returned to say it wasn't a complete rip-off; a few lines had been copied from here and there but the Worcester's Men's *Hamlet* was very different from his own. Shakespeare had the vague sense that they weren't telling him the truth. But what could he do about it? He could crosscheck with some acquaintances at the Boar's Head but that would seem like paranoia. These days he felt besieged by everything. The revelation of Marie's betrayal gnawed at his heart like a bird of prey picking at raw flesh. He felt faint and grasped a chair to steady himself. Fortunately, no one had noticed. Burbage snored gently on a bench in the gallery. He was still under the weather; the long ride from Suffolk had done him no good. His eyes were watering again and his nose all red and itchy. To make matters worse, the sky had begun to darken, threatening to spoil the show.

Alexander Cooke, who was playing one of the lead roles- Helena- was practising his lines in a corner:

"And therefore love is said to be a child,

Because in choice he is so oft beguil'd..."

Shakespeare smiled ruefully. What was he thinking when he wrote those lines? It was one of those times when he was thinking of Marie. He had lamented his own predicament of being bound by family ties. The 'beguiling' was meant for Anne, not Marie, for she was the one that had tripped him. A couple of rolls in the hay and, bang, she was preggers. He was a mere lad of eighteen at the time; she the more mature at twenty- six. She knew the risks, didn't she? Yet she'd submitted easily to his youthful passion. He had done the right thing by her and he did love her at the time. At least he thought he did. But it was nothing, just a pale shadow in comparison with the bright, burning frisson he'd felt for Marie. Yet she, too...

Robert Armin was prancing about the stage doing his turn as Bottom- a nice juicy part for a change- when one of the stagehands called out from the gate:

"Master Shakespeare, sir. Someone to see you. `Says he's your brother."

Shakespeare's heart soared. Drake, at last! He glanced at Burbage and found him sitting up wide-eyed. The stagehand's announcement had woken him, too.

"My brother?" Shakespeare pretended to be surprised. "Can't be. It might be my cousin. Let him in."

The gate swung open.

A thin young man stood there. He had sunken eyes, unkempt hair and a peevish look about him.

"Suppose it was only a matter of time," he said, "Before you start denying your blood relations."

Shakespeare stared open-mouthed. "Eddie," he said, "What...what a surprise! Hello!"

Edmund Shakespeare approached the stage with exaggerated care. His clothes were in tatters and he smelt like the Thames. A scraggly brown beard made him look ten years older than his twenty-two.

"Hello, Will," he said, "Can you spare some bread for a poor relation?"

***

Act Four
One

Winchester goose, they called them, the Southwark prostitutes. The irony was not lost on anyone. It was yet another incongruity in life that the brothels or 'stews' ran in a concurrent line from the edge of the Bishop of Winchester's estate till the boundary of Paris Garden. The brothel owners paid the Bishop taxes in cash and in kind.

The pale, thin girl that stood against the Globe's walls on Tuesday afternoon was a Winchester goose. Pretty features hardening before time, caked with layers of make-up; blue eyes encased in smoky kohl eyes. She's pushed up her small breasts with a tight corset and kept her neckline low to reveal the gathered cleavage. She studied the young man hovering about on the opposite side of the road and decided, gentleman. He had that look about him, of refinement from birth: neat hair, good skin. So what was he doing in a shithole like this?

He had tried to blend in by wearing a cheap doublet and his breeches were mud-spattered but his boots were too fine. An outsider, surely; if he were local, she would've remembered him.

"Lookin' for something?" she drawled.

He glanced at her with a start, as if surprised she should be speaking to him at all.

"A warm bed, praps?" she suggested and ran her tongue over her lips.

The young man smiled. An awkward smile, nearly apologetic.

"I am looking for something, someone, to be precise."

She rolled her eyes. "That someone has a name?"

"Yes, she does but I don't know it."

The girl narrowed her eyes. "You a nutter or something?"

Geoffrey Drake grinned. "No, I'm not a nutter, Miss...?"

"Rosie, I suppose."

"Miss Rosie, how nice to meet you. How do you do?"

Drake extended his hand and she shook it warily.

"She's an old flower-seller who used to hang around here until two weeks ago," he said. "I wonder if you know her."

A flicker of recognition flashed through the girl's eyes but she gave him a non-committal shrug and remained leaning against the Globe's steep white walls. Sounds of a lute striking a plaintive tune came sailing out from the playhouse. *A Midsummer's Night Dream* was nearing its climax. Drake had seen the play advertised on a poster on a wall: 'M. Shakespeare's fantasie-comedie'. The gates would open soon and a ruck of potential customers would stream out. Hence, the girl's vigil.

"Don't you know the flower-seller?" Drake prodded, "Surely you've seen her around, Rosie."

Another shrug.

Drake put his hand into his doublet's inner pocket and fished out two pennies. He held these up for Rosie. She hesitated a moment and then said:

"Old Lily, that's who you'll be wanting."

"Old Lily?" Drake brightened and handed over the coins. "Thank you, Rosie. Now would you happen to know where I can find her?"

"I might."

Drake smiled and gave her another penny.

"She's moved," said Rosie, "Works across the river now in Eastcheap. She's gone from Southwark."

Across the river? Quite an upheaval, he thought. The ferry fare to and fro would be too dear for the woman so she must be doing it on foot over London Bridge. A long and tedious walk. Perhaps she'd relocated lock, stock and barrel.

"Comes home every evening," Rosie added helpfully.

"Really? And where exactly is her home?"

Rosie shook her head. Drake dug into his pockets again but the girl had a resolute look on her face. "Keep your money, I ain't a snitch, am I?"

"A snitch? But I assure you I mean no harm..."

"You're with the Justice of the Peace, ain't you? Or with the Constable? Leave her be, sir, she's not done anything wrong."

"The Justice of the Peace? Good Lord, of course I'm not with him; neither do I work for the Police. Rosie, I only want to ask Lily some questions. I swear she will have no trouble from me."

"She won't talk, sir, she won't; got the fear of the devil in her."

"Fear?" Drake's ears picked up. "What's she afraid of?"

Rosie looked exasperated. "It's why she's done a runner, ain't it? She's `fraid she might get done-in."

"Done-in? By whom?"

The girl's expression changed. She narrowed her eyes again and set her jaw grimly.

"`Ere, what's in it for you? Why should I tell you anything? I ain't sayin' another word, I ain't."

"Rosie, I just need to talk to Lily, to ask her some questions. I want to know a few things about that day."

He paused. The girl wasn't stupid; she knew exactly which day he was referring to so he didn't insult her intelligence by spelling it out. "I only want to talk. Promise."

"Why? You a relative or something?"

"A relative?"

"Of the deceased, the lad that got stiffed here."

"Oh." A thrill of excitement tingled through Drake as he got the first confirmation that he was on the right track. "Yes, I'm kind-of related...I assure you, Old Lily will be well-compensated."

He jingled the coins in his pocket. "Surely she could do with an extra shilling or two?"

"Well, if you put it like that..."

Rosie bit her lower lip and played with the strings of her bodice as she mulled over his offer. He tried not to get distracted and averted his eyes from her chest. She was doing it in an absent-minded manner, scarcely aware of herself.

"Marry, sir, why not?" she said abruptly. "You seem like a decent chap. Come on."

"Where?"

"You want Old Lily, don't you? Then come with me. She'll be back soon."

"Right. Lead the way then, Rosie."

The girl smiled and took his arm. Drake allowed himself to be led, though he didn't relish the idea of visiting a prostitute's lane. He also knew of the borough's reputation as the abode of cut-throats and coney-catchers. So he was alert and a little tense.

"You do know where she lives?" he asked in spite of himself.

Rosie grinned. "I should, shouldn't I? She's me ma."

***

Shakespeare stared at his younger brother seated in a chair across the room and wondered at the transformation in his appearance. Edmund had bathed, shaved off his ugly beard, trimmed his hair and eaten a hearty meal of herring, mashed potato and cabbage stew. His cheeks filled out instantaneously and his eyes brightened. He looked decent now, a stark contrast with his former tatterdemalion self.

Shakespeare's home was spacious enough for a single man but by no means sufficient for two. A Spartan chamber with a single bed in a corner, a wooden cupboard set against the opposite wall, a wooden desk and two chairs. Two big wooden shelves brimming over with Shakespeare's papers and books hung on a wall just above the desk. The only luxury he enjoyed was an attached bathroom. It was a privilege in these parts for tenants to have a separate bath chamber with a jordan and bathtub. The landlady also let him share her maid so he had someone to clean up after him. These living quarters were trifles in comparison with his mansion in Stratford but he liked the place well enough and cherished the solitude it afforded him. So it was with no small measure of consternation that he permitted his younger brother to share his room that night. Furthermore, he knew too well his brother's moonish nature and his penchant for courting trouble.

"I won't bail you out again," he warned Edmund, "If you've run up debts at the Ram's or any other tavern, you will earn the money by good, honest work and repay them. Else, they can throw you in the nick, I don't care. You need to start taking responsibility for your actions, Eddie."

His brother nodded in silence and managed to force his features into a contrite expression but Shakespeare felt certain that the young man was faking it. He was a lousy actor.

"Are you listening to me?" Shakespeare demanded when there was no immediate response.

"Aye, I hear you loud and clear," Edmund replied, "Told you, I intend to find work. Seriously, Will, I just need your support for a week or so."

"I won't give you money; no more of that nonsense."

Edmund made a face. "You won't give me a job, either."

"No chance, Eddie. We're not discussing this again. You cannot act."

"Then let me be a stagehand or...or an usher, anything. I'll do anything, Will. I've acquired some carpentry skills, by the way."

"Ah, then you can be apprenticed to a carpenter. I can set you up with Peter Street; he's the best in the business."

"But why can't I be of use at the Globe?"

"Because you'll keep on at me about letting you act. You won't be contented as a stagehand, don't try to be clever, Eddie. I know all your tricks. This thing- acting- is not your calling. Try something else."

As his brother's face fell into a scowl, Shakespeare placed his hand on Edmund's arm and tried to reason with him. It wasn't too late, he said, Edmund was still young. He could do almost anything he wanted to because he'd attended Grammar School for ten years. He could become an accountant or a physician or an engineer.

"I will assist you in these endeavours but you need to forget about the stage."

Edmund said nothing. He opened and shut his mouth like a goldfish while Shakespeare waited patiently, wondering why, oh, why things had come to this. Everyone else in the family was stable. His three surviving siblings (besides Edmund) were hardworking and reasonably happy. His younger brothers Gilbert and Richard and sister Joan. All three were settled in Stratford. Three sisters had died young but, as far as he knew, none of them had been troublesome. Edmund was the rebel. Perhaps he'd been affected by the family's failing fortunes round the time of his birth. The palpable tension in the house must've weighed heavily on young Edmund. John Shakespeare turned the corner eventually. Good times, bad times, they come and go. Everything passes. What mattered was that John Shakespeare proved to be a survivor. That was the lesson Edmund should've learnt by now. You don't give up when life kicks you in the teeth. You get up, dust yourself, try and correct your mistakes and...you keep going. No use wallowing in self-pity.

Sitting before him in the first-floor chamber of Mrs. Humphrey's house, Edmund bore all the signs of a loser. Downcast eyes, slumped shoulders and a sullen expression. Shakespeare couldn't stand it.

"Get yourself up, Eddie," he said. "I have no sympathy for men who embrace defeat like this. When will you learn to help yourself?"

Edmund said nothing. He remained in his chair with his head hung like a ragdoll's. Then he spoke in a guttural voice that made the playmaker's hair stand on end.

"These...your glory days aren't going to last forever, you know. These are the end times for you, brother."

Shakespeare stiffened. "What's that? What did you say?"

Edmund's lips curled into a sneer. He raised his head slowly and gazed into his older brother's eyes.

"You said it yourself just now. Everything passes; nothing lasts forever. I know all about the deaths in your Company. The invincible Chamberlain's Men, eh? Not so invincible anymore, are you? It won't stop, you know, not until you are destroyed!"

Shakespeare was stunned. He felt like he'd been run over by a speeding horse-drawn carriage: heavy hoofs trampling him to a pulp.

"Until I'm destroyed?" he repeated, "How can you be sure the killer is after me? What do you know about all this, Eddie? Why hasn't he attacked me yet?"

Even as he said this, Shakespeare's memory flashed back to the Suffolk castle killer. Was that linked to the incidents at the Globe and the Mermaid's?

"A direct blow is too easy," Edmund said, "The killer wants you to suffer a slow death; he wants you to see the Company crumble before your eyes."

"How in the hell do you know all this?"

Edmund smiled, all nasty and gloating. "Because that's what I would do if I were the killer! I wouldn't let this end quickly. There must be blood! There must be pain..."

Shakespeare pursed his lips. "I never knew my own flesh and blood..."

"So true, so true!" Edmund cried. "You've never known your own flesh and blood! You don't care for your family. Your wife longs for your affection; your daughters yearn for their father's company; our mother pines for you. But you, the great playmaker, remain holed up in this grubby place, doing what? Writing poetry for your glory and honour? Bah! I tell you, Master Shakespeare, your glory and your riches will be cold comfort when you're on your death-bed."

Edmund paused, red-faced with exertion, and they both sat in silence, seething with hurt and anger. Shakespeare's brow was heavy and his eyes ablaze.

"I don't owe you any explanation, Eddie, but do you really want to know why I do this? Why I labour at this desk hour after hour?"

"Yes, I want to know."

"You really want to know?"

"I do, Will, I do."

Just then there was a knock on the door. Shakespeare was startled. He wasn't expecting anybody. Perhaps it was the landlady inquiring after Edmund. Was he comfortable? Did he need anything? She was being most solicitous, the poor dear.

Shakespeare crossed the room and answered the door.

Geoffrey Drake stood there smiling.

"Evening," he said. "My apologies for landing up unannounced. Am I interrupting something? Have I come at a bad time?"

***

Two

They had intended to stroll along the riverside but it was hardly the place for an invigorating evening constitutional. Brimming over with people: drunks, gamblers and harlots jostled with traders and merchants returning home from businesses in London. Boatmen were ferrying their last few fares for the day, rowing and cursing with equal ferocity. The London watermen were an ill-tempered lot whose profanities could make a true sailor blush. They were quick to take offence and decent folk kept well away. Adding to the crush of people and the rackety din was the all- pervasive stink of fish and rotting fish. Most unpleasant. It was no wonder, then, that the knight and the playwright sought refuge in the nearest tavern, Bear Inn, near London Bridge.

The place was crowded but they managed to find an unoccupied table. Drake ordered French wine and roast duck for both of them and, finally, they sat down for a chat.

"What do you think of Southwark so far, sir?"

Drake shrugged. "It's different, interesting."

Shakespeare nodded. That, it was. No flower gardens here or churches with soaring spires or proud palaces.

Their drinks were served. Drake raised his goblet and said:

"*A ta santé*, William. May your troubles soon be over. That was a close thing with your brother back at your lodgings. Do you think Edmund believed me?"

"I can't say, sir; my brother believes nothing these days and no one, especially me. I have no control over him. In truth, I seem to have no control over anything nowadays."

Drake raised his brow. "A rather despondent remark, William. Surely things aren't that bad. I'm here now and I trust we will find closure shortly of this tragic business. You will be happy to know that we have our first clue: I found the old flower-seller."

Shakespeare was astonished. "Marry, sir, the one that discovered young Smith's body?"

"The very same. Goes by the name of 'Old Lily' and she resides right here, in Southwark. Her daughter is a prostitute called Rosie. `Wonder if you know her?"

He paused, cut into his roast dish, and rolled his eyes in appreciation.

"Umm, wonderful."

Shakespeare reddened and said nothing. Of course he knew Rosie, knew her in the Biblical sense of the word! So the elusive flower-seller was Rosie's mum? Fancy that.

"She hangs around the Globe's gates," Drake continued as if he hadn't noticed Shakespeare's discomfort. "She and Old Lily are quite familiar with you and your players. That's how she knew Jeremy Smith was one of yours. She had a lot to say."

"Did she actually see...?"

"The killer? Yes, she says so."

Shakespeare gasped.

"More importantly, from her point of view, the killer saw her! That's why she fled. It took much persuading to get her to talk. In the end, however, money did the trick. She is, after all, a poor woman."

"So, who was it?"

Drake smiled ruefully. "Sadly, she can't identify him properly because she says his face was hidden. But she did provide some helpful hints."

"Hints? What kind of hints, sir?"

"Patience, William, all in good time."

Drake leaned back in his chair and glanced around the Bear Inn's interiors. Squalid little place, no patch on the Mermaid's but then he was in Southwark, not nice, sophisticated London. `God, what was he doing here? Why had he accepted the Lord Chamberlain's request with such alacrity? The food was good, though, he had to admit.

"How long do we have before closing time?" he asked.

"About an hour, sir. The tavern closes just before the hour of compline. It's now eight o' clock."

"An hour. Good, that should suffice. I must return to London before it's too late. My carriage is waiting at the docks near Paul's Wharf. I'll take a ferry across the river to the Wharf."

"But isn't your residence nearby, at Dowgate, sir? Just across London Bridge?"

Shakespeare gestured with his wine cup in the direction of the Bridge.

"You mean why don't I simply walk across?"

"Or ride across, sir, in your carriage?"

"I could do that but you forget, William, that I'm supposed to be a common fellow, not a knight. Of course I can stroll across to my home. But I'd rather take a circuitous route in case anyone's watching. I must appear to be humble. Lord Carey and I are hoping for an expeditious end to this case because I'm sure my cover won't sustain for long. As I said earlier in Suffolk, I'm not the best of actors."

"Marry, sir, you could've fooled me with your performance back at my lodgings a short while ago!"

"In truth? I don't think your brother was fooled, though. He has suspicious eyes, most unlike yours."

Suspicious and unfriendly.

That was the look in Edmund Shakespeare's eyes when he encountered the tall, fair-haired young man whom Shakespeare claimed was their cousin.

Shakespeare had greeted him with a flash of surprise but then his manner had become warm and effusive.

"Geoffrey! What a pleasant surprise. Come in, come in. I've been expecting you. Meet my brother Edmund. He's the youngest. Eddie, this is our cousin Geoffrey Dupont."

"Our cousin?" Edmund spat out the words as if he were rinsing his mouth. "What do you mean? What cousin? I've never met him in my life, nor heard of him. We don't have a cousin called Geoffrey Dupont."

"We do, we do. Geoffrey's been abroad; that's why you've never met him."

"Abroad? What do you mean?"

"France," said Drake.

Edmund was incredulous. "That's not possible. How come I've never even heard his name before? Will, you've been away from home, I haven't..."

"He's a distant cousin, on father's side," Shakespeare said as patiently as he could.

Drake stood there watching Edmund with an inscrutable expression on his face. Edmund's eyes darted from one to the other. His disbelieving look said it all: he wasn't buying the story for a second. But he was also confused about his older brother's motives for spinning this yarn. Who on earth was this Dupont fellow and why was William trying to pass him off as a relative?

There wasn't much Edmund could do about it except rush off to Stratford and ask their mother about it. But to what avail? Suppose she denied any knowledge of Dupont but William insisted he was their flesh and blood? Mary Arden Shakespeare would probably admit to the possibility since her husband wasn't alive to confirm or deny it.

Shakespeare had turned to Drake as if the matter was settled.

"You're late," he said in a pally tone. "I was expecting you yesterday. Won't you sit down?"

"No, thank you, Will. My apologies for not turning up as scheduled; I was detained by some urgent work. I see you're busy now. We have some business matters to discuss, don't we? Perhaps I should return in the morning?"

"Not at all. Let's go for a walk." Shakespeare picked up his shoes from a rack near the door. "It's a clear night. Great view of the stars and I could do with some fresh air."

The Bear Inn was hardly the place for fresh air but it gave the two men the requisite privacy to discuss the case.

"Never mind what Edmund thinks, sir," Shakespeare said, "You were about to tell me what the flower woman said."

"I'll get to that shortly but first I'd like a clearer picture in my mind about the theatre scene...Tell me about the other playhouses' owners. The Rose and The Swan? I've also heard that plays are sometimes performed in the Bear Gardens? I'm wondering about their owners; they ought to be our main suspects, the ones who wish to ruin your Company by despatching your players to the other world."

"I'm afraid that's quite impossible, sir. We've considered it before, the Lord Chamberlain, Burbage and I," Shakespeare said with a rueful shake of his head. "The Rose is owned by Phillip Henslowe, who manages the Lord Admiral's Men. He also has shares in the Bear Garden. Although neither of these playhouses- if we can call the Bear Garden a playhouse- are as successful as the Globe, I cannot see Henslowe as the one..."

"Neither can I," Drake agreed, "Not at the risk of involving the Lord Admiral, who'd loathe to cross swords with Lord Carey. If it were ever leaked that Lord Howard is trying to ruin the Chamberlain's Company...Fie, fie, I shudder to think of the consequences. No, the nobility is running scared after Devereux's flop show last year. Devereux..." Drake clucked his tongue in regret. "What a fool to lose everything by attempting a half-hearted, ill-planned rebellion like that. Anyhow, he's dead and gone. As to the matter at hand, tell me, are any of your players particularly close to Henslowe?"

"No, sir, not that I know of. Why do you ask?"

"Just a thought. What if Henslowe is not directly involved in a plot against you all- for fear of the Lord Admiral- but has positioned a mole in your midst? We'll have to investigate the players who have joined your Company in the recent past."

"Jeremy Smith was one of them," Shakespeare said in a wry tone.

"Yes, well, we can exclude him from our list of suspects! I have the names of your other young players- Oliver Downtown, Alexander Cooke and Christopher Beeston, if I'm not mistaken."

Shakespeare's brow rose in admiration. "You know this already?"

"Do you trust them?"

"Why, yes, sir."

"Do you know why I didn't show up at the Globe yesterday?"

The sudden change of track surprised Shakespeare.

"No, sir, I've no idea."

"I was on the job at the Boar's Head playhouse in the city watching the Worcester's Men rip off your version of *Hamlet*. You'll be delighted to learn that the crowd spotted the fraud and turned against them. Dekker was forced to return the entry fee. There was utter mayhem; it was wonderful."

"In truth, sir? But I'd sent two of my boys..."

"Yes, I know. Two of the three chaps I've just mentioned: Beeston and Downtown."

Shakespeare's jaw dropped. "Good Heavens, you know everything!"

"Not at all. I just happened to be at a table near theirs and I overheard their conversation with Thomas Dekker. Beeston accepted a bribe from Dekker for keeping quiet about their plagiarizing. Downtown refused the money but, since he clearly did not tell you about this, he must've kept quiet out of loyalty to his friend."

"Unfaithful curs!" Shakespeare's face was dark and angry. "They said it was a false alarm, that the Worcester's version of *Hamlet* was very different from mine. I could wring that Beeston's neck! And Downtown's. Loyalty to his friend? What about the loyalty he owes Dick Burbage and me?"

"Ah, now friendship is a strange thing. `Compels one to do all sorts of things." Then Drake frowned and said: "You only mentioned Henslowe and the Rose. What about the owner of the third playhouse, the Swan? A chap called Francis Langley, I believe? He's dead, right?"

Shakespeare nodded. "Litigious Langley we called him. He had a penchant for getting embroiled in legal cases. But he died in early January this year. The Paris Garden estate, where the Swan is located, was sold to a chap called Hugh Browker. I have no history with him. As far as we've heard, he's not even interested in the business of running a playhouse so I don't think he considers us his rivals."

"But you did have a history with Langley?"

"Yes, sir, Dick Burbage and I. We used to perform at the Swan and the Rose in `Ninety-Five and `Ninety-Six and Langley wanted us to make the Swan our permanent home but we wanted a place of our own. We built the Globe a few years later."

"He must've resented that, the fact that the Globe was such a success. Were you ever in litigation with Langley?"

Shakespeare shifted uncomfortably. "Yes, with him not against him. A fellow called Wayte accused us of using his inn house for...well...immoral purposes. `Dragged two poor women into the fracas, too; Anne Lee and Dorothy Soes. He was a sick bastard. There was no truth in the allegations. Langley and I fought him in court and the matter was later settled privately."

Drake fixed Shakespeare with his gaze. "How so? You paid him off?"

"Er...yes, sir. I didn't want a protracted legal battle. I...I need my peace of mind so that I can concentrate on my work. I can't write if..."

"And I suppose Langley wanted to continue the fight in court?" Drake cut in.

"He did." Shakespeare rolled his eyes. "He was most unreasonable. `Kept pestering me to use my influence with the Lord Chamberlain and persuade him to put in a word to the Justice in the case. Of course I refused."

"You did well to refuse; Lord Carey would not have taken kindly to such a request." Drake pursed his lips and added: "A pity he's dead, this Francis Langley. Were he alive, he would be topping my list of suspects. Did he have any children? One of them might be trying to avenge his father's misfortune?"

"Not that we know of, sir. Langley died without an heir. He might have a relative, a nephew or someone..."

"No, no, not a nephew. Revenge is a powerful and personal motive for a son or a daughter, not for relations one step removed. However, it's worth checking out. I'll have my men look into this angle. I would keep an eye on Beeston as well."

Shakespeare scowled again. "I could wring his neck!" he repeated.

"Come now, Master Shakespeare, you must not let your face betray your feelings. If we are to unmask the killer we must be two steps ahead and twice as devious. My squires are already checking up on all your players. We should have some news soon..."

Shakespeare was surprised. "Our players are being followed? What if one of them spots your men?"

"I don't expect that to happen; my chaps are quite efficient. They're accustomed to my methods by now. I've trained them well. Now, I shall return to Old Lily's story."

Shakespeare sat upright; it had almost slipped his mind.

"She says it was a wet, miserable morning," Drake began,

"You were performing a comedy, *The Merchant of Venice*." Shakespeare nodded. Drake continued: "The old woman was standing directly across the street facing the Globe's walls. It was business as usual at first...The familiar struggle to find buyers for her flowers..."

Lily had some luck. A pair of cloth merchants- pleasant fellows engaged in deep conversation- bought a bunch of roses. Another young woman with a babe in arms expressed her interest in poesy of asters. She sniffed at them appreciatively and started haggling over the price. That's when Lily noticed them, two men from the Chamberlain's Men, Jeremy Smith and another chap. They were walking fast towards the gates of the Globe. Late for rehearsal? Smith had a small cloth bag hung over his shoulder...

"A bag, sir?" Shakespeare exclaimed, "Is Lily sure about this?"

"She is. You never found a bag on him, on his body?"

"No, the killer must've taken it. I think I know what was in the bag."

Drake's brow went up. "You do?"

Shakespeare nodded and went on to tell Drake about the ironsmith Finch's claim of having given Jeremy Smith some hardware items. He also told him about the note and Burbage's forged signature.

Drake listened with rapt attention and an impassive expression; he eyes gave nothing away.

"Interesting," he said at the end. "We're dealing with a very clever and convoluted mind here. The lengths he'll go to...Rather impressive, I must say."

"But none of us can understand it," Shakespeare said, "What was the purpose behind the note and visit to the ironsmith? Wasn't it a clumsy attempt to get Burbage's name dragged into this? I mean, since the note is lost, all we have is Finch's word; that is of little nuisance value."

"I don't think the killer cares about that. Consider it for a moment, William, what purpose did the note serve?"

"I don't know, sir, that's exactly what we're wondering..."

"Be patient. Don't give up so easily. Think, think! What happened because of the note? Jeremy Smith left home and went to the market instead of waiting for his companions and walking with them to the Globe."

Drake paused, letting this sink in.

Shakespeare spent a moment in pensive silence and then said slowly: "The note separated Jeremy from his friends? It ensured that he would be walking alone to our playhouse?"

Drake smiled. "There you have it."

"By Jove, that is devious. So whoever wrote the note used Dick's name just to make it authentic? He could've used John Heminges' name just as well, since he's the treasurer."

"I don't think the killer considered that important. Burbage or Heminges, he didn't care. All he wanted was for

Smith to walk alone, along a certain route, might I add?"

"Yes, sir, and that would've made it easy for the killer to meet him and accompany him all the way to our playhouse without fear of having any witnesses. One of Smith's regular companions was ill, by the way: Alexander Cooke had taken ill the previous night..."

"So he says," Drake remarked.

"The other lad, Oliver Downtown, backed his story."

"Yes, the same young Downtown who backed Christopher Beeston's lies about what happened at the Boar's Head inn? The lad doesn't seem to be big on scruples, if you ask me."

"And yet he refused Dekker's bribe?"

Drake nodded. "Yes, that puzzles me. It doesn't fit in...Tell me, how did Downtown join your Company?"

"Saunders- that's Alex Cooke introduced him to Heminges."

Drake gave Shakespeare a meaningful look. "Why am I not surprised?"

"What is your meaning, sir?"

"Hadn't thought about it before but it is a possibility... what if there's not one but a pair of killers?"

Shakespeare felt his heart going cold. An eerie feeling came over him. Something about the Coroner's inquest came to mind: Henry Condell had told him that the landlord of the Mermaid's tavern had stated that Alex Cooke was missing from his table a short while before Charles Heminges' body was discovered. This was a fact Cooke had neglected to mention before. Shakespeare mentioned this to Drake.

The young knight took a few moments before responding. "This might mean something, or it might not. What does it prove? Only that Alex Cook is not entirely truthful? Isn't that the case with ninety-nine per cent of human beings?"

Shakespeare smiled wryly. He was getting restless now with all this conjecture and supposition. He hated being under this kind of tension. It left him floundering and incapable of concentrating on his work. He needed to find his still point again, the place in is soul where mind and consciousness existed in harmony. That was what enabled him to take off on a flight of fancy and release his creative juices. All this talk of murder and lies and cunning, it was base, horrible. He felt as if sinister forces were sucking the life essences from him.

"You find all this too confusing, don't you?" Drake said, as if reading the Bard's mind. "Wait till you hear the rest of Old Lily's testimony! It might make things clearer and it might even give you a new suspect!"

Shakespeare took a gulp of his wine. "I can hardly wait, sir."

"As I was telling you, Lily says she saw Smith and another fellow walking hurriedly towards the Globe. Suddenly the other fellow puts his arm on Smith's shoulder and Smith stumbles as if he's tripped on a stone. The other chap keeps his hand on Smith's shoulder near the neck as if to steady him.

Now, this is important: Lily says Smith clutched his throat and panicked as if he were choking on something!"

"Choking?" Shakespeare exclaimed, "He was poisoned, too, just like poor Charlie?"

"Precisely my thought. The killer used the same modus operandi both times. Lily says she watched, horrified, as Jeremy Smith collapsed to the ground and lay there writhing for a minute or so. And the other fellow stood over him watching and doing nothing! Can you believe it? The cold-hearted bastard! She says he just stood there as Smith was dying! Surprisingly, no one gave them a second glance. Lily says it was a busy afternoon and everybody was rushing about. The path was slushy because of the rain and passers-by seemed keen on just getting past the two men. The killer murdered Smith in full view of the public and no one knew it! Audacious, isn't it?"

"It...it's evil! I can hardly believe it!"

"Yes, well, Lily says it froze her blood, too. What really terrified her was that after Smith had given up the ghost, the killer glanced around and saw Lily. He caught her watching him, must've seen the look of terror on her face."

He saw me! He saw that I saw- Lily said over and over again. His eyes were like the devil's. I crossed myself a thousand times, and fled from there.

This was quite early in the morning, around nine-fifteen. Lily's gut reaction was to stay clear away from the scene. She said she thought of vanishing right away. She'd never witnessed a murder before. But then she felt remorse for the poor dead boy lying unclaimed in the muddy street. Someone ought to raise hue-and-cry for him; one couldn't leave him there unacknowledged. So she returned to the spot a few hours later and found that her fears were proved right; the corpse was still lying there unclaimed. How come no one had spotted him? How come no one realized he was dead? Or maybe they realized he was dead and quickly passed by, not wanting to be the first finder?

Lily said she gazed at Smith's body from across the street and searched the area for signs of the murderer, in case the man was keeping watch nearby. He seemed to have gone. So she decided to sound the alarm and flee after that. No way was she going to remain there to give witness. The killer knew that she knew and he would surely come after her; what could she- a poor, defenceless old woman- do against a strapping young lad?

"A strapping, young lad?" Shakespeare repeated, "Is that what she said?"

"Indeed but it's pure conjecture because she also says she didn't get a good glimpse of him. He wore a hat pulled low over his eyes and a long black coat, an expensive coat with big buttons."

Shakespeare's face registered surprise. "None of us owns such a coat. Black is expensive. I have a black doublet with a bit of satin in it but that's all. I'm quite sure none of our players...Could this mean that the killer is an outsider, after all?"

"An outsider with access to you and your players and your playhouse? Someone who knows exactly where you'll be at a particular time? That's hardly likely, is it?"

"No, it isn't. But who could it be? Who could afford a coat like that?"

"More importantly, why would someone wear a coat like that while walking through the Borough?"

"To draw attention...to disguise himself."

"Precisely. Misdirection, that's what. He was keen for people to think he was somebody else. He must've borrowed the coat from a wealthy friend or...what about your costumes? Don't you keep special wardrobes?"

"By George, of course we do. And we have a coat like that. That day the player doing the role of Shylock, the moneylender, wore the long black coat. 'God, maybe the killer pinched it and returned it without anybody noticing."

"Who has access to costumes in your Company?"

"Henry Condell, the Wardrobe Manager. They're stored in boxes in the property room. But...oh no, Harry couldn't be involved in all this. He's one of my most trusted friends. He's a gentle soul, our Harry is. 'Wouldn't hurt a fly."

Drake shrugged. "Lily also mentioned that the killer was of medium height and that he had an awkward gait. He walked awkwardly, like he had a bad leg or something."

Shakespeare didn't respond but his face whitened and he

seemed to be thrown into a sudden turmoil. Drake's last bit of information had affected him. Fear and understanding wrestled in the creases of his face. He opened his mouth to speak but then shut it again in silence.

Drake waited patiently.

**

THREE

———

It was nearly closing time. The landlord was banging his palms on the counter to inform everybody it was time to go. Constable Sprat would be coming round soon to ensure that all taverns were closed.

Shakespeare was oblivious to the fuss all round him. He stared fixedly ahead with the expression of one who has suddenly seen the light through a stygian veil.

"It can't be him," he murmured, "It can't."

"I think you'd better elaborate," Drake said.

Shakespeare swallowed hard. "Duncan Sole," he said, "One of our senior players, slipped and fell and hurt his leg a few months ago. His left leg. So he walks with a slight limp now. He's also the one who played Shylock that day...and, yes, he wore a long, black coat during the performance. But it can't be he, sir. Duncan has a prominent black beard- one of the reasons I cast him as the Jewish money lender- and I'm sure the woman would've noticed it if she'd seen him, even if she didn't get a good glimpse of his face."

"That's true," Drake conceded. "One can't help but notice a feature like that. Be at ease, William, I'm not accusing anybody right now. But we must consider all possibilities. That's the only way to solve a case like this. `Never know which clue will lead us to the killer."

"But, sir, Duncan can't be the one. I just remembered that he wasn't even at the Mermaid's the night Charlie was killed."

"How can you be certain of that? All the players knew that you all were headed for the Mermaid's tavern. So this Duncan Sole or anybody else could've lain in wait outside."

"In theory, yes, but how would they know that Charlie would come out?"

"You all were drinking, weren't you? Stands to reason that you'd have to relieve yourselves sometime. But..." Drake held up his hand to cut off Shakespeare's protest. "Like I said, it's too soon to come to any conclusions. I want to know also, do your players take their costumes home?"

"No, sir, never. Condell would sooner give up an arm or a leg than part with a piece of the wardrobe. It's not possible that one of our players would've been strolling around Southwark in an expensive Company coat. No, I'm sure that the coat old Lily saw..."

"What if a costume or dress is damaged? How do you get it repaired?"

"We have a seamstress, Mrs. Dogoody; she was Jeremy Smith's landlady, too. If any dress is damaged, Condell or his assistant takes it to her..." Shakespeare paused and then added with a sigh: "Oliver Downtown is Condell's assistant. And I recall that Downtown was assisting with the props the day Tommy Gray plunged from the balcony. He was also at the Mermaid's, at Charlie's table...I don't know what to think, sir. He's a tiny chap, a boy..."

"At ease, William, this case certainly is hot at hand. We seem to have several suspects; all we're lacking is motive. The 'why' of the case. But, not to worry my good chap, we shall yet catch the murderer and unmask him as surely as my name is Drake! Speaking of masks, have you received an invitation to the Lord Chamberlain's ball?"

"No, sir. I know nothing of it."

"You shall, by tomorrow. The ball is scheduled for Friday evening. It's to be a masque. I trust you and your players will have no dearth of costumes. `Should be fun. `An interesting diversion from your present troubles."

The landlord banged on the counter again.

Shakespeare and Drake glanced up, startled, and realized they were the only remaining customers in the tavern. They downed the dregs from their mugs; Drake settled the bill, and then they left.

***

'We had a surprise today, Eddie Shakespeare showed up.'

'Who is Eddie Shakespeare?'

'The youngest bastard of the family. The brothers aren't close, though, and William seemed properly peeved at the new arrival.'

'Yeah, well, he's a selfish bastard, isn't he?'

'That goes without saying. I've been feeling...it's been too long since the last one. Isn't it time I struck again? Don't want the bastard to think he's safe now, do we?'

'Why not? Lull him into a false sense of security. Then strike. It'll be more fun.'

'That, it might. Whom shall I take down this time?'

'Wait and see.'

'Wait and see? Why do you always say that? It becomes very annoying. You don't want me to be annoyed now, do you? You know how I get...it's not...pleasant...'

Silence.

'Answer me, damn you! Why don't you answer me and tell me clearly what to do? How long can I wait until the big one? Don't you understand how frustrating it is to see him day in and day out and not do anything?'

'You've already done a lot. Patience is a virtue...'

'Who's interested in virtue? I'm all vice; I want only vice...'

***

Shakespeare and Drake strolled towards the boatmen's dock where a ferry was taking its last fares for the day. Shakespeare expected Drake to get on it but the knight continued walking along the riverbank. Shakespeare glanced anxiously at the departing boat and wondered how Drake would get home. He'd said he would be take a boat to Paul's Wharf, so why had he let the last one go? The city gates would shut soon and Drake would have no option but to spend the night in Southwark. Perhaps he was planning on staying at a tavern tonight?

The crowd thinned suddenly; Shakespeare and Drake would soon be the only two men on the street. They were likely to run into Constable Sprat. Now wouldn't he like to extract a fine from the Bard for violating the curfew?

They'd just turned into Brend's Rents, the alley behind the Globe, when Shakespeare became aware of soft footfalls behind them. Two people for certain. Who were they? Cutpurses? Thieves? Murderer? He tensed and didn't dare look over his shoulder. His legs turned to jelly and he thought he'd collapse any moment.

Drake continued walking as if unconcerned. Was he unaware of their pursuers? Was he armed? Did he have a dagger or musket concealed on his person? Why was he looking so casual? This is real life, Shakespeare nearly screamed, not some fancy tournament with rules and heralds to intervene before things turned bloody. He had seen Drake in action in the joust but surely the young man knew that criminals in Southwark were not men of honour that cared for Queen and Country. Here, they'd slice you up with a rusty blade and serve up your entrails to the fish in the Thames!

He quickened his pace and looked askance at Geoffrey Drake, not wanting to be shown up as a coward before the knight but...

All of a sudden, Drake grabbed him by the sleeve, pulled him into a lane off the main street and motioned for silence with a finger to his lips.

Shakespeare was too stunned to react. Drake stood there erect and still.

They heard the footsteps again, crunching on the gravel. To their left, long shadows came creeping across the street. Suddenly Drake extended his left leg and tripped up a man, who fell headlong with a loud cry of alarm. Behind him, another chap also tripped and fell to the ground with a thud. Shakespeare sprang forward to help Drake pin them down but he was taken aback to see Drake helping them to their feet and chuckling with good humour.

"Sir! Long Live the Queen!" one chap exclaimed as he struggled to retrieve his sword from the ground.

"God bless you, sir," said the other.

Drake grinned at them. "Stop sirring me; I'm on a case, remember? Stop saluting me, Rod!"

He turned to Shakespeare and said: "Meet my most

trusted squires, Rodney Peele and Tod Makepeace. Rod and Tod. They're to be my eyes and ears while I'm working on your case."

Shakespeare doffed his hat politely. "Pleased to meet you. I remember Mr. Peele from Suffolk; he was in your pavilion, sir, when the Lord Chamberlain visited."

"Quite right, so he was," said Drake.

Rod, the chubbier one, nodded at Shakespeare and then turned to Drake. "Sire, you'll be pleased to know we have got the information you wanted and we've solved the case."

Shakespeare gasped in surprise.

"Yes, sir, now you can stop pretending to be a commoner and go back to being Sir Geoffrey," Tod said. He was a fellow of medium build with bushy eyebrows. "We know who the murderer is."

"Who is it?" Shakespeare demanded with an excited look at Drake. But he noticed that the latter evinced not the slightest interest in this potentially explosive revelation.

Instead, he said: "Never mind that, tell me what you've learnt today. How many players did you manage to check out?"

"Nearly everybody except one or two," Tod said, "Three, actually. Only three men remain to be investigated. Henry Condell, Thomas Pope and John Heminges."

"Good work. You can fill me in during our journey home. The last ferry is gone so perhaps we can walk tonight..."

"Of course it's gone, sir, we told the boatman to shove off," said Rod, "Couldn't let you take the common man's transport. Your barge is docked nearby."

Drake groaned. "Not my barge. With my colours?"

"The very same. If your barge won't have your colours, sir, then..."

Tod interjected proudly: "And we told the Constable, a tall chap called Brat or Sprat or Something, to keep an eye on it. `Damned if some cut-throat tries to hide on board."

"You told the Constable?" Drake's eyes widened with dismay. "What is wrong with you two? I told you this is a secret mission."

"Aye, sir, we told him that, too, we did," Tod said happily. "Top secret."

Drake sighed. "So much for my cover."

"No matter, Sire, we've solved the case," Rod said with a cherry grin. "You can leave this dreadful borough and return to London anon. We know who's been doin' all the killin'."

"You do?"

"Aye, sir." Rod exchanged a look of suppressed excitement with his fellow squire and continued: "According to our findings there's only one person who had the opportunity to commit murder each time. One man with access to the Company's intimate secrets. One man who knew every detail about the players' whereabouts."

Drake's expression was long-suffering. "All right, so who's this diabolical fellow?"

"Diabolical? Aye, he's El Diablo, the devil hi'self! The gentleman- player Master William Shakespeare!"

Shakespeare's jaw dropped and Drake rolled his eyes towards the heavens.

"Yes, this is what I expected..." he said.

The squires were gleeful.

"...of the pair of you!" Drake added. He thumped Rod on the back. "You've excelled yourself this time, Mr. Peele. Here, meet the devil himself in the flesh, Master Shakespeare! Sorry, William, I neglected to introduce you."

Rod and Tod jumped with alarm.

"Him?" Tod exclaimed, "Ma...ma...Master Shakespeare?"

Drake grinned. "El Diablo, you said."

"But...well...we..."

The two men stared at the Bard as if he were an exotic animal. Dullards, he thought.

"So you're not...?" Rod stuttered, "You haven't ...haven't been topping your actors, then?"

"Of course not. Why would I?" said Shakespeare, "What would I stand to gain from that? Trust me when I say, sirs, I am more sinned against than sinning."

"More sinned against than sinning," Rod parroted, "That's a good line. `Never heard it before."

"I invented it."

"In truth, sir?" Rod was duly impressed.

"I think that should do for tonight," Drake interjected, "I must leave you now, William. I shall see you in the morning. What time should I reach the Globe?"

"Around ten o'clock, sir. We'll all be there. We're putting up *The Taming of the Shrew* tomorrow afternoon. `Haven't performed it for a while so we need to rehearse properly."

"Is it a comedy?"

"Yes, the players don't want to do tragedy until the murderer is caught."

Drake looked bemused to hear this but he made no comment.

"I don't know how long this can continue," Shakespeare said, "The audience will soon tire of comedy. It's tragedy that brings in the crowds."

"In truth, sir?" Tod said in surprise, "Do you mean that people prefer crying to laughing?"

Shakespeare shrugged. "Laughter rolls over us; it's easy to laugh. But tears must well up from our inner being. A man is not easily moved to tears."

"Children cry easily," Rod pointed out with a wise look

about him. "Does that mean they're deeper, more serious, than grownups?"

Good question, thought Shakespeare, wouldn't have expected it of an oaf like you.

He replied: "Children laugh and cry easily because their emotional responses are not fully developed. For them laughter and tears are like other bodily functions. But in the case of adults, we must be moved to the core of our being for the tears to come."

The squires stared and it was clear that Shakespeare hadn't got through to them.

"Never mind the tears, we shall be merry now," Drake said and nodded at his men. "Let us be off. Good night, William. *Rendezvous au Globe a' demain*. I look forward to meeting the rest of the Chamberlain's Men."

"Yes, sir. Have a good night. I am sure the morrow will be eventful. *Bonne nuit*, Sir Geoffrey."

***

FIVE

The invitation to the Lord Chamberlain's ball arrived at the Blackburn country estate early Wednesday morning. Marie found it slipped under her door when she awoke. She took it to her dressing table, sat in front of the mirror and gazed at it admiringly. Lovely black calligraphy and gilded bordering. She wondered if the Queen would attend. Probably not. Elizabeth was still recovering from her Suffolk progress. She was nearly sixty-nine, after all. Her health was becoming increasingly frail. Despite her public posturing and layers of make-up, there was no denying the fact that the Tudor Queen had withered with age. The murmurings were getting louder by the day. Who would succeed her? The general consensus was, her cousin King James of Scotland. He was doing a decent job and seemed to be the least controversial choice. The nobility hoped it would be a smooth transition; Marie had noticed that her husband and other noblemen, who visited from time to time, were quite nervous about the whole thing. They would often talk in low tones about the implications of a change of guard. Some of them were in denial, hoping the Elizabeth would live forever.

But nothing lives forever. People die, feelings die, love... dies.

She recalled the look in Shakespeare's eyes when they'd met outside Suffolk castle; it was horrible. She had never seen him looking so incensed, so repulsed by her. She knew he knew about the others. Well, it had to come out some day. It's only my body, darling, *Ça n'a pas d'importance*. It really doesn't matter.

There were more pressing matters for her to consider now, like how did Shakespeare's portrait get back into her drawer? It had been missing for days. She wasn't imagining things. It was gone and now it was returned. What did it mean?

Nothing good, certainment.

"Cherie, Tu sembles être distrait. A quoi penses-tu"?

"Distrait?"

Marie turned around and replied to the man in her bed in French.

"No, I'm not distracted. There's nothing particular on my mind, Gerard. I was just wondering what to wear to the ball." She held up the invite for him to see.

"George Carey is throwing a masque ball this weekend. Friday night. We're invited. You, too, of course."

Gerard Guilbert gave her a leery grin and patted the bed beside him. "A party? How nice. If you ask me, you should wear nothing at all. You look best in your birthday suit. But I suppose we can't have all the guests walking around with hard-ons! Come here. Come back to bed, *ma lapine*."

"Oh, Gerard, you know it's not safe." Marie's gaze darted towards the door of her bedchamber. "The maid will be knocking soon. Henry will be back any time now."

Guilbert waved dismissively and flicked a lock of blond hair off his face. "We shall hear him arrive. The hounds will precede him. These English nobles make such a noise when they return from a hunt; probably consider it a mark of virility!"

He laughed and the corners of his mouth curved with contempt. "Come on, we have a few minutes before your Lord and Master returns. Let's not waste them talking."

Marie walked across to the bed and slipped off her night dress. She saw her cousin's face glisten in the candlelight like a wild animal. Guilbert reached for her hand and drew her towards him.

"You are exquisite," he murmured, "Has anyone ever told you that?"

"Yes," she said, "In flowery, poetic language. He compared me with a summer's day and with the darling buds of May.

But that was a long time ago. Only memories remain now in the corners of my mind."

***

"Such duties as the subject owes the prince,

Even such a woman oweth to her husband."

When Alexander Cooke spoke these lines in character as Katherine of *The Taming of the Shrew*, the other players burst into applause.

"Great lines, Will," Augustine Phillips exclaimed, "Dick, you lucky sod, getting to enact the ultimate male fantasy!"

Burbage laughed. He was reprising the role of the hero Petruchio.

"If only my Anne would say something like that even once," Phillips added.

"Becky was submissive to me once," Heminges said and they all stared at him. "Just after she gave me permission to leave for work this morning!"

Everyone laughed heartily.

"All right, let's finish this," Shakespeare called them to attention again. "We're almost through. Last scene, please, Dick, Saunders."

So Burbage and Cooke took up their positions again.

Shakespeare's mind was wandering and he had to force himself to focus on the rehearsal.

Where was Geoffrey Drake? He'd given his word that he'd be there around ten. It was nearly eleven; where was he?

"Come now, kiss me, Kate," Burbage said in his concluding lines, and Cooke leaned in for a supposed smooch.

Burbage embraced him and covered their faces with his hat to conceal the 'kiss'.

Shakespeare clapped his hands. "Good work. I think we're ready now."

The playhouse erupted with chatter.

Cooke complained that his dress was too tight so Condell and Downtown took him aside to inspect the garment and see if they could open a stitch or two. Burbage said his throat was hurting because of his long lines in the play, perhaps it was a mistake to take on such a big part so soon after his recovery from the flu. John Heminges suggested he sip a drink of honey and lime in hot water to soothe his vocal chords, and immediately instructed a stagehand to prepare the concoction for Burbage. In the centre of the stage, Shakespeare stood and talked to Augustine Phillips, who was playing Vincentio, an old gentleman of Pisa.

"You're doing well, Phil, but I want to see some more of the madness in this character. You're pretending to be insane so you must make the audience think you're a lunatic."

"I know, I know, but you're the one that keeps telling us to underplay the character."

"Even so, please bear with me, Phil. This is comedy. We're expected to be loony and zany. If it were tragedy, I'd be advising you differently."

"Very well," said the slim, athletic player, "I'll do zany for you, Will."

"Gracias, Senor!"

While they were talking Robert Armin was supervising Nicholas Tooley and John Sinklo as they tried to secure the ropes that held the backdrop in place. For some reason, they weren't getting it right. The painted cloth that depicted a public place in Pisa was either too high or too low or altogether crooked. Armin was getting quite flustered.

Geoffrey Drake stood at the periphery of the playhouse watching the action and feeling like a voyeuristic intruder. He'd found the gate partially open when he arrived fifteen minutes ago and stepped in unnoticed. Everyone, including the boy at the gate, was engrossed in the rehearsal on stage. Edmund was there, too, sitting sullen-faced in the western gallery with another older player beside him. Despite his body language- closed knees, body leaning backwards, arms crossed around chest- he looked like he belonged in the group. Only he, Drake, would be an outsider. He wondered for an instant if he should turn around and abandon the case. This was unchartered territory. Suddenly, he didn't feel like doing it; surely there was another way. So what if the killer wasn't caught? Perhaps the Lord Chamberlain could be persuaded to deploy armed guards to protect the players for a while and that would scare off the murderer...

"Ere, and who are you?" the gatekeeper noticed him finally. "How did you enter?"

"I'm kinsman to Master Shakespeare," Drake said, "His cousin Geoffrey Dupont."

The gatekeeper was surprised. What was going on in the Shakespeare clan? Edmund showed up the day before; now this chap. He hollered for the Bard.

"Master Shakespeare! Someone to see you, sir. Says he's your cousin."

Shakespeare saw Drake and his face lit up like a well-oiled lamp.

"Geoffrey!" he exclaimed, "There you are. I've been expecting you. Welcome to the Globe." He rushed down the stage and shook Drake's hand. Alerted, Burbage played his part as well by embracing the young knight and saying that it had been a long time.

Shakespeare and Burbage's performances were so convincing that the others did not hesitate in warming up to the newcomer. Edmund looked a little less antagonistic this morning. He was still confused about Drake's ancestry but Burbage's reference to a previous meeting made him consider that perhaps his brother was telling the truth, after all; maybe Geoffrey Dupont was part of the Shakespeare family.

As Shakespeare introduced him around, Drake tried to match names with the background information he had.

Augustine Phillips was the first player to shake his hand. An alert and physically fit chap, mid-thirties. Married man with three young children. A musician and senior player, one of the sharers. Stepbrother to Thomas Pope. His apprentices: James Sands and Christopher Beeston.

"Nice to meet you, Geoffrey." John Heminges was the next to come forward. Stocky, bushy eyebrows. A mild stutter. "Any cousin of Will's is brother to us all."

"Thank you, that's most kind," Drake said.

He didn't know much about Heminges except what Shakespeare had told him: senior player, accountant to the Company, married man, father of seven!

"And still counting!" Shakespeare had said, for Heminges' wife Rebecca was heavy with child, their eighth. Alexander Cooke and Oliver Downtown were apprenticed to him.

Rod and Tod were investigating Heminges' background at present. Then they'd move on to Condell and Pope.

Alexander Cooke, Drake learnt, was the chap who'd been playing the heroine. Hardly a shrew. He was tall, willowy, and light-eyed. He had a petulant expression now because of a tight corset.

It became a little confusing as the other players crowded around to get introduced. James Sands, Henry Condell,

Richard Cowley, Thomas Pope, John Sinklo (a very, very skinny chap), William Sly, Christopher Beeston...

Ah, thought Drake, I know you from the other night at the Boar's Head inn.

Beeston had evidently not seen him there for his face betrayed no signs of recognition.

Nicholas Tooley. Also short and dark-haired. Quite young. Apprenticed to Cuthbert Burbage. He lived with Cuthbert and the missus.

"And this is Duncan Sole," Shakespeare said.

Drake stiffened. Shylock; the man with the bad leg; maybe the man in the black coat?

Drake studied Sole's flat, square face and bulbous nose. He gave the impression of being a simpleton . His smile was guileless and reached his eyes easily.

Drake recalled that Sole lived in Rose Alley nearby and that he was a neighbour to William Sly. Suddenly this fact assumed significance. Rose Alley was adjacent to Globe Alley. How convenient for someone trying to target a player en route to the Globe...

A look of understanding passed between him and Shakespeare and he could tell that the playmaker was finding this hard, masking his feelings and making pretence all the time.

Easy, easy, Master Shakespeare. We must be alert and

focussed for we're dealing with a very twisted mind. He's several steps ahead of us.

Drake wondered if one of these nice men was really the killer.

"Oliver Downtown," Shakespeare said next.

Drake nodded, smiling. He remembered Downtown from the other night, too, only he hadn't realized how small the boy was. Downtown was five-foot nothing, stocky in the way that most short people are, and he had shifty eyes. Drake also noticed when they shook hands that the little fellow's grip was surprisingly strong.

Ollie, Ollie, are you the one? Drake had the strong urge to say something like that. Are you the killer, Mr. Downtown? Or are you and Alex Cooke in it together? Or is it you and Beeston? Or is it Cooke alone? Or is it Duncan Sole? Or is it 'x' or 'y' or 'z'?

Drake's mind spun when he realized the number of men he'd placed under suspicion.

Someone tapped him on the shoulder. Drake wheeled around to find a pleasantly plump man of average height and a pointy beard standing there.

"Robert Armin, *a ta service*, Monsieur Dupont." Drake had told them that he was recently returned from France, hence the French. "Call me 'Robin'."

"*Merci*, Robin, Enchante," Drake replied.

"Ah." Armin cocked his head to one side. "Your French is excellent. You're half-Froggie, then?"

Drake grinned. "I'm afraid so. My father's francais. Mother is cousin to Uncle John, that is, late Uncle John, William's father."

"How nice. And are you an actor, too?'

"Good Lord, no!" Drake's response was instinctive. "I'm just visiting. I got back from France last week and I thought I'd spend some time with Cousin Will and..." Drake added with a smile at Edmund, "...by a stroke of good fortune, Edmund's here, too. I look forward to getting acquainted with him. We've never met before."

All eyes turned to Edmund but he only made a face to reveal his contempt for the prospect. Shakespeare bristled with annoyance and was on the verge of ticking him off but Robert Armin intervened and eased the tension.

"Don't mind him, Geoffrey, he's a moonish bloke. You are among friends here. And you're welcome to stay as long as you like."

"Aye, aye," said Heminges.

Drake smiled at them and thanked them.

Despite the sombre and urgent nature of his mission, Drake found himself warming up to these men, and even feeling a trifle uncomfortable about deceiving them. Robert Armin was another player with a squeaky clean reputation.

According to Drake's information, Armin had apprenticed under the famous jester Richard Tarlton, who had died four years back. He joined the Chamberlain's Men in Sixteen Hundred when their principal comedian William Kempe quit. Armin was a more refined comic than Kempe. Like most of the Chamberlain's Men he, too, was a family man.

It was almost unreal; all Shakespeare's fellow actors seemed so normal. Yet one of them was a cold-hearted killer?

"Now you've met everyone," Shakespeare said, "Stay and enjoy the show. We'll talk afterwards, Geoffrey."

"Righto. Can I be of some use backstage? Since I'm not acting, can I lend a hand...?"

Shakespeare shrugged. Edmund called out from the gallery: "Doing what?"

"Pardon me?" Drake said in surprise.

"I said, 'doing what'? What skills do you have, Cousin Dupont? How do you propose to lend a hand backstage? You seem to be a man of leisure."

Edmund's tone was laden with disdain and Drake was tempted to make a retort with the basilard sheathed in his belt. But then he remembered his position. He was supposed to be a spoiled, rich boy. And the truth was, he had no working class skills; he'd never been near a carpenter's saw or a glover's paring knife. All he knew was combat.

"You're right, Eddie," he said, "I might just get in the way if I try and meddle backstage. Perhaps I should join you in the gallery."

Edmund scowled. Thomas Pope, who was seated beside him, threw back his head and laughed.

"You really asked for it, Eddie."

He patted Drake on the shoulder as he made his way towards the bench in the gallery and said:

"Love to stay and talk but I have duties backstage and on stage."

"No problem, I'm sure we'll have many opportunities to chat, Mr. Pope."

"Oh, it's 'Tom', please."

"Right, Tom."

Pope smiled again. "Enjoy the show."

Drake and Edmund sat in silence for a while watching the gates open and crowd stream into the Globe. Hercules made a lonely, stoic figure looking over the entrance with the globe on his shoulders. Beneath the logo, stagehands and gatekeepers worked with practised efficiency to ensure that all those who entered the premises dropped a penny in the boxes held out. No one, as far as Drake could tell, had slipped in without paying. Vendors waded through the audience with the usual fare of cakes, hazelnuts and bottles of ale on offer. The air was buzzing with anticipation and the excitement rubbed off onto Drake. He could hardly wait for the show to begin.

"Will you be at the great ball tomorrow night?" Edmund asked abruptly.

"What great ball?"

"The Lord Chamberlain's. It's an annual event, his masque ball. Will and the other sharers received an invitation a short while ago. It's to be held at Whitehall Palace."

"A masque?" said Drake, "You mean with costumes and disguises?"

"That's usually what a masque implies, at least in this country. Don't know about Froggie-land."

"Oui, it's the same in France. Will you attend it?"

"Probably. Will says I can go as his guest. There's nothing better to do, is there? Will won't let me act; don't know why he's so stubborn about that."

"What disguise will you use?"

Edmund looked directly at Drake and said, "Death. I shall wear the Death Mask. Henry Condell and Downtown will go to the city in a while since they're not required here once the show gets underway, and they'll fetch some masks on hire from a mask-maker the Company deals with. Condell has promised me a death mask. That's all I need; I have a long black coat to go with it."

Drake's ears picked up. "A long black coat? Wow, must be expensive."

Edmund nodded eagerly. "It's my most treasured possession. I don't have much by way of worldly goods but this coat..." His eyes gleamed as he continued: "You've got to see it. It's all velvet and...well...considering the sumptuary laws, it's probably illegal for me to wear it but at a masque-ball, everything is permitted. The coat is in a box back at my brother's place. Would you like to see it?"

Drake smiled. "Yes, I would, Eddie, very much."

***

SIX

What a commotion there was when the play ended! Applause, whistles, lusty shouts from tipsy theatregoers. Thomas Pope came on to present a short, bawdy jig about an old merchant tricked by his clever guests, and sent on a wild goose chase while the guests make off with his young, hot-blooded wife. Augustine Phillips and James Sands accompanied him on the cistern and the lute. The audience howled with laughter.

The playhouse finally cleared around five-thirty, the spectators filing out as a happy, raucous lot. Drake was fascinated. He had never seen this aspect of London-life, or Greater London life, to be precise. William Shakespeare had certainly put a large number of people in very good spirits.

"Behold the happy souls," Armin said to Drake, "And yet the Puritans oppose playhouses."

"Don't you know why?" Drake quipped, "It's because you bring joy to the people! What's the one thing that distinguishes Puritans from other people? Lack of joy. After all, to be a true Puritan you must love mankind but never ever like any man."

Armin chuckled. "That's a pithy saying if there ever was one. `Didn't know you were such a wit, Master Dupont."

Drake coloured. "A wit? I don't consider myself such."

Shakespeare came up to them and inquired if Drake had enjoyed the show.

"I did, very much. But I can't understand how you manage to write so many words, Cousin Will! And how do the players memorize them? You perform different plays every afternoon? How do you do it?"

Shakespeare was pleased with the compliment but he tried to brush it off. "That's the job, cuz. You either do or don't do it. If I don't produce fresh material regularly, my business will dwindle away."

"And as for us actors, we either perform or perish," Armin added, "Simple as that. The competition is getting tougher every day; new boys knock on our gates all the time wanting to work as hired players. We have to turn most of them away."

"And some of us are fated to watch from the sidelines," Edmund cut in bitterly. "Never trusted, never let into the inner circle, just condemned to remain mute spectators."

"Why mute?" Shakespeare retorted, "No one's stopping

you from applauding and cheering a good performance, Eddie. Now stop wailing like a banshee; we've gone over this before."

"The play you performed today..." Drake interjected, steering the conversation away from the sibling rivalry. "Is it one of your more popular comedies?"

"You could say that," Shakespeare replied, "The others also draw in huge crowds, though: *The Comedy of Errors, As You Like It, Much Ado About Nothing, The Merchant of Venice...*"

"Ah, I've heard of The Merchant of Venice," Drake said, "What is it about?"

Shakespeare gave Drake a quizzical frown. What was he gunning for?

"It's er...perhaps my most popular comedy," he said slowly, "It revolves round this young fellow, Antonio, a Venetian merchant, who takes a loan from a mean moneylender called Shylock..."

"What made you set the action in Venice?"

Shakespeare shrugged, still perplexed about Drake's line of inquiry. "'Seemed appropriate for the story, that's all."

"The audience likes different settings," Armin said, "Wouldn't it be dull to have every play set in London or Southwark?"

"But isn't it hard?" Drake persisted, "You must need new backdrops, new costumes all the time?"

At the mention of costumes, Shakespeare brightened; he finally understood what Drake was after. Very clever, very smooth.

"Yes, we need lots of costumes," he said eagerly, "We have wardrobe boxes. Henry Condell is in charge there."

Robert Armin intervened with a fair question: "You seem to be full of queries, Geoffrey. Have you any previous experience in the theatre? Planning on setting up your own Company?"

"My own Company of players?" Drake echoed in genuine surprise, "Perish the thought, Robin, perish the thought. I don't know the first thing about players or playhouses. I'm curious, that's all. I was amazed at the way you all disappeared into the tiring-room and reappeared moments later in different costumes. That's why I'm asking."

"Ah, well, `tis all a matter of practice," Armin said.

"Of course if one were playing Shylock, one would not need to change one's costume at all during the play," Shakespeare said, and received a sharp look from Drake.

No need to make things so obvious yet...

"Ah, that wonderful coat," Duncan Sole chipped in as if on cue, "Wouldn't mind borrowing it now and then, to show off, like. But Harry would never let me."

Shakespeare chuckled. "You can try asking him?"

The gates shook loudly just then. A gateman, who was

snoozing on a chair at the entrance, was jolted awake by the sound. He peered out.

Two men stood there.

"We demand to speak to Monsieur Dupont," one of them said, "We know he's in there."

The gateman felt a trifle uneasy because the men wore serious expressions.

"Why?" he asked.

"That's none of your concern, my good man. Summon Monsieur Dupont. We know he's in there."

So the gateman relayed the message.

Drake put on an expression of surprise. "Summons for me? Who's calling?"

He started to walk to the gate.

Burbage, blissfully unaware of Rod and Tod, asked the gatekeeper to let them in.

The gatekeeper stuck his head out again. "Names, please, and I'll let you enter."

"Names? You want my name?" Rod pushed the chap aside and strode in. "The name's Rodney Peele and I am squire to a brave knight."

"Aye, the bravest of all knights," Tod agreed, "A knight in whom there is no 'night'- that being darkness- but only light."

"In truth?" said the gatekeeper. "And who might that be?"

"Greeting, friends," Drake said quickly to pre-empt his squire's honest reply. "Geoffrey Dupont, at your service. Is this about the money I owe you?"

"Money?" Rod repeated, "Why, is it Quarter Day, sir?"

Drake cringed. Quarter Day was pay day, the last day of each quarter when a nobleman would pay his staff.

What was Rod thinking? Oh, he forgot, Rod wasn't thinking at all! He was incapable of logical thought!

Drake gave them a hollow laugh. "Quarter Day? That's a good one. I know this is about the money I owe your Lord. Shall we discuss the matter outside?"

Before his men could reply, Drake grabbed their collars and pushed them through the gates.

"Greetings, Sire, I hope you are well," Tod said formally.

"I am very well, thank you, I am in the pink of health," Drake shot back with exasperation, "But you two won't be if you pull a stunt like that again! You were not to come inside the Globe? What did I tell you this morning?"

"You said 'Come to the Globe' at six o'clock," Tod said, scratching the top of his head, "Come inside. Then you added: 'Don't'."

"Idiot! Where did you leave your brains? I said: 'Don't come inside,' 'don't call me Sire'. I told you to simply say you wished to speak to Monsieur Dupont about a financial matter. That's the best excuse; it makes me look irresponsible and in debt. In short, one of them! A commoner, with the problems of common people. No one expects a man to discuss financial dealings in the company of strangers." He paused and exhaled deeply: "All right, I think I've said enough. Speak now. What is your news?"

The squires brightened.

"It's about the three remaining players, Thomas Pope, Henry Condell and John Heminges, sir," said Rod, "Condell seems to be clean. He's happily married and goes `ome every night to his wife. Thomas Pope seems all right but he has never married. A bit o'an oddball, to tell you the truth, sir. He goes about doin' good deeds and helpin' orphans, things like that. There is a bit o' bad blood with Cuthbert Burbage. People say Pope wants to become a sharer but ol' Cuthbert Burbage has said 'no'. So he's waiting until someone- one of the six sharers- kicks the bucket or leaves. Then he can fill his shoes, so to speak."

"Only if they're the right size, Rod," Tod cut in, "What if the dead sharer has much bigger feet?"

"That's why I said 'so to speak'," Rod said.

Drake sighed and massaged his forehead. Fond as he was of these two, they drove him bonkers sometimes. Their banter had begun to get on his nerves. But he had to admit that their information about Thomas Pope was interesting. So he wanted to be a sharer; obviously Cuthbert had to refuse. An additional sharer would lead to a cut in the shares of the other senior players. Did Pope want this badly enough to kill?

"What about John Heminges?" he asked.

"Ah, now he should be a suspect," Rod said and exchanged a triumphant smile with his fellow squire. "Heminges seems to be an upright fellow and he is devoted to his wife, regular churchgoer, blah, blah, blah. But did you know, sir, that he and his brother had...differences?"

"Differences? Between him and his brother Charlie who died recently?"

"Aye, sir, the dearly departed. Apparently our friend John bought a small ale house some years back and Charlie wanted a share in it. Or he wanted to buy it off John, something like that. Johnny said 'no' and they had quite a spat over it. People say the brothers loved each other but they also fought like cats and dogs."

"Or like she-dogs and she-dogs," Tod added. "Or like girl-cats and...now what are female cats called?"

"Kitty-kitty," said Rod.

The squires continued their inane talk but Drake wasn't paying them any attention. His mind was churning with the information he'd just received. So John and Charlie Heminges had not got along! It wasn't unusual for brothers to have minor disagreements but he hadn't considered this possibility before. What if all three incidents had not been about the Company or Shakespeare but a devious attempt at misdirection? What if old Heminges had done away with Smith and tried to kill Thomas Gray only to make it look like there was a murderer on the loose? What if Charles Heminges had been the target all along? After all, there'd been no more incidents after Charles Heminges' death.

Who had discovered Charlie's body?

His brother John.

What if he hadn't stumbled upon Charlie's body but actually killed him and then pretended to find the body?

Brother killing brother.

The first murder in the Bible.

Would Charles Heminges' blood cry out like Abel's had?

***

SEVEN

'Geoffrey Drake's List of Suspects:

Unknown subject. Male. Grudge against Shakespeare and the Chamberlain's Men;

Edmund Shakespeare plus unknown insider. Edmund because of his bitterness toward his brother. Problem is he would've had to have had someone on the inside, too. Who is that someone and what is his grudge against Shakesp.? Edmund also has a black coat, remember;

John Heminges. Differences with his brother. Heminges, being the senior most member of the Company, is privy to all its secrets. He was present on all three occasions and he was the one that discovered Charlie's body... He's an accountant and could've forged Dick Burbage's signature on the note sent to J. Smith;

Duncan Sole. Most probable suspect if the flower-seller's testimony is accurate. He had access to the black coat and has a bad leg. (Slight limp, I noticed);

Oliver Downtown and Alexander Cooke. The last two players to have seen J. Smith alive. Something not quite right about the pair of them, especially Downtown. Doesn't seem too keen on acting, so why is he really here?

Christopher Beeston. Amenable to bribery for small favours, hence open to corruption. Is he being paid to ruin the Company by one of Shakesp.'s rivals?'

Drake put his quill down and studied the list under candlelight. Yes, that kind-of summed up his list of suspects. But it was too vague and inconclusive. He felt dissatisfied. What was he missing? Something was staring him in the face but he couldn't see it. He also felt that Shakespeare was holding out on him. There was something he wasn't telling him, something personal but it might have a deep significance on the case. His hunch arose from the incident at Suffolk Castle. Why was Shakespeare so quick to believe that somebody was trying to kill him there? The previous three incidents had occurred in London. Why did Shakespeare believe- wrongly- that someone had followed him all the way from London and tried to finish him off on the night of the banquet?

Of course Shakespeare had been wrong about that. Drake had cleared up that angle the same night. It turned out that the pot-boy who'd attacked-and then been killed by- Shakespeare was nothing more than a common thief. He knew that the Earl had several rich guests staying over, so he disguised as a chambermaid and went about purloining whatever he could. Bleach, the Lord Chamberlain's Secretary was missing a watch; one of Viscount Blackburn's bodyguards reported that six shillings had been stolen from his purse when he'd left it in the servants' quarters while having a wash in the community bath that morning...and so on. Once Drake and the Earl of Suffolk's man Peter Lennox began making enquiries the night Shakespeare was attacked, it transpired that a number of guests had complained about having valuables nicked since their arrival at Suffolk Castle. Drake and Lennox searched the dead pot-boy's quarters and, sure enough, all the missing items came tumbling out from a small box stashed under his bed. It was then that Drake came to the conclusion that the poor boy had attacked Shakespeare merely out of fear of being found out, not because he'd been hired to kill the Bard.

So the question remained: why was Shakespeare so quick to assume it had been an attempt on his life? What was he hiding from Drake?

It annoyed the knight no end when people he was trying to help turned all secretive on him. What was wrong with everybody?

And, what in Heaven's name, was Eddie Shakespeare mixed up in?

Drake could still feel the filth on him after the visit to the Stews a few hours back. He was angry with himself; how could he have not seen it coming?

The labyrinthine corridors, grimy floors, the all-pervasive

stink of corruption- Drake didn't want to admit it but the experience had affected him deeply. It had also revealed a darker side of the younger M. Shakespeare. Edmund was depraved beyond imagination.

But...calm yourself, he chided himself, that doesn't mean he's the murderer.

The invite had come so unexpectedly that Drake hadn't had time to consider his own response.

Edmund smiling guilelessly, as the players packed up and started to leave the playhouse.

Would Cousin Dupont like a night out on the town?

An invitation so innocuous, it was hard to refuse. Nic Tooley and he were planning on visiting some places, Edmund had said, the kind that stayed open all night...

Wink, wink.

Drake hadn't had a clue what they talking about. He'd sent Rod and Tod packing, commanded them to leave him be. He would either take the last ferry across the Thames or check into the Bear's Inn for the night. Whatever the choice, he would do it alone. He needed to collect his thoughts and make a proper list of suspects.

It'll be fun, Edmund had said, enable us to get to know one another. Don't wait up for me, Will, I'll be back late.

Don't care if you don't return at all- Shakespeare had retorted.

"My, my, aren't we just brimming over with filial feeling tonight?" Edmund smirked.

"Where are you planning on taking him?" Shakespeare was right to be suspicious.

"Why? Is there any particular reason you don't want me to spend time with Cousin Geoffrey?"

That did it. Shakespeare backed off and Drake found himself being led into narrow alleys and a heavy wooden door which, when opened, revealed a large-breasted ugly woman called Pearl (of all things!), who flung her ample self into Edmund's arms and exclaimed:

"Eddie! Eddie, my dear! You're back? How lovely to see you again!"

Edmund had replied in the same vein and then introduced Nic Tooley as his 'mate' and Geoffrey Drake as his 'cuz' and Pearl stepped back to admit the three men in.

"Come on in and enjoy yourselves," she sang.

The young men entered a narrow courtyard that was flanked by rooms on three sides, two stories high. Laughter, loud voices, and the clanking of glasses combined in an awful din that made Drake's ears ring. He felt he'd develop a headache if he lingered too long in a place like that.

And then Drake saw her.

The girl with the golden hair.

She must've been no more than thirteen or fourteen. Lovely, fresh complexion and sapphire-blue eyes. She looked like a doll, peering out of a window on the first floor.

Drake stopped dead in his tracks and stared at her. Pearl followed his gaze and screamed:

"Get inside, you wicked girl! I told yer, no lookin' out."

The girl disappeared.

Pearl gave Drake a look full of cunning. "She send the blood rushin' to the 'ead, doesn't she?"

Drake turned his face away, shamefully aware of the colour rising to his cheeks.

"Is she...?" he asked, unable to articulate it for the prospect was too sickening to consider.

Pearl rolled her eyes in her fat head and laughed. "Is she on the game? Now, wouldn't you like to know that?"

He was aware that the pimp-woman was mocking him and he had half a mind to knock her yellow teeth in but...

Get a hold of yourself, Geoff; you're on a mission, stay focussed.

Pearl laughed again and strode on ahead of them into a large room with wooden chairs and tables and a bar at one end. Bottles of ale, wine and other colourful liquids twinkled on shelves behind the counter.

"Sit down, have a seat, gentlemen," Pearl said. "Here's

where one enjoys oneself after the curfew hour."

"Doesn't the constable object?" Drake asked, his eyes surveying the room warily. He understood that Edmund had brought him here for the specific purpose of making him uncomfortable. It was a game. Drake was on their territory; what kind of message would they give him?

If there was one talent Geoffrey Drake had been born with, it was the knack of sensing danger. It had saved his life on a number of occasions in the past, that split second when instinct told him to duck, or thrust, or run. He wasn't experiencing any such prescient feelings right then so he wasn't really worried. Just alert. His right hand checked for the comforting feel of his dagger at the right side of his belt. It was concealed by his knee-length brown coat.

"The constable?" Pearl echoed. "Constable Sprat, you mean? Why, the good copper is upstairs with Ruby as we speak! Take my word for it, Mr. Dupont, he's in no position to object!"

Drake raised his brow. Of course. What a stupid question. He was certainly not covering himself with glory tonight. He studied the fat woman for a moment and saw, beneath all those layers of padding in her face, a look of cunning mendacity.

"So, what's it going to be tonight?" she asked Edmund and Nic Tooley. "Your companion seems a bit of a monk to me but surely you two are ready to roll?"

Edmund gave her a long-lost look. "I was hoping for Ruby but now that she's occupied...I could wait but I don't want her directly after Sprat..."

"Ah, now there's no sense in gettin' sentimental, Eddie. Ruby's a workin' girl; you'll always be the next man."

"I know, I know," Edmund conceded. Then he clicked his fingers as if a thought had suddenly struck him. "Pearl, what about the girl at the window?"

Drake started and fixed Edmund with a hard look. Surely he would not...!

"Suzanne?" Pearl's lips parted into a lascivious smile. "Ah, she's a beauty now, ain't she? Lovely long golden ringlets and all. But she'll cost you, Eddie. She's pure so I'm holding out for the highest bidder."

"What was the last highest bid?"

"Five pounds."

"Five?" Edmund's jaw dropped.

"Aye, you'll be surprised at what people are willing to pay for someone like her. I'm sure I'll get double..."

"Come now, she's just a child," Drake burst out through clenched teeth. He was unable to contain his disgust any longer.

"That's none of your business," Fat Pearl said sharply. She turned to Edmund and asked: "Who is this chap? I don't think I like `im."

"She can't be more than twelve or thirteen," Drake persisted.

"She's nearly fifteen, if you must know. She's old enough. I've had girls in here as young as nine and ten, so don't go all high 'n mighty on me. Do you know what it's like to be poor, sir?"

"How much will it cost to...to...?"

Drake couldn't get himself to use the word 'buy' though that's what he meant. He would buy her freedom and release her from this hell hole.

"What would it take to liberate her?" he asked.

Pearl shook her head. "I don't sell my girls."

No, you just ply their bodies like some reusable object in the market, like...like a jordan! That was the only thought that came to mind and it repelled him.

"I think a round of drinks is in order," Edmund interjected with a smile to relieve the tension. "Pearl, wine please for my cousin; ale will do nicely for Nic and I."

Pearl rolled her eyes. "Thought you was never going to order." She clapped her hands for the bar man and hollered: "Gordon, one mug of Bordeaux, two ales." Then she ruffled Edmund's hair and patted Nic Tooley's cheeks. "Have fun, lads."

Drake got no more than a derisive smile.

Their drinks came immediately.

Drake took a cautious sip of the French wine and was

surprised to find it top quality. A lotus in a pond. Life was full of surprises. He glanced up, aware of two pairs of disapproving eyes on him.

"What's the matter, Cousin?" Edmund said in that same mocking tone that had begun to grate on Drake's nerves. "Don't they have harlots in France?"

"That girl is a child; there should be some limits..."

"She's not a child for long. There's always a first time for everything."

"And Suzanne's first time will come sooner or later," Tooley added for good measure. "Then it'll be routine for her."

Drake said nothing but he had a sudden vision of decapitating Nic Tooley with his sword Verbera and it made him feel better.

Two drunken fellows rose from a neighbouring table and began to stagger out unsteadily. As they plodded past Drake's table, one of them brushed past Edmund and nearly fell on him. Edmund sprang up, grabbed the man's throat and punched him in the gut. The man howled in pain. Drake and Tooley got to their feet, anticipating a counterattack from the man's companion but none was coming. Edmund patted himself down to make sure his purse wasn't missing.

"Uh...sorry, I took you for a thief," he mumbled to the frightened fellow on the floor. "Here, take my hand."

Drake watched as the two drunks scampered off mumbling

about madmen and suddenly he understood where Edmund must've spent the past year or so.

Tooley chuckled. Edmund sat down again with a sheepish look about him.

"Take it easy," the barman said gruffly.

Edmund nodded at him and then faced the other two with a supercilious smile on his face.

"Don't know what came over me. I thought he'd made a move for my purse."

"Been keeping company with the likes of him?" Drake said, "Where have you been recently?"

Edmund hesitated before replying. Then his lips curled into a sneer and he said:

"Wouldn't you like to know that? I'm sure you'd love to run off carrying tales to my big brother."

Drake shrugged. "If they're worth telling. But I doubt you've been doing anything worthy of note. Tell me, why do you resent your brother so much?"

Edmund was taken aback at the sudden change in subject.

"I like him well enough but I loathe him, too. He isn't very likeable; you don't know him yet."

"He seems pleasant enough," Drake said, "And the players hold him in high esteem." Drake turned to Tooley. "Don't they, Nic?"

"Oh, aye. In general. His talent is unquestionable. He has vanquished all opposition by the power of his quill. No other company can match our popularity so, yes, we're all in awe of him."

"I expect his rivals hate him."

"Naturally. They wish he'd drop dead tomorrow."

"Tomorrow? At the Chamberlain's ball?"

Tooley reddened at his unfortunate use of the word. "I didn't mean 'tomorrow' with reference to a particular day, sir. It was a general remark."

"Yes, but tomorrow would be a good day for murder, wouldn't it? All those masks and disguises..."

Edmund eyed Drake over the rim of his mug. "So many questions. Is it natural curiosity, cuz, or something else? Just what do you do for a living? You don't seem to be in any financial distress?"

"But two men came to demand money from him at the playhouse," Tooley reminded Edmund.

Edmund nodded and turned his inquiring gaze towards Drake again. "That's true. What is it you do?"

Drake looked unflappable. "I get by. I like to spend my father's money."

"Like I said earlier, a man of leisure?"

"You could say that."

"So what are you doing at the Globe? You said you were visiting Will; haven't you visited enough? Why don't you leave?"

"Why? Does my presence offend you, Eddie?"

"Not really but I don't get you. I can't believe you're related to us and I don't understand why Will is insisting you are. I have an idea, though. Would you like to hear it?"

"I'm all ears."

Edmund leaned forward. "You're in trouble and he's shielding you. He's a respectable gentleman, the Queen's favourite playmaker so his word carries weight. In fact, his words literally bring in hundreds of pounds every month for the Chamberlain's Men. You, on the contrary..." Edmund waggled a finger at Drake. "I suspect you've been sent here for a reason and brother Will is helping you because of his own... sympathies."

"What sympathies?"

Drake played innocent but he guessed what Edmund was implying and he didn't like it at all.

"Fie, fie, Geoffrey, don't play games. We all know that Will is a closet Catholic. Our father was a recusant all his life. He was fined heavily for non-attendance in Church but that didn't deter him. I think you're one of a kind, you and Will. We've all heard of how Henry the Fourth keeps pushing collaborators from France into England in the hope of stirring up the faithful against Her Majesty."

Drake was nonplussed. Edmund's allegations were outrageous but unnerving. Being accused of collaboration with Catholics was high treason and it would send one immediately into the terrible hands of Richard Topcliffe. The treatment he would mete out would be just a shade better than what a damned soul would endure in the hot sulphurs of hell, the only difference being that Topcliffe's torture would end with the victim's death. Of course the chances of Drake's arrest were slim since he could reveal his true identity and his mission any time. But he was loathe to let down the Lord Chamberlain in such a way. There was also the small chance that the treason charges would stick anyway. Such was the level of paranoia in those days that a mere four or five witnesses stating that they'd heard a man profess the Catholic faith was sufficient ground for his arrest and preliminary investigation. In short, the avoidance of such an eventuality was clearly in Drake's best interests.

"Oh, Eddie," he said loud enough for any spies that might be lurking about and eavesdropping. "What's this really about? You're angry at your brother for not giving you a part in his plays so you're cooking up false charges against him and me? You know what? This broth is hard to digest. You're well aware that we're all faithful Protestants and unquestionably loyal to the Queen of England. This is a waste of time. Why don't you go and look for the real traitors?"

Edmund coloured and Drake knew he'd touched a nerve.

"Who put you up to this?" he demanded. "Did someone approach you and bribe you to implicate your brother? Let me guess: you've been in the nick for a while. You were doing time for some petty crime and someone suddenly realizes- or you begin to boast- that you're William Shakespeare's brother. Then what happened? They made you an offer; prove that the Lord Chamberlain's playmaker is a practising Catholic, and all charges against you will be dropped. Who approached you with the offer, Eddie? Which prison was it? Aldgate? Ludgate?"

Edmund sat very still. His face had crumbled and his eyes glistened with tears.

"It was Bedlam," he said in a strained voice.

"Bedlam?"

This was a surprise. The mental asylum up in North London? Drake hadn't expected this. Nic Tooley looked astonished, too.

"What happened, Eddie?" he asked.

"What do you think, Nic? The great William Shakespeare decreed that his brother Edmund can't act, that's what. He left me high and dry and refused to support me. I was on the streets and the Justice of the Peace arrested me for vagrancy, ironically because I was an actor! When I protested, he threw me into the madhouse. Can you imagine that? Do you have any idea what it's like, Cousin Geoffrey? Worse than hell. We...the inmates shared our cells with rats and fleas! No one cares if the entire place is infected with the plague. It would simply give the authorities an excuse to burn down the damned place! That is where I spent nearly one full year."

Edmund paused, red-faced, his eyes moist and his throat dry. Nic Tooley's lips were pursed and Drake could tell that he was deeply moved by Edmund's narrative. Drake, however, refused to get drawn into sentimentalism.

"Who approached you at Bedlam?" he asked again.

"Why should I tell you anything?"

Because the same person might be responsible for the incidents at the Globe! Drake almost blurted this out but checked himself in time.

I'll find out, he promised himself, as surely as my name's Drake. No, Dupont. Whatever. The lines blurred suddenly and Drake felt fuzzy in the head. He had to force his mind to focus.

"Don't tell me; I don't care," he said, "But it seems to me that you blame your brother for everything. William is an experienced dramatist. If he feels you don't have what it takes to be a player, then he must be right. Nic, did you ever watch Eddie perform on stage?"

"Er...I don't remember," Tooley said lamely.

"Weren't you in the Company a year back when...?"

"Aye, I saw Eddie perform once."

"Well? What did you think about his acting prowess?"

"I don't know," Tooley said, sitting on the fence. "He was all right, I suppose. But he has a bit of a problem learning his lines..."

"I do not," Edmund said hotly. "No more than the rest of the players. That's not fair, Nic."

"Apologies, Eddie, but you do. Of course that's not such a problem considering we have prompters, like. Master Shakespeare could have given you small parts; that's what we all feel. He could've accommodated you."

"Why should he?" Drake countered. "Eddie, why can't you do something else? Why do you have to act?"

"Because it's my dream."

"Then join some other company. The Admiral's Men or the Worcester's."

"Don't you think I've tried? I approached Henslowe but he turned me down because of Will. No other company will hire me because they suspect I would spy for my brother. You know, steal their plays for him. See, Geoffrey? I'm ruined, utterly ruined."

Drake shook his head. "Again, I don't see how your brother is to blame for everything. He's putting you up now, isn't he?"

"I don't give a fig for what you think."

"I know, but it would be better for your health if you did care."

At that Drake stood up, put a couple of shillings on the table to pay for his drink and said:

"I must be off; it's late. `See you at the Globe in the morning. Any more traps laid out for me, cuz?"

***

EIGHT

———

Later that night.

Near London Bridge.

Two men stood at the riverbank talking and watching the river flow gently by. Their dress indicated that they were merchants or doctors out for a late night stroll. It was just past the hour of compline so one would assume they lived nearby; close enough to make a dash for their homes when the Constable came round checking. Alternatively, they could be wealthy enough to pay, without hesitation, the fine for violating the curfew. On closer inspection, the discerning eye would note the hardened, rough features of a man known as Swindon the Slicer or Swindon of Southwark. His companion, a young man with elegant features, looked not noble but genteel. His English had a trace of a foreign accent.

They were nearing the end of a conversation.

"...so you understand why it must be tomorrow?" he was saying to Swindon.

"Aye, I'm not an imbecile, am I? Don't like the disguise, that's all."

"My employer is not paying you to like this."

"I know but a death mask? It's too common."

"That's the whole idea, Mr. Swindon. You have to blend in, not attract attention. Remember, I'll be waiting for you outside Whitehall Palace. I will get you in."

"How? You said entry is by invitation only."

"Invitees are permitted to bring a companion. You will accompany my employer. He will be wearing a mask, too. He will identify the target for you..."

"That's not necessary. I know what Shakespeare looks like; told you, I'm a regular at the Globe. Your employer even showed me a portrait of the man last time we met but I assured him it wasn't necessary."

"What if Shakespeare is wearing a mask? My employer will need to ferret him out and then let you know."

"All right, if he so wishes but I am well acquainted with Master Shakespeare and his work. There's lots of fightin' and bloodshed in his tragedies. Do you know the players use real sheep's blood?"

The other man screwed up his nose. "Gross."

"Oh? And shedding human blood is not?"

"I have never killed anybody, Mr. Swindon, and neither has my employer. Our hands are clean."

"Your hands, eh? What about yer heart? Don't get all sanctimonious on me; I know what I am. My soul is blacker than coal."

The other man glanced at him in mild surprise. "Why do it, then?"

"Because it's what I do. Don't know anything else. I have needs, too." Swindon added, much to the other man's surprise, a quote from one of Shakespeare's plays: "As long as I have a want, I have a reason for living. That's from *The Merchant of Venice*. Good one, ain't it?"

The other man nodded grudgingly.

A heavy silence followed. Both men gazed into the river's dark waters. It was so quiet now. All the ferries and boats were docked for the night. But beneath the surface was a throbbing, vibrant riverine ecosystem with its own cycle of life and death. Big fish ate the small fish; small fish ate smaller organisms; and these fed on even smaller organisms. A predatory world, much the same as the one inhabited by human beings above.

"Do not be anxious; tell your boss the job will be done," Swindon said presently. "I like Shakespeare but I like money more. I only wish I knew why. It's personal, isn't it?"

"Of course it's personal. Do you know the story of the Trojan war?"

"Trojan? Where's that?"

"Troy, Greece. It was chronicled in a Greek epic."

"A Greek epic? How in the world would I know that? I am not a learned man. You were telling me why..."

"That's the reason. The age-old story of Troy. Helen, the Queen of Sparta, was kidnapped by a Trojan Prince and she fell in love with him. It led to a great war. Oh, I remember, Shakespeare presented some part of it in his play *Troilus and Cressida*."

"Troilus and Cressida?" Swindon exclaimed. "I know that one; I saw it. Aye, I recall there was someone called Helen in it."

"That's right." A reflective look came into the other man's eyes as he added: "Shakespeare described her as a pearl, whose price hath launched a thousand ships. `Same case here. My employer has launched you to deal with the situation."

Swindon nodded. "It will be done."

"Remember to be careful. Draw Shakespeare out so that no one else is hurt. My employer will help you with that."

"All right. But I still don't get it; if your boss is not the one, then who's been topping the Chamberlain's Men?"

The other man's eyes widened in surprise. "I know nothing of this."

"I mentioned it the last time I met your employer or whoever it was. You all really have no idea?"

"We know nothing, I'm sure of it."

"Strange world you inhabit. Success has many enemies, eh? Marry, `tis no concern o' mine. I'll meet you outside Whitehall tomorrow evening."

"Six o'clock precisely."

"Yes. And then it's curtains for Will Shakespeare! A real pity, if you don't mind me sayin'."

The other man made a face. "Just keep your mind on the money, Swindon, your mind on the money. `Till tomorrow, then. Adieu."

***

For the man on the street, the Globe playhouse was an oddity the next morning. Friday, ten o'clock, and no flag up? Neither black for tragedy nor coloured ones for comedy.

Eleven o'clock, still no flags up. Finally, at a quarter past eleven, a small notice appeared on the outer wall near the entrance:

'Playing suspended today on account of the Lord Chamberlain's Ball. Shall recommence Monday afternoon with the tragedie of Prince *Hamlet* by M. Will Shakespeare.'

The news was received with disappointment. Three days

without a performance? What would the people of Southwark do for entertainment? Yes, there was bear-baiting but it wasn't as much fun. Some people wandered down to Rose alley to check out the shows there. Nothing there, either. Henslowe had apparently rented out the playhouse to a local fencing group for the weekend. What a bummer. Dull weekend in store.

The general public didn't know it but the Globe was all agog with activity that morning. The nine players who were to attend the Chamberlain's Ball had turned up to try out their costumes and to chat about the evening. The anticipation of an event is much more exciting than the event itself. Of the nine players, six were the sharers (Heminges, Shakespeare, Condell, Cuthbert, Richard Burbage and Augustine Phillips). In addition, Robert Armin and Thomas Pope would go as companions to Heminges and Phillips respectively, while Edmund had also been invited (albeit grudgingly) by Shakespeare. Drake dropped in around noon and found that some of the other players were there, too, per force of habit. They were conditioned for the theatre five days a week; it didn't feel right to be any place else on a Friday afternoon.

Cuthbert opted out round Three o'clock when a servant arrived from his home in North London with a message from his wife saying that her mother, who lived in Nottingham, had suddenly taken ill and was not expected to pull through. He left the playhouse immediately and proceeded home from where he and his wife would hire a wagon and head off on a northerly route.

The rest of the invitees clowned about in their costumes for a while.

"I do wish you'd chosen another outfit," Robert Armin said to Richard Burbage.

Burbage glanced down at his Roman toga and said: "What's wrong with being Julius Caesar?"

"You are Julius Caesar, that's what. It's hardly a disguise."

"It's a fancy dress ball, Robin; we don't need to go in disguise. We just need to wear interesting costumes. Besides, you're hardly in a position to comment, Mr. Green!"

The others laughed.

"I beg your pardon, sir," Armin responded in mock-indignation. "You happen to be speaking with Sir Robin of Locksley, also known as Robin Hood. He's a gentleman that's run afoul of the Law. All I need is someone to be my fair maid, Marian."

Burbage scoffed at him. "Robin Hood without arrows? Do you know how ridiculous you'll look carrying a bow without arrows?"

Armin nodded with a pout. "I know, but what can I do? We won't be allowed to bear arms at the Lord Chamberlain's ball. You know how tight security will be."

"Do arrows qualify as 'arms'?" Edmund exclaimed, joining in the banter. "I would think the only real arms of combat nowadays are swords and muskets. Surely bows and arrows are outdated."

"Who cares?" said Armin. "It's just a masque ball." He

glanced at Heminges and chuckled. "You couldn't look sillier if you tried; Janus, of all things?"

Heminges, who was walking around in his mask that had two heads front to back, replied: "Which one's my front? Go on, tell me."

His companions howled with laughter.

"One doesn't need to look at your head to know that!" Henry Condell exclaimed.

"Come now," said Heminges, "You'll have to agree I'm more dignified than you are, Mr. Unicorn!"

Shakespeare was going as Zeus and he strode around the stage trying to look grave and imposing but the 'thunderbolt' kind of gave him away. A wooden stick covered with white paper- that was the best he could do.

Edmund picked up a sword that was lying near the entrance to the tiring-room, a real long sword. It was not very sharp and it was one of six that they used during performances. The rest were in the property boxes. This one had been left out because its sheath needed to be replaced; the old cover had worn out.

Edmund ran his forefinger along the blade and said he'd like to try and take this into the ball. He was going as Death, after all, shouldn't he be carrying a sword?

Shakespeare objected. "Forget it, Eddie. The guards will never allow it into the ballroom."

"Why not? It's Whitehall Palace. A man would have to be a proper fool to try and create trouble there."

"And there's no dearth of fools in this world," Drake remarked from the sidelines.

He'd been sitting there quietly and observing the players.

Edmund started as if he'd just remembered Drake. He narrowed his eyes and brandished the sword with both hands, cut the air sharply, and advanced towards Drake. His manner was so menacing that the other players jumped out of the way in alarm.

Edmund swung the sword in Drake's direction again.

"You always look so calm," he said with a nasty smirk. "'Never afraid of anything, eh? I'll bet nobody has ever challenged you to a real duel. Let's have it out once and for all. What about it, Cousin Geoffrey?"

"Edmund!" Shakespeare cried, "Have you taken leave of your senses?"

Edmund ignored him.

"What about it, cuz? Afraid now? Won't you rise to the challenge?"

"Edmund, stop it." Shakespeare grabbed his arm.

Geoffrey didn't move. He remained seated where he was and regarded Edmund with an unaffected air, which only infuriated the younger Shakespeare all the more. Edmund's nostrils flared and his eyes became bloodshot. He tried to break free of his older brother's grasp.

Burbage also intervened and tried to wrest the sword's handle from the belligerent young man. But Edmund was not to be deterred. He shook himself free and swung the sword around him in an arc that narrowly missed Burbage's protruding midriff. Burbage shouted in surprise and alarm.

Everybody tensed as they realized that Edmund was not fooling around. He was hell bent on duelling with his newfound cousin.

"What do I have to do? Insult your mother?" he railed at Drake.

"You have a bone to pick with me?" Drake asked. "What is it?"

"I don't like you; that's what," Edmund spat out. "I refuse to accept you as my cousin."

"Eddie, don't be an idiot." Shakespeare tried to keep the desperation out of his tone. Edmund was challenging the best jouster in the realm! He could lose his head...literally. How long would it take for Drake to decapitate his opponent?

"Please take no notice of him," Shakespeare begged of Drake. "He has no idea..."

"No idea? Of what?" Edmund demanded. "He's a spoilt, rich boy who likes to spend his father's money. What do I have to fear? Come on, Froggie, take up the challenge."

"Eddie, you don't want to meet him in real combat," Burbage said.

"At ease, all of you. This is going to be fun," said Edmund. "I'm not going to hurt anybody."

He tottered at the edge of the stage with the sword just a foot away from Drake's chest. If he thrust right now, the blade would run right through.

Shakespeare grimaced. Why was Edmund so keen on committing suicide?

"You lily-livered, or what?" Edmund continued tauntingly.

Drake rose. His patience had finally run out. He climbed up to the stage and asked in mild irritation:

"You want to do this with or without swords?"

"Do you even know how to hold a sword?" Edmund asked in a voice dripping with arrogance.

"Yes," said Drake.

"Oh? Ever been in a sword fight?"

"Yes."

Drake's calm exterior and staccato replies rattled Edmund. A hint of uncertainty crept into his eyes for the first time. But there wasn't much he could do about it; having committed himself thus far, he could hardly back down.

"Someone get him a sword," he said, "Chris? Ollie?"

Christopher Beeston sprang up from his perch in the gallery and rushed into the tiring-room to fetch a sword.

"This is unlawful," Burbage said anxiously. "If anybody finds out..."

"Please spare him," Shakespeare murmured to Drake.

"Stop whinnying," Edmund snapped. "Anyone can tell he's never..."

Edmund paused mid-sentence. Beeston had given Drake a long sword like the one in Edmund's hand. The way Drake held it and the attacking position he'd assumed were clear indicators of an experienced swordsman. Legs slightly bent, left hand open, the perfect angle of the blade- a sudden jolt of reality for the cocky Eddie Shakespeare. Like a bout of epiphany sans its accompanying joy.

Edmund knew it was a foolhardy thing to do but he rushed at Drake anyway, waving the sword wildly and shouting like a crazed Hun. Drake had to stifle a guffaw. He knocked the sword out of Edmund's hand with the first blow. Edmund stood there stunned as Drake's blade ripped through the buttons of his doublet in one swift move. Not a scratch on the flesh but all the buttons gone.

The applause was loud and instantaneous. The Chamberlain's Men were dumbstruck; they had never seen anything like this.

Edmund's face stung with shame. He glanced around in dismay at the players' gleeful expressions.

As Drake returned the sword to Beeston's outstretched hand, Edmund attacked from behind, trying to deliver a blow to Drake's solar plexus. Drake spun around, grabbed Edmund's attacking right hand, followed up with a left-handed blow to Edmund's right jaw and puff! Shakespeare's brother went reeling across the entire length of the stage.

A collective gasp went up from the players.

Edmund lay motionless on the wooden floor. Shakespeare and Heminges rushed to his side and felt for a pulse. It was faint.

"Water!" Shakespeare shouted at Beeston.

"Geoffrey! Where on earth did you learn to fence like that?" Armin exclaimed.

"Water, Chris. Hurry," Shakespeare said as Beeston fumbled with a glass tumbler and jug at the side of the stage.

"You knew he was an expert swordsman, didn't you?" Armin said to Shakespeare. "That's why you were so worried."

"Yes, I knew. He...he's..." Shakespeare stuttered.

"Master of Fencing from L'ecole d'escrime, Toulouse," Drake said helpfully.

"That's the one," Shakespeare said. "I tried to warn Eddie but he wouldn't listen. Thank you, Geoffrey, for sparing his life; he's such a fool! Please accept my apologies in his behalf."

"Oh, no apologies are required, Will. I am not about to

take a man's life for immature behaviour. What would that make me?"

Armin was still in a daze. Shakespeare and Heminges splashed water on Edmund's face and tried to revive him. Armin stared at Drake.

"Never seen anything like it," he said. "The way you moved...Geoffrey, it's a natural talent. I know; I tutor the players in fencing all the time. No school can teach your kind of skills."

Drake grinned. If only he knew...

"Believe me, Robin, the skills I've acquired have come only after long hours of practise."

"To what end?" Armin asked.

"I beg your pardon?"

"To what end? Why did you become a Master of Fencing if you were going to succumb to a life of leisure? A strapping young chap like yourself should have a proper job instead of loitering around his cousin's theatre all day."

"Loitering around?"

Drake could scarcely conceal this amusement. He glanced at Shakespeare and Burbage and saw that they, too, had pursed their lips tightly to stifle smiles.

Oblivious to this, Armin continued in his big-brotherly way: "Yes, loitering around, doing nothing. Have you ever given serious thought to your life, Geoffrey? Have you ever considered what you'd like to do in life? To become somebody?"

"Er...no."

"I know you haven't. There's still time to change, young man..."

"Ease up on him, Robin," Augustine Phillips interjected. "You're sounding like an old crone."

"Never you mind," Armin retorted. "The lad needs to hear this."

A dull moan escaped from Edmund's lips just then and everyone was relieved to have him come round at last. Shakespeare patted his face and told him to open his eyes.

"Uh...what happened?" Edmund mumbled. "My head...I feel like I've been trampled upon by an elephant."

"Not elephants but a steed called Geoffrey Dupont!" Shakespeare quipped.

Edmund's eyes snapped open and he sat up with a start to find a number of familiar faces looming all round him.

"By Jove, I made a royal fool of myself, didn't I?" he said with a sheepish smile.

"Aye, a fool," said Burbage. "But there was nothing royal about it!"

The others laughed. Edmund rose unsteadily with his brother's assistance and rubbed his forehead.

"He's a Master of Fencing," Armin said of Drake.

Edmund shook his head in wonder. "That'll teach me to make assumptions about people. A man of leisure, eh, Cousin Geoffrey?"

Drake shrugged.

"Forgive me." Edmund extended his hand in a conciliatory gesture. "I don't know what came over me. A mismatch in my bodily humours, I suppose. Can you forgive me, cuz?"

"Let's just forget about it," Drake said magnanimously. "Let's move on. And the rest of you, those who are attending the ball, had better get on with it. It's nearly five o'clock."

"Would you like to come?" Edmund asked with newfound eagerness. "I'm sure you could come as a companion to..."

"No, thank you, Eddie. I would be out of place at the Lord Chamberlain's ball. Geoffrey Dupont has no role in the English Court."

"I see. The French connection, hmm? Didn't think of it. Well, that's a pity, isn't it, Will?"

Shakespeare smiled. The rapid turnaround in Edmund's attitude was amusing.

"Geoffrey, would you clobber him over the head again?" he exclaimed, sending the others into peals of laughter.

***

NINE

Swindon had a bad feeling about this, a real bad feeling. Whitehall Palace! What in the hell was he doing at Whitehall? This was not some dank, dark alley where his deeds could be concealed under the cover of darkness. Here he was, a common killer, rubbing shoulders with Lords and Knights and, yea, the Lord Chamberlain himself. Robert Cecil was present, too, all pompous and puffed up. Everybody was wearing fancy clothes; they seemed luminous and glittering in the light of candles and torches that hung on the walls. His own eyes gleamed through the eyeholes of his Death mask as he craned his neck to gawk at the huge Venetian paintings adorning the walls of the ballroom.

A band was playing at one end, a lovely symphony of lutes, dulcimers and harpsichords played by a group of six musicians. They were led by a young man who played the lute and looked every bit a gentleman. Occasionally he broke into song in a clear, strong tenor.

Everyone wasn't wearing masks; most of the guests were in fancy costumes that did not conceal their faces. Two gentlemen had come dressed as Merlin the Magician and they were none too pleased about the coincidence; they steered clear of each other. There were two or three Achilles as well and they glared at one another across the room. One tall man had pasted a 'third eye' on his forehead and claimed to be Cyclops, the Greek monster. Swindon also saw a ridiculous 'Unicorn' talking to a man in a bull's mask. What would they come up with next? The ladies fared better. Greek goddesses, the Lady of the Lake and the Faerie Queen ruled the evening but most of them just wore pretty gowns with lace neckpieces that were in fashion because of the Queen's fondness for them.

"That's him- William Shakespeare," Swindon's companion hissed, nudging him in the ribs.

Swindon started. It was the first sentence the man- who also wore a Death mask like Swindon's- had spoken since they'd entered together. In accordance with the plan, Swindon was received outside Whitehall by the same man who'd met him near the river the previous night. Wordlessly, the man had given him a Death mask, which he put on, and then another tall man emerged from a waiting carriage, his face hidden behind the unimaginative Death mask. He had beckoned to Swindon to follow him. Swindon had obeyed but he felt annoyed at being treated like this: ordered around through gestures. He had half a mind to walk away or to stick his knife into the masked man.

Don't you sods know who I am? What I'm capable of?

But he forced his mind on the money and decided to look upon this as nothing more than an inconvenience. It was just role-playing. So what if he had to pretend to be footman to some nobleman? It was just a lucrative little game.

I'm a professional; I must be prepared to adapt. In fact, he would consider it a step up in life; killing someone in a palace! How that would puff up his resume. Maybe his alley cat days were over.

"God, what is he supposed to be?"

The second sentence from his companion.

Swindon realized the man was referring to Shakespeare's dress: flowing white robes and a white rod in one hand.

Lamb to the slaughter, Swindon mused. White was the colour of sacrifice. He studied the intended victim in silence.

Shakespeare was at the centre of a group of people, his fellow players, probably. One man was the two-faced Janus; another wore the Unicorn headpiece. A slim chap of slight build wore Greek robes and held a model of the globe on one shoulder (Augustine Phillips as Atlas). A stocky chap (Thomas Pope) had his face painted like a joker's. There was a Robin Hood, too, and- Swindon groaned- another man with a Death mask. A heavy-set man stood beside Shakespeare clad in a Roman toga and sandals and wore a laurel on his head.

"Who's that?" Swindon asked his companion.

"I have no idea."

"Who is he disguised as?"

"Julius Caesar, of course. What's it to you? Stay focussed on the Bard; remember no one else is to be hurt."

"I know, I know. Leave it to me."

"I will ensure that he is drawn away into the corridor adjacent to this room in a few minutes' time. You go and wait there. We will not meet again. My man will see you at the Bridge at ten o'clock tonight to give you the rest of your money if you-know-who has ceased to exist by then."

"Ten o'clock? He will be done-in as soon as he steps out of this room."

Swindon's companion nodded. "I'm counting on that. Go now. Let us not waste any more time." He added with a snigger: "His last few moments alive, and he doesn't even know it."

***

"Hail, Caesar!"

Burbage swung around in surprise and found a man in a Death mask standing there. Not another, he groaned.

The mask was removed to reveal a smiling Henslowe.

"Mr. Henslowe? Couldn't you do better than that?"

Henslowe laughed. "Look who's talking. Julius Caesar?"

"But you've got a large stock of masks and disguises in your property boxes," Augustine Phillips joined in and shifted the globe to his other shoulder. "More than ours. Why didn't you choose something special?"

Henslowe chuckled. "Marry, I didn't have the time...we only just received the invitation. But Ned's done a good job; have you seen him?"

Burbage and Phillips shook their heads.

"No? There he is. See? Will. Harry, is that you in the Unicorn's head? You, too, take a look at my son-in-law."

Shakespeare and co. glanced in the direction he'd indicated.

A tall, swarthy man stood there in conversation with the Lord Chamberlain. He wore the exotic robes and bejewelled turban of an Indian prince.

"That's Ned?" Thomas Pope exclaimed, his joker's smile widening.

"Aye, brilliant, isn't he?" Henslowe sounded proud as a peacock. "It took us a good two hours to paint his face but it was worth it. I wish Her Majesty was here; she'd have been so impressed."

"So she's not attending the party?" Pope asked.

"Afraid not. She's indisposed."

"Who's that standing beside them?" Burbage asked.

A slim figure in a Sphinx mask.

Henslowe shrugged. "Nobody we know. `Must be one of Carey's acquaintances; they've been hobnobbing for a while."

"I was wondering if it's Ben," said Shakespeare.

"No, no. Ben is- believe it or not- disguised as a ghost!" Henslowe said with a laugh.

"A ghost?" Shakespeare echoed.

"Yes. He just wore a white sheet and made two slits for eyeholes. `Looks quite creepy, actually."

Cymbals clanged just then and all eyes turned towards the band. A Steward of the ball stood there. He bowed and then called everyone to attention. The first official dance of the evening was about to commence, he said, the Branle (pronounced 'brawl' from the French verb branler- to shake). This would be followed by the Gaillard, which was the Queen's favourite dance. But first, there'd be a song by Robert Johnson, lutenist to Her Majesty Queen Elizabeth. The Steward requested the guests to utilize this time to choose their dance partners.

"On behalf of the Lord Chamberlain Sir George Carey, the Baron Hunsdon, I wish you good tidings and pray your Lordships and Ladyships enjoy the rest of the evening. Our heartiest gratitude for accepting the invitation and for gracing this ball with your presence." He bowed again.

The ballroom erupted with applause.

Shakespeare and his group gathered to one side to listen to the song since none of them were planning to join in the dance.

Robert Johnson was a gifted musician in his early twenties and a good friend to the Chamberlain's Men. His father John had been the Queen's lutenist and when he died eight years back, Robert was invited to join Carey's household as an apprentice. He displayed a prodigious talent that soon caught the Queen's attention and he was appointed her official lutenist. He also directed the music for a number of plays at the Globe.

Johnson caused a bit of a stir that night when he announced the title of the song he was going to sing: Flow My Tears by John Dowland, not one of his own. The very mention of this sent ripples through the audience for Dowland, who was once a popular composer had recently left the country for Denmark after being frustrated in his attempts to obtain a position at Court. This, despite the Lord Chamberlain's patronage. All because he'd converted to Catholicism during a visit to the French Court in the early Nineties.

Johnson's choice of song was a poignant reminder of a lost opportunity due to a questionable choice of ideology. The lyrics seemed to be autographical.

"Flow my tears, fall from your springs," Johnson began,

"Exiled forever, let me mourn;

Where night's black bird her sad infamy sings'

There let me live forlorn..."

Shakespeare loved this song. It never failed to bring a lump to his throat. There was something plaintive about the tune and, of course, Johnson's melodious voice, that tugged at his heartstrings. He thought of Marie; how could he not? He wondered if she was here. She ought to be. He'd caught a glimpse of Blackburn. But he hadn't really looked for Marie for fear of finding her. He couldn't bear to face her anymore, not after knowing what he did. How could she...?

Someone tapped him on the shoulder. Another steward of the ball.

"Master William Shakespeare?"

"Yes."

"There's a gentleman who wishes to meet you, sir. He's wearing a black mask and he's gone into the corridor beside this hall. He asked me to give you this."

A small folded piece of paper.

Shakespeare's heart stopped. He knew what it was even without opening it.

The steward glanced at him in mild surprise, noting his hesitation in accepting the missive.

"Er...thank you," Shakespeare finally found his voice and took the paper.

Sure enough, it was the drawing of the heart with an arrow through it.

Bugger it! Why can't she let me alone? There were no words this time, just the drawing.

Heminges, who was right beside him, saw the folded note and inquired about it.

"Down vain lights, shine no more..." Johnson sang.

"Nothing," Shakespeare said gruffly.

He was in two minds. A man wanted to meet him, the steward said. Who was it? Blackburn? Why would he want to meet in such a clandestine fashion? Shakespeare remembered Marie's previous warning.

Attention! Il sait.

But, surely not. Blackburn would surely not try and harm him at the Lord Chamberlain's ball. No way. That was too bizarre. No man in his right senses...What if it was not a man, but Marie herself in disguise?

That was possible. She had a flair for the dramatic; she often wore masks. She had never disguised as a man before, as far as he knew, but it must be she.

But why would she want to meet him?

"No nights are dark enough for those

That in despair their lost fortunes deplore..." the song continued.

How appropriate, Shakespeare mused bitterly, as the chorus struck up again. This time, several guests joined in:

"Flow my tears, fall from your springs!

Exiled forever, let me mourn..."

Shakespeare sighed.

Damn, damn, damn. But he'd better get it over with.

Without a word to his companions, who were all engrossed in the band anyway, Shakespeare quietly left the ballroom.

***

Act Five
One
——

"Ere, sir, could we `ave words with yer?"

The man started as he gazed into the wide-eyed expression of the chubby man before him.

"Yes?" he said.

The chubby chap gave him a conspiratorial wink. "You're our sire, aren't you?"

"I beg your pardon?"

Rodney Peele made a face and glanced at Tod Makepeace with a look of disappointment. It wasn't Sir Geoffrey; the voice was too gravelly.

"What are you?" Rod demanded sonorously.

"What am I? Why, I'm a man, of course."

"No, I mean this." Rod grabbed the nose of the man's mask and shook it hard.

"How dare you? Who do you think you are?" the man said angrily. "Let go."

"I have the honour of being squire to a brave knight. Now, will you tell me what this contraption is?"

"Pegasus," the man responded, clutching his nose. "It's a mythical creature, a horse. Now will you kindly excuse me?"

Rod and Tod watched with baleful expressions as their quarry beat a hasty retreat into the crowd.

"Why couldn't Sir Geoffrey tell us straight out?" Rod grumbled. "How will we find him in this crowd?"

"Time's running out," Tod said grimly. "Now that we know who the killer is...Hey, Rod, `e did tell us. `Said he'd be in disguise, didn't he?"

"Marry, Tod, you amaze me. How's that suppose to help?"

"Didn't `e say `e'd be wearing a pink mask?"

Rod shrugged his heavy shoulders and gestured towards the guests in the ballroom.

"Can you see any men in pink masks? No, Tod, he said that only to throw us off-scent. He doesn't want us bothering him today. But we must tell him, mustn't we?"

"Oh, aye, we must. Say, let's ask that fellow, that mask has two faces. Maybe he meant 'two-faced' when he said 'pink'?"

Rod gaped at his companion. "What does 'two-faces' have in common with 'pink'?"

"I don't know but...oh, come on."

Tod, being considerably lighter in weight and on foot, succeeded in bouncing through the crowd and reaching the man with the two-face mask. Rod was a few moments late in catching up. They both stared for a while, trying to find out which was the front. Finally they got fed up and decided to stand on either sides as they accosted the person concerned.

"Got you, sir!" Tod sang, "Got you. We know it's you."

The masked man did an about turn.

"Aren't you our sire?" Tod asked.

"Certainly not," the man replied. "I have not had the fortune...Who are you look...looking f...for?"

"Our Master, a brave knight. He's in disguise but we don't know which."

The masked man chuckled. "I get the feeling he doesn't want you to know."

"Oh yes, he does. He said he'd be wearing a pink mask."

"A pink mask?" The masked man paused, and then added with another chuckle: "I w...wonder, could he have meant 'Sphinx' instead of 'pink'?"

"Sphinx! Yes, that's what he said," Rod exclaimed from behind. "Yes, Tod, that's what he said; Sphinx, not pink, you oaf."

"Good," said the masked man. "Now, perhaps you could leave me..."

"Er, one more favour, good sir," Rod said. "What is the Sphinx? How will we know it?"

The masked man glanced around the room and then pointed. "That's him, beside the Lord Chamberlain."

"Ah, we should've guessed," Tod exclaimed in delight. "He would be next to Lord Carey, wouldn't he?"

"Who is he, your brave knight?" the masked man asked and then let out a sudden exclamation of surprise: "Weren't you two at the Globe the other night?"

"The Globe? We're all in the 'globe'," Rod said, making air quotes, and Tod slapped him on the back to congratulate him.

"You were, you were," said the masked man. "You came searching for young Geoffrey..."

"Geoffrey?" Rod and Tod echoed with indignation.

"What do you mean?" said Rod. "You can't call him by his name like he's some common fellow."

"Like yourself, I'm sure," Tod added in his haughtiest tone.

"Of course I'm a commoner. I'm a mere player but... who...?"

"You're a player?" Rod said.

Suddenly he was on guard.

"Yes, I'm an actor. But, tell me, what am I supposed to call Geoffrey...?"

"Could we know your name, sir?"

"My name? Yes, of course. I'm...er...Janus."

"Janus?"

"Janus."

"What kind of a name is that?" Tod wondered aloud. "Sounds Greek to me."

"In actual fact, it's Roman," said the masked man.

"Oh, well, good even, Janus. Thank you for pointing out our sire," Rod said. "We must be off. Come on, Tod."

They scampered off.

Behind the mask, John Heminges watched them go with a queer feeling of unease. Who were these men? What had they meant by the reference to Geoffrey? Was there another Geoffrey floating around? He glanced at Shakespeare, who was chatting with Henslowe and Burbage. What's going on, Will, between you and your newfound cousin?

"Sire, sire, we've found you!" Rod and Tod greeted Drake with the enthusiasm of the Biblical shepherd who'd found his lost sheep.

Drake grinned behind his mask. "Good work, men, I didn't think you'd work out what the Sphinx is."

Tod scratched his head. "And the Sphinx is not pink."

"Pink?" cried Drake. "Do you think I'd be caught dead in pink?"

"N...no, sir."

"We have news," Rod said, hopping from one foot to the other with excitement. "It can't wait. I think...we know who the murderer is. He might be in this room as we speak."

"Or even if we don't speak," Tod added.

Drake saw the look of ardour in their expressions and his curiosity was piqued. He nodded, stepped aside, and took off his mask.

His squires grinned when they saw his face and the joy in their eyes warmed his heart. He was fortunate to have such loyal servants.

"What is it?" he asked.

"The boy is dead," Rod said. "The boy that fell...Thomas Gray. We found out a short while ago. You wanted us to check and see how he was doing because you wanted to talk to him, remember?"

"Of course. How sad. Yes, I wish I had spoken to him."

"Well you can't, sir, not now," Tod said. "Not until...you know..."

"What?" Drake asked in genuine surprise.

"Well, I don't want to be the one sayin' it, but I only mean that you can't talk to `im until you...join him someday..."

Drake smiled wryly. "Thank you, Tod, I'd never have guessed. So what's the urgency, chaps? If Gray is dead...how did he die, by the way?"

"Chest infection," Rod replied. "His ma told us he got a cough and that his body was too weak and broken to fight back. But...now here's the important part: she says that some time back when two of the players visited him, Tommy told them who he suspected!"

Drake was surprised. "In truth? Now this is interesting. No one's mentioned this to me. Which two players visited him?"

"Henry Condell and Robert Armin."

"Condell and Armin. Hmm, and they didn't mention... Did Mrs. Gray say whom he'd suspected?"

"Yes, she did. And she wanted to know why that devil had not yet been arrested and put on the rack."

Drake let out a low whistle. "Well, who was it?"

"The brother," said Rod. "The brother of the man killed at the Mermaid's."

"John Heminges?"

"Aye, he's the one."

"Did she say why Thomas Gray suspected him?"

The squires nodded, their faces gleaming with conviction.

"Poor Tommy's mum says that the dearly departed Tommy had overheard John and his brother, Charlie arguing one day," Rod explained. "John said 'Sometimes, Charlie, you make me so angry, I could kill you!'"

Rod paused for effect. "That's it?"

Rod's face fell. "Isn't that enough, sir?"

"He said the word 'kill'," Tod pointed out.

"Yes, but we often say things in anger that we don't mean," Drake countered. He raised a finger to stall their protests. "I know this seems to confirm our earlier suspicions about Heminges but we must be sure. Tell me, did Mrs. Gray say anything else? Did she mention if Tommy said Heminges knew he'd overheard the argument?"

The squires shook their heads.

A pity, thought Drake. For if Heminges had caught Gray eavesdropping, it would've given him a motive for attempted murder. Now, it was all supposition. A far-fetched theory of misdirection. Could it really be true that Heminges had killed Jeremy Smith and then attempted to kill Thomas Gray only to create the smokescreen of a serial killer, to conceal the real target- his brother, Charles? It was possible, of course, but suddenly Drake felt the theory was too convoluted and the explanation- paradoxically- too simplistic. Why would John Heminges go to such great lengths to conceal his motive for murdering his brother? He could've felled Charles anytime. Why choose such a public spot as the Mermaid's? Wasn't it too much of a risk? And how would he be sure that Charles would leave the tavern alone at a particular moment? There were too many loose ends.

Drake glanced towards the Chamberlain's Men's group. The Branle had begun and they were standing in a cluster and watching it. Suddenly Drake realized that Shakespeare wasn't amongst them. He scanned the room quickly. On his advice, Shakespeare hadn't worn a mask; Drake wanted him easily spotted so that he could keep an eye on him. But where was he now? Drake had warned him against leaving the ballroom alone. He'd extracted a promise from him to remain with the group all through the party.

"But it's the Lord Chamberlain's ball, sir," Shakespeare had protested. "Only a mad man would..."

"Oh? So you think the killer is perfectly sane?" Drake had replied. "He must be suffering from a touch of madness to do something like this. The ball is dangerous because it gives everybody an excuse to wear a mask. I don't feel comfortable about your presence there. Please promise me you'll be careful. Do not go anywhere alone. Do you swear it?"

Shakespeare had sworn.

So what had possessed him to leave the room?

"Fan out and search for him," he ordered his squires. "Now!"

***

When Shakespeare entered the corridor outside the ballroom, he was surprised to find it deserted. It was a large passageway with sturdy white pillars and tall doors on the left that opened into a square courtyard. The doors were bolted from the inside. Shakespeare was surprised to find no guards anywhere. Then he heard the steady beat of the music from the ballroom and knew that the Branle had begun; everyone, including the guards, must be engrossed in watching the dance. He waited, standing still and alert in the silent passage. Was he imagining it, or did he hear a rustling sound behind him?

"Is anybody there?" he called out.

No response.

He gazed at the note in his hand with a puzzled frown creasing his forehead. Why had Marie drawn him out of the ballroom if she didn't want to meet him? He thought of calling out her name but then decided against it. Perhaps the steward had been mistaken; perhaps the note wasn't meant for him at all. But who else could she be sending this drawing to? Sharp pangs of jealousy singed his heart and he had to take deep breaths to control the tight feeling in his chest.

This is ridiculous. I should never have come. I'm through with Marie Blackburn.

He turned to leave.

All of a sudden a figure in a black Death mask stepped out of the darkness and appeared before him.

Shakespeare let out an exclamation of surprise and took a few steps back.

"Who are you? What do you want?"

All he got in response was a grunt. The figure advanced in quick, self-assured strides and Shakespeare was shocked to see an ugly brown rope coiled around the person's hands.

"Wha...at?" he cried in disbelief.

The man moved swiftly. He surprised Shakespeare with an unexpected blow to the side of his head that sent him reeling against a pillar and then to the floor. As he tried to recover from the shock, Shakespeare felt the rope sliding around his neck. He squawked in fear. An agonizing pain hit his throat and he thrashed his limbs about in panic. He tried to wrench the rope away but it was too tight. His flailing hands hit the mask half off his assailant's face.

The man paused and released the pressure on Shakespeare's neck. An exquisite feeling of relief washed over the Bard even though he knew it was only a temporary reprieve.

What a feeling, to be able to breathe again! The sweetest, best feeling in the world!

"Want to know my identity, eh, Master Shakespeare?" His attacker spoke for the first time in a gruff, common accent. "A reasonable desire, I suppose, to know who your executioner is."

He yanked his mask off.

Shakespeare stared in surprise for he had never seen the man before! All along he'd expected it to be one of his fellow players...This fellow had small, mean eyes that peered rat-like in a fleshy, scarred face.

Who the hell was he?

The killer read his expression and laughed.

"Expected to be someone you know, eh?"

"Why?" Shakespeare croaked. His throat felt like it had been scraped with a sharp knife. The pain was excruciating. "What have I...done...?"

"What have I done?" the killer mocked him. "Marry, sir, nothin'; I mean nothin' to me. This is not personal, it's business."

He picked up the rope again and made for Shakespeare's throat again.

"Wait, wait!" Shakespeare hissed, although his throat was on fire. "Who is it? Who has hired you?"

The killer smirked. "As if I'd tell you even if I knew the name. The answer's in the note, my friend."

Shakespeare's heart lurched. Marie? Or her husband? Could it really be one of them?

The killer lunged for Shakespeare again and he got the rope around his neck again with practised efficiency. Terror filled the Bard's heart as the crushing pain returned. He struggled with all his might but the man had him in a vice-like grip. Then, just when he thought it was all over, the killer's grip slackened. Shakespeare's hands went to his throat and he tried to pull the rope off. But he was losing consciousness and his hands went limp. He heard the sounds of a scuffle. In a haze, he saw hands and legs thrashing about. His heart was thumping away like a horse in a canter and he slowly felt his breathing returning to normal. He tried to rise slowly on his hands and knees but his legs gave way and he collapsed against a pillar.

When he came to, he saw the familiar faces of Rod and Tod staring at him.

"There, there, now Master Shakespeare," Rod said. "How do yer feel?"

"Here, a sip o' ale," Tod said, putting the mouth of a bottle to his lips. "It'll make you feel better."

Shakespeare took a big, thirsty gulp but it set his throat on fire again and he coughed and retched.

"Easy, easy," Rod said, "Don't drink so fast. Back from the dead ye are."

"Sir Geoffrey's just saved yer neck," Tod said, handing

him the bottle again. "That makes you his man now. One o' us; how `bout that?"

Then Geoffrey Drake's face came into view, taut and flushed with exertion.

"You okay, Will? I hope you recover quickly. Drink some more ale and try and sit up. We really need to talk."

***

Two

———

When Drake and his squires had entered the corridor and seen Shakespeare with the noose around his neck, Drake knew he had just a couple of moments to save the Bard's life. Shakespeare's body was limp and he seemed to have given up the fight. Not a good sign. Drake covered the twenty-odd feet's distance between him and the killer in two long strides and grabbed Shakespeare's assailant around the neck. The man was taken by surprise and released Shakespeare immediately in a reflex action. He tried to prise Drake's arm away. Drake yanked him to his feet and sent him headlong into a wall. Rod and Tod stood rooted to the spot, confused and undecided.

Drake jerked his thumb towards Shakespeare and shouted at them to attend to him. Shakespeare looked dazed and incoherent but at least he was breathing.

Rod and Tod obeyed and rushed to Shakespeare's aid.

The killer had collapsed with blood squirting from his nose and mouth but, much to Drake's consternation, he stood up again and pulled a dagger from his waist belt. Drake understood that he was facing a man hardened by years of street fighting. He also noticed that the Lord Chamberlain's security had not been foolproof. The guards at the main entrance had ensured no one entered with swords, lances, arrows and guns but they hadn't searched the guests for hidden knives and daggers, which could be easily concealed in the folds of their clothes. They'd assumed that no one would actually try and create trouble here.

Assumptions, assumptions: the cause of death of many a good man. Drake had learnt long ago to hope for the best but prepare for the worst.

The way the killer brandished the dagger left Drake in no doubt about his professional abilities. This wasn't Edmund holding a sword as if it were a stick to beat a child with; the man in front of him was prepared to kill. Drake knew he must avoid getting cut at all costs for even a small gash would give his opponent a huge advantage. They sparred for a minute or so like boxers in a ring. Then the killer grunted and rushed at Drake full pelt, head forward, knife aimed at Drake's gut. A good strategy. Aim for the face or neck and chances are you'll miss if the target is reasonably quick on his feet. But the gut is a substantial area and the chest is directly above- perfect spots for debilitating upward thrusts.

Drake anticipated the attack. His reflexes were better

than ninety-nine percent of his peers and a hundred percent superior to a man in his mid-thirties like Shakespeare's assailant. He waited until the fellow had expended his energy in the forward rush. Then, instead of ducking or trying to avoid the blow, Drake grabbed the man's knife-wielding hand, twisted it in the opposite direction towards the fellow's exposed midriff and knocked him on the face with his left forearm. The killer howled as the knife sliced into the area between his ribs, crunching through the sternum and knocking the wind out of him. Drake twisted it further upwards and deeper in and the killer was gasping for breath as his life ebbed away.

For a moment, everything went silent. Drake and his squires stared at the killer's still body. They heard the music change inside the ballroom. The Branle was over; the tempo picked up for the next dance, the Gaillard, which was an energetic style involving jumps and quick steps.

"He's dead," Tod said unnecessarily.

Drake nodded with a rueful frown. He was furious with himself for killing the man; now they'd never know who'd paid the fellow for attacking Shakespeare.

"Damn," he muttered. "I must be losing my touch. I haven't been in a brawl like that for years."

"Losing your touch, sir?" Rod repeated in surprise.

"Yes. I needed the bastard alive. Dammit!"

"We'll `ave to report it to Lord Carey," Tod said.

"Bugger it," said Drake. "Yes, I'll do that in person. But first let's see about Shakespeare. How is he?"

The three of them turned to the playmaker. He was sitting now but his gaze was still disoriented.

"Marry, sir, what do we `ave `ere?" Tod said, crouching down beside Shakespeare. He'd found the piece of paper with the heart and arrow drawing crumpled on the floor. He smoothed it and handed it to Drake.

The young knight studied it wordlessly. At last! The clue he'd been searching for. A wounded heart: a woman? He'd suspected this all along. She was a noblewoman; that's why Shakespeare had been so cagey. He wondered, for a moment, if she might be Marie Blackburn for he recalled seeing them talking outside Suffolk castle. But he dismissed the thought. Surely not she...A viscount's wife...

He leaned over Shakespeare and told him to gather his wits about him and recover quickly for they had much to talk about.

Shakespeare registered the note of disapproval in Drake's voice before he opened his eyes and he knew, with a sinking feeling, that he would have to confess all about Marie.

"Your attacker is dead," Drake said with terse edginess in his tone. "Did you know him, William?"

Shakespeare shook his head. His throat was dry and sore and his neck felt like it had been wrenched out of its socket. He remained sitting on the floor with his back resting against a pillar. He was weak and fuzzy-headed, certainly in no position to hold lengthy conversations.

Drake shoved the paper under his nose and said: "Tell me about this. Who's the woman?"

"Marie," Shakespeare whispered and then grimaced as a sharp pain racked his throat. It felt like he'd swallowed a porcupine whole.

"More ale," Drake said and Tod supplied it dutifully.

"Marie who?" Drake asked as Shakespeare downed the drink. He had the uneasy feeling it would be Lady Blackburn but he didn't want to admit it until Shakespeare spoke the name. "Why is it a wounded heart?" he added,

"Failed love affair," Shakespeare said painfully. "Countess Marie."

"Dear Lord, not the Countess Marie Blackburn?"

Shakespeare nodded.

"Marry, William, you do get around! You had an affair with her?"

Shakespeare bobbed his head again.

Rod and Tod stared agape at him, then at Drake, who rolled his eyes to share their feeling.

"For how long has this been going on?" he demanded.

"Many years. From before she was married."

"Why didn't you marry her?"

"I...was already..."

"Ah, I see. You were already married, with children, I presume?'

"Three."

"By Jove. I would never have...Does the Viscount know about you and his wife?"

"She says he...knows."

"O God! Do you realize what this means?" Drake exclaimed. "Do you understand the implications? Viscount Henry Blackburn is now our prime suspect for today's attack on you and- who knows?- maybe even the three dead players in your Company."

"Three?" Shakespeare glanced up sharply.

Drake nodded. "Gray is dead, too. We just found out."

"Oh no! How?"

"Got a chest infection, poor boy. His body was already weak and broken from the fall; he died yesterday. His mother said she wanted to inform you all but she was too distraught."

Shakespeare shut his eyes and pursed his lips sadly. This was terrible news. Poor Tommy. How he wished there'd been something he could've done...He felt badly about not having visited Gray after he was discharged from hospital. Two or three other players had been over and their reports had not been cheerful.

"By the way, Mrs. Gray told my squires that Thomas had suspected that John Heminges had murdered Charles. Any thoughts on that?"

John Heminges? Shakespeare mouthed the words soundlessly. No way, that was impossible.

"I can't believe it," he whispered.

"Apparently Armin and Condell felt the same way," Drake said. "That's why they kept this information to themselves. I'll have to question them later." Then Drake sighed and pinched his forehead with his fingers. "Lord Henry Blackburn! This gives me no pleasure, you know. This was not the denouement I was hoping for. But I can't ignore it, either. How many people know about you and the Countess, William? Anyone in your Company?"

"Only Dick Burbage. He found out during our visit to Suffolk."

"Last week? Then he couldn't be involved in any way."

"No, sir."

"How do you and the Countess communicate?"

Shakespeare dithered. Drake's patience ran out.

"Hurry up, man!" he snapped. "It's bad enough that you've been holding out on me. I asked you earlier if there was anything I should know, any secrets, and you said 'no'. Do you realize how much time and effort we've wasted because of that? If I had the slightest inkling about your affair, I would have tailed the

Viscount and discovered his connection with this killer. What were you thinking, William? Is this a sodding game to you?"

Shakespeare didn't answer. He just sat there with his head hung low. Of course Drake was right; he should've come clean with him from the beginning.

"It has ended," he whispered. "Last week in Suffolk. I ended it."

"Why?"

"I discovered...there'd been others..."

"Other lovers? Of course she's had other lovers. Marie Blackburn is one of the most promiscuous women in all of England! It's common knowledge. Marry, William, she's made a proper fool of you. Do you realize that?"

"Yes."

Drake sighed. "Even so, she is nobility. I hate to break this to Lord Carey but it must be done. Rod, Tod, remain here with Master Shakespeare; see that no one else tries to knock him off! I'll go and fetch the Lord Chamberlain."

***

He knew it had all gone tits up when Swindon didn't return within fifteen minutes. How long would it take to squeeze the life out of a man? Surely not that long. He stood in a corner and kept his gaze peeled to the door of the hallway. Come on, Swindon, come on. You're Swindon the Slicer, a bloody killer; it's not like you're doing this for the first time. *Merde! Merde!* What use was it hiring a murderer if he can't even murder? A tailor stitches; an ironsmith fashions weapons; a lowly farmer draws out crops from dry land; so why in the hell can't a pro like Swindon complete a simple task like this? *Imbécile! Crétin! Le diable l'emporte à l'enfer!* Damn him to hell!

Then he saw Geoffrey Drake walk through the door. Drake, of all people! Bloody hell. What had he been up to? When did he show up? The Sphinx mask in his hand made the man in the Death mask realize that Drake had been around all evening. Not a good sign. Geoffrey Drake meant nothing but trouble.

He watched Drake's eager eye sweeping over the ballroom; then he saw Drake wading through the crowd of guests doing the Gaillard, and going up to the Lord Chamberlain.

The man's heart burned with curiosity. What had gone wrong? Why was Carey following Drake? O Hell, they were proceeding towards the corridor again. What had happened? Was Shakespeare dead? What about Swindon? Had he been captured? Or killed? Had he got away?

Whatever the outcome, surely the note would be out in the open by now. The thought of this warmed the cockles of his heart.

He smiled inside the Death mask.

One way or the other, his purpose might yet be achieved...

***

"Good Heavens! What's this all about? William? Geoffrey? Who's the dead fellow?"

The Lord Chamberlain's outburst was only to be expected. He'd come alone at Drake's request; his personal guard, armed with swords and muskets, stood in the doorway keeping an eye on them all.

"We don't know his identity yet, My Lord," Drake said. "He tried to kill Shakespeare and I arrived just in time. Unfortunately, in the scuffle that ensued, I killed him."

"Unfortunately? Why do you say that? You live by the sword, you die by the sword, and so on."

"Yes, My Lord, but he could've been useful to us alive. I could have extracted a confession from him."

"Oh, yes, you're right. Well, that can't be helped now. William, do you have any idea who he is or why he tried to kill you?"

Shakespeare shifted uneasily. He was standing now but he felt awful.

"I have no idea, My Lord," he whispered.

"But this time we have a clue," Drake interjected and showed Carey the paper with the drawing.

"What sort of clue is this?" Carey said with a frown. "Was the killer an artist? Not much of a drawing, if I may say."

"No, My Lord, that's not it," Drake said slowly. "There's something you ought to know..."

He paused and swept a glance over the hallway. There was no one apart from Carey's guards, and they were too far to hear the conversation. Rod and Tod knew already.

"Well? Go on," Carey said impatiently.

"Er..." Drake cleared his throat, not sure how to break the news. "Master Shakespeare has been...closely acquainted with Countess Marie Blackburn for several years. This drawing is their personal sign..."

He let his voice trail off as Carey's eyes widened with understanding.

"Marie? You, William? You and Marie? Does that mean the two of you were lovers?"

Shakespeare nodded, keeping his head down.

"By George, that's almost unbelievable. How...? When did you two meet?"

"Long ago in Stratford," Shakespeare said in a low, rasping voice. "She was visiting..."

"Why are you whispering?"

"I..."

"The killer tried to strangle him with that rope," Drake explained, pointing to the noose that lay beside the dead man's body. "Nearly broke his neck."

"Fie, fie! That must've been terrifying. I am sorry to hear that, William. All right, since you can't be very communicative right now, I'll spare you from giving me the details. Geoffrey, tell me what we're assuming now: that Henry Blackburn hired a killer to eliminate him?"

Drake nodded.

Carey's face fell. "Damn. Henry was in Suffolk, too, the night William was attacked."

"Yes, but as I informed Your Lordship, that incident does not seem to be related to the other incidents at the Globe," Drake said. "The pot-boy was a thief; he'd stolen from other guests, too."

"I know, but that doesn't prove conclusively that the attack on William wasn't a hit." Carey pursed his lips and rubbed his chin. Behind his thoughtful eyes, one could tell that his brain was ticking away like a clock at double speed. "But does Blackburn even know about you and his wife, William?" he asked. "I'm sorry to break it to you but Marie Blackburn has several lovers. You're not the only one, William."

"I am aware, My Lord," Shakespeare said stiffly.

It still hurt to think of all the men that had shared her bed. He had tried and tried to push these thoughts from his head but...

"She's lovely, a goddess in bed," Carey continued. "But as a wife? No, thank you. I'd sooner trust the Witch of Endor or that woman who was eaten by dogs in the Bible."

"Jezebel," Rod and Tod said.

Carey started. "Glad to know you all know the Bible. Jezebel, it was. I'd trust her but not Marie Blackburn. The point is, since she's been bonking so many fellows, why would Blackburn single you out, William, to vent ire? Are you sure he knows about the pair of you?"

"She says he does," Shakespeare croaked. "But... it's over. The affair, I ended it."

"You ended it? You dumped her?"

Shakespeare nodded.

"When?"

"Last week in Suffolk. I found out..."

"You mean you didn't know until last week?" Carey exclaimed with a laugh. "By George, she's really strung you along. What is it about women? They can really get you by the bollocks and..."

He paused, seeing the others redden, and laughed again. "Am I embarrassing you all? But it's true, isn't it? Why are we men such fools? William, how did she take it? Your ending the affair?"

"I don't know, My Lord. We didn't talk much afterwards..."

"What if she's the one?"

"My Lord?"

"You heard me. Suppose she's the one that hired this dead fellow to bump you off? Perhaps she's full of fury at being dumped."

Shakespeare shook his head. "I can't believe that," he said

hoarsely. "She tried to warn me in Suffolk, sent a warning note."

"In truth? But mightn't that have been a clever ploy to throw you off guard? She's a foxy thing, William."

"So should we treat the Countess as a suspect, then?" Drake wondered aloud.

"Please, sir, I know her..." Shakespeare pleaded.

"Yes, I know her, too," Carey said with a twinkle in his eye. "Did I ever tell you that I've had her, too, on a couple of occasions?"

Shakespeare nodded balefully. Carey had evidently forgotten his conversation with him and Burbage in Suffolk.

Carey let out a small sigh. "Well, I'm in no mood to arrest the woman. But we must confront Blackburn. Let's see his reaction. Could he be the one behind all the trouble at my playhouse, as well?"

"We can't say at this stage," Drake said cautiously. "There's no indication yet..."

"Yes, but he might hate Shakespeare's guts enough to try and ruin him by ruining the Company," Carey said. "All right, let's haul him in."

He gestured to the guards at the door. "One of you go and fetch Viscount Lord Blackburn. Tell him I need to see him right now in private. Escort him here."

"Very good, My Lord," one soldier said and went inside.

***

THREE

It's not every day that you come face-to-face with your wife's lover and are then accused of plotting to murder the bloke. Shakespeare wondered at Henry Blackburn's composure and, in spite of everything, his heart went out to the man. What ignominy! To have strangers tell you that your wife's been bonking another fellow and, excuse me, but do you happen to be the one that hired the deceased would-be killer? A bizarre situation. Shakespeare knew he would've crumbled like a loaf of stale bread, were he in Blackburn's place. But the viscount just stood there in silence and listened as Carey confronted him with the wounded heart drawing. He was an intelligent man and evidently saw no profit in denying his knowledge of the affair. But would he confess to hiring the murderer?

"The truth, please, Henry," Carey said in a tone that was firm but not hostile. "Did you pay this chap to top

Shakespeare? Do you know him?"

Blackburn stared at Swindon's body but he wasn't really looking. Shakespeare saw the expression in his eyes: apprehension. A man weighing his options. He was not bothered about the body, only about what his reaction should be.

"Yes," he said finally, surprising them all. "It was me. I... er...wanted Shakespeare dead."

His voice was toneless; he could've been talking about a dead rat in his kitchen.

Carey looked distressed. He had expected Blackburn to deny everything. "Why now?" he demanded. "The affair has been going on for years, even before you married Marie. So why did you target Shakespeare now?"

Blackburn swallowed hard. His eyes shifted from Carey to Drake and then to Shakespeare. It was fairly obvious that he didn't know the details. His expression was rigid; an iron man.

"I only just found out," he said finally.

"But their affair ended recently," Carey said. "Didn't you know that?"

"No."

"Why are you doing this, Henry? Confessing to a crime you did not commit? I am interested in justice, you know. Are you aware of the ramifications of accepting this charge?"

"I am aware of the consequences of not confessing,"

Blackburn shot back. "You'll go after her, won't you? I see the look in your eyes, in all your eyes. Wanton woman; French; the perfect scapegoat. I won't let that happen. She's my wife, George; she won't spend one day in the Tower!"

Blackburn's face had turned red with emotion and they could all see the veins throbbing at his temples. But he soon recovered his poise and said to Carey:

"Why would anybody disbelieve me? I'm confessing to hiring the killer. I don't know his name. One of my men was the mediator. No one else is culpable."

"And what about the previous attack on William at Suffolk?" Carey asked. "Were you behind that, as well? The chambermaid that tried to stab him?"

Blackburn gave him a wry smile. "As I recall, it was a pot-boy disguised as a chambermaid. Don't take me for a fool, George. Yes, I paid him to finish off Shakespeare but, as you can see, my plans failed both times."

"That wasn't a hit, Henry. The pot-boy was just a common thief who saw an opportunity and tried to rob William." Carey was getting agitated now. "Why are you doing this? Don't you realize that you stand to lose everything if your guilt is proven? Maybe even your life?"

The Lord Chamberlain's anxiety was understandable. He didn't want to make a faux-pas in this case. The idea of humiliating a powerful nobleman without sufficient evidence was not a pleasant one. It could backfire on him with frightening consequences. Yet he couldn't ignore Blackburn's confession, either, for there was the niggling doubt: what if Blackburn was in fact telling the truth?

"Where's Marie?" he asked. "I haven't seen her tonight."

"She didn't come. She's indisposed. What are you waiting for, George? Arrest me."

"Not tonight. Not at my ball!" Carey snapped. "I'll take a decision tomorrow. Go on and rejoin the party. I can arrest you whenever I wish. Where will you run?"

Blackburn shrugged. "Why would I run when I'm prepared to go to prison?"

Carey stamped his foot in annoyance. Blackburn turned away and strode down the hallway through the door, back to the ball.

"What can I do?" Carey exclaimed, stamping his foot again and, no doubt, wishing that Blackburn and Shakespeare were under it. "That man is not guilty. I'll wager my finest robe on my conviction that Henry Blackburn is not a scheming murderer! How can I send him to the gaol? Why is he doing this?"

"To protect his wife, My Lord," Drake said gently.

"Yes. I know that. He thinks she's guilty! But he's so damned noble that he'll protect her at the cost of his own title, his lands, his very life. Think about it, William, if Marie's own husband thinks she's capable of conspiring to murder you- a man she has supposedly loved for many years- how can you be convinced of her innocence?"

"I...I can't give a reason that makes sense but I know she would not..."

"Bah! That's no use."

There was a flourish near the door just then. Carey's guards were barring someone's way. John Heminges. He and Augustine Phillips were peering into the corridor and trying to enter.

"Will? Ah, there you are," Heminges exclaimed. "We've been wondering where you'd gone. Hallo, Geoffrey. Why won't these brutes let us pass?"

Carey nodded at the guards so they stepped aside and allowed Heminges and Phillips to go rushing into the hallway. They stopped dead in their tracks when they saw Carey, Drake's squires, and the dead man.

"My Lord." They bowed at Carey.

"Geoffrey, what are you doing here?" Heminges asked. "You said you weren't coming."

Drake shrugged noncommittally. He'd left his Sphinx mask in the ballroom when he went to fetch Carey. Heminges had taken off his Janus mask as well.

"You two?" Heminges exclaimed at Rod and Tod. "Weren't you looking for your Lord a while ago? You thought he was disguised as the Sphinx?"

"Aye, we found `im," Tod said happily.

Heminges looked confused.

"What's going on? Who's the stiff?" Phillips asked.

"He's a man who just tried to kill William," Drake explained. "I arrived in time and killed him."

"Good Lord!" they chorused and rushed to Shakespeare's side.

The Bard made a choking sound and stuck his tongue out to explain that he'd nearly been strangled. The two players were full of concern. They examined his neck in a most solicitous manner and grimaced at the ugly red welt round it.

"Did you suspect William would be attacked?" Heminges asked Drake. "How did you reach him in time?"

"Just lucky, I suppose."

"Well, that's it, then," Carey said abruptly and rubbed his hands together. "What an eventful evening. I shall get back to my party. Geoffrey, I'll send the Constable around to deal with the corpse. But tell your squires to remove it from here, will you? Let them take it to the courtyard."

Drake nodded and Augustine Phillips exclaimed: "Your squires? What does that mean? Who are you, Geoffrey?"

"Aren't you Will's cousin?" Heminges asked.

Carey laughed and then tut-tutted, realizing that he'd just blown Drake's cover.

"Ouch, the cat's out of the bag, I suppose," he said with

a wink at Drake. "It wasn't such a good cover, anyway. You- a commoner? Didn't work well. You can tell them, Geoffrey, I'm sure they can keep a secret. They're my servants, after all. Heminges, Phillips, remember, not a word to anyone."

"My Lord?" The players were nonplussed.

What on earth was this all about?

Carey grinned at the squires. "Would you like to do the honours?"

"Oh yes, My Lord," Rod said and cleared his throat in a self-important sort of way. "Good men, you have the honour of meeting Sir Geoffrey Drake, the bravest knight in the realm."

Heminges and Phillips stared in surprise.

"Sir Geoffrey?" Phillips exclaimed. "The Sir Geoffrey? Sir Francis Drake's nephew?"

Drake nodded, smiling.

"By George, I'd never have guessed," Phillips said. "Will you forgive us for not giving you due respect? We had no idea. Wait till the others find out!"

"No," said Carey. "Let's try and keep up this pretence a little longer. The killer has been despatched to hell but we still don't know who hired him. The case is not over, not by far. Only the four of you know the truth about Geoffrey's identity; try and keep it that way."

"Four of us?" Heminges repeated.

Drake replied: "Shakespeare and Burbage were in on this from the beginning…"

Just then Robert Armin and Edmund appeared in the doorway.

Drake rolled his eyes. "Marry, I think that's the end of Geoffrey Dupont."

How many people could be trusted to keep a secret?

Carey laughed and went back into the ballroom, while Shakespeare, Drake and the others went through the rigmarole of explaining everything to Armin and Edmund.

"Sir Geoffrey?" Robert Armin exclaimed. "You're one of the best swordsmen in the land! No wonder you worsted Eddie in less than a minute. Oh dear, I made such an ass of myself by lecturing you. Forgive me, sir. Eddie, you're lucky to be alive." He turned to Shakespeare. "So that's why you were terrified for your brother's life?"

Shakespeare nodded.

Edmund didn't look amused. He was silent for a beat and then he said: "I knew you weren't a relative, Sir Geoffrey. A knight in our midst? Fancy that. I took you for an adventurer or a coney-catcher, never a knight."

Drake smiled.

"What's to become of the body?" Armin asked, eyeing the dead man suspiciously as if he might suddenly spring to life again.

Rod and Tod started, remembering their obligation to remove the body. They did so, while the others continued talking animatedly. Burbage, Pope and Henry Condell arrived soon after and there was yet another round of explanation. All the while, Drake kept Edmund under observation.

The man was disturbed. His ferret-like eyes, tongue that kept darting over his lips, and the frown on his brow were indications of a man in turmoil.

What's eating you, Eddie boy? Drake wondered. Aren't you happy that your brother's life was spared? Why aren't you delighted to discover my true identity? Any player who is innocent would be excited to find a blue-blooded knight in the Company. So why aren't you jumping with joy?

Shakespeare noticed Drake watching Edmund and his heart sank again.

Now, what? Surely Drake didn't know something about Eddie, something bad? Surely Eddie wasn't involved in this mess?

Was he?

Drake's eyes were burning into Edmund's. What did the knight know that he- Shakespeare – did not?

Dear God, when will this end?

William Shakespeare despaired of ever getting his life back to normal again.

***

The ball ended late at half-past ten and it was a rare occasion to find so many people travelling home after curfew hour. The Lord Chamberlain had informed the Sheriff in advance, so the hour of compline was relaxed until midnight for guests of the ball. If they were stopped by the police all they'd have to do was present their invitation cards and the cops would let them go. Of the Chamberlain's Men who'd attended the ball Shakespeare, Edmund, Augustine Phillips and Thomas Pope were Southwark-based and Carey had arranged special passes for them to return to the Borough on foot via London Bridge. The option of crossing by water was not viable since the docks had closed at nine as usual. It would be a long walk; Whitehall Palace was a good distance from the Bridge and when the ball concluded, the London-based players- Burbage, Heminges, Condell and Armin- insisted on the others lodging with them for the night. Edmund, too. So Shakespeare went off with Burbage; Phillips and Pope accepted Robert Armin's hospitality; and Edmund went home with John Heminges.

The players were on a high, discussing the attack on Shakespeare and the revelation of Geoffrey Drake's identity, and they made a noisy group as they strolled northwards towards Shoreditch and St. Bishopsgate. None of them noticed the shadowy figures following them at a safe distance...

Shakespeare did not take part in the conversation because of his painful throat and neck. He was exhausted and just wanted to crash into bed. When he arrived at the Burbage residence, however, he had to endure another round of excited chatter as Richard Burbage narrated the events of the night to his wife. Naturally she was both shocked and excited and she fussed over the Bard for a while.

Would he like a hot drink? Some brandy? How about a glass of lime juice and honey?

Shakespeare thanked her for her concern but begged to be excused. "I just want to rest," he said.

"Of course, that's understandable, you poor thing," Winifred gushed. "Give me a moment; I'll make up the bed in the guest room. `So pleased to have you staying over tonight."

She rushed off to get things organized and her husband stared after her with a look of such love and affection that Shakespeare wanted to be sick! But he chided himself for his cynicism. Just because he didn't fancy his wife, it didn't mean he should begrudge others' happy marriages. A quotation from Marlowe's Hero and Leander sprang into his mind:

'It lies not in our power to love or hate,

For will in us is over-ruled by fate.'

He wondered if that was true: were people just puppets in some strange, cosmic game?

But hadn't he written in *Julius Caesar* that men at some time are masters of their fate? Well, tonight was certainly not such a time. His escape from death was fortuitous; it had nothing to do with his own efforts. Unlike that night at Suffolk castle when he'd fought off and killed his attacker, tonight he'd been overwhelmed easily. Yet he'd escaped thanks to Geoffrey Drake. So what should he make of it: narrowly cheating death on two occasions within the space of ten days? Was there really some divine purpose to his life?

What if he had not made it? Where would he be now? Rotting in some cold and icy hell? Or bathing in a fiery flood? He realized with a start that he hadn't even considered the possibility of heaven.

Richard Burbage was a fine painter. One of his oil works was hanging on a wall in the guest room. It was a picture of nature in fury, a sail boat struggling against rough winds on a choppy sea. Burbage had let his imagination run wild so the sky was crimson red and the sea water had streaks of red as if on fire. Above it all, however, at the top right corner was a cherubic white angel smiling benignly.

Shakespeare shook his head with a wry chuckle to himself. So typical of Dick; he was such a decent chap that he couldn't accept that anything was wholly evil. Even in the midst of nature's fury, he'd placed an angel to ensure that the little boat would not be destroyed.

It didn't work, Shakespeare thought. Were he the painter, he would never have put the angel in.

What good can come of anything when woman plays false with man?

After meeting Henry Blackburn, his image of Marie was shattered beyond repair like a looking glass crushed by a rock. For Blackburn had dignity and integrity. He, Shakespeare, had felt like a low life-form before him, scum on the surface of stagnant water, that's what he was. And how Blackburn had loved her in spite of everything.

Treacherous woman!

But, O, how could he absolve himself? He'd been part of that treachery for years. The pain of her betrayal still hurt but now it was compounded by his self-loathing. He, too, had stained a marriage bed. Did he deserve to have his life saved twice under such providential circumstances?

Perhaps it was a sign. Will Shakespeare mend thy ways!

"Rotten effort, isn't it?"

Burbage's voice startled him from behind.

"The painting," Burbage added as Shakespeare wheeled around. "It's downright embarrassing but the missus likes it. She insisted on putting it up."

Shakespeare smiled. "It's very good," he whispered and then winced in pain.

Burbage put a restraining finger up. "Don't talk, for Goodness' sake. I just came to see if you're comfortable, if you want anything. There's a bottle of ale on your bedside table in case you should get thirsty at night. See? Now lie down and rest."

Shakespeare nodded.

"You've had a terrible experience. You need all the rest you can get. Thank God you're alive, Will. You really are a blessed man."

Shakespeare nodded and said: "I wonder why. I don't deserve..."

"Shh! Do not stress your vocal chords. Marry, Will, none of us deserves anything. Thank the Lord for His Grace, that's all. There's no answer to the 'why's. Now we see through a glass darkly, remember? Who knows? Perhaps the Good Lord has a plan for your life."

Shakespeare raised his brow.

"Why not?" said Burbage. "I don't know what the plan is but there must be a reason He's spared your life twice in the recent past. Perhaps He wants you to write more plays."

"For what purpose," Shakespeare whispered. "They'll all be lost after I'm gone."

Burbage let out a sigh of exasperation. "I'd better leave, or you won't get any rest. No, your plays won't be lost. They're printed now. I'm sure my children will read them. The Company will keep performing them long after we're both gone, Will. We still do Marlowe and Kyd's stuff, after all. Of course they were our friends and bloody good playmakers. But you're better than them. I wager you won't be forgotten, not for a long, long time."

Shakespeare smiled and mouthed 'thank you'. Then Burbage said good night, went out and shut the door behind him.

Who knows the future? Would his words really be remembered by the next generation? Or would they be stamped out by 'the inaudible and noiseless foot of Time'? His metaphor in the last part of *All's Well That End's Well*. The thought of this title brought a pensive frown to his face. Would this end well? Would the real killer ever be caught? Or would it end...with his end?

***

The Chamberlain's Men's seamstress Mrs. Dogoody had a face that had once been pretty and a figure that had once been comely. Both these traits had enabled her to obtain a well-to-do husband who died ten years later, leaving her with two small children and a big double-storey house. She used this asset wisely, letting out the top floor to tenants and using her drawing room as a tailoring chamber from where she operated as a seamstress. She was now well into her forties and her figure had filled out. Her children Gwen and George were young adults. Gwen helped her in the shop and George was apprenticed to a grocer. Mrs. Dogoody was contented, pious and usually quite cheerful.

The unexpected death of her previous tenant had, however, cast a shadow over her happiness. Jeremy Smith had been a sweet boy. Ever polite and helpful, always ready to run errands for her in his spare time although, she suspected, that was partly due to his desire to chat up young Gwen. Not that Mrs. Dogoody minded, not, not in the least. She was a pragmatic woman and, having been widowed at a young age, she knew the value of a good husband. Smith had had prospects since being employed by the Chamberlain's Men.

In fact, it surprised her when Gwen played hard-to-get. Her daughter usually put on a haughty air whenever Smith came round but Mrs. Dogoody also noticed how the young girl sucked in her stomach and stuck out her breasts in the boy's presence.

Girls had no shame nowadays; what was the world coming to?

Now, when Smith was gone forever and his replacement was a ruder, older chap who seemed to do nothing all day, Gwen was all coy and eager and much too keen on going upstairs at every opportunity.

"Be careful, girl," the woman warned her. "If you let this chap have his way with you, you'll end up with one in the oven and no husband."

To this, Gwen had replied that the time for exercising caution had passed and what was the point of life if one could not have the occasional adventure?

It was only natural that such an attitude gave the seamstress no end of anxiety for her daughter's future so when a fancy carriage pulled up in front of her house on a sunny August morning, and two men sprung out of it, then a third- an elegant young gentleman- she thought Gwen had gotten into some kind of trouble.

What had she done?

Neither of her children was home.

She answered the authoritative knock on the door with trembling hands.

The young gentleman stood there flanked by the other two men, who were attired in humbler clothes. His servants, no doubt.

"Mistress Evelyn Dogoody?" one of the servants asked.

She nodded wordlessly, her rabbit eyes revealing her nervousness.

"I have the honour of introducing Sir Geoffrey Drake," the servant continued. "May we come in?"

The seamstress's eyes widened and she didn't react immediately.

Her silence left the men nonplussed.

"Madam?" the squire said with a raised brow.

"Oh, yes, please come in." She finally found her voice and stepped aside so they could enter. "Welcome, sirs."

Her stomach was in knots and she had to clasp her hands together to stop them shaking. But the knight had a kind face and she began to feel easier, now that they had entered politely.

There was an awkward moment as the three men stood in her grubby little drawing room unsure of how to proceed. Then she remembered her manners.

"Won't you sit down, Sir Knight?" she said, patting a chair

and coughing in the cloud of dust that rose up from it.

The knight hesitated but then accepted the seat with grace and spoke for the first time.

"I'm sorry to come calling like this, Madam, without prior intimation. Please be at ease. We'll be out of here in no time at all. I just want to ask you some questions."

"Questions?" Her dark round eyes darted from the knight to his squires, who were still standing and surveying the room.

"Is this about Gwen?" she asked.

"Gwen?" the knight repeated.

"My daughter."

He chuckled. "No, I'm not acquainted with your daughter. Please, won't you be seated in your own home?"

"Yes, yes, of course, Sir Knight."

She took the chair opposite him, positioning herself at the edge with her hands resting on her knees in what she hoped was a genteel fashion.

Geoffrey Drake gave her an encouraging smile. "You are seamstress to the Lord Chamberlain's Men, are you not?"

"The L...Lord Chamberlain? Yes, sir, I am. Is there a problem? Did I make a mistake?"

"Not at all. Please don't be anxious, Madam, it's nothing like that. I only have some questions about one of their players, the boy who died. Jeremy Smith. I believe he was your tenant?"

"Jeremy?" Mrs. Dogoody's face lit up. "Ah, such a nice lad. Very fond of him, I was. His death was so...tragic. I still can't believe..."

"What can you tell me about his last day? You were one of the last persons to see him alive. Is it true that he left early that morning?"

"Aye, sir. He would usually have his breakfast- boiled eggs, porridge and two slices of bread- down with us in our kitchen at around eight o'clock. His friends would come by round nineish...You know his friends? Alex and Ollie. Nice lads, very polite, as are all the Chamberlain's Servants. Anyhow, the three of them would stroll off together to the Globe, where they worked."

She paused, relaxing now, and pleased to find that she'd engaged her guests' attention; they were hanging on her every word.

"But that morning Jeremy came down early, just before eight, I think," she continued. "And he was in a right state, he was. `Said that Mister Burbage, the one that owns the Globe, had given him some important work. `Said he had to visit the ironsmith nearby and pick up some hardware on credit. Apparently he'd found a note under his door signed by Mister Burbage when he woke up that morning. He was so excited. Poor lad."

"Did you see the note?" Drake asked. He was delighted at the way she was clearing up things. Her story had confirmed the ironsmith, Benjamin Finch's account of Jeremy Smith's actions on the day he died.

"No, sir. Gwen and I were preparing breakfast so we were busy, like. We didn't take much notice at the time, just gave him his meal and then he ran off."

"What time did he leave?"

Mrs. Dogoody frowned reflectively. "Not sure, sir. Might've been eight-thirty. Maybe eight-forty? Something like that. It was just before Oliver showed up."

"Oliver Downtown?"

"Aye, that's the one. Downtown, the wee chap. He came round asking for Jeremy. `Said Alex had taken ill. He wanted to know why Jeremy wasn't in his room."

"Are you sure about the time? Downtown came well before nine? Wasn't that unusual?"

Mrs. Dogoody looked confused. "I don't know, sir. Never gave it much thought, to tell the truth."

Why would he do that unless he knew that Smith wouldn't be there? Drake mused.

"This is important, Mrs. Dogoody," he said, leaning forward. "Please think carefully before answering. What did you tell Downtown about Smith's whereabouts?"

The woman seemed to be taken aback. "I don't need to think about it; I remember the conversation well. I told him about the note and that Jeremy had gone off to the ironsmith's shop."

Drake was surprised. Ah, if this was so why had Downtown neglected to mention it? He'd only confessed to learning that Smith had left home early; he then claimed to have gone directly to the Globe. Why didn't he mention that he knew about Smith's visit to the ironsmith Finch's shop?

"Are you certain about this?" Drake asked her. "You told Downtown that Smith had gone to the ironsmith's?"

"Aye, sir, of course I'm sure. I'm prepared to swear on it."

Drake sat there for a moment immersed in thought. The significance of this bit of information was not lost on him. It proved that Oliver Downtown knew that Jeremy Smith had taken a detour that morning before heading for the playhouse. So why the charade? He and Smith were supposed to be together anyway. There would have been nothing unusual...unless, of course Downtown had concealed this fact deliberately so that he could pretend to turn up at the Globe ignorant of his friend's whereabouts? A careless attempt at dissembling. Didn't he know that someone might question the seamstress? And what of the note? Had he written the note and forged Burbage's signature? He lived nearby. He could've easily walked to Smith's place under the cover of darkness and slipped the note under the door.

In this context Alex Cooke's illness was also a trifle too convenient. Was he really ill that day? Or was he and Downtown in this together?

But Drake kept returning to the same question: Why? What would a young player like Downtown or Cooke stand to gain from killing their fellow players? Were they on somebody's payroll? John Heminges, for instance?

Drake pursed his lips with dissatisfaction. He got the feeling, again, that this theory was too convoluted. There were too many suspects. All of them couldn't be killers! He had got his men to trail the players the previous night when they walked to their homes in North London after the ball. One man each was posted outside the residences of Richard Burbage, John Heminges, Harry Condell, and Robin Arminge. None of them had anything suspicious to report. The night had passed quietly; there'd been no dubious visitors at anybody's place. In the morning they'd all surfaced round seven-thirty, converged at Burbage's place at nine o'clock, and then left for Southwark on foot.

Saturday morning. They must be rehearsing for Monday afternoon.

Two of Drake's men had remained outside the Globe to keep an eye on things, while the other two returned to his residence at Dowgate to report back.

Satisfied that everything was under control at the playhouse, Drake had set off for Dogoody's place in his carriage with Rod and Tod. No more travelling on foot through the Borough. Now that everybody knew who he was, he could boldly question the players and anybody else connected with the case.

Now he wanted to get to the Globe as soon as possible and question Oliver Downtown.

"Mrs. Dogoody, that will be all," he said, rising. "Our business is concluded. Thank you for your time."

The seamstress sprang from her chair and mumbled the usual- that he was welcome, that she was honoured to have met him and so on.

As he turned to leave, an item of clothing caught his eye. It was a shabby black coat hanging from a nail at one end of the room.

"Is that yours?" he asked, a tad too sharply, and the anxious look returned to the woman's eyes.

"Mine, sir?" she said.

"That coat."

It was dirty, nothing like the one Old Lily had described.

"Oh. No, sir, it's not mine. I couldn't afford something like that! It's a customer's, Mr. Darlington's..."

"The Chamberlain's Men have one like that, don't they?"

"Aye, Sir Knight. I mean, no, theirs is very fancy. Shylock's coat, worn by whoever plays Shylock, the greedy moneylender of *The Merchant of Venice*."

"So I've heard," Drake said and asked the next question as casually as possible. "Have you seen it around recently?"

"Why, yes, sir. Downtown brought it across about two weeks ago. There was a tear and I mended it."

"Do you remember exactly when he took it back? How soon before or after Jeremy Smith's death?"

"Yes, sir, it was the day before Jeremy's death, I'm sure of it. Ollie said Harry Condell was anxious to get it back because they were doing The Merchant...in a few days' time."

The day before? Drake didn't know what to make of it. If Condell was so particular about the Company's wardrobe, he would've known if the coat had gone missing. If Downtown returned it the day before Smith's death, it couldn't have been used by the killer.

Was he jumping to conclusions about the little chap's involvement? Wasn't he forgetting the important fact that Old Lily said the killer in the coat had been of average height. Downtown was tiny; she would not have missed a characteristic like that. Also, she'd said that the killer had walked awkwardly...Duncan Sole had a bad leg; shouldn't he concentrate on him? As far as the coat was concerned, perhaps it was another coat altogether.

Drake sighed. He was going round in circles again. One moment he considered Downtown as the potential murderer, the next John Heminges, and then he thought it might just be Duncan Sole and...oh, had he forgotten about Edmund?

"If I can be of any further help..." Dogoody was saying.

Drake was shaken out of his reverie. He thanked her abruptly and strode out of her house. Taken by surprise, his squires hurried after him.

***

FOUR

"I feel faint; I think I'm going to pass out," Richard Cowley exclaimed. "This news is too much to digest in one go. Slowly please, Dick, Robin, John. Let me understand this: the chap we've known as 'Geoffrey Dupont' is actually a knight called 'Geoffrey Drake'?"

"Dear God, we've been so pally with him, calling him 'Geoffrey'!" John Sinklo said, covering his face with his hands. "What will we say to him now?"

Burbage and Armin grinned. "Nothing," said Burbage. "He knows you didn't know his true identity. Why wouldn't you be pally with him?"

"But it's so embarrassing!" Sinklo said. "You knew it all along, Dick? You and Will? And you lied to us all?"

Burbage cringed. He'd known that some of the players would react like that, with expressions of hurt and betrayal. Shakespeare had a good excuse for keeping quiet: his painful throat, so he exercised this option and kept quiet, leaving Burbage to do the explaining.

"We didn't have a choice." Burbage tried not to sound too defensive. "We were under orders from Lord Carey. The success of the plan depended on Drake's cover."

"In truth? Well, his cover is blown now," Richard Cowley said, joining in the protest. "What did he achieve?"

"He saved Will's life, didn't he?" Burbage said hotly. "What's the matter with you all today? You ought to be grateful that Drake reached Will in time last night; else, he wouldn't be among us today."

"We are grateful for that," Cowley said. "But Drake also killed the only man who could tell us who was pulling the strings. That doesn't seem like a great strategy. And who was this killer, anyway? We don't even know his identity..."

"His name was Paul Swindon and he was a contract killer." Drake's familiar voice said from the entrance. "He was thirty-four-years old and he also went by the name 'Swindon the Slicer'."

All eyes turned on the tall, slim figure of Geoffrey Drake attired in a dark blue doublet with satin cuffs and black breeches that tapered off into a pair of fine leather boots; a far cry from the simple clothes they'd seen him in earlier.

Cowley reddened. "Sir Geoffrey! My apologies, I..."

"He was hired for the sum of six pounds to eliminate Master Shakespeare," Drake continued, ignoring him and, thus, squashing him like an ant. "His employer's identity is still unknown but I shall find out and let you all know quite soon. Any further questions, Mr. Cowley?"

Richard Cowley's face resembled the colour of a beetroot. "Er...ah..." was all he could manage.

"Forgive him, sir," John Heminges said. "We're all grateful to you for saving Will. It's just that the revelation of your true identity came as a surprise to some of us; that's all. Please forgive us if..."

"All is forgiven," Drake interjected brusquely. "But you must understand that this case is far from over. Swindon was hired to kill Shakespeare, only him. It turned out that the fellow had a loose tongue, especially after one too many mugs of ale and he was accustomed to boasting about his assignments. He told his pals that Shakespeare alone was his target. So that leaves us with the question...?"

Drake paused for effect.

"Who killed Jeremy and Charlie?" Robert Armin filled in the gap.

"*Voila*," said Drake. "And Thomas Gray, too. He's dead, by the way."

"Dead, sir?" Heminges exclaimed and the other players looked stunned, too.

Drake noted the expressions of dismay all round and thought, admirable; one of you is a very good actor. He decided to put the cat among the pigeons and see how they'd respond.

"Yes, he died a few days ago," Drake said without adding that he'd told Shakespeare about it last night. The Bard kept silent, too. "Tragic, isn't it?" Drake continued. "Interestingly, I've also learned that two of you visited the boy before his death and that he told you whom he suspected of being the murderer."

"What?" Heminges said and glanced at Condell and Armin. "What's this? You were the ones, weren't you? Is it true? Gray had his suspicions? Why didn't you share them with us?"

There was an uncomfortable silence as everybody stared at the two players in question. Drake thought it ironical that Heminges was the one demanding to know the name; did this mean he was innocent? Or was this a double-bluff?

"Go on, tell them," Drake prodded.

His newly revealed authority had transformed his demeanour; gone was the polite carapace. Geoffrey Drake was a man on a mission today and there was urgency in his manner. No more dawdling about. Drake was set on a particular course of action and he was determined to see it through.

Condell and Armin exchanged uneasy glances.

Then Condell cleared his throat, looked askance at Drake and said: "We're sorry to break it like this, but it was you, John. Tommy suspected you of being the murderer."

"Me?" Heminges cried with bulging eyes. "Wha...at? Why?"

The astonishment on his face was so real that Drake wanted to exonerate him right there and then.

"He was delirious, rambling," Condell said quickly. "We took no notice of it because the idea seemed so ridiculous. Tommy said he overheard you and Charlie arguing one day and that you said you could kill him..."

"I said I'd kill him?" Heminges echoed. His eyes were wild and baleful.

"No, you said you could kill him."

"Of course I said that," Heminges cried. "He was my younger br..brother! Don't br...br...brother's fight? Charlie c... could he a p...ain in the arse sometimes. Yes, we fought. He wanted a partnership in my alehouse but he didn't know the f...f...first thing about business. I said no. It was a spat, that's all. O God! He was my brother; I loved him."

"We know, we know," Armin said and put a soothing arm around the distraught man. "That's why we dismissed Tommy's allegations."

Condell turned to Drake. "Sir, John can't be the one. If we're assuming that the same man was behind all three incidents, then it isn't John. On the day that Smith's body was discovered he walked with Robin and I from Shoreditch to the Globe as he always does. We were in this playhouse all morning rehearsing. He could not have nicked out, killed Smith- Marry, I can't believe I'm even saying this- and doubled back here without anybody noticing. It's just not possible."

"And then there's the question of motive, sir," Burbage joined in. "John is a sharer in this Company; why would he harm our own players?"

Drake raised his hand. "All right, let it rest for now. But I want you all to know that this is not child's play. Sooner or later you must face up to the fact that one of you is a murderer! These incidents could not have occurred without an insider's involvement. There's no room for righteous indignation. One of you has killed twice no, thrice, considering that Gray's death was directly related to his fall during the play. You are either working alone or at someone's behest."

Drake paused and swept his gaze over the group of anxious players all round the theatre.

"Turn yourself in now and you might escape a long and painful death," he continued in a tone of steely resolve. "Otherwise I will find you and then I'll show you no mercy. I will seek you out and finish you as surely as my name is Drake!"

The young knight's declaration had a sobering effect on the players. It was impossible to miss the searing heat of his glare. No one spoke for a while. Then Drake himself broke the silence.

"Which play are you rehearsing for?" he asked Shakespeare.

"We haven't decided, sir. We were going to do *Hamlet* on Monday but I think the consensus is for *Romeo & Juliet*, considering that it was abandoned half-way last time."

Shakespeare's throat was still hoarse but it didn't hurt as much to talk as it did the previous night.

"Oh, so you're doing a tragedy again. I suppose you'll all be on guard this time?"

Shakespeare nodded.

"I don't want to disrupt your rehearsal but I want to talk to some of you in private now," Drake declared. "Where can we talk?"

"In private, sir?" Burbage repeated.

"Yes."

"The tiring- room is best, then."

"All right," said Drake. "William, I want you to stay with me. Condell, you first. Come on."

Henry Condell started but he didn't have time to recover from his surprise. He just followed Drake and Shakespeare into the tiring-room with a stunned expression on his face.

"This should not take long," Drake began without ceremony. "I paid a visit to Mrs. Dogoody this morning and I have some questions in connection with your responsibilities as Wardrobe Manager."

Condell listened intently with a puzzled frown knitting his brow.

"Mrs. Dogoody?" he parroted as if Drake had named some obscure Mongol warrior.

"The seamstress," Drake said as gently as possible, although his patience was wearing thin.

He hadn't realized how stressful it had been to go undercover as a commoner, to constantly be on guard against revealing something he oughtn't. He had never assumed another identity like that before, without his aristocratic trappings. He was very relieved to be free of that mask but he also felt that time was running out. It had been over a week since Charles Heminges' death; he felt the killer would strike again any time now. As Monsieur Dupont he had faced several constraints. He couldn't, for instance, have interviewed the seamstress personally without arousing the players' suspicions. Similarly, he couldn't interrogate the players. But as Geoffrey Drake he could revel in the authority given him by the Lord Chamberlain.

"Oh, her," Condell said in a tone still vague. "Pardon me, sir, but I don't usually interact with her. It's young Downtown who takes our costumes from our playhouse to her house most of the time. He lives close by, you see."

"Yes, I am aware of that. Now, I want you to think back clearly to the days just before the day of Smith's death. Do you recall sending a black coat to Mrs. Dogoody for repair?"

"I do, indeed, sir. Shylock's coat, we call it, though we also use it for the Duke in Much Ado and in a number of other plays. There was a large tear under the left sleeve near the armpit. Some buttons were also missing. Downtown and I noticed it a few days before we were scheduled to perform *The Merchant of Venice*, so I sent it off for repair immediately. As I recall, it was returned the day before the play."

Drake smiled. "That would've been my next question: when did you get it back? Tell me, Harry, who put it back into the wardrobe box when Downtown brought it back? You, or Downtown?"

Condell considered this for a moment and then he said: "Downtown did."

"Did you ensure it was in the box? Did you see it?"

Condell flushed for the first time. "I...er...no, sir, I did not. But I am sure Ollie would have put it in. He's very conscientious, sir. 'Gives me the keys every evening after locking the boxes. I am very particular about the keys, sir. I keep them on my person at all times."

"No doubt," Drake said wryly. "But you also leave your assistant in charge of putting away costumes and taking them out. It's all right, Harry, I'm not questioning your management style, just trying to ascertain the facts. You see, from what you've told me, it is possible that Downtown did not actually return the coat to the box that day but kept it with him and returned it the next morning just in time for the show."

Condell looked stunned. "But why would he do a thing like that? What has the coat got to do with anything...?"

"You'll know soon. One more question: would any other player, such as Duncan Sole, for instance, have had access to the coat?"

"Duncan Sole?" Condell exclaimed. "Why would he...?"

"Would he have had access?"

"No, sir, not unless Downtown or I gave it to him. But that didn't happen, sir, I'm sure of it."

Condell threw an inquiring look at Shakespeare but the Bard did not respond.

"Did you see Downtown enter that morning?" Drake asked. "Did you notice whether he was carrying something, say a small package, under his arm?"

"No, sir, I don't believe I saw him enter." Condell looked perplexed with all these queries. "Did you, Will?"

Shakespeare shook his head. "I was busy with the rehearsal. I don't recall when he entered exactly."

"You may go now," Drake said abruptly to Condell. "Do not breathe a word of this to anybody. You'll know everything quite soon, I promise. As for now, please keep my confidence and send in Oliver Downtown. Remember, not a word about this interview to anybody."

Condell exited the tiring-room with the same dazed look on his face that he'd worn when he'd entered. Shakespeare said to Drake in low-tones:

"Aren't we forgetting something, sir? The flower-seller said that the killer was of average height; Downtown is tiny..."

Drake nodded. "Patience, William, patience. All will be revealed anon. It won't take much longer now, mark my words."

Downtown entered.

He was shifty-eyed, nervous, perspiring, which was only to be expected, so Drake didn't read too much into it. And, yes, he was very short. `Must've been hard growing up in a rough place like Southwark. But Nature is a great leveller. What one lacks in one faculty, she compensates through other attributes. So blind people tend to have excellent hearing; the deaf have finely-tuned powers of observation; and short people...?

"Oliver, tell me how you came to be hired by the Chamberlain's Men," Drake said directly and Downtown's brow shot up as if the query threw him off-balance.

"Why, Saunders recommended me, sir. That is, Alex Cooke. He recommended my name to Mister Heminges."

"I know that but how did you come to know Saunders?"

Downtown tugged at his doublet's sleeves and fiddled with them. "We live close by in Margaret's Hill. We just happened to get acquainted, sir, I think it was at the cock-fighting one day. Saunders is very fond of cock-fighting and bear-baiting. We go there whenever we can afford to."

"How did you earn your living before you joined this company?"

"Er...my...er mum died. Her name was Agnes. She left me some money and I didn't really do anything, sir. Just got by on that amount, I suppose. She would've been very happy that I'm finally part of a proper company..."

"When did your mother die?"

"Last year, sir." The boy's face clouded as he spoke. "She was the one that raised me. I never knew my pa. She told me he'd died a long time ago."

"I'm sorry to hear that. What was your mother's profession? How did she earn her living? Do you have brothers and sisters?"

"No, sir, I'm an only child. My mum worked as an accountant's assistant in Paris Garden."

Drake was surprised. Not many women worked in such professions; she must have been a woman of learning. Funny, he mused, Downtown doesn't strike me as well-to-do.

"What was the name of the accountant?" he asked.

"Mr. Radcliffe, sir, but he's gone, too."

"I take it you attended St. Saviour's Grammar School?"

"Yes, sir, for five years."

"So why didn't you apprentice with an accountant? You could've earned good money. Why choose to act, instead?"

Downtown shrugged. "I suppose Saunders made it sound interesting. I'm not much of an actor but I'm learning slowly."

He threw a glance at Shakespeare in the hope of receiving confirmation of his acting prowess but the latter said nothing.

"Are you an honest man, Downtown?" Drake demanded, suddenly changing track.

The player blinked. "Pardon me, sir? Honest? Yes, yes. Of course I am."

"Then why did you lie to everybody about Jeremy Smith?"

"Lie, sir? About Jeremy?" Downtown looked horrified.

"You knew that he was headed for the ironsmith Finch's shop on the morning that he died but you told no one. Why? You only said that you'd called at Smith's place and that his landlady, Mrs. Dogoody, said that he'd left home early. Why didn't you tell the truth?"

Downtown said nothing for a few moments. He stared at Drake and the knight could almost hear the wheels churning in the boy's brain. His black eyes rolled about in deep thought. What was he thinking? Trying to make up some excuse?

Finally he expelled a long sigh and said: "Yes, Mrs. Dogoody told me about the note and about Jeremy's plan to visit Finch. But I proceeded directly here because I didn't want to be late for rehearsal. When we found his body, I was too sorrowful, I suppose. I didn't think these little things were important at the time."

"But you knew that I was worried about Jeremy's absence," Shakespeare said slowly. "Why didn't you tell me that he'd gone to the ironsmith's shop? We could've sent someone to call him from there."

"I was busy backstage, sir. I was working in the tiring-room upstairs with Mr. Condell. I don't think I even knew if Jeremy had come or not."

"And when his body was found, you still didn't say a word," Drake said.

"I was too overcome, sir, with grief. Jeremy was my best friend. I never thought all this would be important. I am sorry, sir..."

"All right, you can go," Drake said, cutting him short.

Downtown started, taken by surprise again. His eyes flashed and then he nodded and kind-of skulked out.

Shakespeare turned to Drake. "You didn't ask him about the coat, sir."

"No, I didn't," Drake said flatly. He consulted his pocket watch. "I must be off. You all continue with the rehearsal. I'll see you later tonight. Something else requires my attention right now. Got to get organized."

"Yes, sir. Any instructions for me, sir?"

"None whatsoever. Just continue with your work like it's business as usual. Try and rest your voice. It's better today but you'll suffer later if you don't take precautions."

Shakespeare nodded obediently.

Then Drake strode off with a confident, near-jaunty gait, leaving Shakespeare to wonder what he was so pleased about. It almost seemed like Drake had figured out who the killer was. He wished he could share the brave knight's enthusiasm; as far as he could tell, they had learned nothing important from Condell or Downtown. Drake's method puzzled him. But he reminded himself that the Lord Chamberlain had reposed complete confidence in Geoffrey Drake. And the Lord Chamberlain was no fool.

Patience, he told himself, be calm. I'll be as patient as a gentle stream. It was a line from his play *Two Gentlemen of Verona*, and it brought a smile to his lips. 'Gentle stream', indeed. What had he been thinking of? In his experience, streams were rushing, gushing and tripping over pebbles at full pelt, they were anything but gentle!

***

FIVE

——

Late evening the same day.

The Blackburn estate in Hereford, outside London.

The viscount and his family had just finished supper and were relaxing in the drawing room when they heard it from afar, the unmistakable sound of galloping horses. The sound became louder and louder and Marie Blackburn tensed. She exchanged an anxious look with her cousin Gerard and then sought her husband's gaze but he seemed to be engrossed in the book he was reading, a volume of Holinshed's History of England. She strained her ears to listen for the sound of carriages. Yes, there were two. Their wheels made a ruckus on the gravel on the path leading to the estate's gate. Then the sound stopped abruptly. She imagined them talking to the guards at the gate, presenting their credentials. Moments later, the horses and carriages were on the move again, getting nearer and nearer.

"Henry, who could it be?" Marie's face was drained of colour.

Blackburn lifted his eyes and saw that a terrible fear had overcome her.

"What is it, my dear?" he asked in a sang-froid tone. "Has something disturbed you?"

"Can't you hear them?" she railed. "Two carriages have arrived at our door. We have visitors, Henry, at this hour! It cannot be a good thing."

"No, dear? Well, I expect we shall soon find out."

The door of the drawing room opened and their manservant entered with a self-deprecating cough.

"May I beg Your Lordship's pardon but I am constrained to say Your Lordship has a visitor. Sir Walter Raleigh. He requests an audience urgently."

"Sir Walter?" Marie's hand flew to her mouth and she sprang from her chair.

Raleigh was Captain of the Tower Guard.

Her husband seemed unperturbed. "By all means, Ian, show him in."

The servant retreated. Marie wrung her hands as if they were on fire. Gerard Guilbert rose, too, and begged her to calm down. Then in stepped Walter Raleigh, valiant knight, veteran of many battles to defend Queen and Country. He was a tall, well-built man much like Henry Blackburn.

"Hello, Walter."

"Good evening, My Lord. Countess. Monsieur Guilbert. Lord Blackburn, I beg forgiveness for this intrusion but I've come about the Queen's business."

He paused and Blackburn looked him in the eye, calm as the sky before a storm.

"Indeed? Won't you sit down and share a drink with us first?"

"Your Lordship is too kind but I pray to be excused on this occasion."

Raleigh then rolled open a small scroll he was carrying in his hand.

"Lord Blackburn, I have the painful duty of arresting one of your relatives," he said.

No, thought Blackburn, not her! I won't let them. Muscles tensing, he steeled himself for the inevitable.

To his utter astonishment, Raleigh proceeded to turn away from him and say:

"In the name of Her Majesty Queen Elizabeth I am arresting you Mister Gerard Guilbert on suspicion of conspiring to murder Master William Shakespeare, gentleman playmaker and servant to the Lord Chamberlain."

"What?" cried Marie.

Guilbert's jaw dropped and he froze in stunned silence.

Henry Blackburn smiled quietly.

"This is preposterous!" Marie said. "Sir Walter, please. There must be some mistake. Gerard is my cousin. He would never..."

Her voice trailed off as the pieces came together in her mind. But, of course it was Gerard! He was the one who had stolen Shakespeare's portrait to show it to the hired killer! Then he'd returned it. He was in her room (and in her!) far more frequently than her husband was. Although she had suspected Henry, she had also thought that stealing a portrait of her lover was far too demeaning for him. Why had she never considered Gerard as a suspect?

Now she rolled her wide eyes at him and said: "Is it true? *C'est toi?*"

"Of course not," Guilbert snapped. "Henry, this is unacceptable. I haven't had anything to do with anybody's murder. Who is Shakespeare anyway? Why would I wish to murder the fellow?"

"Mister Guilbert..." Raleigh tried to interrupt.

"*Non, non, non.* I must protest. I am deeply offended. Lord Henry, if you cannot prevent a man from being insulted in your house, I shall leave immediately. Why would I try and harm Shakespeare, of all people? He is nothing, a mere actor. He is nothing to me."

"Mister Guilbert..." Raleigh tried again.

"O my God, it is you!" Marie screamed at her cousin. "How could you, Gerard? You've been jealous of him all along? How could you...? *Je te detest!*"

"Marie, don't be silly. These are vicious lies."

"These are not lies," Raleigh said in a loud voice. "We have François in custody, Mr. Guilbert. He's been singing like a canary."

"François?" Guilbert echoed and for the first time, his facade cracked. Apprehension flashed into his eyes.

"François? Your servant?" Marie said, putting another nail into his coffin.

"Yes, well, the man under arrest says his name is François Legrand and that he's servant to one Gerard Guilbert, cousin of Countess Marie Blackburn." With the unpleasant part over, Raleigh was having fun now. "It might be a strange coincidence, Mr. Guilbert, but I'm sure we'll get it all sorted out once we bring you face-to-face at the Tower. You see, taking out your frustration on Master Shakespeare's brother was an error of judgement. You did not account for Geoffrey Drake's involvement in the case. You did not know that Drake had kept a number of players under surveillance, including Edmund Shakespeare."

"Who is Edmund Shakespeare?" Blackburn asked.

"William Shakespeare's younger brother, My Lord." Raleigh continued: "It appears that Mr. Guilbert has been trying to destroy Master Shakespeare for some time now because of...well...Shakespeare's friendship with Countess..."

Marie blanched. Blackburn set his jaw grimly but said nothing. Guilbert's face darkened.

Raleigh continued oblivious to their reaction: "First, he tried to recruit Edmund to spy on William Shakespeare and prove that Shakespeare was a closet Catholic. By sheer chance the warden of Bedlam hospital, where Edmund had been incarcerated, was friendly with François Legrand. It appears that they met at a tavern one night and became friends. The warden mentioned that the famous playmaker's brother was an inmate at Bedlam. François passed on this information to Mr. Guilbert over here, and you, Mr. Guilbert, saw an opportunity to have your revenge. You bailed Edmund out and told him to plant himself inside the Chamberlain's company and to gather proof of Shakespeare's Catholic leanings. But that didn't work. A week went by and there was no news from Edmund. You weren't unduly perturbed because you had hired Swindon, a contract killer, by then to murder Shakespeare. François was the middleman. But he says that the first time it was you- Guilbert- who met Swindon. You wanted to be sure he was up to the task. You met him in a churchyard, of all places! By George, you have a twisted mind, Mr. Guilbert! Unfortunately for you, all that scheming came to nought since Swindon was felled by Drake last night, Shakespeare was saved, and you were so frustrated that you sent François to pay Edmund a visit earlier this evening. That proved to be your undoing. Now, will you please accompany me...?"

"I am a French subject," Guilbert said in his haughtiest

tone. "The laws of your land do not apply to me. I shall leave for France..."

"You're going nowhere except to the Tower of London," Raleigh replied and barred the doorway for effect. His right hand rested on his sword handle. "Yes, you're a French subject; so is François Legrand. But when you start murdering Englishmen on English soil there are consequences. Come on, now, you don't want to make a scene, do you?"

"Just one question, Walter," Blackburn put in. "You said someone's been murdering players at the Globe. If Gerard is guilty only of conspiring to eliminate Shakespeare, who's responsible for doing away with the others?"

"We don't know yet, My Lord," Raleigh replied. "But with Drake on the case, I'm confident that the murderer will be exposed shortly."

"I agree."

Then Blackburn turned to Guilbert. "Farewell, Monsieur. This is the second time you've committed an offence in my home and abused my hospitality. Last time you tried to steal my mother's will. I knew it was you; Drake told me. But he's such a discreet young man that he left it to me to mete out whatever punishment I thought suitable. I let you go then for Marie's sake. And, yes, there was the question of family honour and so on. But this time you tried to take a man's life! I trust justice will be done. I hope I never see you around again. Do your duty, Raleigh, and take this man away. Many thanks to you, to Lord Carey and, of course, to

Geoffrey Drake."

Raleigh bowed gently. "I will convey Your Lordship's sentiments with all speed."

Guilbert backed away from Raleigh and his eyes darted all over in search of an escape route. There were large bay windows in the room but Raleigh's soldiers would, no doubt, be waiting outside. It was no use; escape was not an option. Guilbert's shoulders slumped and he walked slowly towards Raleigh. Then he paused and said to Marie in caustic French:

"You are a fool, you know, always pining for a common poet while your true love waits patiently beside you. How could you not recognize love when it was right next to you all the time?"

He was referring to himself but Marie made a smart retort: "You're right, I've been a fool. I shall learn to appreciate my husband more after this episode."

Guilbert snarled at her and took a menacing step in her direction but Raleigh was quick to seize him by his lapels.

"Enough histrionics for now. Let's go."

They departed immediately with Guilbert dragging his heels in a manner most unbecoming of an aristocrat.

As the carriages rode away noisily, Marie turned to her husband with baleful eyes and a quivering lip.

"Oh Henry, can you ever forgive me, my darling?"

Blackburn smiled. "There is nothing to forgive. You are my wife; it's my duty to protect you. Let us put this dreadful business behind us and go away someplace for a holiday. What do you say?"

"A holiday? What a marvellous idea, darling. Where shall we go?"

"Wherever you wish."

"Alright. How about...umm... Greece?"

"Greece?"

"Yes. It will be warm and romantique this time of the year and I've never been there."

"Very well, Greece it is. I shall get everything organized first thing in the morning."

"Wonderful!"

Marie clasped her hands together and beamed at her husband. He had that look in his eye. She knew he would be sharing her bed tonight. Her smile didn't waver; she hoped it would disguise the sense of dread she was feeling.

A holiday in Greece with Henry Blackburn? What an incurably dull prospect! There were fewer men with a colder disposition than he had. Of course he was a noble man, the salt of the earth but what of love, of emotion? What of deep affection and the madness of making love with your entire being? Living with Henry was like being tied to a limp doll for the rest of your life.

Mon Dieu! She could not face it.

William, dear William, must we part like this forever? What will you do- go back to dull, old Anne? What's the use of living if you can't feel passion and high emotion and the madness of love? I am a hot-blooded woman; is it wrong for me to long for pleasure?

Greece with Henry? Ugh.

But weren't the Greeks supposed to be passionate lovers?

She smiled to herself.

Why, I might yet salvage some pleasure out of this dead marriage...

***

A few hours before Guilbert's arrest, three men had followed Edmund Shakespeare from the Globe to the Stews nearby. He was alone and on foot and they were happy about that. All they had to do was wait until Eddie had done it- how long could he spend in there? Half-an-hour? One hour at the most? They knew he wasn't a hired player; he was living off his brother so he couldn't have many quids to spare. Yes, one hour was the outer limit.

"Why can't we go inside and wait?" one of the ruffians said to the man in charge, a slim chap with aristocratic airs about him.

"Because I'm paying you to teach the bastard a lesson, not for your own sporting pleasure," the man retorted.

"Aye, but if we go in maybe we can get adjacent rooms and catch him with his pants down! Won't that be a sight?"

The ruffian and his companion laughed raucously but their employer gave them a sour stare in reply.

"I have no wish to see him with his pants down."

The ruffians chuckled. Then the first chap said: "There it is again: your accent. You're a foreigner, ain't you?"

"That's none of your business. Keep your mouth shut and your eyes peeled. We don't want Edmund to slink away unnoticed."

"We're right opposite the entrance," the ruffian replied. "How can `e escape, gov? Ease up, will you? You just don't `ave a sense of humour. Hey, I've even thought up a song for us:

'Waitin' for Master Eddie,

Who's doin' it in a beddie,

With a comely lassie,

But we're lingerin' here wi'out a sign of any...'"

The man in charge screwed up his nose as the two ruffians chorused "Pussy!" and said: "You are disgusting. But, then, what else can I expect in this Godforsaken borough? Be quiet now and concentrate on the door."

The news of Edmund's visit to the Stews made Drake sick in the heart. He knew instinctively which brothel Edmund must be visiting and his stomach churned in disgust. The lovely young girl's face leapt before his eyes. Suzanne, the girl with the golden hair. She was just a child; surely Edmund would spare her.

Drake had a bad feeling about it and he immediately departed from the Falcon's Inn, where he'd been waiting with Rod for information on the players' movements and rushed towards Madam Pearl's house on foot.

Drake had an elaborate network of spies in place, who were following the players that he considered as suspects: John Heminges, Duncan Sole, Oliver Downtown, Alex Cooke, Christopher Beeston and Edmund. Shakespeare, too, had a shadow for his own safety. The network worked as a relay with Drake's men posted at strategic points so that they could carry information forward without abandoning their charges. Tod and another squire called Gerald Gunn had been assigned to follow Edmund. They knew they were onto something when they saw that three strange men were also on the Shakespeare sibling's tail. When Edmund stepped into the brothel and the three strangers took up positions directly opposite the entrance, Tod instructed Gunn to go and fetch Sir Geoffrey from the Falcon's Inn at once. He felt certain that the strangers would accost Edmund as soon as he came out.

Drake arrived panting just in time to see the three fellows drag Edmund into a deserted alley by the side of the brothel and deliver a body blow that took the wind out of him. Gunn was following close behind, while Rod had brought Drake's carriage and parked it out of view.

"What should we do, sir?" Tod whispered. "Do you want us to save Master Eddie?"

To Tod's surprise, Drake ignored the question and asked in a rough tone: "How long did the bastard spend inside?"

"In the Stews, sir? Er...not sure. He was in and out really fast. No more than fifteen minutes, I suppose."

"Are you sure of that?"

"Well...it couldn't `ave been much longer, sir. Shouldn't we get closer and try and hear what the attackers are saying?"

Drake nodded absently and Tod could see that his master's thoughts were preoccupied elsewhere. He was relieved to see Gunn and Rod inching closer to the alley where Edmund had just received another blow, this time to the side of his left jaw. Rod and Gunn would be able to hear them now. Edmund was moaning and begging for his life.

"Sir, are you all right?" Tod asked Drake in concern.

Drake just said: "Hmm."

He was faraway, chastising himself for having neglected the issue of Suzanne for so many days. If she was to be saved, he would have to act fast. Finances weren't a problem. The madam of the brothel had mentioned an offer of five pounds; Drake would pay three times that, not to deflower the young girl, of course but to...No, that wasn't feasible. It was too much of a responsibility. Get real, Geoffrey, he told himself. You can't afford to pay for the release of every harlot in

Southwark. Manumission isn't your mission. And, remember, most of these women are there by choice. Surely not Suzanne, though. She was fourteen-years-old! The very thought of her consumed him with the desire to do 'something' to get her out of there.

Eddie, if you've touched her, I'll kill you with my bare hands.

He stood by and watched as the ruffians in the alley let Edmund have it, and imagined himself kicking the blighter in the bollocks.

Rod overheard most of their conversation.

"What did you think, Eddie?" the tall, slim man was saying. "That you could get away with it? Monsieur Guilbert pays your bail and you ignore us like we're nothing to you? Don't you remember your side of the bargain? You deliver Shakespeare to us! We paid your bail; you belong to us!"

Edmund was on the ground, shielding his head with his hands and arms.

"Please! Please!" he gasped. "I can't do it. There's nothing to tell! No evidence...I'm sorry. Please...no!"

Another kick in the side.

Edmund assumed a foetal position and begged for mercy.

"No more, please! But...what can I do? My brother's not Catholic! There's simply no evidence...argh!"

Whack. Another kick.

"Sir, we must intervene," Rod whispered urgently. "They'll kill him!"

Drake and Tod had joined him and Gunn at the entrance to the alley.

The man in charge was shouting. His accent was unmistakably French.

"You are a liar, Edmund, a vagrant, useless fellow. You promised us! You said you'd give us a weekly report at the Boar's Head Inn. What d'you think? That we'll forget it? Your freedom cost us money, Eddie, money. We want to nail the Bard. You will help us!"

Suddenly they caught sight of the flash of steel in the cold moonlight. One of the ruffians had pulled out a knife. He gazed inquiringly at the Frenchman.

"Oui, why not?" said the French chap. "Perhaps Master Eddie thinks he has no need of one ear!"

"Oh God, noooooo!" Edmund's scream ricocheted off the alley's walls as the ruffian pressed the sharp blade against his left ear.

Drake and his squires intervened and the alley erupted with shouts and exclamations as the ruffians were subdued at once. They offered no resistance. The French chap tried to fight off Rod but he soon laid down his sword when he realized whom he was dealing with.

Sir Geoffrey Drake.

Damn it! He knew the name too well. He'd seen Drake that day at the Blackburn estate when the knight had ruined things for Guilbert and Marie at the old hag Countess Blackburn's funeral.

Damn him! *Merde*! Drake was a troublemaker if there ever was one. And he was well-connected. There was only one thing to do: surrender and make a full confession. So he replied boldly in response to Drake's query about his identity:

"I am François Legrand, manservant of Monsieur Gerard Guilbert, cousin of the Countess Marie Blackburn."

Drake was not surprised. He'd finally got his man, at least the one who'd hired Swindon to kill Shakespeare. His informants had already told him that Swindon had been dealing with some foreign chap, who was probably French. Drake had instantly suspected it might be Guilbert and co.

"Master Eddie, how are you feeling?" Tod asked Edmund, who still lay there moaning and half-conscious.

"I'll live," Edmund muttered. "Thank you! Thank you!"

His face was bloodied and swollen and he could hardly move.

"He needs a doctor," Tod said.

"He'll have to wait," Drake said with barely a glance in Edmund's direction. Instead, he took Rod aside and gave him urgent instructions. "Take my carriage. I want you to present this Legrand chap before the Lord Chamberlain at once and make his confession there. Tell him that way, he might save his neck. A full confession, particularly about Guilbert's role in all of this, is his only way out. They're the ones that hired Swindon to knock off Shakespeare."

Rod's eyes bulged. "Of course! They must be the ones, sir. Swindon's friends said..."

"Yes, yes." Drake cut him short. "We have no time to waste. Proceed immediately."

"Why aren't you coming, sir?"

"I'll join you shortly. Be quick, Rod, because Lord Carey is all set to despatch the Captain of the Tower Guard to Hereford to arrest Viscount Blackburn for the attempted murder of Shakespeare!"

Rod gasped.

"He told me so this afternoon," Drake went on. "We can't let him arrest the wrong man. Ha, I had the feeling it would be that snake Guilbert. Lord Blackburn is too kind-hearted; should've turned him out the day he and Countess Marie tried to cheat him out of his inheritance. But, I suppose the situation is complicated with Guilbert being Marie's cousin and all."

Rod didn't know. He had a vague idea about the incident at the Countess Blackburn's funeral but Drake's discretion ensured that no one, not even his closest assistants, knew the details about what had transpired that day. Rod did, however, appreciate the urgency of presenting Legrand before the Lord Chamberlain. It was already six o'clock; Walter Raleigh must be getting his men ready for the hour long journey to the Blackburn estate. He gestured to Gunn to march Legrand to Drake's carriage.

"Tod will remain with you, sir?" Rod said, since Drake seemed to be preoccupied with some other matter.

Drake gave him a dubious look. "You think I need protection?"

"Aye, sir. It's dark now. This is Southwark, no place for an aristocrat to linger at night. I'll take Gunn along if that's all right with you, sir? He can return for you with your carriage after dropping me off at Whitehall."

Drake chuckled. "Well, well, Rod, I didn't know you had such a level head on your shoulders."

"Indeed, sir, I'm sure you didn't even know he had a head at all!" Tod quipped.

Drake laughed. Rod gave him a dark look and said: "Look who's talking. You think you're Socrates, eh?"

"Socrates? Who on earth was `e?" Tod exclaimed.

Rod hesitated.

Drake teased him. "Go on, tell him. You started it, Rod."

"Er...wasn't `e that Greek bloke, sir, that used to say clever things n' all?"

Tod whistled and Drake raised his brow. "I'm impressed, Rod. And I thought I was the one spending time in the company of smart men like William Shakespeare. Very well, go ahead as planned. But hurry."

"What about these low-lives?" Tod asked with a jerk of his head towards the ruffians, who were sitting in the alley with subdued expressions, awaiting their fate.

"You remain with them until the constable arrives." Drake said. "Rod, tell one of our chaps en route, to find the Southwark constable and send him here on the double."

"Right, sir, will do. Nathan is at the Southwark end of the Bridge; I'll give him the instructions." Then Rod frowned again and asked: "But why are you staying behind, sir? What's keeping you here?"

Drake smiled. "A matter of the heart, Rod, something you know nothing about! I have to see about a girl..."

***

SIX

Fat Pearl nearly slammed the door in Drake's face when her doorman announced him.

"You, again?" She eyed him suspiciously. "I know all about you, Sir Geoffrey. What will you be wanting with the likes of us, Sire?"

Her tone was heavy with sarcasm and Drake thought it amazing how a nasty woman can look even nastier and uglier when she spews venom. The effect of words on the one who speaks them was vastly underrated. A woman's language defines her in the same way her actions do.

"Who told you about my true identity?" Drake asked with one foot firmly in the doorway. "Eddie, or someone else?"

No way was he going to get bullied by a common prostitute.

"Eddie and two other players." Pearl gave up their names without any qualms. "You forget, Sir Geoff, that my girls are very popular with the Chamberlain's Men. Tom Pope was in here late last night, bursting with the news. Ditto Chris Beeston, this afternoon. You'll be surprised to find how horny news like this makes some men. Now what d'you want with us, sir? I've paid my taxes. We have the Bishop of Winchester's protection, you know, so we don't need to fear knights or lords or anybody else. State your purpose plainly, sir."

Drake looked the woman in the eye but the truth was he was surprised at how her defiance had unnerved him; he was not accustomed to such churlish behaviour.

"I'm going to come in," he said in his brashest tone. "You'd better not try and make a scene. I'm armed with a sword and dagger and you don't want your doormen getting hurt or our girls getting slashed accidently, do you?"

He hit a nerve. Fat Pearl looked anxious for the first time. Her manner transformed in an instant.

"Sire, why this talk of knives and swords in a peaceful house like mine?" She immediately stepped aside to admit him in. "This is a place for pleasure, sir, I am honoured to have you. Now, tell me, which of my girls do you desire? Shall I bring you a couple, so you can choose?"

Drake grinned. The woman was a class act; she ought to be on stage at the Globe, no less. What a pity women weren't allowed to act in playhouses.

"There is someone I'm interested in," Drake said, as she

led him by the arm to the bar. "The young girl I saw during my last visit. Suzanne."

Pearl's face darkened. "Not possible. I've already promised her to someone."

"What? To whom? What d'you mean 'promised'?"

"Come now, Sir Geoffrey, you're a man o' the world, aren't you? Suzanne is not yet...she's not been initiated- shall we say? I've been offered a large sum for her..."

"Five pounds, I know, you told me last time."

"The bid went up just now. Eddie came in and promised me seven quid. `Said he'd deliver the money by tomorrow."

"Eddie? But he has no money!"

Pearl shrugged. "That's not my concern. He said he would arrange it. He can beg, borrow or steal, I don't care."

Drake set his jaw grimly. I'm an idiot, he mused, why did I save the bastard's neck just half-an-hour ago?

"I'll double the offer," he said, trying to keep the desperation out of his tone. "I can pay you within the hour."

Pearl's brow shot up. "You are taken with her! Well, you can have her within the hour, then. For that kind of money, I'll give you my best room."

"No, you don't understand." Drake felt he was going to be sick. "I don't want to...I want to take her from here."

Pearl stopped dead in her tracks. "Are you a nutcase, sir?"

"No, I'm deadly serious."

"Impossible. Why should I let her go?"

"Because she's a child!"

Pearl smiled in a diabolical way. "Not for much longer."

"Marry, I'll pay good money. Make an exception; give her to me. I'll ensure that she has a good life."

"Oh? And how will that benefit me, sire? Haven't you heard of the goose that laid golden eggs?"

"Fie, fie, Madam, do something good for once in your life!"

Drake's passion left Pearl unimpressed. She glared at him and replied:

"Don't talk to me like that; you don't know the first thing about me, sir. I provide my girls with good living. They're happy here. Nobody is detained by force. Suzanne is an orphan. She's been cared for ever since her mother died in the plague ten years ago. So don't talk to me of good deeds. And what makes you think she'll want to go with you? What are you offering her, anyway?"

"A better life; a life of decency."

"Will you marry her- a girl raised in a whorehouse?"

Drake hesitated. This was the part his hadn't worked out.

It was awkward. He'd just turned down a proposal from the Pompadours in France and his mother was hopping mad at him; the prospect of Suzanne as a daughter-in-law, even in the distant future, was unlikely to alleviate the situation.

"She's too young for marriage," he replied cleverly.

"In truth, sir? Then what do you intend to do with her? Raise her on your charity? What happens when she grows up?"

"We'll see; there's time yet. If I can't...don't marry her, I'll ensure that she marries well. You must see my point of view: anything is better than letting her get ravaged by some lecherous pig at the age of fourteen!"

Pearl sighed. She said nothing for a moment but Drake saw in those small eyes of her, the first hint of compassion.

"Marry, sir, you're a romantic; I would ne'er have thought of it. You, of all people?"

Drake grinned. "Me neither. I wasn't, until I saw her."

"I'm not surprised. She is a beauty." Fat Pearl exhaled deeply. "But what shall I do about Eddie? He's an old customer."

"Eddie is in no position to do anything to anyone for some days to come. He has just suffered a beating directly after departing from this house."

Pearl looked shocked. "Alack! Is he all right? Who beat him? Why?"

"Never mind all that. He's fine. I saved his skin."

"You, sir?"

"Yes, but if I'd known about him bidding for..."

"But why was he attacked?"

"He got involved with the wrong people. `Ever heard of the saying: when you sup with the devil make sure you use a very long spoon'? Eddie didn't. Anyhow, the constable has taken him to the infirmary. He'll survive."

"Poor chap." Pearl went quiet for a while. Drake waited impatiently, pacing the floor and stamping his feet about. Then she nodded heavily, and said:

"Give me a day or two to prepare her. I'll have to talk to her and try and convince her. You may not believe it, but she's been loved and taken care of all these years. But, yes, she doesn't know about what is to come if she remains...If she agrees, I'll release her into your charge for the sum of...fifteen pounds."

"Agreed."

"Can I get the amount in gold sovereigns?"

Drake thought about this for a moment. He wasn't sure if he wanted to arrange that. "I'll see what I can do. You get Suzanne ready; I'll come round tomorrow evening."

"That's too soon. Make it the day after, sir. There are things to be arranged. If she agrees, she'll have to get her things together...It'll be a big change for her, Sir Geoff."

"Done. The day after, it is. Monday evening. Good night now."

"You will return, sir? I'll be refusing other bids for her until Monday night, then."

Again, Drake's stomach churned. The very idea of men bidding to defile the young girl, it was repugnant. Worse still, was the casual manner in which the madam was discussing it.

He decided he'd better give Pearl something as down payment so he fished in his pocket and found two pounds in change.

"Here, keep this as a deposit. Look after her and don't let anyone touch her, Pearl. I'll be back the day after with the rest of the money, as surely as my name is Drake!"

***

Sunday morning.

The Chamberlain's Men based in Southwark were filing out of St. Saviour's church after the eight a.m. service. They'd all turned up: Shakespeare, Augustine Phillips and his family, Thomas Pope, Alexander Cooke, Oliver Downtown, John Sinklo, Richard Cowley, Duncan Sole, James Sands and Christopher Beeston. The priest had said a special prayer for Edmund, thanking the Lord for sparing his life and also petitioning for his speedy recovery. Drake had broken the news to Shakespeare the night before after his visit to the Stews, about the attack on Edmund and the subsequent revelation of Gerard Guilbert's role as conspirator. He also informed Shakespeare about Edmund's complicity in the matter, how he had got out of Bedlam by promising to betray his brother.

"But he did not go through with it," Drake said in spite of himself, to soften the blow. "Guilbert's men set upon him because he did not sell you out, William."

He'd left it at that, knowing that the Bard would need some time to come to terms with what he'd just learnt.

Shakespeare didn't react. He just thanked Drake with a vacant stare as if the knight wasn't even there.

"You can visit Edmund in the infirmary, if you like," Drake said. "They say he'll be discharged in the morning. He has a broken nose, a swollen jaw and aches and pains all over but I fear it's his pride that has suffered the most. I've taken care of the costs, by the way, so he can simply walk- no, limp- out in the morning."

"Thank you, sir. Your kindness leaves me speechless. Please let me repay you, permit me to cover this." "No need, my good fellow. These are trifles, as far as I'm concerned. I only hope that Edmund learns his lesson. He ought to know that if you play with fire, you will get burned. I suppose he didn't have much of a choice, though; Bedlam is an infernal place. A man will do anything to get out of it."

Why am I making excuses for the bastard? Drake wondered even as he spoke these words. He doesn't deserve it. Think of Suzanne; think of what he intended to do to her!

Shakespeare nodded quietly. "Thank you again, sir."

"Do you want to see him tonight?" Drake inquired.

"Not tonight. Maybe in the morning, after Church. I'll have to tell the others..."

Shakespeare's voice trailed off again and the glassy look returned to his eyes.

Drake bade him good night and then departed.

There were so many occasions in life when words become powerless, impotent and like empty gongs clanging away soundlessly. No one could help Shakespeare, Drake mused. He had to wrestle with his inner demons and work things out for himself. Only he could decide how to deal with his deceitful brother. It must be so painful for him to consider that Eddie had joined hands with the very men who'd tried to kill him! A terrible nightmare. Drake thought the Bard would do well to wake up and face reality. But what does one do when the real world is more frightening than the world of dreams?

After greeting the priest and complimenting him on the sermon, the players huddled together in the churchyard to talk; everyone except Shakespeare, who found an empty bench and sat on it alone, in a meditative mood.

"Wish there was something we could do to cheer him up," Phillips said with a cluck of regret. "By George, I could wring that bastard Eddie's neck! How could he do that to his own brother?"

Shakespeare had told them everything just before the service.

"I always knew he was a sneaky fellow but I never expected this," Thomas Pope agreed. "Why did Sir Geoffrey save his skin? He should've left Eddie to the mercy of those ruffians. `Would've served him right."

"Hmm, that was a stroke of undeserved luck for Edmund," said Phillips. "I wonder, though, how did Drake happen to arrive on the scene at precisely the correct time?"

"I was about to say that, too," Pope said. "He does seem to be kind of omnipresent, doesn't he? Arriving in time to save Will; then reaching in the nick of time to rescue Eddie...Very strange."

"It's not strange; he must've had Eddie followed," Beeston said abruptly.

"Oh my goodness, you're right," Pope exclaimed. "That would explain it. He's been following Eddie. He's a knight, after all, and he's on a mission blessed by Lord Carey himself. So he's not short of manpower. He must have suspected that Edmund was up to no good."

"My word, isn't he a crafty chap?" John Sinklo said with a laugh. "I wonder if he's had any of us shadowed?"

"You know, I think he has," Duncan Sole said slowly. "I've had a feeling during the past few days that someone's watching me. I mentioned it to you, James, didn't I?"

Sands nodded.

"What have you done to make him suspicious?" Phillips said. "You must be mistaken, Duncan. Why would Drake have you followed? You have nothing to be guilty of."

"In faith, I do not. But maybe Drake thinks I do! I can't explain it, but I swear I've caught a man tailing me once or twice in the past few days."

"It sounds unlikely," Phillips said. "You must be mistaken."

"I don't think he is...mistaken, that is," Christopher Beeston piped up. "I, too, have felt I'm being followed. Drake is up to something."

"That's very odd," said Phillips. "I wonder if Will knows anything about it. Anybody else felt they're being shadowed? Ollie? Richard? Jim?"

Downtown, Cooke and Sands shook their heads, as did Cowley, Pope, and Sinklo. They hadn't noticed anyone on their tail.

"You know what? Let's ignore it," Thomas Pope said. "If Sir Geoff is having us followed, it must be for a damned good reason. He's under orders from Lord Carey, remember? And if we're not up to anything illegal, how does it matter? Let Drake's men or the whole of Southwark follow us around to their hearts content; what difference does it make?"

"None, I suppose," Duncan Sole said. "It's disconcerting, that's all. But I suppose there are worse things to be endured.

Think of poor Will, being betrayed by his brother like that..."

All eyes turned on Shakespeare, who was still sitting on the bench statue-like, with one hand under his chin. A forlorn figure. He hadn't seemed to have moved in ten minutes.

"The private wound is deepest," Pope remarked, recalling a line from *Two Gentlemen of Verona*. Then he smiled, and added:

"Where would we be

Without Will's lines

To comfort us

 In trying times?"

His companions chuckled. Richard Cowley made a show of clapping without making a sound.

At that moment, a sonorous voice cracked the air.

"The Chamberlain's Servants! Is anybody here from the Lord Chamberlain's Servants?"

The owner of that authoritative tone was a hefty man dressed in official liveries. Green breeches, plain brown doublet and a brown hat. He carried no sword but the sheath of a dagger hung from the side of his leather belt.

His cry had shaken Shakespeare out of his reverie but he made no move to rise from the bench so Augustine Phillips stepped forward in acknowledgement.

"We're here, sir."

The official waded through the crowd of churchgoers and went up to Phillips. He had a scroll in hand.

"You are a member of the Lord Chamberlain's players?"

"Aye, sir. Augustine Phillips at your service. I'm the Company Manager."

The official consulted a paper in his hand. "Where is Mr. Richard Burbage?"

"Mr. Burbage lives in Shoreditch and he attends St. Leonard's Church there. I expect you would find him outside ..."

"No, it's all right, you'll do. I bring summons from Lord Tilney, Her Majesty's Master of the Revels. Here."

He handed Phillips the scroll.

Phillips opened it and the others crowded around him. It was an order for a command performance of *Richard the Third* at Whitehall Palace on Friday next week.

Shivers of excitement passed through the players. Such an honour! Summons like these delighted them always.

"Dick will be thrilled," Phillips exclaimed. "He considers Richard the Third his best role."

Shakespeare ambled across, curiosity having got the better of his melancholy, and he read the summons. A broad smile spread across his face.

"Do you have a response?" the messenger inquired.

"Yes, yes, of course," Phillips said eagerly. "Please thank Lord Tilney for this honour. Tell His Lordship we shall obey with all our hearts."

The messenger nodded. The expected reply, obviously. "Lord Tilney has also instructed me to warn you not to deviate from the approved text. He will, of course, be present to monitor the performance."

"That is only to be expected," Phillips said, not letting his smile turn into a scowl. "It will be as he orders."

"Very good. Please present yourselves at His Lordship's office at ten o'clock tomorrow morning to discuss the details, costumes, set pieces, and so on. He requires Mr. Burbage and Mr. Heminges to be present."

Phillips nodded. "We shall convey the message; they'll be there."

The messenger tilted his head. "That's all. Good day to you all."

They wished him the same and then he left.

The little group began to chatter excitedly. A command performance again! At long last. How their hearts had burned when the Admiral's Men were invited to perform for the Danish King; now it was their turn again. The order was a sign of the queen's renewed confidence in the Chamberlain's Men. Thomas Pope let out a whoop of joy.

"To work, gentlemen!" he exclaimed. "Sunday or not. By George, we have our work cut out. We need to prepare for tomorrow's show and then start working for the palace performance. Someone has to inform the others. Ollie, you and Chris go now and tell them all in Shoreditch to get their arses down to the playhouse on the double. We have a lot to do. Don't forget to tell Robin Armin, too."

Downtown and Beeston grinned. "Certainly, Mr. Pope."

Augustine Phillips turned to Shakespeare. "This should cheer you up."

"It's wonderful, yes," the Bard replied with a glum look. "But what do I do about Eddie? I don't want to ever see his face again, let alone take care of him."

"Forget and forgive, Will, your words in *King Lear*," Phillips said.

Shakespeare grimaced. "'Hardly an original line. And why do you all insist on throwing my words back at me?"

Phillips grinned. "That's our revenge for your making us memorize so many difficult lines!"

"In faith, you are most kind today."

Phillips put an affectionate arm around the Bard's shoulder. "Come now, Will, let us be merry. Let's focus on the joy of this event. A command performance before Her Majesty! It doesn't get better than this. As for Edmund, let him be. He must be feeling remorse for what he's done; besides, he's in real pain now, physical pain. Try and forgive him."

"Forgiving is easy but how do you forget when it's your brother...? He's always before my eyes."

"Send him back to Stratford?"

"To do what? Be a burden on my aged mother and younger brothers? No, when a man casts off his shame and kills his conscience, there's not much anyone can do. I'll have to endure him until he finds something to do."

"Then why don't you relent and give him bit parts in our plays?" Phillips suggested.

"What? And pay that ungrateful cur?"

"Why not? Do it for your mother's sake. And the money will come out of the Company's coffers, not yours. That way Eddie will fulfil his heart's desire of being on stage, and he might stop bothering you."

"But he cannot act."

"Marry, he's not that bad. Bit parts, I said. Give him a walk on part to begin with. Any man with half a brain can walk across a stage and make faces. Be reasonable, Will."

Shakespeare sighed. "Oh, well, I'll think about it."

"Good," said Phillips. "Now let's put this aside, and head for the Globe. We have our work cut out but I wager it'll be the most pleasurable thing we've done in a long, long time."

***

SEVEN
———

Speaking of pleasure, few things could match the epicurean delights of dining at the Lord Chamberlain's table. Food and drink, like all other aspects of everyday life, were regulated by laws that were more common in their breach than observance but the limitations were commonly accepted due to monetary compulsions. The common people were allowed no more than two dishes and soup at a meal. At Lord Carey's private quarters, however, nine or ten dishes were served at breakfast, lunch and supper. The leftovers or broken meats would suffice to feed the lower ranking servants of his household.

Geoffrey Drake had been invited to dine with Carey that Sunday afternoon and the sight of so much food filled him with awe even though his family were by no means the two-dish subjects. Drake was amazed at the variety of meats. Mutton prepared with Claret, roasted crane, fried stork, boiled eggs, three kinds of bread, spinach tarts, blueberry cheesecakes...the food kept coming and he had to beg the Lord Chamberlain's leave for not taking seconds since he really thought his clothes would burst at their seams. French wine was served to wash the food down.

"But you've hardly eaten a thing," Carey said.

It was only he and Drake at the table, which was decorated with flowers and pretty candle stands. His secretary Bleach was in attendance in the adjacent room.

"A young chap like you," Carey added, "Come on, have some more cheesecake. Eat something more."

"I beg Your Lordship's leave but I am completely full; couldn't manage even one more morsel. I've eaten enough for a week!"

"Nonsense," Carey pooh-poohed. "Don't you spend hours in fencing practise? Where will you get the energy from if you don't eat properly?"

"I have eaten, My Lord, the food was delicious. `Never had a better meal in my life. As for fencing practise, I fear it has been neglected for the past week because of my mission in Your Lordship's Company."

"Ah, coming to that." Carey raised his finger for emphasis. "I'm glad you mentioned it; I think it's time we talked business."

They hadn't discussed the ongoing investigations during the meal. Carey had been the perfect host, chatting away about sundry things that affected the nobility: palace expenses, problems of peerage, relations with King James of Scotland, and so on. Now since dinner was over and they relaxing in is drawing-room, the Lord Chamberlain got to the point quickly.

"I must congratulate you first, Geoffrey, for apprehending Legrand and for saving me the embarrassment of arresting poor Blackburn. A wonderful job. I am considering a suitable reward."

"Oh, but I assure Your Lordship, I want nothing. The honour of being of service exceeds any reward."

Carey smiled. Well said, he mused, the boy was intelligent.

"Even so, there will be compensation for your efforts," he said. "However, as we both know, the man who murdered my players is still at large. Your work is not yet done."

"I am aware of that, My Lord. Rest assured, the matter shall be concluded shortly. My men are making inquiries and we're keeping some suspicious players under surveillance. It will all come to a head shortly."

"I hope so because I'm convinced that this Guilbert fellow was involved only in the attempt to do away with Shakespeare, not with the rest of the murders."

"I agree, My Lord. Has he made a full confession yet?"

"Not a full confession." Carey gave Drake a pained look. "It's a somewhat delicate matter. The Queen, Topcliffe and I had a chat this morning. Her Majesty wants us to tread cautiously for diplomatic reasons. Guilbert is a French subject and he's distantly related to the monarch." Carey waved dismissively. "Many levels removed, but there are a few drops of royal blood so we really can't have his head off. In any case, he's guilty of attempted murder, not murder. We're expecting the French to send an envoy any time now to plead for his release. That didn't stop Topcliffe from pulling out a few fingernails, though. Guilbert is a delicate chap, says Topcliffe, and he fainted at the mere sight of the screws and rack!"

Drake made a face as of in derision but he secretly empathized with Guilbert's dread of torture. It would surely make Samson himself turn jelly-kneed.

"He was quite voluble," Carey continued. "He confessed to having bedded Countess Marie nearly every day. He also confessed to hiring Swindon to kill Shakespeare because he was tired of hearing her go on about our Willie being her one true love! Fancy that, eh? She beds so many noble men but her heart beats only for a poet! Words, words, words. Anyhow, that's all Guilbert admitted to. He was adamant about not wanting to harm anybody else."

"I thought as much, My Lord. So what's to become of him?"

Carey shrugged. "I suppose we let Topcliffe have some fun for another few days and then banish Monsieur Guilbert back across the English Channel. It'll be the Queen's decision."

"A just one, if I may say. Shakespeare is alive, after all and we can hardly expect Guilbert to pay for the death of a no account fellow like Paul Swindon."

"No, of course not. So, coming back to the main reason why I asked for your help, Geoffrey: who is the murderer at the Globe?"

"I can't give Your Lordship any names right now but I've narrowed it down to a few players..."

"Geoffrey, I don't need to emphasize the urgency of having this matter resolved, do I? Her Majesty has just issued summons for a command performance of *Richard the Third*, one of Shakespeare's histories. She wants it performed the coming Friday. I instructed Tilney to send word to the players this morning." Carey leaned forward. "This show must go off smoothly. It'll be here at Whitehall. God forbid anything should go wrong! I'll be the laughing stock of everyone. Robert Cecil would love it. I want the murderer caught before Friday. You may resort to any trick in the book. You need to push money in, to bribe some people? I'll provide you with it. You want more spies on the ground? I'll supply them. Just say the word..."

"My Lord, none of this will be necessary. My men are in place already and we're following up some leads. Rest assured, sire, the matter will end by then."

Carey narrowed his eyes. "Do I have your word on it?"

"Yes, My Lord, as surely as my name's Drake."

"Good." Carey exhaled with relief and leaned back in his chair. "Good," he repeated. "I have confidence in you. My apologies if I'm sounding anxious but..."

The door opened and Bleach entered with a gentle bow.

"Forgive the intrusion, My Lord, but Sir Geoffrey's squire Rodney Peele is here. He wishes to speak to Sir Geoffrey about his findings in the ongoing investigation into the troubles in Your Lordship's players' Company."

"Ah." Carey brightened. "Just what we need; send him in, send him in."

"Pardon me but I fear the squire might become tongue-tied in Your Lordship's presence," Drake interjected before Bleach could withdraw. He didn't want Carey's interference at this stage. Carey, in his present nervous state, was liable to jump to conclusions and try and fix responsibility on the first suspicious person that came along.

"I see," Carey said. "You wish you confer with your man in private?"

"If Your Lordship permits."

Carey was clearly not pleased but he was sensible enough to back down. "Very well;you are in charge of this, Geoffrey." He rose, causing Drake to jump up, too. "Far be it from me to interfere. Just find the bastard who's doing this. I shall retire to my bedchamber for a rare afternoon nap. You may carry on as you please."

Drake thanked him for his kindness, for the excellent meal and then left the drawing room to meet Rod, who was waiting in the hall.

As usual, the chubby squire was nearly walking on air, levitating with the joy of possessing valuable information.

"Sir! Sir!" he said breathlessly. "I have interesting news; I think you'll be delighted. In fact, I know you will. Guess what, sir? That beastly fellow Christopher Beeston is planning on taking flight tonight! We followed him and caught him meeting the Worcester's chap Thomas Dekker at- where else?- the Boar's Head tavern. I think he's suspicious about us. He knows Tod and me so I sent Gunn and another chap to tail him. Beeston is a nervy chap and he spotted Gunn. Tried to shake `im off, `e did. But the second man Fielding managed to stay on `is tail right up to the tavern. Overheard them talkin', too. Beeston was driving a hard bargain regarding his salary, whining about the big risk `e was takin' since he's signed a bond with the Chamberlain's Men. `Said he'd have to pay Mr. Burbage a heavy fine. There was some discussion about playbooks, too."

"Playbooks?" Drake repeated in surprise.

"Aye, sir. Dekker said `e would increase Beeston's salary if `e would bring along as many playbooks as possible. `Bring? Ye mean steal `em?' Beeston said, all high n' mighty, to which Dekker replied that he didn't care so long as `e got his hands on `em playbooks. At this, Beeston whined again about how difficult it would be, considering Old John- Heminges, we presume- keeps `em under lock n' key and hands `em out personally whenever they're required for rehearsals. Heminges also collects them immediately after. So, how will Beeston succeed in hiding his copy from 'Ol' Hawk-eye'? He also complained about you, sir."

"About me?"

"Aye. Said it had become a dreadful bother now that they all know you are Sir Geoffrey and not plain ol' Froggie Dupont. Sorry, sir, but those were his words."

Drake smiled. "Good. That means I'm getting somewhere. When a man is criticized, it means he's making progress. What else did Beeston say? Did he reveal when he's likely to quit the Company?"

"Not precisely, sir, but Fielding says all this 'appened a short while ago and Beeston complained about 'ow 'ard it was to get away. 'Said that Thomas Pope had sent him and Downtown to Shoreditch to inform Burbage, Heminges and the others who live in London city, that the Queen has ordered a special performance by the Chamberlain's Men on Friday. Pope wanted them to tell the others to convene at the Globe this afternoon. Beeston said he delivered the message and then excused himself from Downtown, saying he had some work at the market and that he would return to the Borough later in the afternoon. Then he went off to meet Dekker."

"So they didn't decide when exactly Beeston is to leave?"

"No, sir."

As Drake thought over the matter with a pensive frown on his brow, Rod said: "What do you make of this, sir? Do you think Beeston is the murderer? I mean, this is the second time he's betrayed the Chamberlain's Men."

"I'm not quite sure yet but of course he is a major suspect. Perhaps he abandoned his plans to kill more players because of my arrival on the scene. I'm not convinced about his motive, though; why would he kill his fellow players?"

"We don't know but we must consider that he was at the scene in each of the three incidents, sir."

Drake raised an admiring brow. He was pleased with Rod's attention to detail and his line of reasoning. He hadn't thought his squires capable of anything more than menial work and physical labour.

"You have a point, Rod, of course but that still doesn't mean Beeston is guilty for certain."

"Mightn't Dekker be paying him, sir, to ruin the Chamberlain's Men?"

"I don't think so. We've considered this before. Dekker would not have sufficient resources at his disposal to pull off so many incidents; neither does he have enough money to pay off someone on the inside. This means someone high up in the Worcester's Men would have to be involved. I think that's improbable. The only one who has that kind of power is Somerset, the Earl of Worcester himself. Would he risk a direct attack on the Lord Chamberlain? No, Somerset wouldn't dare. If he were to be found out, he'd be in deep trouble. No, I can't get over the feeling that these incidents are intended to ruin Shakespeare, not Lord Carey."

"But, sir, we've caught the man that wanted to kill Shakespeare."

"Yes, but I think there's more than one man who wants to see the Bard's downfall. This other man...he's diabolical. He doesn't care whom he destroys so long as he bleeds Shakespeare slowly. `Know what I'm saying?"

Rod nodded but the dubious look in his eye told Drake that he wasn't convinced.

"What are we going to do about Beeston, sir?" he asked.

"I'll inform Shakespeare; let him deal with it. I don't care which company Beeston works for but I do care about the playbooks. Master Shakespeare's work shouldn't be distorted. Remember what the Lord said about pearls before swine?"

Rod grinned. "Aye, sir."

"Keep Beeston shadowed anyway, until we find out exactly what his role is in all this. Oh, did Tod get back to you about verifying Oliver Downtown's antecedents?"

"Ah, that! I almost forgot to tell you, sir!" Rod exclaimed, hitting his forehead with his palm. "Most important. Yes, sir, Tod went to Paris Garden liberty this morning after church and inquired about Downtown's mother Agnes and her accountant boss, a Mr. Radcliffe, as Downtown said. They both lived once upon a time, of course, and they're dead now. Tod got this info from a woman that runs a pawn shop, a Mrs. Watson, I think. She said she had known Mrs. Downtown very well. 'And did Mrs. D `ave a son called Oliver'? Tod asked. 'Aye', said the woman. 'And is she in touch with `im now?' 'In touch wi' him?' she says, takin' a turn, 'How can I be in touch with `im? How can anybody be in touch wi' him?

He died, didn't he? Drowned in the Thames with his poor ma on St. Valentine's Day last year!'"

"What?" Drake whistled. "My word, this is unexpected."

Rod grinned. "Ain't it, sire?"

"By my troth, I would never have thought..."

"...that Oliver Downtown is a ghost, eh, sir?"

Drake laughed. "No, Rod, Downtown is not a ghost."

"Then a demon, sir?"

"Perhaps."

Drake's tone was light, but his mind was racing. Now here was an unexpected twist in the case. Oliver Downtown was rumoured to be dead? Was it the same boy who was a player now? Was there some reason why he wanted his former acquaintances to assume he was dead? Was Mrs. Watson's information correct? Or was the player Downtown someone else who had taken on the dead boy's identity?

Drake decided he had better interview Mrs. Watson herself to find out how reliable she was.

But whatever the outcome of that interview, young Mr. Downtown had some explaining to do...

***

NINE

——

The Chamberlain's Men were rehearsing *Romeo & Juliet* when Drake arrived at the Globe around four o'clock that Sunday afternoon. He'd been torn between a desire to interview Mrs. Watson in Paris Garden and the need to warn Shakespeare about Beeston's intended flight to the Worcester's Men. Finally he decided in favour of the latter. Mrs. Watson could wait. In any case, his squires would remain on Downtown's tail so there was little chance of him getting up to mischief if he was, indeed, the killer.

James Sands was playing Romeo this time and Alex Cooke was Juliet again. Drake felt the atmosphere was a little tense. No wonder, too. The last time they'd performed this play, Thomas Gray had fallen to his death. This time round, the players were on guard and they were watching each other's backs. That made them jumpy. Oliver Downtown was busy backstage as usual. Christopher Beeston was reprising the small part of Juliet's suitor Paris and Drake felt a sense of foreboding when he saw Beeston standing in the wings with a playbook in hand. His intentions were suspect for none of the other players were holding playbooks; they all had foul papers in hand only, which contained their sides. So how had Beeston managed to convince Heminges to give him a playbook? Moments later, Drake had his answer.

Beeston was doubling up as prompter for the rehearsal.

Will you leave everyone in the lurch and run off tonight? Drake wondered.

Shakespeare and Burbage were sitting in the gallery and watching the players on stage. They waved and greeted Drake warmly when they saw him. Both of them rose to climb down but Drake motioned to them to remain in their seats; he would join them there. He wanted to speak to them in private.

They were in good spirits and told him about the summons for a command performance. He congratulated them and told them he knew about it since he'd just had lunch with the Lord Chamberlain. They were looking so pleased that he felt sorry about having to break the news about Beeston. He inquired about Edmund instead and Shakespeare's face darkened at once. He said that Eddie was better and that he'd fetched him from hospital that morning and deposited him at their lodgings.

"God knows he doesn't deserve my support," Shakespeare

grumbled. "But I can't abandon him, either. For what it's worth, he kept begging my forgiveness."

"That's good," said Drake. "A contrite heart is the first step towards true repentance, I should think. Let us hope Edmund's remorse is genuine." Then he paused and added: "I'm afraid I have bad news."

Shakespeare and Burbage sat upright.

"Yes, sir?" Burbage was alert and all ears. Shakespeare looked a little weary.

He told them about Beeston's meeting with Dekker and his stated intention to leave the Chamberlain's Men along with stolen playbooks.

Burbage clenched his fists and muttered all kinds of expletives that were not complimentary to Beeston or his parents, whoever they were! But Shakespeare took the news calmly.

"Leaving us for the Worcester's?" he said. "Clearly he is foolish as well as deceitful. Which attribute outweighs the other, I cannot tell. And the playbooks..." Suddenly Shakespeare brightened, laughed and said: "I say, let's turn this around and have some fun."

"Fun?" Burbage said incredulously.

"Yes. I have an idea. Thomas Dekker wants our playbooks? Let's give him playbooks."

"What on earth do you mean?"

Shakespeare grinned, his brown eyes dancing with amusement. "Exactly what I said. Let's give him playbooks. There are many kinds of playbooks, aren't they?"

Burbage looked confused. "I don't know what you mean."

"I said I have an idea. All we need to do is get a message across to our printer, Valentine Simms…"

***

'Now is the winter of our discontent

Made glorious summer by this sun of York;

And all the clouds that lord upon our house

In the deep bosom of the ocean buried…'

Drake was reclining in bed at home and reading a quarto edition of *Richard the Third* that Shakespeare had given him that afternoon. The words made him sit up in surprise. This was really good stuff. He'd watched different performances during the past week and listened to several beautiful lines but he hadn't really concentrated on or appreciated the beauty of Shakespeare's verse. When Shakespeare gave him a copy of the play and said: "Read and enjoy, sir," Drake had accepted it without much enthusiasm. He wasn't much of a reader. He understood the language of war and combat but the pleasures of the literary life were lost on him. When he flicked through the pages, he felt the play was exceptionally long. Still, he picked it up out of curiosity. Ten p.m. Sunday night. He'd tried to interview the pawn shop woman Mrs. Watson earlier in the evening but she was out visiting a friend somewhere. A neighbour said she'd be available at the shop in the morning after nine-thirty. So Drake had gone home for a quiet evening, a rare thing. He wanted a bit of space to sort his thoughts. His network of spies was in place following all the suspect players so he could rest easy for now. The Lord Chamberlain's demand to have the case wrapped up in the next few days weighed heavily on his mind. He'd given his word but how was he going to accomplish that? The murderer had proved to be most elusive and surprisingly clever, maintaining a low-profile when the heat was on.

Who are you? He wondered aloud. Why did you kill three players and then stop? What have you achieved?

The girl kept interrupting his thoughts, as well. Tomorrow night he would rescue her. Then what? Tomorrow night was really bad timing since his mother was scheduled to return from France the next day. He was already in the doghouse as far as she was concerned because he'd rejected the alliance with the Pompadours in France; his mother had been very keen on it. But he'd found the girl in question, Edith de la Pompadour, a young noblewoman to be dull and self-centred. She talked only of herself and during the course of one afternoon they'd spent together, Drake found out everything about her. He realized that life with her would be inexorably boring and, besides that, he didn't even find her physically attractive. None of these factors impressed his mother, however, and she was very angry when he said 'no' to young Edith. Now she'd return and find him taken up with Suzanne...He cringed at the thought. How on earth would he deal with the situation? He had no idea. Instead of thinking it through, he pushed it out of his mind and started reading *Richard the Third*.

The opening speech fascinated him but he also found its length quite daunting. Shakespeare certainly had a penchant for writing long soliloquies. The language captivated him and he imagined Burbage delivering the lines with power, making people squirm and revel in equal measure during the show.

'I am determined to prove a villain

And hate the idle pleasures of these days...'

Richard declares before he becomes King, when he's still the Duke of Gloucester.

The lead protagonist's character was wonderfully convoluted. He was scheming, villainous, capable of dissembling, even of courting the widow of a man he had murdered, and yet one experienced a sense of poignancy when, unhorsed in battle at the end, he cries:

'A horse, a horse, my kingdom for a horse.'

Drake wasn't certain if Shakespeare had based this character on a real person or not. Was the real Richard the Third a deformed hunchback? True or not, this feature seemed to define Richard's character all through the play. He called himself 'rudely stamped', 'deformed, unfinished, sent before my time'. It was little wonder that such a person would have a grouse against the world, against people in general. This set Drake thinking: the same must be true of the murderer. The fatal assaults upon Jeremy Smith and Charles Heminges, the 'accident' that eventually killed Thomas Gray- what did these reveal about the killer's nature? That he had utter contempt for other people, for human beings in general. Nothing connected the three dead players except their occupations. There was a certain randomness about their choice as victims. The killer could not have decided to do them in more than a few days before the incidents for the Chamberlain's Men didn't plan their performances much in advance. They usually chose the plays they'd perform just a day or two before the show. So he- the killer- couldn't have known, for instance, that Smith would play a role in The Merchant...more than a few days before that Monday morning. Similarly, Gray's selection as Romeo was done only three days before the show. Ditto the case with Charles Heminges. He'd been Burbage's understudy for a while but he didn't know he'd be doing *Hamlet* until a day or two before. His murder was committed even more spur of the moment than the others' because no one knew that the players would be visiting the Mermaid's Tavern that evening. The plan was spontaneous. Drake felt certain that the three dead players had been targeted only because they were convenient victims. Any of the other players could just as well have been killed.

So what did this say about the killer?

That he didn't really care whom he killed so long as it was a player.

Because his real target was the ruination of William Shakespeare.

That was the only possible explanation.

Which of the players had a deformity? None, really.

Duncan Sole's bad leg was a minor injury; John Heminges' stutter wasn't so pronounced as to give him a complex about it; John Sinklo was thin but Shakespeare had used this very feature to his advantage and Sinklo had benefitted. What about Oliver Downtown? Ah. As usual, the boy's name gave pause. Not only was there something dubious about the chap (if only he could get hold of Mrs. Watson) but Drake also wondered if his small stature had given him grief during childhood. Children can be cruel and unforgiving; Downtown must have been bullied because he was short. Of course that didn't mean that all short people turned out to be murderers. But in Downtown's case, Drake felt that this physical trait might be a significant point in defining the boy's character.

That did, however, bring him back to the same problem of the flower-seller's testimony. She said the killer was of average height and that he walked with a slight limp.

Drake sighed. Bad leg- Duncan Sole. That's all he could think of.

And what about Suzanne? What would he do after picking her up from the Stews the next evening? Where would he keep her? How would he explain to his family that their new guest or ward or whatever, had been raised in a ... a brothel?

He cringed at the word and suddenly wondered if he'd acted rashly. What was he thinking? He needed to have his head examined. A mere glimpse of a pretty girl had thrown him into turmoil.

Dear Lord, what have I gone and done?

Imagine what her manners must be. What if she turned out to be a swearing, foul-mouthed little shrew?

Should he back out? Simply not turn up tomorrow night? What on earth could he do?

These thoughts continued to torment him and the brave young knight fell into a fitful sleep.

***

Nicholas Tooley, the young player apprenticed to Cuthbert Burbage and living with him and his family, went down the street to Richard Burbage's house at eight the following morning as per his daily routine. Cuthbert and his wife Elizabeth were still in Nottingham keeping vigil beside Elizabeth's mother's death bed.

Nic Tooley and Richard Burbage strolled to Henry Condell's house like they did every day, fetched Condell, then met John Heminges and Robert Armin and they all chatted amiably while proceeding towards London Bridge. Instead of following a straight route towards the Bridge that would lead them across the river to Southwark, Burbage and Condell turned right and announced to the others that they'd be stopping by at the printer's shop in St. Paul's churchyard to pick up some playbooks they'd recently ordered before going to the Globe. Heminges and Armin would carry on to the playhouse and get the rehearsal underway. Tooley was asked to accompany Burbage and Condell so he could help carry the playbooks.

A visit to the printer's shop was not unusual but Tooley couldn't help feeling there was something odd about the whole thing because Burbage and Condell kept exchanging amused winks and talking in low tones as they neared the huge cathedral. It was brimming over with shops and people and the priest, who stood in a corner exhorting the faithful few that showed up, to turn from their wicked ways and repent. The printer Valentine Sims greeted them in the same way- with grins and an air of connivance that truly perplexed Tooley.

What on earth was going on?

Tooley also gathered from the snatches of conversation he overheard between Burbage and Sims, that these playbooks had been printed in haste and that Burbage had given the order only the previous evening. It wasn't a big order, just one hundred playbooks. Sims divided them roughly into three bundles and the three players carried one each and set off for the docks from where they'd take a ferry across the river. Much more convenient than taking the circuitous path along the river's northern banks on foot. What surprised Tooley even more was the way the other two treated the playbooks' bundles once they reached the Globe. Whereas they'd usually be maniacally careful to hand them over to John Heminges directly, today Burbage and Condell simply put the packages down on a bench in the eastern gallery and called out to Chris Beeston, asking him to deliver them to Heminges.

Tooley took the set he was carrying upstairs to the first-floor of the tiring-room where John Heminges was hunched over a desk doing the previous week's accounts.

"Mr. Heminges sir, here are the new playbooks," Tooley announced.

Heminges waved his hand absently and didn't give them a second glance. "Put them down on that chair, please, Nic. I'll get to them anon."

Curiouser and curiouser, Tooley thought, scratching his head. Aren't they concerned that somebody might nick one of 'em books? Tut-tut, the Chamberlain's Men had become too lax in matters of security.

He met Beeston on the way down. Beeston's eyes were gleaming strangely and there was a half-smile fixed on his face. He was chuffed about something.

'Wish I knew what it was,' Tooley thought.

***

TEN

Mrs. Watson wasn't at her pawn shop.

Mrs. Watson wasn't at home.

Her neighbours were a little surprised; she ought to have returned by now since it was Monday morn and she had a business to run. No cause for concern, though, not yet. Perhaps she stayed on at a friend's place. She'll be back sometime today for sure, sir, the neighbours said to Geoffrey Drake.

He tried to conceal his annoyance and thanked them. But he was beginning to worry. The situation was slowly getting out of hand. He had never been involved in a case like this before, where the suspects changed like shifting shadows. One moment he felt sure it must be 'x', the next minute it was definitely 'y'. Then, as he tried to reason things out, 'z' became a solid murder suspect.

He almost wished the murderer would strike again so that he could investigate the case when it was still hot!

He went to the Globe and spent some time watching the first few scenes of *Romeo & Juliet*. The playhouse was packed to capacity and the players were looking good. Great atmosphere. Shakespeare and he shared a private laugh over the playbooks. Wait till Beeston hands them to Thomas Dekker! Shakespeare said he sorely wished he could be there to see Dekker's expression. Then he informed Drake that if all went well with the show the players were planning a small celebration at the White Hart Inn that evening; would Drake be able to join them? Drake replied that he'd love to but he had a prior engagement (Suzanne, ahem!).

The clock was ticking. It would soon be time for Drake to visit the Stews and fetch Suzanne. He was becoming increasingly nervous about the whole thing. Really, he should call it off. We're all born with our own destinies; Suzanne would have to face her own fate... Marry, what on earth would he tell his family? Forget the whole thing, Geoffrey boy, forget it. You don't even know the girl. You owe her nothing.

Six o'clock.

Drake was at the Bear's Inn with Tod. His nerves were on edge and he couldn't tolerate anyone else's company. He didn't want to be with Shakespeare and co. It was time. Fat Pearl would be expecting him to arrive any time now. He had the money in gold coins but he felt he'd sooner throw the purse into the Thames than go through with the scheme of rescuing the girl. He hadn't mentioned it to anyone, not even to Rod and Tod. He ordered another goblet of wine. Best to deal with contentious matters when the red liquid is coursing through your veins.

Six-fifteen. Rod burst through the inn's entrance with news that Mrs. W had finally shown up. He'd been waiting outside her home. She had arrived on the five-thirty ferry from Eastcheap, where she'd been visiting an ailing aunt. How was the aunt? He'd inquired out of politeness. Not much improved, she said, but she had no choice but to return because the shop could not be left unattended.

Rod informed her that a famous knight wished to meet her; would she kindly stay in until Sir Geoffrey could be escorted to her place?

A knight? Visiting a poor woman like me? Mrs. W was all flustered. How could she entertain a knight, of all people? How could she be of assistance? Her house was a mess; she had nothing to offer Sir Knight.

He wants nothing, good lady, Rod assured her, just to talk to you.

Was it about the boy that drowned? She asked.

Aye, said Rod.

She said she thought as much, since a squire Mr. Makepeace had been asking about it just the other day. Well, she would be happy to be of service except that...well, Oliver Downtown was dead; what could she do about it?

Rod smiled and asked her to remain at home. He would be back on the double with his knight.

And so, by six-thirty-five p.m. Drake finally met Mrs. Watson with Rod and Tod in tow. His carriage parked in the street in front of the row of tenement houses and it was instantly surrounded by urchins and curious onlookers. 'Langley's Rents'- declared a battered old signboard. Rod reminded him that Augustine Phillips and Thomas Pope had houses nearby.

Mrs. Watson was a bird-like woman, nimble-footed and alert and she looked far less than the forty-nine years she claimed to be. She was a childless widow and quite self-sufficient. Drake noted that her ground floor flat although tiny, was neat and clean and the furniture didn't look as worn out as he would've expected. She offered them cake and ale, which they declined, and then sat opposite Drake in an armchair and declared that she was ready to answer any question he asked.

"I told your man about the Downtowns," she said with a nod at Tod, before Drake could put forth his first query. "Agnes and her boy, Oliver. They drowned in the Thames on St. Valentine's Day last year, Sixteen Hundred and One. Very sad business, sir. They were returning from evening revels in the city when a sudden squall came and two ferries were overturned in the river. Don't you remember, Sir Knight?"

Drake said he vaguely recalled something like that but he was abroad at the time, in France.

"How old was the boy when he drowned?" he asked.

"Sixteen or seventeen, I think, sir."

Drake nodded. Age wise, it was the same boy they knew.

"Can you describe him for us?"

"Marry, sir, of course I can. I remember him well. He was just a common boy. Quiet. A stout chap, well built, a strapping boy like his ma. Agnes was a large woman. They say Mr. Radcliffe had his eye on her, Mr. Radcliffe being her boss, but he also passed away soon after. Got the fever, I heard..."

"You said Oliver was a strapping boy," Drake said carefully, without revealing an ounce of excitement. "Do you mean to say he was a tall chap?"

"Tall? Not especially tall, sir, but not short, either. Average height, I suppose one could say. He was taller than me, anyways."

Drake smiled in triumph. A breakthrough, at last. Mrs. Watson was at least five-foot-four. If the Oliver Downtown she knew was taller than she, it could not be the player at the Globe.

It was now proven beyond doubt that Downtown had assumed the dead boy's identity. But, why? He didn't inquire further about the drowning and all because it didn't matter. The only question of importance was: why had Downtown stolen the dead boy's identity? He must've known the real Downtown. And, more importantly, there was something about his real identity that he wanted to keep hidden.

"It must've been big news in Paris Garden," Drake remarked. "A local boy and his mother drowning like that. What about Mrs. Downtown's husband?"

"No one knew him," Mrs. Watson said candidly. "Some said he was a sailor and that he had drowned years back. I never met him. But she was a good woman; must've been properly married and all."

"Were the bodies ever recovered?"

"No, sir. That's the tragic part. Five or six people drowned in that accident but only two bodies were washed up the Bankside. The rest? Carried out to sea, or worse....eaten by the fish!" She grimaced. Rod and Tod exchanged a horrified look and went green. "God alone knows what happened," she continued. "But there was a proper funeral; Mr. Radcliffe saw to it."

"And did Mr. Radcliffe have a son?"

"No, sir. He never married. He was a good man. A little mean at times but..."

"But he paid for the funeral?"

"Mr. Radcliffe? No; he wasn't that generous. No, it was his boss Mr. Langley that bore the costs. We had a lovely service..."

"Francis Langley? Owner of the Swan?"

"Aye, sir."

"Mr. Radcliffe worked for him?"

"Aye, sir. And Mrs. Downtown, too. Mr. Langley was quite prosperous once, as you might've noticed from the board in front of the house. These properties belonged to him."

"Who owns them now? Did Langley have an heir?"

"No, sir. I'm not sure who owns them. Maybe the Bishop does; he seems to own everything in this area!"

"What was Langley like as a person?"

"He was all right, I suppose. Always in trouble with the law but then some people are like that, aren't they? Always getting caught up in some entanglement or the other. They say his conduct towards the ladies was improper but I met him a few times and he behaved like a proper gentleman."

Drake nodded. He would for Mrs. Watson had that air about her- alert, no- nonsense. No man would take liberties with a woman like that.

"And Agnes never complained, either," the woman continued. "She worked for him and said he could get hot-tempered at times but he was always decent towards her."

Drake considered this for a moment. The question was hovering about in his mind: why did the player they knew as Oliver Downtown choose that particular identity? He has to have known the real chap.

"Did Oliver have any close friends?" he asked.

"Aye, some. There was this chap Patrick, Ann Lee's son. He and Ollie were inseparable. Two peas in a pod, we would say. He was awful cut up when Ollie died."

"Patrick Lee? Can you describe him?"

"Of course, though I must say, I didn't know him well, him or his mother Ann."

Drake noted a trace of disapproval in her tone. The name 'Ann Lee' seemed vaguely familiar to him but he tried and failed to place it.

"Pat was a tiny chap," Mrs. Watson said and Drake nearly let out a whoop of joy. "Prematurely born, they said. He was all right. Crazy about Ollie, he was."

"Tiny chap?" Drake said, his pulse going ninety beats per minute. "You mean he was short?"

"Aye, Sir Knight. Couldn't have been more than five feet tall, if that. He was a few years older than Ollie but one wouldn't have thought it."

Drake tried to suppress his broadening smile. "Have you seen him around lately?"

"No. Come to think of it, I haven't seen him since his mother passed away six months back. Everyone dies, don't they? Agnes, Ollie, Radcliffe, Langley, Ann..."

"Indeed, that's the only thing we're sure of when we're born," Drake said tritely. "Tell me, Mrs. Watson, what was Patrick Lee like?"

"Quiet boy," she said. "Much like Ollie, though Ollie was louder and more confident. Preferred to remain in the background, did our Pat. I wonder what he's got up to now."

He's a player in the Chamberlain's Company! Drake mused. Yes, it had to be the same chap. But why, O why, was he pretending to be a dead boy called Oliver Downtown? What was wrong with being Patrick Lee?

"You don't seem to have been too fond of Ann Lee," Drake observed.

Mrs. Watson pursed her lips. "Well...one shouldn't speak ill of the dead..."

"How did she die?"

"No idea. One of her experiments must've gone wrong. They say she had a mysterious fever...I don't know."

"Experiments?"

"Aye, sir. She fancied herself some sort of doctor, kept mixing herbs and all. I think she was really a witch and nobody knew! `Half expected her to fly off on a broomstick one day. But, as they say, one always gets one's comeuppance in life..."

She paused and Drake felt the hair rise on his arms. Patrick Lee aka Oliver Downtown's ma was a kind of witch? The Globe victims- two of them- had been poisoned. Could it be that the boy had learnt about secret poisons from his mother? Ah, the evidence was piling up nicely against Mr. Ollie Downtown.

"What about Mrs. Lee's husband?"

"Missus?" The woman sounded scornful. "She was no 'missus' anything. Never married Pat's pa, whoever he was. I don't think anybody ever saw him."

Could that be the reason why Patrick Lee had hidden his real identity? Drake wondered. Because he was illegitimate? It was not an argument that satisfied him entirely but he had to admit the possibility.

He consulted his pocket watch. Ten-past-eight. The Chamberlain's Men would be at the White Hart Inn, which was a good twenty minutes away, just off the Borough High Street. Downtown ought to be there, too. If he hurried, he might be able to corner him there.

Drake also remembered that Suzanne must be waiting for him. So where should he go first?

The White Hart, of course.

And that had nothing to do with his attempt to avoid a visit to the Stews? Go on, Geoffrey, tell yourself another.

He thanked Mrs. Watson for her help, told her that he might need to talk to her again, and then left in his carriage with Rod and Tod.

"Where to, Sir?" Tod asked, so he could tell the driver.

"The White Hart Inn." Drake added as an afterthought: "I wonder how Beeston is getting on. We've got someone on his tail, don't we?"

"Yes, sir, we do," said Tod. "Fielding and Nathan. They're reliable. We also have two people watching the Chamberlain's Men so they must be at the White Hart, too. Why is the 'heart' white, I wonder?"

"It's 'H-A-R-T', not 'H-E-A-R-T'," Drake explained, "Another name for 'deer', the animal."

"Ah, I see. The other heart, the 'H-E-A-R-T' is also a 'D-E-A-R' thing, sir."

Drake chuckled. "So it is. I would never have made the connection."

"Most people have black hearts," Rod put in.

"I agree," said Tod. "That's what I meant when I said is anyone's heart white? Like this chap who has been knocking off the players. And Master Shakespeare's brother, who got his just desserts last night. They've both got black hearts, I'm sure. Black as the river at night."

"What makes their hearts black?" Drake asked lightly.

"Envy," said Tod.

"Envy and hatred," Rod added.

"And a desire to 'ave what Mr. Shakespeare has," Tod said.

"That's good," Drake said. He enjoyed these moments,

when his mentally-challenged squires displayed rare sparks of brilliance. "So who could it be- the murderer?"

Tod rubbed his chin thoughtfully and then said: "Someone who had it all and lost it because of Shakespeare."

Drake stared at him. Tod Makepeace's logic was unassailable. The man behind him was someone who had had it all and then lost it because of Shakespeare's success?

Only one name came to mind: Phil Henslowe.

Could he have dismissed Henslowe from his list of suspects too easily? Perhaps Patrick Lee (or Oliver Downtown) was the one who did the killing but Henslowe was pulling the strings? Was there a connection between the two men? The theory was plausible. Phillip Henslowe, theatre impresario, owner of the most successful playhouse the Rose, the one who gave Shakespeare his first big breaks; the same man who was forced out of the Bankside because of the Globe's monster success- could he be nursing a grudge powerful enough to murder the Chamberlain's Men?

It was possible, Drake mused, as his carriage rode through the busy Southwark streets. The only problem was that he'd had Henslowe checked out thoroughly and the man came out clean. He seemed to be a straightforward chap, wholly involved in running the Fortune, in managing the Rose although it was on the wane, and in various other business activities. He was a generous moneylender, too. Could he have some kind of hold over Patrick Lee? Was the boy in his debt and, hence, obliged to do Henslowe's bidding?

Theories, just theories.

(And try as he did, he couldn't get his appointment with Suzanne out of his mind!).

Drake's carriage had just turned into the street that contained the White House Inn when it lurched violently, nearly unseating him and his two squires. His horses neighed and then stopped. The sound of running footsteps cracked on the road, followed by shouts of "Stop! Halt right there, lad!"

Drake, Rod and Tod recovered their composure and opened the carriage door. They caught a glimpse of the fleeing figure with a familiar squire giving chase.

"Fielding!" Rod hollered when he recognized the man. "What's happened?"

Fielding, a tall man with a hooked nose, paused in his tracks but his eye remained on his escapee.

"Nathan's at the inn," he shouted back. "He'll fill you in. Gotto go. The bloke's getting away!"

And he was gone in a blur.

"What on earth...!" cried Rod.

The carriage driver got off his perch and apologized to Drake for the awkward stoppage. He said that the fleeing boy had run into the carriage's path and nearly got trampled to death; it was all he could do to rein in the horses.

"That's all right," said Drake. "Park the carriage. We'll proceed on foot. The inn is directly ahead."

There was a commotion outside the White Hart. When Drake peered in, he spotted Shakespeare, Burbage, Heminges and a number of other players talking excitedly. His squire Nathan was there too, talking animatedly with them. He bowed gently when he saw Drake.

"Bad news, sir," he said. "Two more players are dead and one is absconding. Fielding's gone after him."

"Who died?" Drake demanded.

"A chap called Duncan Sole and one Oliver Downtown."

Drake's jaw dropped. Great! His two main suspects!

"Sole and Downtown?" he exclaimed. Rod and Tod exchanged surprised looks. "What happened?" Drake asked.

"I...we were outside, Fielding and I, so we didn't actually see what happened," Nathan said, his face flushed and his eyes rolling all over. "Apparently they were seated at a table drinking ale along with a third chap, Alex Cooke, when, all of a sudden, they dropped dead! That's what everybody says!"

"Just like that?" Tod exclaimed, "Dropped dead?"

Nathan shrugged. "It's what the others say."

"Who was the boy that ran?" Drake inquired. "Alex Cooke?"

"Aye, sir."

"Good Lord."

Drake sighed deeply. How nicely this complicated everything.

"Why did Cooke run? Did anybody accuse him of anything?"

"Don't know, sir. Fielding and I ran in when we heard shouts. I've no idea why he made off."

Drake searched the crowd and caught Shakespeare's eye.

"Sir Geoffrey!" Shakespeare looked relieved to see him and quickly made his way towards the entrance.

"They're dead, sir, dead! Two of them this time," Shakespeare said breathlessly. "Duncan and Ollie; can you believe it? This time it happened right before our eyes! Sole and the lad were guzzling ale and, suddenly they dropped dead! No one touched them, I swear it. Then Saunders rose, cried, 'God have mercy!' and dashed out of the door! Why did he run off? We have no idea. What's going on? Is there really a curse upon us? Perhaps we should all be in church praying for our souls! I just don't understand..."

"William, William, calm yourself." Drake put his hand on the Bard's shoulder. "I understand you've had a bad experience but..."

"They were sitting and laughing just like us!" Shakespeare said with a cloudy look in his eyes. "How could this happen? Are none of us safe? They just collapsed! Harry's gone to fetch a physician, Dr. Moreley, who lives nearby. By my troth, sir, it happened right before my eyes..."

"William, I need you to try and think clearly," Drake said in a steady, calm voice. "Tell me exactly what happened? I have to say, these developments have left me flummoxed, too. I was all set to pronounce Downtown the killer!"

"Downtown? But he's dead, sir, he..."

"I know; you've just told me. Slowly now, tell me what happened. I don't want to know that they dropped dead. Tell me clearly what they were doing. How many drinks had they had? Did they just order a new drink? Was the same servings boy attending them? Tell me whatever details you can remember."

"In faith, I'll try, sir." Shakespeare took a deep breath, sighed, and said: "I can hardly believe it; the strangest thing happened..."

***

ELEVEN

Christopher Beeston felt the noose tightening around his neck. It was a horrible, choking feeling even though there was no real rope there. He could hardly breathe. The heat of Thomas Dekker's glare burned his eyes.

"What's this?" Dekker hissed. "What the hell have you brought me, Beeston?"

His chubby fingers leafed through the playbooks at high speed.

"A Comedy of Errors," he read from the title page. "Page one, wonderful; page two, very good, very good; and then, what is Henry the Fourth doing in the damned Comedy of Errors? Ah, look who we have on page ten: Puck! How nice that he's come to visit us from A Midsummer's Night Dream! Damn you, Beeston. This is shit!"

Beeston sat down heavily and cradled his head in his hands. What a mess. He'd been taken for a ride. Served him right, of course. He'd smuggled out ten playbooks and transported them across the river to the Boar's Head Inn with all the stealth and secrecy of a cabal. He was so relieved when his fellow players went off to the White Hart after the show. It had given him the opportunity to sneak away to meet Dekker. But now, as they examined the books in the tiring-room of the Boar's Head Inn, they found that each book was a melange of different plays, two pages from this one, another page from that one, tragedies and comedies all mixed up. In short, they were completely useless to Dekker or anyone else. Beeston was astounded when he realized that Burbage had placed a special order for these the night before. It was a well-planned hoax! Now he'd burned his bridges with the Chamberlain's Men and the Worcester's were hardly likely to give him a hero's welcome, either.

Thomas Dekker was pissed off and he rubbed it in by reading aloud from each book and taunting Beeston.

"The quality of mercy is not strained. Ah, beautiful line. Wish I'd written it! I love Portia. But...ouch, why is she professing undying love to our Greek friend Troilus, now? And, oh, this is a real gem, Beeston. Get this: Juliet meets Romeo in her bedchamber on page thirteen and on page fourteen she has *Hamlet*'s head in her lap! Talk about promiscuous women!"

"Mr. Dekker, I'm sorry," Beeston mumbled. "I...I don't know how this happened. How did they find out?" That bloody Drake, he mused, he knew he was being followed! But he thought it wise to refrain from mentioning this to Dekker just now. The fellow would go bananas at the thought that Drake's men might be waiting outside the inn. "I realize I've been had; believe me, I had no idea. But I should've known it was too easy. Burbage and Heminges are never so casual about playbooks..."

"You're an idiot," Dekker snapped.

"I know, I know. Please accept my apologies, sir."

"What do we do? This is worth less than toilet paper. And it means that Shakespeare's onto us. I will be screwed if he reports this to Tilney..."

His voice trailed off as his gaze fell on a strange little ditty written in haste in Shakespeare's hand:

'Once the merchant of Venice

Declared he'd play tennis

If only he'd find an owl;

That wuld tell him which beast

Had a ton o' the meet'st

Hot air to fill in `em balls.

It isn't ol' Chris

He has nothing o' this

Outwitted by Mr. To-mas

Whose decks are aplenty

Wi' typhus not gently'tis better he were grazin' the grass!'

Dekker's face darkened. His humiliation was complete. Shakespeare was laughing at him.

Never mind, he consoled himself, who knows how long Shakespeare will last? The murderer hasn't been caught, after all. He hoped that there was more killing, many more death before the fellow was caught. He wondered why Shakespeare had not been finished off yet.

What are you waiting for?

Enough of the small fry; go for the big fish now. Stop messing about...

***

The evening had begun well. The Chamberlain's Men had descended upon the White Hart in high spirits since the show had been such a success. All of them hadn't come. Robert Armin opted out because one of his kids was ill and he felt he ought to spend some time with her; Richard Cowley had a toothache and said he'd prefer to sleep it off; John Sinklo and Nic Tooley chose to go bear-baiting instead. Young Tooley was a little too fond of bear-baiting, Burbage observed quietly, he'd better have a word with Cuthbert after the latter returned from Nottingham. Christopher Beeston excused himself saying he had a prior engagement in London city (ahem!).

Burbage and Condell tried to keep straight faces while saying:

"Right, then, see you tomorrow. Don't be late for rehearsal."

"No, Mr. Burbage, I won't. Good night," Beeston responded and slunk away.

The show had received such a good response that John Heminges estimated their earnings at five pounds. He wasn't sure since he hadn't counted the money yet but his guesses were usually spot on. He'd know the precise amount after doing the accounts the next morning. The players revelled in the fact that their hard work had paid off and that there'd been no mishap during the show. This put them in an unusually good collective mood.

Burbage, Condell, Heminges and Shakespeare were at one table, while Augustine Phillips, Pope, James Sands and Will Sly took a table to their left. On the opposite side were the trio of Duncan Sole, Oliver Downtown and Alexander Cooke.

For a while, everything was fine. The players chatted about the show, about the crowd's applause and about James Sands' wonderful turn as Romeo. He had exceeded everybody's expectations and hadn't faltered even once. Christopher Beeston, his prompter, had twiddled his thumbs all through the show.

It was nearing closing time when Sole and Downtown had met their end, Shakespeare told Drake. Sole had ordered one last pitcher of ale. The youngsters said they didn't want any. Cooke said he was full up to his neck. Downtown said he'd burst if he had another drop. But Duncan Sole filled both their glasses and then put the remnants of the pitcher to his lips. Downtown drank a little.

"All of a sudden, both men began to make strange, gurgling sounds," Shakespeare said. "They clutched their throats, thrashed about for a few moments, and then fell forward with their heads on the table. Dead! See? Their bodies are still in the same position."

Drake went across to the table. It was a rectangular wooden table littered with used plates, the pitcher of ale, three mugs and spilt ale. Sole and Downtown were slumped over with their eyes closed, tongues protruding and- as Drake expected- white froth at their mouths. He picked up a mug of ale and sniffed it. `Couldn't tell if the odour was any different.

"What did Alex Cooke do?" he asked.

"Oh, him? I was coming to that," Shakespeare replied. "Saunders sprang to his feet when Sole and Downtown collapsed and gazed at us as if in mortal terror. He exclaimed: 'It wasn't me, I didn't do it! God have mercy!' and ran out of the door! He behaved as if we'd accused him of murdering the other two, but we hadn't."

"None of us said a word to him," Will Sly added. Like the others he, too, was ashen-faced. "Saunders just jumped up as if he assumed we all thought he was guilty!"

"That's not surprising," Drake said. "Three men at the table and two are dead. It's only natural to think of the survivor as the murderer."

"But he didn't touch them," Heminges said. "I'm sure of it, sir. If this was poison, and Saunders is the killer, how did he inject the substance into Duncan and Ollie? He did not pierce their necks, or anything like that. We were right here."

Drake frowned thoughtfully. He had a theory but one thing puzzled him: all three mugs were empty; if all three men had drunk from them and the ale was poisoned, Alex Cooke should've been dead, too.

"Did any of you notice if Cooke, or Saunders as you call him, drank from the mug filled by Sole? The last drink Sole poured?"

The players glanced at one another.

"We were too far away to see anything," Phillips said, "Tom, Will Sly, James and I. Our table was on the other side."

"I don't think Saunders took more of than a small sip, if that," Burbage said, as he dredged his memory. "No, sir, he didn't drink in the end. As Will told you, he said he was full. So was Ollie; silly boy. He shouldn't have had any more. You're certain that the ale was poisoned, sir?"

"It's the only explanation," Drake said. "How else can two men drop dead suddenly? I'll have to send word to the Justice of the Peace and Constable Sprat. They'll have to question the landlord and the servings boy, although it's rather far-fetched to consider their involvement. How could they have known that you all would be visiting this particular tavern tonight?"

"They couldn't have known," Burbage said, "We decided

to come here during the show, if you recall, sir. Will and I mentioned it. But the plan was firmed up only after the performance. The landlord couldn't have known...unless one of our players ran on ahead and told him. But that didn't happen, either. Saunders, for instance, was with us at the playhouse until we departed; he was washing the paint off his face. All of us left together except Beeston, but..."

"No, Beeston is not the one," Drake said. "He wouldn't rush here, bribe the landlord or servings boy to poison the ale, and then disappear! The killer would've wanted to remain here all the time."

"But, sir, not being here would make an excellent cover," Shakespeare pointed out.

"It would but that still doesn't make sense. How would the landlord know whom to poison, if he had, indeed, been paid off by Beeston? Why not poison the lot of you? Why single out Downtown and Sole; why not you, William, and Richard? You both are surely more important..."

There was a small commotion at the door. Harry Condell had returned with Dr. Moreley, who was a mousey little man with sparse hair that stuck out like whiskers on his head. He greeted everybody with a nod and went about his business at once. His professionalism impressed Drake, for the doctor went directly to the table where Sole and Downtown were slumped over the top and began examining the bodies without asking any questions. He placed expert fingers against the side of Sole's neck, then checked for a pulse, and said:

"Dead."

He repeated the procedure with Downtown's body, paused, and then pressed his fingers against the boy's neck again.

"There's life in the boy, yet," he declared tonelessly. "You need to get him to a hospital."

The others were startled.

"You mean he's not dead?" Shakespeare cried.

"He's nearly there but there are faint signs of a throbbing in his neck. Not good because I don't think he'll make it through the night but you could try taking him to the infirmary if there's some means of transport..."

"Rod, quick," Drake exclaimed, his heart thumping with excitement. "Get my carriage. Take this player to the infirmary. Move now!"

"Let me help," James Sands cried, so he and Rod heaved Downtown over the table and carried him out.

"Marry, sir," Tod mumbled under his breath, "If this isn't becoming a hospital carriage!"

Drake felt elated. Downtown aka Patrick Lee was alive! So he was right about Downtown being the murderer! The 'why' of the case still needed to be cleared up. Alex Cooke had to be found. Suzanne had to be fetched...it was turning into a long night.

Soon after Drake's carriage left with Rod, Tod and James Sands accompanying the near-dead boy, Constable Sprat showed up with an assistant to arrest the landlord and servings boy. They both protested their innocence and begged for mercy. Drake instructed Sprat not to treat them harshly because they were probably telling the truth. A night in the clink ought to loosen their tongues if there was anything to be revealed. Sprat nodded in agreement. He was so in awe of Drake that he became tongue-tied in his presence.

"Now to find Cooke," Drake said to Shakespeare and the others. "Where do you think he's gone?"

"Can't imagine, sir," Shakespeare said.

Drake turned to John Heminges. "He's apprenticed to you. So tell me, where could he be headed? My man is following him but I have no way of knowing where they are until they reach their destination and my squire gets word back."

Heminges shook his head in agitation. "I...I don't...don't know..."

"What about his parents?"

"They're long dead, sir, b...b...but he has a br...brother who works at the Falcon Glass Works near Paris Garden. They're n...not cl...close but I think he's someone Saunders might turn to."

"Sounds right. Would you go, Heminges, to look for him? I'll send my squire Nathan along."

"Yes, sir, of course I will. But don't you want to question him?"

"No, he's not the killer. I think his mug is empty because he spilled its contents on the table when he jumped up. I want you to look for him only to tell him that he need not fear; nobody's accusing him of murder. He can come back. I only hope he doesn't do himself harm in the meantime."

"In that case, I'll leave now," Heminges said.

Condell also offered to go with him so the two players and the squire Nathan set off in a north westerly direction for Falcon Glass Works. Dr. Moreley also left for his own home.

Constable Sprat, while leading the landlord and waiter away, reminded Drake and the others as gently as possible, that it was nearly curfew hour.

"I think there are extenuating circumstances tonight," Drake said.

Sprat hesitated. "Yes, sir, well...I cannot permit the whole of Southwark..."

"A handful of players can hardly be said to constitute the whole of Southwark," Drake said.

Sprat blushed. "No, sir. It shall be as you wish. Any man who is not a player or your squire and is found loitering on the streets after the hour of compline shall be fined."

Drake nodded. "A wise decision, constable."

Bowing politely, Sprat and his team departed from the inn taking their two prisoners along.

"Players being exempted from curfew?" Burbage said with a chuckle. "Now that's a novelty!"

"Enjoy it while you can," Drake quipped.

"Sir, I don't understand what transpired here," Burbage said, sobering up again. "You seem to be satisfied with the outcome, but I don't get it."

"Don't you?" Drake said in mild surprise. So much had happened and he'd done most of his reasoning in his mind so he hadn't realized that none of the players knew what he'd worked out.

"We've got the murderer," he continued. "I only need to wait until the morning once he recovers, if he recovers, to find out if he acted alone or at someone else's behest."

"But who is it?" William Sly asked with a baffled look on his face.

"Isn't it obvious? The one that supped the cup o' hemlock and survived. A clever trick, indeed, although it seems to have gone awry for him. It's one of the oldest tricks in the book: make the world think you're a victim, and you're home and dry. Only, I never imagined he'd go so far."

"Downtown?" Sly said in surprise. "Wee Ollie?"

"That's right. Tiny little Downtown. He was sitting beside Sole. It would've been so easy for him to slip some poison into the ale pitcher, shake it around for a bit, and no one is any the wiser. In any case, Duncan Sole must've been too drunk to realize that the ale tasted a little different."

"Ollie?" Sly said again. "I would never have guessed! But why would he do it?"

"Ah, that is where we hit a brick wall. Why? I hope he recovers sufficiently to make a confession. By the way, his real name is Patrick Lee. Oliver Downtown, the name he goes by, belonged to a lad that died over a year back. He is Patrick Lee and his mother was a woman called Ann Lee, who also died some time ago."

"Ann Lee is dead?" Shakespeare said with a start.

"You knew her?" Drake asked at once.

"Yes, I did. She…and another woman, the late Francis Langley and I were embroiled in a controversy…"

Drake snapped his fingers. "I knew her name was familiar. You told me about this: some bloke dragging you all to court. If I recall correctly, Langley was annoyed with your refusal to ask Lord Carey to influence the case?"

"That's correct, sir."

"But that was Langley and he's dead. His offspring isn't the one trying to ruin your company; it's Ann Lee's. So what could Ann Lee or her son have against you?"

Shakespeare shook his head. "I'm at a loss for words, Sir. I barely knew the woman. She was a bit strange; there were rumours about her involvement in the black arts, that she grew all kinds of dubious herbs…"

Shakespeare paused, realizing the significance of what he'd just said. "Strange herbs! Is that where her son learnt about poisons?"

Drake nodded, his face aglow with excitement. "See how it's all coming together? Strange herbs- that's exactly what Mrs. Watson said. Go on, William, what else do you recall about her?"

"Nothing much, I regret to say. We hardly met once or twice during the course of the trial."

"What were you accused of?"

Shakespeare's gaze fell. "Indecent behaviour, sir, that's what we were accused of. But it was a lie. Upon my word, sir, I never touched the woman, neither her nor the other one, Miss Soes. I'm not claiming to be a saint; you know otherwise. But she was just not my type. I'd gone across to the Swan to speak to Langley because he wanted us to use his playhouse as a permanent home but we'd decided to erect our own place. I went over to break this to Langley. The two women were there, along with the chap who later accused us of immoral acts, a fellow called Thomas Wayte…"

Drake narrowed his eyes. "Thomas Wayte? Now he's someone I haven't investigated but it's hardly likely that our friend Pat would act at his behest when he'd accused his mother of cavorting with other men. Besides, you settled the case out of court. So Wayte must've gained from it financially."

"He did, sir, a sum of twenty pounds! Langley and I paid half each."

"Twenty…? My word, that's a handsome amount!"

"Yes, sir, but I didn't see we had any choice. The cost of protracted litigation would've worn me down if the case had dragged on."

"The women didn't contribute towards the costs?"

"No, sir, they did not."

Drake fell silent. Here was another brick wall. He'd been thinking that perhaps Patrick Lee/ Oliver Downtown held a grudge against Shakespeare because his mother had to pay her way out of the case. But that was not so. He also believed Shakespeare when he said he had never been involved with Ann Lee. So, why would Pat Lee go about murdering his fellow players and try to ruin the Bard?

"It's all here, the clues," Drake murmured, almost to himself. "I'm missing something. Please keep your thinking cap on, William. If anything comes to mind about Ann Lee…"

Just then his carriage came into sight, the horses at a canter, and Rod hanging out of the coach precariously.

"Sir, sir, we're back," he exclaimed.

Drake grinned. "I would never have guessed."

Rod jumped off even before it came to a halt. James Sands alighted after him.

"Sir, we made it back as soon as we could," Rod launched into his report directly. "Knew you'd need your carriage. Tod has remained at the infirmary a little longer. It's touch n' go with the lad. The physician says he might survive, he might not. Dumb chap, ain't he, the doctor? I asked `im, what's the third alternative? And `e stared as if I was loony, `e did. Anyhow, there's still the breath `o life in young Downtown so we know he's not dead. But chances are, he's soon be departing for…" Rod pointed upwards and then downwards. "…God alone knows where!"

"Is he conscious? Can he talk?" Drake asked.

"Nay, sir, the doctor says there's little chance until the morning. Tod is with him in case he regains consciousness; he'll get word to us."

"He's very pale," James Sands added. "His lips have turned black and the physician says he can never recover fully. Any news of Saunders, sir?"

This last query was directed at Shakespeare.

"Not yet but Sir Geoffrey sent his squire and John in search of him."

"Hope he's all right. Alex Cooke is a good lad; he has no reason to be afraid."

"Trust you're right about that," Shakespeare said evenly. "Poor Duncan; I can't believe he just dropped dead like that."

"You'd better inform his family," Drake said.

Shakespeare's brow clouded again. "So many lives wasted," he said. "For what?"

"That is the question," Drake agreed. "But, not to worry, everything shall be revealed very soon. You all ought to visit Duncan Sole's family and break this terrible news. The constable will have deposited the body at the mortuary by now; Sole's family can claim it from there."

"I'll go, sir," Shakespeare said. "What a terrible business. Like an endless night without stars."

"Yes, but the sun shall rise in the morning, just wait and see. I'll be off now since there's nothing more to be done tonight regarding the case. See you at the Globe tomorrow, William. If all goes according to plan, everything will be sorted out by then."

Shakespeare and Burbage nodded but Sands and Will Sly looked perplexed.

"How…?" They began.

Shakespeare cut them short. "Have patience and trust Sir Geoffrey. Will either of you accompany me to Sole's home?"

"Yes, of course," they both agreed.

"It's late already; let's not waste any more time. What must be done, t`were best done quickly. Good night, Sir Geoffrey. I share the same hope as you but not your optimism."

"There's no harm in exercising caution," Drake said and the others looked askance at the Bard, as if he and the knight were talking in riddles. "But I trust that, after tonight, it won't be necessary. I bid you all good night; *a demain*, then."

Rodney Peele was taken aback when Drake ordered the driver to proceed not north east towards London Bridge and thence home to Dowgate but in a north westerly direction towards the Stews.

"At this hour, sir?" Rod said in spite of himself.

"Is there ever a better hour to visit a brothel?" Drake teased.

His squire was aghast. "But…but, sire, surely you have no need…There's no dearth of comely young ladies that are only too willing…"

"At ease, Rod, it's not what you think." Drake permitted himself a little sigh and then said: "There are times when a man commits himself beyond a reasonable limit and then finds no way to back out of the declared course of action without losing one's honour and causing a great deal of misery to other people."

He paused and Rod stared back blankly.

"You won't understand, Rod, so don't overstrain those grey cells of yours," Drake said, "It's a matter of the heart, something you know nothing about."

***

TWELVE

——

The attending physician at St. Saviour's hospital was a thin, bleary-eyed man with a goatee beard called Dr. Foster. He was overawed by the knightly visitor, the clean-faced, strapping young Geoffrey Drake, who showed up at dawn (or so it seemed) with one of his attendants in tow, asking about the patient brought in last night, one Oliver Downtown. The doctor nearly stuttered as he led the knight and squire to the general ward where about twenty-five inmates occupied two rows of beds facing each other.

Downtown's bed was in a corner and there was a chair beside it courtesy Tod, who'd commandeered one while keeping vigil beside the bed all night until Drake arrived. Now he was gone. Drake had sent him home.

"Doesn't look good," Dr. Foster said gravely. "There are all the indications of poisoning and your man said it was so but, unless I know what kind of poison he's ingested, I can't give him the antidote or start the right treatment."

Drake stared at the pale-faced young man in the bed before him. Downtown's eyes had sunken in and he looked skeletal. His lips were black and he was lying so still that Drake wondered if he had passed away.

"Won't you have a seat, sir?" the doctor motioned to Drake.

"Thank you." Drake sat down and leaned forward. He called out Downtown's name. No response except for a slight quiver of the lips. Drake tried again and met with the same response. Then he whispered:

"Patrick Lee."

The boy's eyes snapped open.

"Hello, Patrick, how do you feel?"

The boy didn't reply but a curious frown knitted his brow. Drake knew what he was thinking. How did you find out?

"Which poison was it?" he asked.

The boy averted his eyes.

"Patrick, if you don't tell us, we can't help you. We all want you to pull through so please make an effort."

Downtown's mouth contorted into a bitter smile. "The Deadly Nightshade," he hissed.

"The...what?" said Drake.

"Fie, fie, that's Belladonna," Dr. Foster exclaimed. "I...I'm not sure about the antidote; in fact, there's nothing anyone can do if it's been consumed in large quantities. He must know all about it." He addressed Downtown. "How much did you ingest, lad?"

"Too much, obviously."

So it wasn't attempted suicide, Drake thought. Why wasn't Downtown dead yet? Because he'd been taking it all his life in small portions to develop immunity against the poison!

"One does not play around with poison," the doctor said with a baffled expression. "What was he thinking? How did he take it?"

"Mixed with ale," Drake replied when Downtown made no response.

"Deliberately, then?" the doctor exclaimed. "By George, 'tis a terrible sin, boy, a terrible sin."

Downtown turned his face away and assumed a foetal position, clearly in great pain.

"It preys upon your internal organs and then causes paralysis of the limbs and the heart," Dr. Foster went into graphic details. "A horrible way to go. It would've been better if he'd taken a stronger dose and died in minutes."

"He didn't intend to die," Drake said wryly.

"Yet he drank the poison knowingly, Sir Knight?"

"It's complicated; is there anything you can do for him?"

"I'm not sure, sir, but I'll try to find the antidote. I'll ask around."

"How long does he have?"

The doctor shook his head. "Not long, sir. Minutes, one hour, I'm not sure. It depends on his constitution."

"Then get on with finding the antidote, doctor. I'll give you a shout if his condition deteriorates."

"If ?" the doctor said with a raised brow, and left the knight and squire beside the dying boy's bed.

"Heard that, Patrick?" Drake said in a ruthless tone.

He realized he hadn't much time and this might be his only chance to extract the boy's confession.

"Are you ready to meet your Maker?"

Downtown grunted. Then he said hoarsely: "Do I have a choice? Let me die in peace; go away."

"There's no peace for you; wouldn't it be better to tell the truth now?"

"What are you, a Father Confessor now?"

"For you, I might as well be. Why did you do it, Patrick? Why did you take so many innocent lives?"

Downtown grunted. "Figure it out for yourself; you know everything anyway."

"Not everything but, yes, I know that you nicked the black coat from the wardrobe box after pretending to put it back, and then you wore it to draw attention away from yourself when you stabbed Jeremy Smith with poison-tipped needles. That was your first kill. Why did you choose Smith? You made Alex Cooke ill the previous night when the three of you were out drinking together. You could've poisoned him like you poisoned Duncan Sole last night. Why keep Cooke alive and kill Smith?"

No reply. "I don't have to say anything," Downtown snapped and then his body jerked violently.

"Make a confession, lad, unburden your soul," Rod implored him. "Have you no fear of God?"

Downtown ignored him.

Drake continued, talking quickly since the boy was fading fast.

"Thomas Gray. You loosened the railing of the balcony, didn't you? It must've been so easy since you were helping out with the props that day. But when you didn't succeed in killing him right away, you reverted back to your preferred method of killing, that is, poison. You got poor Charlie Heminges outside the Mermaid's. And now, Duncan Sole. Why, Patrick? That's what I want to know. It's clear that you wanted to ruin the Chamberlain's Men; but, why?"

"Sod off," Downtown said.

"Look `ere," Rod said angrily. "Watch yer lip, boy?"

"Or what?" Downtown returned. His face was red and he was perspiring with the strain. "You'll...kill me?"

Rod took a step towards the dying boy but Drake put out his hand to restrain him.

"Easy, Rod. Patrick, I know it wasn't really the Company's ruin that motivated you; it was Shakespeare. You hate his guts; why?"

"Don't you know why?"

"No, I don't. What's he ever done to you or to your mum?"

"My father, you fool, I did it for my father."

"Who is your father?" Drake asked in astonishment. Rod leaned forward eagerly.

"The man Shakespeare ruined, utterly ruined."

"Who?" Drake asked and then said slowly as a ray of light flashed through his brain. "Francis Langley?"

Downtown smiled. "At least now someone knows."

"By George, I would never have guessed," Drake exclaimed. "I kept saying that Langley or his off spring are my prime suspects but...he and your mum; you blame Shakespeare because he wouldn't assist them in a court case? And because he wouldn't use the Swan as his base? And because the Globe's success sent all competition into ruin?"

"One year more," Downtown said hoarsely, "That's all my father asked but the great Bard of Avon would have none of it. Father lost everything…even his life. He died of a broken heart. He promised to acknowledge me as soon as the Swan's fortunes revived but…"

Now Drake saw it clearly. Langley and Ann Lee had had an illicit affair and Patrick was a bastard child. He must've learnt quite late of his father's name. For some reason Langley, when confronted by his son, promised to give him his name only when the Swan recovered. But that didn't happen. In Patrick's twisted scheme of things, it wasn't Papa Langley but William Shakespeare who emerged as the villain of the piece. Because of Shakespeare, Patrick would never have his father's name.

"Why link your legitimacy with Shakespeare?" Drake reasoned. "He wasn't responsible for your parents' affair."

"He is responsible for all my father's woes. He killed him," Downtown exclaimed, writing in pain. "Father was going to tell the world…he promised to own up. `Just let me get my business back on track, he said, won't do for the Puritans to find out I've fathered a child out o' wedlock. It's a sin, Pat. My God, I'm a child of sin. But it would've been all right if it wasn't for Shakespeare. Father tells me all the time; he talks to me still."

"He talks to you?" Rod repeated. "You communicate with dead people?"

"He's not dead…to me. I hear his voice. Take this fellow

down, he says, Smith is no good, no. But he'll do all right as Nerissa. Stop him. You can do it, Pat. Take him at the gates. Let the mighty Shakespeare's company see that one of their players is dead and he can't do a thing about it! Arrgh!"

Downtown's scream was horrible. He thrashed around in the bed, his mind going insane with agony, and Drake couldn't help but pity the deranged boy.

Dr. Foster came running with a bottle of wine in hand.

"Something to dull the senses," he said. "It's all I can do. I've been searching for the antidote; it's physostigmine, by the way, but we have none in stock. It's a plant- Belladonna. You can grow it in a pot anywhere. Dangerous thing. Its flowers, leaves and roots are highly poisonous. I'm surprised a young chap like he could've known about it."

"His mother knew about these things," Drake said as the doctor tried to pour some wine down the boy's throat. But it was too late. Downtown had stopped struggling. His chest heaved with the effort of breathing but his head was limp. Slowly his breaths became fewer and farther between and then he stopped breathing.

The doctor sighed. "It's over."

"Yes," said Drake, "In more ways than one."

He suddenly felt emotionally drained and physically exhausted. The strain of the past two weeks hit him. He'd kept his nerve and tried not to let the pressure get to him. Now, finally, he could tell the Lord Chamberlain that the killer had been caught and killed and that the one pulling strings had not been Henslowe or Dekker or another player but the ghost of a dead man or, rather, a young boy's hallucination.

"Whom do we inform as next of kin?" Dr. Foster asked.

"I don't think anyone will be claiming this body," Drake said.

"But, Sir Knight, you spent the past hour at his death bed."

"I was simply doing my job. The fellow was a killer, so spare no tears for him, doctor. He killed four men before accidently taking his own life."

"In truth, sir? I can hardly believe it; he looks so tiny."

"That's another thing: it isn't hard to imagine that young Patrick here was bullied and ridiculed as a child on account of his short stature; that must've given him a grouse against the world in general. He was the perfect specimen for diabolical counselling."

"Diabolical?" the doctor's face lost colour. "You don't mean…?"

"No, not he. His mother, they say, used to practise black magic. Anyhow, the fellow is dead as you can plainly see. You have nothing to fear. Report his death to the Coroner; he'll take it from there."

Once they were out of the hospital and back in their carriage, Rod remarked that it was a pity the fellow had died without making a full confession.

"A pity for him, not for us," Drake said. He had instructed his driver to head for St. Margaret's Hill, Downtown's tenements. He wanted to inspect the late player's quarters before going to the Globe and breaking the news there. A couple of more pieces of the puzzle remained to fall into place.

"I got everything I wanted out of him," Drake continued. "But if he had confessed, perhaps he would've entered the afterlife a better and lighter soul."

"What do you expect to find in his quarters, sir?"

"Evidence. Downtown's confession- whatever he did tell us- was conclusive but since he was the killer, there are certain things we ought to find at his place."

"Like what, sir?"

Drake smiled mysteriously. "Three things; you'll see."

He was officious again, fully focussed on the job at hand. After allowing himself that moment of weakness beside Downtown's bedside, Drake had rallied again. He was anxious to have the case closed so that he could return home to the girl. There was another battle front he'd opened. His mind was still reeling from what she'd told him and he had to speak with Shakespeare in private. She consumed his thoughts and weighed heavily upon his heart.

Fat Pearl had been her usual nasty self when he arrived at the Stews late at night with his stomach in knots and his mouth dry with apprehension.

What have I got myself into?

"You said you were a man of your word, Sir Knight," Pearl snapped. "She's been waiting four hours."

"I know I'm late but there were unavoidable reasons for my delay; in any case, the night is not over yet. So she agreed to leave?"

Pearl made a face. "She's fourteen but she's not stupid. Of course she agreed to leave. Where's my money?"

Drake handed her the bag of gold coins.

Pearl's eyes gleamed. She was nearly salivating and Drake imagined her retreating into her den and spending the rest of the night counting and fingering the money.

"Wait here; I'll fetch her," Pearl said and waddled out of the courtyard.

Drake stood there examining his shoes and wondering what in the hell he was going to say to the girl.

Then she appeared and all his fears evaporated like a blue lake's water on a sunny day.

Her golden hair fell in ringlets around her shoulders and her wide blue eyes bore deep into his in an imploring, beseeching way that made him all gooey in the legs. She was not tall but her figure was perfectly proportioned; at first sight, she brought to life the nymphs of folk lore.

"Hello, Suzanne," he said.

"Hello, sir."

Her voice was soft and her manner coy. She wore a light grey dress that clung to the contours of her firm and shapely body and Drake found himself unexpectedly aroused. He felt ashamed.

Have a heart, man, she's just a child!

But...take heart...just a few years more...

Suzanne carried a small box in one hand- all her worldly possessions. Pearl patted her on the head.

"Run along now and be a good girl. Don't give the gentleman any o' your lip."

"No, Madam."

"I'm warning you, she can be a handful," Pearl added nauseatingly. "Gets all high n' mighty, she does."

"That's quite all right," Drake interjected. He decided he would not take another moment of this. Suzanne belonged to him now and he would not let anybody talk her down.

"Come, Suzanne, shall we go?" he said.

She nodded and came forward. He put his hand out and she took it. He grinned; she felt so good! A frightened little rabbit in need of reassurance.

"Farewell," he said brusquely to Pearl, who stood there watching them with an envious expression.

"Farewell," she returned. Then, just as they were going through the door, she added: "What about the others?"

Drake wheeled around. "What others?"

"The others, other girls like her. There are six more girls about the same age waiting to be...initiated. You going to rescue them all?"

"Would you let me, if I paid you?"

Pearl grinned her evil grin. "Course not, sire. I can't close down my establishment. You can't save everybody. This is the oldest profession in the world."

"So you're telling me this only to make me feel bad?"

Pearl shrugged.

Drake shook his head in wonder. "People like you...they make a person wonder why the Good Lord rescued Noah and company from the Flood! Why did He bother? You know, Pearl, just because I cannot rescue everybody doesn't mean I should not rescue the one I can! Never avoid doing the good you can do for fear of what you cannot do. Farewell, and I pray our paths never cross again!"

He left quickly, escorting Suzanne by the arm to his waiting carriage. Rod and the driver stared in surprise. He introduced her as 'Miss Suzanne' and instructed Rod to ride in front with the driver so that he and the girl could get acquainted.

The coach door closed. Suddenly Drake and Suzanne were alone and it was an awkward moment for the both of them.

Neither knew what to say. The girl looked out of the window for a while and then she rattled him by saying:

"Madam said I must do anything you ask. Do you...do you want me to kiss you?"

Drake cringed. So the bitch had tried to teach the girl to behave like a whore!

He leaned forward. "Suzanne, let's not talk about Pearl now? Try and forget her and everything she might have taught you. You're free now. You don't have to do anything you don't want to. I promise you will be treated kindly and with respect in my home. You can study if you like; I'll engage a tutor. You can do anything you want."

She smiled. It was such an innocent and guileless smile that his heart was instantly warmed.

"You are very kind, sir," she said and then added after a moment's hesitation: "Can I ask you something?"

"Sure. Anything."

"If I'm very good will I...can I get some sweets?"

Drake's face broke into a broad smile. "Of course you can. Lots of sweets; you can eat them all day until your teeth fall out!"

Suzanne giggled. "You are funny, sir. Oh, I forgot...She-the person we don't want to talk about- said I can tell you the names of my parents."

"Your parents?" Drake echoed in surprise. "I thought... they're dead?"

"They are; she says they are but I don't know. I don't remember them at all. She said that my mother's name was Marie and my father's name was William. Do you know anything about them?"

So Drake was anxious to ask Shakespeare about when he'd begun his affair with Marie Blackburn. It was a long shot, since there were thousands of 'William's in the land and several called 'Marie'. 'Marie' being the French form of 'Mary' wasn't as common but it still didn't follow naturally that the William and Marie, parents of Suzanne (if Pearl was to be believed), were William Shakespeare and Marie Blackburn. But Drake couldn't get the idea out of his head. Even when they reached Downtown's one-room flat, thoughts of Marie and Shakespeare and Suzanne were crowding the corners of his mind, not the three items of evidence that he hoped to find. Fifteen minutes later, they'd found all three and Rod's mouth was agape in wonder.

"How, in Heaven's name, did you know, sir?"

"Reason, my dear Rod, it all stands to reason," Drake said smugly.

The first item- a flower pot with the Belladonna plant growing in it.

If Downtown had been a regular user and if he had easy access to this poison, it was only logical to assume that he'd keep the plant close at hand. His mother would've taught him how to extract the poison from the plant's leaves and flower.

The second exhibit: stacks of small needles that Downtown had required for stabbing his victims.

The third: the one that really excited Drake although he'd expected it- a pair of clogs, high-heeled shoes like the Romans had once worn.

"What did he use these for?" Rod exclaimed.

"How else does a short man appear to be taller than he is?" Drake said.

That was something which had puzzled him for some time: Old Lily's assertion that the man in the black coat had been of medium height. How could she have not seen that Downtown was tiny in stature? There had to be only one explanation: that he was not short that day! Hence the clogs and hence the awkward walk 'as if he had a bad leg'.

"Amazing, sir," Rod said. "You are the greatest investigator in the world!"

"Oh, you're too kind, Rod. It's all very logical. I should've seen it sooner. It had to have been Downtown; everything pointed towards him. Yet I allowed myself to get distracted with thoughts of Edmund and John Heminges, Duncan Sole and others."

"You were just being thorough, sir."

"Thoroughly slow, you mean to say! How could I have not known sooner?"

Rod found a small box under the bed that contained some

papers. He handed it to Drake. Sifting through the stuff, Drake was pleased to find the note that had sent Jeremy Smith to the market on the day of his death, the note with Richard Burbage's forged signature on it. Downtown had evidently taken it from Smith after killing him.

What about the hardware items? Rod asked. They were nowhere.

Probably thrown in some garbage dump or sold off in the market, Drake guessed, more likely the former. For Downtown didn't really care about money. Remember how he refused Thomas Dekker's bribe? That was the first thing about Downtown that had struck Drake as odd. The fellow was an apprentice, he hardly earned any money. So why did he refuse Dekker's offer? It wasn't out of loyalty for Shakespeare; he didn't report Beeston, after all. No, he had refused the money because he wanted to remain in the Chamberlain's Men so that he could carry out his revenge against Shakespeare. He'd acted out of character for a normal apprentice.

Drake pursed his lips and chided himself again for getting distracted. Let that be a lesson for the future, Sir Geoff, he mused to himself. Now, focus on the task at hand. Talk to Shakespeare and Co. Report to Lord Carey. And then go home to Suzanne.

The mood at the Globe was sombre. The players had observed two minutes' silence in Duncan Sole's memory before commencing their rehearsal for the command performance of *Richard the Third* scheduled for Friday. They would finish this by eleven o'clock and then do a quick practice for the two o'clock show of *Julius Caesar* that afternoon. Richard Burbage and Augustine Phillips had just returned from meeting Lord Tilney to discuss details of the command performance.

Business as usual, Drake mused as he walked through the Globe's gates.

Alexander Cooke was the first to greet him. Rushing to the gate, he inquired urgently about his friend Oliver Downtown.

"He's not with us anymore," Drake said bluntly. "Died about an hour ago. Don't cry for him, Saunders, he was the killer."

"I know; that's what Master Shakespeare said. I can hardly believe it, sir. I thought he and Duncan had died and I would be blamed for it since I was the only one alive. That's why I ran. Thank you, sir, for sending your squires and Mr. Heminges after me."

Drake regarded with a wry smile. "You shouldn't have run like that. Marry, you led them all a merry dance, didn't you? Where did you go? To the Glass Works' factory?"

"Aye, sir. I just about managed to waken my brother when your man Fielding came. Then your other squire and Mr. Heminges arrived. I'm so sorry about causing all that trouble." He paused and then asked: "Tell me, sir, do you have any idea why Ollie went about killing our friends? I still find it incredible..."

"I do know. `Had a chat with him before he gave up the ghost."

"So, why...?"

"I think we'd better gather everybody together so that I can tell you all the truth. I don't want to go about repeating myself."

"Aye, sir, of course."

So Cooke announced to the others that Sir Geoffrey was about to reveal the details of the case and that they should gather around if they wanted to hear it all.

"Why don't you take the stage, sir?" Shakespeare said teasingly.

Drake smiled. "No, William, you will never make an actor out of me! A bench in the gallery is fine, thank you."

So the young knight sat on the first level of the western gallery and the players crowded around him as he told them all about Downtown's death, his confession, and about his own visit to Downtown's flat. The revelation of the dead boy's parentage stunned them all.

"So he was Litigious Langley's boy?" Burbage exclaimed. "We would never have imagined it. The bastard Langley kept pursuing us even in death, sending his evil child to drive stakes through our hearts!"

"Oh, I hardly think it's fair to label Patrick Lee, or Oliver Downtown as we knew him, as an evil child," Shakespeare said. "He was a victim, Dick. A victim of birth, of circumstance; I think his life and death were tragic."

"You mean we should condemn the fault, and not the actor of it?" Burbage said, quoting from *Measure for Measure* and, for once, Shakespeare did not object.

"Precisely," he said. "Can you blame him for what he became, reared as he was by a mother like Ann Lee and fathered by a disreputable fellow like Francis Langley? The boy never had a chance, not from the moment he was born."

"I don't know how you can harbour such charitable thoughts towards a murderer," John Heminges interjected with a scowl. "That tiny devil snatched my brother from me. He killed innocent boys like Jeremy and Tommy and poor Duncan, too. How can you stir up any compassion in your heart for him?"

"He would've got you, too Will, in the end," Robert Armin said, agreeing with Heminges.

"It's not compassion I feel; just sorrow," Shakespeare clarified.

"Un-just sorrow, I'd say," Heminges retorted.

"I'm only glad it's over," Henry Condell said and there was a chorus of 'ayes' all around. "Now we can get back to our usual work without fear of being felled. Sir Geoffrey, how can we ever thank you? Without your investigative skills, we would've still been under fear and death." Condell's remark changed the subject and instantly, the mood changed. All the players burst into spontaneous applause and they tried to shake his hand and thank him profusely.

"We'd really like to do something to show our gratitude, sir," Burbage said.

"Perhaps we could offer you free passes to all our shows as long as the Globe stands?" Heminges suggested.

Drake laughed. "I'm afraid your generosity would be wasted on me. I never was a theatre aficionado and I'm still not! It's been a pleasure meeting you all but plays still don't hold my interest. Sorry."

"But you will attend the command performance at Whitehall palace on Friday?" Shakespeare asked.

"Ah, that I won't miss; Lord Carey won't let me go so easily!"

Everyone laughed.

Then after chatting some more, Drake declared that he ought to leave for Whitehall right away to inform Carey that the murderer had been exposed and that the case was solved.

"He ought to be pleased that the matter is concluded successfully," Shakespeare said.

"Yes, he'll be very happy. He will also be relieved that it wasn't the Lord Admiral's Men nor the Worcester's who were behind all these deaths. Their involvement would've been very awkward politically. Anyhow, it's all sorted now. Farewell and all the best to you all."

The players responded with genuine feeling and exclamations of farewell. Shakespeare walked him to the gate, which was just as well, since Drake wanted a word in private.

"William, I must put to you a difficult and personal query," he said, feeling suddenly awkward, "And I can't give you the reasons behind it."

Shakespeare looked at him with mild surprise. "Yes, sir?"

"How long ago exactly did you and Countess Marie begin your affair?"

"Marie and I...?" the Bard was understandably taken aback. "I...er...why, sir?"

"I told you, I can't say why."

"Oh, er...well, it was the summer of 'Ninety-two when theatres had closed because of the plague. I had gone home to Stratford and..."

Drake smiled and put his hand up to stall Shakespeare. Ten years ago! So Suzanne couldn't possibly be his and Marie's child.

"Thank you, William, that's all I needed to know."

Drake experienced an odd combination of relief and disappointment. Relief to discover that unfaithful Marie's blood was not coursing through the young girl's veins; disappointment over the continuing mystery over her ancestry. Why bother about it? He reasoned, it doesn't matter to me.

He and Shakespeare bade each other a fond farewell. Both of them felt emotional and awkward and they were glad when that was over.

"I can never thank you enough," Shakespeare said, barely able to speak because of the lump in his throat. "You saved my life and my company, sir. I don't know what to say..."

"Nonsense, William, you're the Bard; you always know what to say!" Drake said lightly. "Fear not, I see it all in your eyes; you don't have to say a word. Have a good life and continue writing well. I wager you'll be remembered for generations to come."

"Why, thank you, sir. That's most kind. See you Friday at the palace."

"Yes, see you then."

When Drake returned to his carriage, he leaned back in his seat and stretched his long legs. He was a picture of a man at peace but inwardly he was still in turmoil.

"All's well at last, eh, sir?" Rod said with a cheerful smile.

"Is it? I have yet to overcome the most formidable obstacle in my path."

"In truth, sir? What is that?"

"Not 'what' but 'who'? My mother! She returned from Paris early this morning; fortunately she got delayed and didn't make it home last night. Tell me, how on earth do I explain young Suzanne to her?"

Rod chuckled. "Why don't we turn around, return to the Globe, and ask Master Shakespeare for his advice? They say he knows all about the matters of the heart, sir."

Drake shook his head. "No, Rod, I'm afraid this is one instance where even the Bard of Avon will be at a loss for words! Onwards to Whitehall now; let me meet Lord Carey first and then go home to face my fate. What will be, will be. Tell the driver to speed up; I have a busy day ahead."

***

EPILOGUE

———

Monday morn.

One week later.

Rodney Peele reported for duty at Geoffrey Drake's residence at Dowgate, London city at seven a.m. Tod Makepeace, who'd been on night duty, was about to leave for the day.

"Good morrow, Tod," said Rod. "How goes it with you? Everything's peaceful this morning?"

"Aye, all appears to be well. Last night's revels were wonderful. Everyone seems to be sleeping inside, yet to recover from the party. We stayed up till midnight."

Rod grinned. "Must've been great fun. Did the Queen attend as well?"

"She did, she did. And she danced in such an energetic manner that it was hard to believe she's nearly seventy."

"In truth? She danced? Well, I think everybody is happy about Sir Geoffrey's investiture as a Knight of the Garter. It's not every day that so young a knight gets admitted into that elite company. What about the other thing? The girl...Lady Suzanne?"

A broad smile creased Tod's face. "She is lovely, Rod, quite lovely. All of us squires and guards long for a glimpse of her! And she conducts herself with quiet dignity that's surprising for one that's been raised in a...you know... I trust the Lady Drake will come to accept her by and by. It's not easy but our Sir Knight possesses such a good and clean heart that it's hard to refuse him anything. And who would know his heart better than his mother?"

"True," Rod agreed. "What about the Chamberlain's Men? I heard that they'd all been invited?"

"You heard right. Invited, they were all and they turned up as well. Master Shakespeare recited some lines from a new play he is working on and he received thunderous applause."

"A new play?" Rod's face lit up. "What was it about? Did he say?"

"Aye, he informed the guests that it was a tragedy about a Moor called Othello. Marry, I even recall two or three lines that he quoted for they were so appropriate under the circumstances:

If after every tempest come such calms,

May the winds blow till they have waken'd death!"

Rod chuckled. "So now is the calm after the tempest, eh? All very well to say since things went our way. `Wasn't the command performance smashing? Burbage's turn as Richard the Third- now that is something I can watch over and over again."

"I agree, and so can the Queen. Did you notice how she sat glued to her seat for nearly three hours on Friday night?"

"Indeed, she did, she did. Marry, `tis all on account of Shakespeare's genius. Which other playmaker can hold an audience's attention like that? Know something, Tod? I've tried writing a few lines- nothing fancy, just a few verses about the events of the recent past. Would you like to hear `em?"

Tod gave him a dubious look. "If I must...I was about to go home, you know, been on duty all night..."

"Come now, be a sport. Lend me your ears for five minutes and then you can go."

Tod rolled his eyes in a good-natured, exasperated way and said: "My ears are yours; go ahead, friend."

Rod thanked him, cleared his throat, and said:

"Valiant knight Sir Geoffrey Drake

Knew it would be no piece o'cake

When summoned by Carey for honour's sake

To seek out the enemy that was drivin' a stake

Into the hearts o' the Chamberlain's Men.

Could it be Heminges? Or could it be Ben?

Was it young Downtown? Or was it the gen

That played Shylock in the Merchant of Ven?

The end came swiftly o'er a pitcher of ale;

Ollie Downtown was Pat Lee, `twas the twist in the tale.

The events set in motion

By his murderin' and envy;

Gave Sir Geoff a promotion

And the Bard, hale and hearty,

Keeps writin' and, oh what commotion

At his playhouse, there's always a party.

So welcome, welcome, One and All

To the Globe play hall.

Bring yer elders, bring yer spouse

For fun n' games at Shakespeare's playhouse!"

He paused and asked his fellow squire: "Well? What d'you think?"

Tod laughed. "Methinks Master Shakespeare would not approve! But it's not bad, not bad at all."

"He ought to approve," Rod shot back. "For `tis his fault. Makin' poets out o' ordinary men like me; I tell you, sir, I am a poet and I did not know it."

Tod chuckled and began to walk away. "I'm bound for home. Not for me all this rhyming and jiving. `Tis a madness most meet when every man on the street starts talking in verse; Good Lord, is this a blessing or a curse?"

Acknowledgements

Writing about Shakespeare is a daunting task and putting him into a work of fiction is probably sheer madness. There's a profusion of research material, which serves to complicate the matter: where does one begin? Which commentaries to read? When to stop? Here are some of the works I drew upon: *The Shakespearean Stage* by Andrew Gurr; *Shakespeare in the Theatre*: compiled and edited by Stanley Wells; *Shakespeare & Co.* by Stanley Wells; *Diary of Phillip Henslowe* by R.A. Foakes and R.T. Rickett; *Cambridge Companion to English Renaissance Drama* edited by A.R. Braunmuller and Michael Hattaway; Bill Bryson's *Shakespeare*; Commentaries on *Shakespeare's* plays by Harold Bloom; *Soul of the Age* by Jonathan Bate, and *The Age of Shakespeare* by Frank Kermode. And to those who might consider this effort presumptuous, I assert humbly Anthony Burgess's view of 'the right of every Shakespeare-lover to paint his own portrait of the man.'

Sharon Gupta is a Delhi-based Civil Servant and writer working in the Ministry of Communications. She graduated with English Honours from St. Stephen's College, Delhi and acquired a Master's Degree in English Literature from Delhi University. She joined the Civil Services in 1994 and is currently posted in Chandigarh. Besides writing thrillers, she loves reading, music, and playing the guitar. Among her favourite writers are Ian Rankin, Lee Child, Mark Billingham, Robert Goddard, Stephen Booth, Simon Kernick and, above all, William Shakespeare.

You may visit Sharon at her website: *www.sharongupta.com* and at her blog: *sharonwriter.blogspot.com*. She is represented by the Red Ink Literary Agency.